THE COURT

"Mike Shevdon stri[...] core of English folkl[...] can relate to finds he's part of an incredible and scarily believable parallel realm. If you've been thinking urban fantasy has nothing fresh to offer, think again."

   Juliet E. Mckenna, *author of the* Hadrumal
   Cycle *and the* Tales of Einarinn

"If you're a fan of urban fantasy – or even if you're not – I'd recommend this book."

   Spellmaking

"Shevdon's prose is elegant and simple and winds up being invisible. We notice the story, not the writer. And that's a rare and pretty fantastic thing."

   Kate of Mind

"Mike Shevdon gave me just what I need: main characters that I feel for, care about and could get invested in. Thanks for something new, sir, that has renewed my faith in modern fantasy."

   Deadwood Reviews

"The Courts of the Feyre is swiftly becoming one of my favourite series. There is a fantastic quality to Mike Shevdon's work that I've yet to discover anywhere else. A great example of modern urban fantasy executed perfectly."

   The Eloquent Page

ALSO BY MIKE SHEVDON

The Courts of the Feyre
I: Sixty-One Nails
II: The Road to Bedlam
III: Strangeness & Charm

MIKE SHEVDON

THE EIGHTH COURT

THE COURTS
OF THE FEYRE
VOL. IV

ANGRY
ROBOT

ANGRY ROBOT
A member of the Osprey Group

Lace Market House,   4301 21st St., Ste 220B,
54-56 High Pavement,   Long Island City,
Nottingham, NG1 1HW   NY 11101
UK   USA

www.angryrobotbooks.com
Eight into one won't go

An Angry Robot paperback original 2013.

ISBN 978 0 85766 227 9
eEbook ISBN 978 0 85766 228 6

Printed in the United States of America

9 8 7 6 5 4 3 2 1

For Jo and Peter

ONE

The fair was an assault on the nostrils. The press of bodies intermingled with the sickly scent of spun sugar over
diesel fumes from the generators, cut by the ozone tang
of sparking electricity from the rides, gave him indiges-
tion, not helped by the thumping bass of the music. It
had Marshdock feeling sick even before he'd found the
meeting place.

One of the oldest of the travelling fairs – originally
they'd been a nexus for information exchange and maintaining contacts, but these days they were merely an
amusement for those who liked such things. The dark
came early this time of year, and the last of the families
were drifting towards the edges of the fair; kids clinging
with sticky fingers to trophy bears and being rewarded
with toffee-coated apples and doughnuts laden with
sugar and cinnamon. Soon the families would be gone
and a teenage crowd would slip in between the rides and
the shooting galleries in search of a different kind of thrill.

"Scream if you want to go faster!" That was the call.

No one did business here any more. Normally he
would not grace it with his presence but he'd received a
tip-off that there would be something special for him, as
long as he collected in person.

Information like that always carried a premium, and being the sole source would mean that he could pay off favours that were long overdue and start to build up some capital again. The last year had been lean. Nothing was said, but he had the distinct sense that someone had put the word out that he was no longer to be trusted. It had been like that ever since the girl – Blackbird – had brought him an unwanted visitor. It hung on him like a curse, and it rankled with him that he had helped them and got nothing in return. It showed weakness, and in his line of work that was a luxury you couldn't afford. He walked past the dodgems and threaded through the crowds heading for the darker edges of the fair between the rides and the caravans.

Since the incident in Covent Garden, Carris had been a refugee. She appeared when it suited her, and where she went in the meantime no one knew. In truth, no one really cared. She would drink and curse and swear revenge against the one who had killed Fenlock, her lost love, but everyone knew she would not face his killer directly. The word these days was that Fenlock's murderer was Warder-trained and everyone knew the Warders stuck together. No one wanted that kind of trouble, even for a price; not that Carris had anything to offer.

So the invitation to meet Carris had been intriguing. Delivered through numerous proxies to ensure that her location wasn't discovered, it was pitched well beyond anything she could normally demand, indicating that she thought she'd stumbled on something worthwhile. His initial scepticism had been tempered by the condition that he meet her here in Nottingham, while the fair was in full swing, making Marshdock wonder if she'd been travelling with the fair all along. It would explain her erratic appearances.

There were hints in the message that she was onto something big – something that the Lords and Ladies would be interested to know, and that kind of favour was always worth cultivating. Carris couldn't take it to them direct because that would mean dealing with the Warders, and she was understandably shy of that. Since Carris trusted no-one else to act as go-between, Marshdock could earn favour on both sides by bridging the gap.

Wrapping himself in glamour to remain unseen, he slipped between the penny-falls and the hall of mirrors, merging with the shadows behind the stalls and letting his eyes become accustomed to the dark before moving on. He was early, but it always paid to scout out the location of a pick-up before the meeting. He might rarely stray from his fireside these days, but many years of collecting information in dark alleys had taught him caution. Even so, he almost stumbled into the figure lingering in the shadows behind the hall of mirrors.

He retreated back into the gap between the stalls, realising that the lurker was watching the area behind the stalls so intently they had not noticed him. He wondered for a moment whether Carris had also turned up early, but then realised that the figure was male and not inclined to the gothic fashions that Carris adopted. As Marshdock's eyes adjusted to the dark he nevertheless began to think he recognised the person lurking there. There was something familiar about them, the way they hunched their shoulders and cocked their head on one side as if listening. A suspicion formed in his mind, just as the figure stepped out into the light that striped across the grass between the hall of mirrors and the candyfloss stall.

It was a facsimile of himself. Marshdock's pulse began to race as he wondered why anyone would be impersonating him. It wasn't as if he was a regular at the fair – he couldn't recall when he had last been here. That meant that someone knew that he was going to be here. He'd told no one where he was going, so unless he'd been followed – no, more likely someone had heard about the

9

meeting from Carris. One of the go-betweens must have blabbed and now someone wanted to get the jump on him. Someone was trying to steal his prize.

He considered confronting them, right there, but caution was ever his watchword. He would see what they did and make his judgement then. His hand slid to his belt and eased the long knife from its sheath. He held it down behind his leg so the blade would not catch the light and give him away. Better to be ready.

"Marshdock?" The call came from the shadows beyond the waiting impersonator.

"Well who else would it be?" his twin asked, impatiently.

"Were you followed?" asked the voice.

"Certainly not!" said his twin, with conviction.

Carris edged into the light. Since he'd last seen her she'd lost even more weight. Her stick-thin legs in skinny jeans looked too spindly to bear her and she moved in short bursts like a frightened cat, ready to dart into the shadows at the first sign of trouble. Her skin took on a sickly tone in the coloured lights from the fair that no amount of face powder and black eyeliner could disguise. Her black hair hung lank around her face. Marshdock thought he could smell her.

"You know the price?" said Carris, peering into the shadows so that Marshdock was obliged to keep rigidly still or give himself away.

"We can negotiate on that," said his twin. He even sounds like me, thought Marshdock.

"No negotiation! I want the wraithkin Warder dead! Understand?" Her anger was fierce, but short-lived. "I want my life back," she said, quietly. "I want some respect." She faded fast; it was hard to imagine anyone giving her regard in her current state.

"Then you'll have to produce something worthy of blood-price, won't you?" said his twin. "A favour for a favour, you know how it works."

"How can I trust you?" she asked. "This didn't come from me, understand?"

"Who else can you trust?" said his twin. "And my sources are always anonymous. Now, either you tell me something worth knowing, or I'm leaving. Which is it to be?"

"It concerns the High Court," said Carris. "That's gotta be worth something?"

"That depends," said his twin, cautiously.

"The Seventh Court, they're here," she said. "Not just one, there's a group of them."

"That's news indeed," said his twin, "but hardly a surprise. You'll need more than that to be worth a blood-debt against a Warder."

"I've seen them," she said. "They didn't see me, though. They were meeting someone from the High Court – the who and the why, that's worth the price, isn't it?"

Marshdock was close enough to see her fingernails were scraping her palms as she spoke. The need in her was like an addiction. She badly needed this and the negotiator in him saw that the time was right. Now was the moment to strike a deal.

"Well," said his twin, "that's interesting information. I'd love to know how you came by it."

"I told you, I saw it myself," she insisted. "This is the good stuff – it's first hand."

"And who else knows of this?" his twin asked.

"No one except me," said Carris, "and you, if you agree the price."

"Good," said his twin. It was indeed good stuff, thought Marshdock, if no one else knew of this.

His twin turned away for a moment, as if weighing up the worth of the offer. Then he twisted in the air, spinning on the spot. Something flashed in the light and Carris gave a soft, "Uh!"

Standing before her was no longer the hunched figure of himself, but a tall figure with dark hair and sharp, pale

11

cheekbones in a long Edwardian coat. In his hand was a bright blade, the end of which was embedded in Carris' chest. She looked down in shock at the place where it pierced her breast.

"The price of that particular nugget of information is rather higher than you imagined," he said, his rich voice finding amusement in this sudden turn of events.

"Raffmir?" Carris whispered. "But how...?"

Raffmir pushed the blade a little harder, and she gasped in pain. She clung to the blade with her hands where it entered her chest, as if it were the only thing supporting her. Her blood welled through her fingers.

"The price is agreed," said Raffmir, "with the small rider that you will not tell any one else. You won't tell, will you?"

He allowed her to topple backwards so that the blade slipped from her with a sucking sound, and her slight frame collapsed onto the grass. She kicked once or twice and was still. Raffmir took a white kerchief from his sleeve and wiped the blade, then dropped the blood-soaked kerchief on top of the corpse. Carris' magic was already claiming her, her body turning to ash as Raffmir watched.

"Good," said Raffmir, "so that's settled." He sheathed his sword. "Well, one might as well enjoy the fair, since we made the journey." He stepped between the stalls, leaving the body to decompose on the grass.

Marshdock stood then for some minutes, his heart hammering in his chest less the wraithkin return to check on his victim. For once, Carris'd had the real deal, but it had cost her everything. A secret meeting between the Seventh Court and someone from the High Court meant only one thing – treachery at the highest level. Information like that could be hard to sell, though. It would take all his art to broker such a deal. If only she'd named the traitor... still, the fact that there was a traitor was valuable enough.

He needed proof, though. He needed some token to verify his claim.

Cautiously, he moved to the edge of the shadows, towards the rapidly decomposing corpse. Carris' magic would burn through her, and within minutes there would be little left but some skinny jeans and a few goth trinkets. Checking the gap between the stalls, he could see no sign of the wraithkin's return. Steeling himself, he darted to the corpse, snatched the kerchief from atop the remains and ran for the gap between the caravans, away from the fair and away from the wraithkin and his sword.

The goth trinkets were worth nothing, but a wraithkin's kerchief soaked in Carris' blood – that was proof.

"What do you think?" asked Blackbird.

"That's one of those questions again, isn't it?" I said.

She swept across the floor in the dress, the heavy folds of damask rustling as she moved to stand before the tall mirror, turning one way, then the other. "It's a simple question, Niall. Do I look the part, or am I going to be mistaken for an extra from a costume drama?"

"You look splendid." In truth, it was a fabulous dress, cut from heavy turquoise cloth and fitted to emphasise her curves. "I expect it's the height of fey fashion." She caught my reflection in the mirror, her expression souring at my teasing, and turned. "This really isn't me, is it?" she said. She held the wide skirt out sideways.

"Mullbrook thinks this is a good idea," I said. "Trust his judgement. He knows the High Court better than anyone except perhaps the Warders, and we only wear grey."

"Oh, I don't know," she said. "I quite like you in plain grey. It suits you." She held up the hem of the skirt and sidled over to me, leaning up for a kiss and sliding her free hand under my jacket. "I could take it off?" she suggested.

"If you do I'm going to be late," I said, "and Katherine is not known for her patience and understanding, at least as far as I'm concerned."

She sighed, returning to the mirror. "I feel like I'm going to a fancy dress ball. Maybe I'll take it off anyway, wear something simpler, save it for formal occasions."

"What, and offend Mullbrook? No disrespect my lady, but you know what happened last time no one paid any attention to his suggestions. I'm not a fan of tripe at the best of times."

"There you go, you see? You start calling me, My Lady this and My Lady that. It's not me, do you see?"

I moved behind her, turning her shoulders so that the light caught the pattern in the material. "You are the Lady of the Eighth Court," I told her, "and Mullbrook is right. The more you look the part, the quicker they will get used to the idea. The first step to being treated as an equal is to act like one. Kimlesh and Yonna dress formally for the High Court. So does Barthia, come to that. Mellion is the only one who comes as he is, and even he wears the silver chain of the Horde-Master."

"I suppose," she said. "But don't you think it's a little over the top?"

I teased back the twist of copper from her shoulder and kissed the nape of her neck from behind, feeling her tremble as my warm breath passed over her bare skin. "I don't know," I said. "I rather like it. Maybe you could wear it later?"

"You are not to be encouraged, Niall Petersen," but she was smiling as she said it. In the mirror her eyes had a sparkle of green in them. She leaned back against me, and I folded my arms around her.

"You won't fight with Katherine, will you?" she said, suddenly serious.

"I am simply going to drop Alex off," I said. "I'm not stopping long enough for an argument. Hello, here's your daughter. Don't let anyone know she's here because she's supposed to be dead. That's it."

"That's what I mean, I'm sure she already knows that she can't tell anyone about Alex."

"This isn't my idea," I said, "but everyone keeps telling me that Alex is grown-up. Frankly I've given up trying to stop her doing things she wants to do."

Blackbird did not look convinced. "It's only natural that she will want to see her mother. Better you take her than she just turn up on the doorstep unannounced, don't you think?"

"This doesn't have anything to do with what I think. Besides, I rather feel my place is here with you."

"You can't be present when the court is in session, Niall."

"Why not?" I asked. "Fionh is."

"Fionh is there at the invitation of the court. Someone has to attend, and they trust her."

"And they don't trust me, you mean."

"That's not what I meant and you know it. Even Garvin isn't normally invited, and they trust him implicitly. It's a matter of roles, that's all."

"As you say, My Lady."

She turned and met my gaze directly, determination in the way she lifted her chin. "We will have a court. We will be recognised. The Eighth Court will be home for any fey with mixed blood. They will have to accept us eventually."

"When you say it like that, I believe you," I said, "but you need to say it to them, not me. I wish I could be there to help you convince them."

She shook her head. "Angela will attend me. She'll have to wait outside, but her presence will be noted. She unnerves them enough for it to make the point."

"She's becoming quite an asset. I would never have guessed she'd adapt to life at court so well. She'd lived alone so long, I thought she'd find it daunting."

"I think she's finally found somewhere she can be," said Blackbird, "Which convinces me even more that we are doing the right thing. Besides, they think she knows something."

"What?" I asked her.

She shook her head. "I'm sure if she knew, she'd tell me, but it's as much a mystery to her as to me. If she does know something then she's not aware of the significance of it."

"So we negotiate on bluff and hope they don't know the difference?" I suggested.

"You don't bluff the Seven Courts, Niall, even in jest." She smoothed the dress, "You'd better go before you make us both late. I'll see you when you get back. Give Katherine my regards. Will you ask Angela to join me when she's ready, and we'll walk down together?"

"Yes, Lady." I bowed, accepting the instruction.

Blackbird frowned at me. "Don't tease," she said.

"You'll have to get used to it," I reminded her. "A lot more people are going to be calling you that before we're done."

"Don't remind me," she said, turning back to the mirror.

I took my leave and went to find my daughter.

Alex's room was still at the end of the west wing. I'd offered to find her a room closer to ours, but she'd insisted on being left where she was. Still, there were more visitors these days and she was rarely there alone. I was also trying to be more accepting of her wishes and to treat her as an adult, even when she didn't behave like one.

As I passed along the hallway, Angela emerged and then retreated to her doorway so that I could pass without brushing against her – a courtesy and a necessity with a seer like Angela, since any contact could lead to her seeing flashes of my future – or in her case, my past. Teoth said her power was corrupted by her humanity, but I wasn't so quick to judge.

"Blackbird asked if you'd walk down with her." I told her.

"I was just heading there," she said. "We have two new people coming in this evening. I was hoping Blackbird would spare the time to meet them?"

"I'm sure she will if she can. You'll have to arrange it with her, though. I'm going out with Alex and I'm not sure how long I'll be gone. It should only be a couple of hours, but you never know."

"I'll try and catch her now, then," she said.

I walked on to the end of the corridor where Alex's room was, and knocked quietly on her door. There was no answer. I knocked again more loudly, "Alex? Are you ready?" There was still no reply.

I tried the door handle and the door opened easily. "Alex, honey, we're going to be late." I looked around the room. There were a few clothes laid out on the end of the bed, and an Alex shaped heap underneath the duvet. "Alex, are you OK?"

I walked round to the side of the bed. All I could see was the top of her head. The curls of her dark hair spread across the white pillow were twitching with agitation. Alex's hair had a will of its own and generally reflected her mood.

"What's wrong? I thought you were getting ready?"

"I'm not coming," said the muffled voice under the duvet.

"Not coming? But I thought you wanted to see your mum? I've arranged it especially."

"I'm ill. Tell her I'm s-s-sick and I c-c-can't come," said the muffled voice.

I could hear the lie in that, "Alex, come out from under the quilt," I said firmly, "I'm not talking to the top of your head." The duvet edged downwards until I could see her face.

"What's the matter?"

"I feel sick," she said. From her voice, that at least was true.

"Is it something you've eaten? What did you have for lunch?" I asked her.

"I didn't eat lunch. I felt sick."

"That's probably why you feel ill, then. You need to

17

have something in your stomach or you're going to feel bad."

"If I eat, I'm going to throw up," she said miserably.

"When did all this start?" I asked her. "You were OK this morning."

"I can't see Mum. You'll have to tell her I am ill." She tried to pull the duvet back over her head but I caught the edge of it, and after a moment she let go.

"Is this about seeing your mother?" I asked her. She shook her head, but she couldn't deny it. "Alex, you were keen to see her. What on earth could be the matter?"

"I don't know," she said. "I just feel bad. Tell her I'm not well. Tell her I'll come next time."

I shook my head. "I'm not going to see her without you," I said. "You're the one she wants to see, not me."

"I can't," she said.

"Why not?"

She pulled the quilt more tightly around her, hugging it to her.

I sighed. "I spoke to her yesterday. She was excited about you coming to see her and she's made special arrangements. If you're worried about being spotted, don't be. Your glamour will take care of it. No one will know you were there except your mum and Barry, and they're not going to tell anyone."

"It's not that," she said quietly.

"Then what is it?" I asked her. My question was greeted with a long silence.

"Alex, your mum and me…" I sighed, and tried again. "Your mother and I both love you very much. When you disappeared, it was hard for both of us – harder than you realise. We thought… they lied to us, Alex, in the cruellest way imaginable. They told us we'd lost you, and it broke our hearts – both of our hearts. Your mum, she couldn't cope with seeing your empty room every day. She didn't know you were still alive."

Alex sniffed and wiped her nose on the duvet. I pulled a tissue from the box on the chest next to the bed and gave it to her. She blew noisily.

"Maybe I did wrong. Maybe I should have told her that I'd found you, but I wasn't even sure myself. I thought maybe I was cracking up – hearing your voice when it wasn't there. And then, when I knew you'd been taken away, I didn't know where you were or how to get you back."

A hand crept out from under the duvet and I held it in mine.

"We cope with loss in different ways, and for your mum, having your things in the house with her every day was just too much. It reopened her wounds, and the only way she could cope was to clear it all out and try and move on. I know it was your stuff, but you have to understand – try and see it from her perspective. It wasn't that she wanted to forget, it was that the memories were too fresh, and too painful to bear."

"How can I go back?" said Alex. "How can I go back there when there's nothing left for me?"

I squeezed her hand. "Things are not important. It's all just stuff, Alex. You can replace it, or do without it. What's there for you is your mum. I was wrong to keep you from her, and it's time you re-connected with her. I'm not saying it will be easy. You've both been changed by what's happened and you'll have to work out where you are with her. You'll both carry the scars for as long as you live, but she's still your mum, Alex, and that's what really matters."

She sniffed, and then said, "OK."

"Good," I said. "Now, you have ten minutes to get up and dressed and be downstairs ready to go. I'll wait for you at the Ways."

She sat up in bed. "Ten minutes! I can't get ready in ten minutes! What am I going to wear?"

I stood up and went to the door. "You have clothes on

19

the bed. Your mother won't care what you're wearing. It's you she wants to see, not your clothes."

"But–"

"Ten minutes," I repeated, and shut the door behind me.

Outside I took three deep breaths and went downstairs to wait for her.

The figure slipped into the open-sided barn, melting into the shadows within. "Are you there?"

"Are you sure you weren't followed?" The voice was almost a whisper.

"Don't be ridiculous."

There was a long pause.

"Tell me," instructed the voice.

"What about my side of the bargain?"

"All in good time."

"There's nothing happening. Nothing significant."

"I'll decide what's significant," said the voice.

"The discussions are endless. The courts are in stalemate. Teoth and Krane are opposing them, while Kimlesh, Yonna and Mellion are in support. Barthia doesn't know which side to choose. It's the same as last time."

"That in itself is informative," said the voice. "And you?"

"I don't have a choice."

The voice laughed softly. "No, you don't. How is it?"

"The same."

"Nothing is certain. The sooner the better."

"I need to know."

"And risk exposure? The time will come soon enough. Have faith."

"Easy for you to say."

There was another long pause.

"Are you there?"

When there was no reply, the shadow slipped away.

• • • •

In the basement, ten minutes had come and gone. I paced up and down, wondering how long to wait before I went back up and tried to oust Alex from her bedroom. Going back up would re-set the clock and she would be at least another 15 minutes after that, but equally she could have retreated back under the quilt with no intention of appearing, leaving me to pace up and down.

I glanced again at the door, steeling myself to go back up there, when it opened. Standing nervously in the doorway was an Alex I'd never seen before. She'd somehow tamed her hair into a style that framed her face with dark curls. There were gold studs in her ears, which I couldn't remember ever seeing. She had a royal-blue sweater over a long, flowing maroon skirt that came down to her ankles, and she was wearing a pair of low-heeled court shoes.

"What do you think?" I shook my head and she looked panicky. "You think it's too much?" she asked.

"No, no. It's not you, it's me. For some reason I thought I was the father of a young girl. Then this woman appeared and I... Your mother's not the only one who's got some adjusting to do."

She smoothed her hands down her skirt and smiled hesitantly at that. "We should go," she said.

I stepped forward to the Way-node, glancing back to her. "You know where we're going?" I asked her.

"I'll be right behind you."

I stepped forward onto the Way and felt the power rise beneath me. In a moment I was whirled away across the deepest night.

The advantage of using the Ways is that you can cross a great distance in no time at all. The disadvantage is that they don't always end up where you want to go. While Alex and I were soon in the suburbs of London, we still had to walk to our destination.

"How much further is it?" Alex asked me. "These shoes aren't meant for walking."

"Aren't they?" I asked her. "I thought you'd just, you know…?"

"What?" she said.

"I thought it was just glamour – all the clothes and make-up?"

"It's real," she said. "Which is why I'm going to have blisters."

"I could give you a piggy-back," I told her.

"We are not doing piggy-backs, not when I've gone to all the trouble to look nice for Mum. Have you any idea how much this skirt will crease?"

"No one has to know. You can hide it all if you want to."

"Mum will know."

"How?"

"How the hell do I know? She just will, that's all. It can't be that far, surely?"

"If we cut through here, it'll be quicker," I said, heading for a grassy pathway between some houses.

"Dad!"

"What?" I said, threading my way past the brambles that overhung the path. She stood at the entrance to the pathway, her hands on her hips in exactly the pose that her mother used when she was exasperated with me. "What?" I repeated.

"You're not expecting me to go through there in a skirt and these shoes, are you?"

I glanced down the path. It was rather muddy in the middle and a self-seeded elderberry had taken most of the width of the path about halfway along.

"OK, maybe not," I agreed, returning to her. "I was just trying to save your feet."

"Next time," she said, "We'll ask one of the drivers to bring us down." It made her sound just like her mother.

When we reached the avenue where Katherine and I had once made our home together, I deepened the glamour around us. Given the changes in her these past few months, I thought it unlikely that Alex would be recognised as the girl who'd been killed in a tragic accident, but it didn't hurt to be cautious. I rang the bell and there was a long pause.

"Maybe she's gone out," said Alex. "Maybe they were called away to attend to a sick friend. Maybe…"

A shadow grew through the translucent glass and I recognised Katherine's outline. She unlocked the door and opened it, standing back to let us in, and then stopped. I watched her look from me to Alex, and then back to me.

"Hi Mum," said Alex.

"Alex? I thought, that is… come in, both of you."

In preparation for this moment, I had spent time with Katherine, briefing her, explaining a little about the gifts that Alex had inherited from me and what that might mean. She had greeted the whole thing with scepticism and had been adamant that it made no difference. Alex was still her daughter, nothing had changed. But now that her daughter was there in front of her, I could see that wasn't true. Lots of things had changed. She pushed the door closed behind her, turning her back on it and assessing us both.

"I was just… I need to finish getting your room ready." The lie was apparent to both Alex and me. I'd warned Katherine that Alex would be able to tell if she was untruthful, but it clearly hadn't sunk in.

"What's wrong with my room?" said Alex.

"Nothing, darling. It's just–"

Alex turned and bounded up the stairs, despite the sore feet and impractical shoes.

"Not yet!" said Katherine. "It isn't… ready." It was too late. Alex was upstairs before either of us could react.

"I was trying to… you might as well come up and see for yourself."

She led the way upstairs to the room at the back of the house that had been Alex's until the accident. I knew Katherine'd had it redecorated and fitted out as an office for Barry. I hadn't expected what she'd done with it since discovering that her daughter wasn't dead.

Alex was standing in the room turning round slowly, taking it all in. Katherine watched her. From the doorway I could see the boy-band posters on the walls, the way the light from the new pastel-blue curtains caught on the sparkly headband on the mirrored dressing table. I could see the new bed with the matching duvet cover. She had gone to a great deal of trouble to re-create a teenage girl's bedroom, only to have a young woman stand in it with an expression of complete bemusement on her face.

"Ah," I said, breaking the silence.

Alex looked at her mother and must have seen something there because she leapt forward and hugged her fiercely. "Thanks, Mum." She said. "It's... lovely."

"Well, we can change things," said Katherine hurriedly. "You can choose your own decorations. We'll have a man in to do it properly, you'll see." She hugged her daughter back and kissed her hair. They were almost the same height, I noticed.

"It's a bit..." I started to say. Alex glared at me over her mother's shoulder. "...smaller than I remember." I finished. "But I guess you'll get used to it."

"It's fine," said Alex, releasing her mother. "Right, Dad, it's time you were going, isn't it?"

"Is it?" I asked. "There were a few things I thought we should talk about," I suggested.

Alex side-stepped her mother and steered me towards the stairs. I found myself being propelled gently down to the front door. "You will remember to be careful," I said to Alex over my shoulder. "You're not supposed to be here, remember?"

"I'll be invisible," said Alex. "You can come and get me in a few days. It'll give Mum and me some time together."

"I meant to talk to you about Kayleigh," I said, remembering that I hadn't explained to Alex what Kayleigh knew.

"Don't worry. It'll all sort itself out." She opened the door pointedly.

"OK, I give in. I'll leave you to it."

She stood on tiptoe and kissed my cheek. "Thanks, Dad."

I shook my head. "If you need me to come and get you…"

"I'll come back when I'm ready. Mum knows I'm not staying forever."

"OK. Have a good time." I stepped outside and she closed the door after me. I couldn't escape the feeling that I'd just been evicted by my own daughter.

I straightened my jacket and evaluated options. I would actually be better walking down to the tube station and then finding a Way-node in the centre of town. It would take slightly longer, but would involve a lot less walking.

I turned out of the drive and set off for the station, only to have Katherine run out of the house after me. "Niall, wait!"

I turned and waited for her. "That didn't take long. What's the problem?"

"No problem," she said, "but this came for you. It's been behind the clock in the lounge for a week or so, but I didn't have a forwarding address." She handed me a white envelope with my name and Katherine's address written out longhand in scrawling blue script. I turned it over and there was a serious-looking crest on the back of the envelope.

"It looked like a summons," she said. "You haven't been speeding again, have you?"

I slit the top of the envelope with my finger and pulled out a sheet of carefully folded heavy white notepaper. The crest was repeated on the letterhead – it gave the address as The Royal Courts of Justice, The Strand, London. The same scrawling hand had written the letter.

Dear Niall, if that really is your name.

Please forgive the unorthodox method of contacting you but I have no other way. I've checked the archives, and read the notes of my predecessors, and there's no precedent for this. I got this address from Sam – you remember him, I'm sure. He said this was the last address you were known at. I hope to God it reaches you.

It's happening again. They've been here, I know it. It feels wrong and there are things in places where they shouldn't be. It shouldn't be possible, but I swear it's them.

"Niall?" said Katherine. "Is it bad news?"

"May I come in for a moment?" I asked her. "I'd like to use your phone."

I followed her back to the house. Alex was holding the door half open. "What's wrong, Dad? You look like you've seen a ghost."

"May I?" I asked Katherine, nodding towards the phone in the hall.

"You can use the one in the lounge if you'd like privacy," she said.

I stepped through to the lounge and took the sofa seat next to the telephone, opening out the letter to read the rest of it.

They don't know I'm wise to them yet, and I'm not sure what they're after, but they've been here more than once. I'm making a point of not staying after dark, but I need your help. I can't deal with this alone. I've taken limited precautions, but there's only so much I can do.

Please come,

Claire Radisson, Chief Clerk to the Queen's Remembrancer.

Picking up the phone, I dialled the number on the letter. The phone rang twice.

"Royal Courts of Justice," said a voice. "How can I help?"

"I'd like to speak to Claire Radisson," I said.

"One moment, I'll put you through."

The phone went quiet for a moment, and then rang again. It continued ringing. Eventually the voicemail picked up. A recording started: *You are through to the Queen's Bench Division of the Royal Courts of Justice. Unfortunately there is no one available to take your call. If you would like…*

Katherine watched me from the doorway as I dropped the call and pressed redial.

"Royal Courts of Justice," said the same voice. "What can I do for you?"

"I called a moment ago," I said, "I was trying to reach Claire Radisson in the Queen's Bench Division. Can you tell me if she's in today?"

"I'm afraid I can't give out details of people's whereabouts," said the voice. "I can take a message if you'd like me to ask her to call you, or I can put you through to her voicemail?"

"No, it's OK," I said. "Thanks for your help."

"That's OK. Have a good day." The call dropped and I put the phone back on its cradle.

"Would you like some tea?" asked Katherine.

"That would be nice, thanks," I said. Katherine headed for the kitchen and was replaced by Alex in the doorway.

"What's up," she asked.

"Nothing, I hope. While you're here I want you to look after your mum. No one knows you're here, and let's keep it that way, but take some precautions. Set wards on the doors and windows, that kind of thing."

"Against what?" she asked.

"Unwelcome visitors," I said, tucking the letter into the inside pocket of my jacket and moving back into the hall. Next to the stairs there was a mirror. I placed my hand on it. "Claire Radisson?" A stillness crept into the hallway, broken only by the sound of a kettle boiling from the kitchen. "Claire, are you there?"

The sound wavered in the mirror and then set up a

jarring vibration so that I pulled my hand away sharply before it damaged Katherine's mirror. "She did say she was taking precautions," I told Alex's enquiring look.

"Who did?"

"An old acquaintance."

"What does she want?" she asked.

"I'm going to have to go," I told Alex, as I went to the front door. "Give my excuses to your mum."

"She's making you tea," she told me.

"You drink it." I watched Alex made a face. "Look after each other," I told her.

"You're not going to start with the whole, *don't talk to strangers thing*, again are you?"

"It's good advice," I said, "especially at the moment." I reached out for her and she gave me a brief hug. Then I slipped out of the door and headed for the tube station at a brisk pace.

Two

The Royal Courts of Justice has a portal entrance of pale
stone on the north side of the Strand opposite the church
of St Clement's Dane. It has iron railings along the front,
which are opened to allow the public inside, but if you're
fey they still make your teeth ache when you walk between them.

Joining the file of people going through the metal de-
tectors and full-body scanners, I walked through without
raising any alarm. Once past security, I strolled past the
central reception confidently and mounted the steps to
the first floor. I turned right at the top of the steep stairway and followed the corridor to the end. The door to
Claire's office was closed. I tried it, finding it locked. I
placed my hand upon it.

"Can I help you?" The voice came from a young woman
in a doorway I had passed. I let my hand drop from
the door.

"I was looking for Claire Radisson," I explained. "This
is her office, isn't it?"

"Claire isn't here today," said the woman. "If you'd like
to make an appointment I'm sure reception can help you."

"She asked me to come and see her," I explained.

"She's not there," the woman said, bluntly.

The woman was telling the truth as she saw it. "May I leave a message for her?" I asked.

"I'm sure reception could help you with that." She had emerged from the office and was now standing in the corridor.

"Perhaps I'll go and ask them," I said.

"I think that would be best," she said.

She watched me head back towards the stairway. I took three steps down and waited out of sight for a count of thirty. Then I leaned back around the top of the stairway, finding that the woman had retreated to her office. Wrapping myself in glamour I re-entered the corridor and ghosted past her door to Claire's office. Placing my hand on the door I felt the lock tumble. I pushed the door open and slipped inside. Being careful not to touch the inside door handle, I leaned against the door and pushed it shut with my foot.

Some time ago, Blackbird and I had returned to Claire's office to find it booby-trapped with darkspore, the mould used by female wraithkin to consume the flesh of the unwary – at least it looked like mould. It was actually part of them, a living remnant which could consume organic material, feeding the host. If Claire said they had been here then I had every reason to be cautious.

Taking shallow breaths, I tested the air for the heavy scent of rot and decay. Edging into the room, I could see that the outer office had changed little since I'd been here last. There was a picture – modern art – that had not been here before. Claire had acquired a new office chair with a flexible mesh back, and a chrome coat-stand. The doors to the Queen's Remembrancer's office were closed, but I suspected that even if there were small changes in the outer office, the inner sanctum would remain as it had always been.

I glanced across Claire's desk and that's when I noticed the open cupboard. There was an empty square on the floor of the cupboard. The indentation was rectangular. It was where the safe containing the knives and the horse-shoes for the Quit Rents ceremony was kept. The safe had gone. There were marks in the plasterwork where the plaster and bricks had been chipped away to expose the bolts that anchored it, and dust on the floor where the anchors securing the safe to the wall had been levered out. Someone had taken their time and neatly removed the safe, which must have taken a while and caused a fair amount of noise, but no one had raised an alarm.

Scanning the room, I noted the scuff marks in the carpet. Checking the door handles to the Queen's Re-membrancer's office, I opened it and scanned the room from the doorway. There was no one there and the room hadn't changed at all. Even so, there was no sign of the safe or the people who'd taken it.

"What do you think you're doing?" The voice came from the outer door. The woman from the other office was standing there looking severe.

I turned to face her. "The safe, where is it?" I asked her.

"I don't know what you think you're doing in here, but if you do not leave right away I am calling security," she threatened.

"This is not a game," I told her. "Claire asked me here. Now where's the safe?"

She went to shut the door on me, but I moved too quickly. Wrenching the door from her, I propelled her backwards. As she staggered back I caught her by the lapels of her jacket and lifted her up the wall with one hand. She squeaked in surprise, the seams in her jacket crackling as they took the strain. She tried to kick me but I pressed in close so our breath mingled, allowing her only limited movement.

I spread my glamour around us, deadening sound. "You can scream, no one will hear you." She took that as an invitation, screaming her head off. True to my word, though, we remained alone.

I waited until she realised it too, and her screams petered out. "Earlier, you asked if you could help me. Now's your chance. Where's the safe?"

"Fuck you," she said, through gritted teeth. You had to admire her. A foot off the ground, pinned to the wall and she was still spitting abuse.

"You don't understand," I said. "I risked my life for the contents of that safe. I know damned well that Claire wouldn't let it out of her sight, so where is it?"

She glared at me.

"I'd play these games if it weren't so fucking serious," I said. "I'll ask you once more."

She shook her head, clamping her lips tight.

The air shifted in the corridor. The light faded, and dappled moonlight grew and shifted across the wall. Her eyes went wide, the whites around them stark in the pale light. My hand was outlined against her jacket, the purest black. Looking into her eyes I knew she was seeing me as a lightless hole in the world. A song hummed in my veins, a long note, low and loud, calling to me. I could feel tendrils of darkness, spreading from my hand under her clothes. Her eyes went wide. She screamed again, uninhibited, kicking and thrashing in my grip. "They came and took it! Some men. From a company. They took it away!"

I held back the tide rushing into me, gritting my own teeth against the flood that pressed for release. "When?"

"A little while ago. For pity's sake!" she squeaked.

"Who took it?"

"Some men. They're replacing it with a newer one."

"How long?"

"Fifteen minutes. Twenty maybe?"

"Where?"

"I don't know," she wailed. Tears were running down her face. There was the certain knowledge in her eyes that I would kill her. A small part of me believed her. A small part of me wanted to, but she was telling the truth.

I released her and she collapsed like a sack of sand onto the floor. Her head lolled to one side. I forced back the wave of power and let the magic fade. Looking down at her, I wondered what was becoming of me. There were some things ordinary people weren't meant to see and she'd just come very close to dying. Looking at her made me think of the stories that Claire had told us when we first met. She'd said that not everyone who dealt with the Feyre walked away unscathed, and I was beginning to see why. I needed to get better control of myself. I had almost killed her for no other reason than she wouldn't give me what I wanted. That was what Raffmir would do, and I would not let myself sink to his level.

I squatted down in front of her. Her eyes were not focusing. She was in shock. Fifteen or twenty minutes maximum, she'd said. They'd only just gone – for a moment I wondered what would have happened if I'd walked in on them while they were cutting the safe loose.

If I left her where she was, someone would soon notice her. Perhaps they would call an ambulance or a doctor. It was more than I could do for her. I'd already done too much. Whoever had been here, they had a heavy safe containing the horseshoes, the nails and the two knives from the ceremony. Fifteen minutes with a heavy safe in this warren of a building.

There was every chance they were still here.

I jogged down the corridor, swerving round someone emerging from an office with a pile of folders, nearly knocking them off their feet. "Don't run!" they called after me.

Ignoring them, I paused only to look through the windows into the courts along the hall. They had a safe, now where would they take it? Not into court. Out the front door? No, I would have encountered them already. They could cloak themselves in glamour but the safe would remain as it was. The iron inside it would protect it – that

33

was why it was there. The iron in it should prevent them carrying it, so where were they? They must have found a way to counter it, to mask the nature of it.

Reaching the end of the corridor, I stopped. There were numerous stairways, up and down – difficult to get a heavy safe downstairs. If you were fey you couldn't hold it with the knives inside it. Someone else was moving it. They must have human collaborators. It was the only way. Sprinting around the corner, I slipped between two gowned barristers in conversation. They shouted after me, but I was already past. There were display cases left and right – somewhere close there must be a goods lift. Somewhere, but where?

I rounded a corner and was presented with more corridors. I was running out of time. I could run around this maze all day and never find them. There must be a better way. My eyes settled on a small red box on the wall – fire alarm. Crude, yet effective. Now I was thinking.

Using the heel of my hand, I smashed the glass. Immediately sirens echoed down the corridor. There was a moment's pause while everyone wondered whether it was a false alarm, and then they began moving. I kept ahead of the crowd, searching for misfits, the odd ones out, allowing myself to be shepherded towards the exits with the rest. Once outside I watched the doors, but no one emerged with a heavy object. There were lawyers, jurors, members of the public, police, but no one who looked like they would remove a safe. I moved down the street, heading for the side entrance. The restless autumn leaves swirled around my feet in the fickle breeze.

I peered through the iron railings under the stone arches into the courtyard of the Royal Courts of Justice, looking for anyone struggling with a heavy load. A wooden guard post was just beyond the railings manned by two security guards. This close, I could feel the dissonant hum of the iron railings between me and them. There was no way I could touch them, never mind climb

34

over them and slip inside, and the proximity of so much iron was disrupting the glamour that made me less noticeable, drawing curious glances from the guards.

Moving back from the railings, I watched as one of them answered the phone while the other went to attend to a grey van that had pulled up beside the guard station. With luck and good timing, I would be able to slip into the courtyard unnoticed when they let the van out. As I moved in towards the iron gates, the guard went to speak with the driver, who wound down his window. I waited by the exit, watching them. There was a reflection on the windscreen: the monochrome image of bare branches of the trees above distorted by the curve in the glass. The clouds thickened, dimming the meagre sunlight so that the reflection faded. I caught a glimpse through the windscreen of the person in the passenger seat. The long face, high cheekbones and black hair were familiar.

It was Raffmir!

He must have seen me too. Suddenly the guard was thrown back and the van gunned its engine, leaping into motion. It crashed into the gate, swinging the heavy ironwork directly out at me. I dived, but the gates hit me, hurling me away with a force beyond their weight. I felt the dark pulse of power as they struck me, the jolt of pain as the iron sent a numbing shock through my body.

I landed heavily, and for a long while the dark swallowed me. After a while, though, I began to sense sounds, and lights, and cold, and it came to me that I must be dreaming.

The rain descended in sheets in the dark, depressing the branches of nearby trees and drumming on the ground. Everywhere tiny rivulets slithered through the grass, pooling in hollows and merging, joining to form the beginnings of streams, meandering towards the river.

I stumbled across the uneven ground. Though the rain did not touch me, it curtained my vision so that I nearly toppled over the bank into the flood. Even in the limited light under the clouds I could see the river was swollen, testing its banks and pulling at tree roots. Out in the stream, leafy branches emerging from the brown water gave testament to comrades already fallen to the flood.

Out on the river there was a light, swinging and bobbing. It hung over the flow, seemingly floating, as it edged towards me.

Alerted by the sound of hooves, I turned, alarmed. A horse galloped into view, then skidded and slid as, seeing the barrier too late, the rider tried to turn away from the river. The horse toppled onto its side with a solid thump, whinnying in protest. The rider slipped deftly from the saddle, rolling to the side, but failed to account for the treacherous ground and tumbled into the mud, coating himself in it all down one side.

The horse twisted and clambered to its feet, then trotted away sulking before halting at the limit of visibility. The horseman swore in a language I did not comprehend, but his meaning was clear. He ignored me, coming to stand at the bank's eroded edge to stare into the dark. He was young, stoutly built and muscular. His long hair was twisted across his face and he pulled it behind him, plaiting it quickly into a loose braid in a practiced gesture. He was not dressed for the weather, wearing only light trousers and a loose shirt which clung to his skin, revealing muscular arms.

He saw the light on the river and ran back to the horse, which stood shivering in the dark. He pulled a small package from the saddle, slapping the horse's rump so that it trotted away into the dark.

Returning to the riverbank, he called out in a harsh foreign tongue, raw and guttural, to the source of the light. It hung there in the dark, and then edged towards the bank. As it neared, a boat resolved behind it, pointing upstream. A figure in a long cloak stood in the craft, balancing easily as it rocked and swerved in the current. There was no sail, and no one rowing, yet it leaned into the current and danced between the flotsam being dragged downstream. As it neared the bank, the hood was pulled back.

"Kimlesh?" I said, and then realised she could not see me.

She answered the young man, her clear voice carrying across the water.

"What do you wish for?" she asked.

He answered her. His words were incomprehensible whereas hers were plain, but his gesture at the far bank was clear.

"There is a bridge a few miles downstream," said Kimlesh. "If it still stands."

He said something under his breath and then held up the bag he had taken from the horse's pack. He shook the package, which chinked, and though the sound surely did not carry to the craft bobbing in the current, his meaning was clear.

"You are lying. You will steal my boat and slit my throat, if you can," she said.

He shook his head and climbed carefully down the bank to the water's edge where the brown water sucked at the bank.

"Your voice betrays you," she said.

He searched the bank, then, looking for something but not finding it. After a moment, he called out, again.

"There is no tether, Guillaume, nor any needed. This boat finds its way in any flood."

His expression was bemused. He called a question to her.

"You already know that, son of Herleva. Why are you here, then?"

He shrugged, glancing over his shoulder.

"First we bargain, Guillaume, and then we will see," she said.

There was a drumming over the persistent pattering of the rain; hoof-beats splashing through the wet. His expression changed at the sound of hooves, and his entreaties became more persistent, though he lowered his voice so he would not be over-heard.

"What will you give me in exchange, Guillaume? What will you offer me in return for escape from your pursuers?" Her voice was quiet, but it carried across the water.

You had to admire the man. It took nerve to stand on the bank with the horsemen riding up and down the river looking for him while the bargaining went back and forth. At one point

*there was a cheer as they found the loose horse, but he never
looked back. His attention was focused on the woman. Everything else, even the rain, might as well not have existed.*

*"We are agreed then," she said. "I will take you to the far
shore, and you will grant me a single boon when I come before
you and petition in person, be it within your power?"*

*A jingle of harness behind us sealed the deal and the boat
dived to shore. Guillaume tried to step into the shallows and
sank up to his thigh in the deep water where the shore was cut
away by the current. He was nearly swept away, but the craft
was alongside, and she held it firm while he scrambled over the
gunnel and tumbled in. Immediately the bow turned out into
the current and it bobbed into the flow, the light dancing at the
prow. A shout went up and horses pounded over, spilling men
with spears. Guillaume was briefly visible, lying in the bow
while the hooded Kimlesh stood in the stern as they faded into
the rain.*

*The men peered into the dark, one casting a spear out across
the water, which fell short and slipped into the flow and was
not seen again. The men swore among themselves, but none
tried to enter the stream after the young man. They gathered up
their horses and rode away in a mass, downstream, heading for
the bridge that Kimlesh had mentioned.*

"Is he dead?" said a voice.

"You don't see living people that colour," said another.

"What's that on his face?" said the first voice.

"It's where the gate hit him. You see the pattern from
the ironwork?"

I tried to move. I felt numb, as if my whole body had
pins and needles. My body was twitching with the effort.

"He's moving!" said the voice.

My body continued to twitch and jerk. "Nnnnnnngggh,"
I groaned, trying to get my tongue to obey me.

"He's alive," said the second voice. "Call an ambulance! Get some help!"

People were shuffling around me. Across my vision, blobs of luminous colour slid past. It was like being inside a lava lamp. The light intensified and my eyes jerked open. "T-t-t-t-t...." My teeth were chattering, though I had no sensation of cold.

I could hear people moving, but I couldn't focus. I could see vague shapes swimming in and out of my field of vision; the light burned into the back of my brain, but now my eyes were open I couldn't close them. Someone was using a mobile phone, calling an ambulance.

"He's lying on the floor," he said, and then after a pause, "No, not as far as I can see."

It felt like my arms and legs were quivering as sensation returned. I managed to twitch my arm over my eyes in a rag-doll spasm, shielding them from the intense light.

"Are you all right?" said the second voice.

I swallowed, and managed to roll over onto my side. As soon as I did, I puked noisily onto the pavement, my stomach cramping and my knees jerking upwards with the effort of chucking everything up. It was some minutes before I could hear anything other than the sound of my own retching.

"Here, I have a tissue somewhere," said the voice.

A middle-aged lady squatted down beside me and fished into her handbag, pulling out a small pack of tissues. "Can you breathe now?"

I nodded, accepting the tissue and wiping my mouth. It was coming back to me now. I'd been next to the gates. The van had driven straight through them, flinging the gates into me and knocking me flying. Raffmir had been the passenger in the van.

"Give me a hand," I asked hoarsely.

"I think you should wait," said the lady. "There's an ambulance on its way. They won't be long."

"I have to get after them," I said.

"Who? The van? They're long gone – nothing you can do about it. Just you rest there."

I pushed myself up onto my elbow. Now that sensation was returning I could feel the bruising down my face, chest, arms, thighs… I was going to be a patchwork of black and blue.

"Get me up," I said to the lady.

"I don't think you're in any position to–" said the lady.

"I said, get me up," I growled. Something in my tone must have overridden her concern because she offered her hand and I half-crawled and half-staggered to my feet.

"Have to think…" I said, mostly to myself.

"You're in shock," she said. "It takes some people like this. You need to sit down and have a nice cup of tea."

"A cup of tea… not what I need right now," I said. "Which way did the van go?" I looked up and down the street. She was right. They were in a vehicle, with the safe. I was on foot, and I had no idea where they were going.

In my head I could hear a voice echoing hers. You are in shock. You don't know what you're doing.

I knew one thing, though. I couldn't afford to be around when the ambulance arrived. I staggered away from her, into the street. A taxi swept by, horn blaring. I had a brief impression of the face in the cab, a fist raised.

"Where are you going?" the woman called after me.

I lurched into an unsteady jog, weaving towards the big stone church across the paving. Veering around, I could see I was leaving a line of red spots on the pale paving. I was bleeding from somewhere – I held out my arms to see where it was coming from, whirling around wildly, leaving a trail of bloodspots. It was like they were following me around. I wrapped my glamour around me in a vague attempt to disguise my path, knowing that the trail of blood-spots would give me away regardless. I wanted to turn people away, to get them to ignore me, but I was incapable of such subtlety. Instead I slammed together a ward of *Leave me alone!* and hoped for the best. Crashing open the doors into the church, I collided with an old man in the entrance porch. I barged him aside, taking the steps down to the crypt in ones and twos. I could hear the commotion behind me.

The crypt of the church of St Clement's Dane is not a great place to hide, but there is a Way-node there. That much I remembered. I stumbled onto it, feeling it rise up under me, and it swept me away from the sounds of pursuit and unwelcome attention. The Ways welcomed me, lifting me and carrying me across the void, my direction unknown, without focus or purpose. I found myself drifting, hanging in the blackness with the sounds of lost souls echoing around me. I wavered in and out of consciousness, without sense of direction

"Something I have to do…" I heard a voice say, then recognised it as my own. I watched my out-flung hand; blue fox-fire was dancing from my fingertips. "…have to focus."

Groaning with effort, I pulled myself through the emptiness, searching for a way out. Shadows drifted near me, edging away into the blackness as soon as I faced them. Suddenly space and gravity returned and I found myself falling forwards in complete darkness onto a hard stone floor. I remember the cool of the hard paving, the rough texture under my cheek, just before I passed out.

The square was large and open, dominated by the huge church at one end. It looked like a medieval pageant, except that the horses, the coaches and the people standing around watching were beyond what anyone would wear outside of a film set. The buildings gave the lie to that, though. These were half-timbered, but clean, with bleached wood beams and whitewashed plaster. The bells in the campanile were tolling and calling the faithful to prayer, but those answering the call weren't just any faithful. It was a procession, the wealthy of the city gathering to make their peace with God. People were held back by ranks of men, while those in open-topped coaches and on horseback progressed slowly past. I looked around, finding the architecture uncharacteristically grand and flamboyant, at odds with my impression of the time.

At that moment I heard horsemen coming into the square – not the gentle walk of horses but an urgent clatter of hard-shod hooves on the cobbles. There was a change of mood in the crowd, a murmur that grew into alarm as the crowd scattered before mounted men. They pushed into the square – between fifty and a hundred hard men with lined faces and grizzled beards, their mouths set hard and eyes narrowed. Their weapons were undrawn, shields slung from saddles and swords sheathed, but the impression that this could suddenly change and turn into a massacre was in the forefront of my mind. Is that what I was here to witness? A slaughter?

The arrogance of the wealthy came to the fore as they turned to see these interlopers, watching them as one might watch a spectacle or a sporting event. Footmen moved in to seal the gap between the horsemen and their patrons. They had spears raised in defiance and their ranks were well-disciplined, but they might as well have stood before a tidal wave. The horsemen rode easily through them, the screams of the fallen echoing in the square, as spears were swept aside by swords that were suddenly bared, and axes hefted in battle-scarred hands. The footmen were not prepared for a mounted assault and either stood aside or were run down by the horses. Anguished cries came from the men, as unease spread through the wealthy. Suddenly their assurance was undermined, but they had nowhere to go.

The mounted men pushed into the open square in loose formation, their horses disciplined, their movements ordered. They halted twenty feet from the procession, their horses champing, shaking their heads, excited at the prospect of action. They edged into a long row facing the nobles, and halted. Questions were called from the coaches, but the line of horsemen remained tight; the silence of grim-faced men only broken by the whinny of the horses or the cries of the trampled footmen as they were carried away behind them. The crowd was silent, expectant and waiting. No one knew what would happen. They only knew they would be witnesses.

Behind the line of horsemen, a man dismounted. He was big, broad-shouldered, his face hard and his muscles lean. He carried no sword or axe, but without a word the silent horsemen parted before him, edging sideways as if his mere presence were enough to move them. He walked through the line of men and across the space between the procession and the line of horsemen.

As he approached, a footman leapt down from a carriage to protect his charges, and then stopped. The big man looked at the servant and then looked back at the line of horsemen. Along the line were several mounted archers. Bows ready, arrows nocked, they stood ready to draw, eyes focused on the footman. The big man met his stare and he looked back to his coach for guidance. I could see it cross the servant's face: this wasn't bravery, this was stupidity.

The big man walked past him, nodding an acknowledgement of the bravery of a lone man prepared to stand against the line of mounted men. He swept his long hair back from his face in an unconscious gesture, plaiting it into a loose braid, and it was then that I recognised him. He'd grown since the incident at the river, putting on weight that wasn't all muscle. He had stature that had been absent when he was being pursued, that came from more than the line of men behind him. This man was used to command, used to being at the centre of events. Townsmen and visitors, noblemen and women, servants and soldiers – they all watched him.

He walked along the row until he reached a young woman in a line of wealthy men. She was no more than a girl, and sat side-saddle on a beautiful grey horse, immaculately groomed and dressed with ribbons in its mane. She faced forward, and looked at the church across the square, not down at the man now standing beside her. The wealthy men around her moved restlessly, trying to decide what to do, but she ignored the man looking up at her completely.

He spoke to her. His voice was heard clearly across the square, but the words were alien to me. Her eyes didn't waver. He spoke again, and this time he caught hold of the reins of her horse.

43

She wrapped her hands in the reins and tried pull them from him, but he tugged them hard and she was wrenched from her saddle and pitched at his feet, skirts and petticoats trailing over the saddle as she slid to the ground. The fall was hard and she landed awkwardly, but she neither cried out, nor begged for assistance. She stood slowly, gathering her dress, brushing at smeared marks on her elbows and arms, and pulling her dignity together. She turned and faced the man, who watched her with apparent amusement. She drew back her arm and slapped him hard across the face.

There was utter silence. Neither the mounted men, nor the merchants moved.

He said something quietly to her that I did not hear. She replied in cold tones. The big man regarded her for a long moment. Then he drew a knife from his belt. One of the men behind her went to draw his sword and found himself the focus of the mounted archers. He took his hand away from the pommel very slowly.

The big man reached in and slipped the knife under the girth of the saddle, severing it in one smooth cut. He stepped in and pitched the saddle from the horse, dumping it behind her mount and making the horses behind hers dance back restlessly. Her horse stepped sideways and then recovered, standing shivering beside her. He regarded the girl, but she neither flinched nor gave way. He looked up at the merchants behind her, but not one would meet his gaze.

He stepped back, and gave a courtly bow quite at odds with his demeanour. With that he strode back through the lines and found his own mount, swinging easily up into the saddle. He surveyed the procession and the square for a moment as if he were committing it to memory, and then turned his mount and rode out of the square. The line of men followed, until the clatter of their passing faded from the square. Everyone waited until the last of them had gone and then let out the breath they'd been holding.

The girl, who had been left standing beside her unsaddled horse, was suddenly assailed by offers of carriages and assis-

tance. She ignored all of them and, leaving the saddle where it had fallen, took the reins of her horse and walked with it along the line of the procession to the very front, passed the reins to a waiting footman, and with the all the grace she could muster, entered the church.

THREE

I came to on a cold stone floor. My cheek felt like it had been sandpapered. I tracked back through my memories, setting aside the dreams of stranger encounters, and tried to figure out what floor I was lying on. It was dark and cold, but not damp. Swallowing as I licked my dry lips, I winced in pain as I lifted my hand to my face, feeling the crusty trails of dried blood. I probed it with my fingers. Dry was a good sign: at least I'd stopped bleeding.

I pushed myself up from the hard stone, listening in the darkness for any signs of habitation around me. It was mercifully quiet. Tentatively I reached inside myself and let my power spill out, illuminating what turned out to be a small cellar with a shifting milky light. Rolling into a position where I could prop myself up on an elbow I swallowed several times before trying to sit. I sat like that, hands on knees, while I gathered my thoughts and figured out what to do next.

Exiting via St Clement's Dane with a posse of do-gooders in pursuit hadn't been too clever. In my confused state I'd just staggered in there and thrown myself down the Ways. I was lucky I hadn't become lost there. I might never have found a way out.

My fingers traced a pattern of wheals and blisters on

my face where the iron gates had hit me. No wonder I'd been disorientated. Being hit by half a ton of swinging iron, I was probably lucky to be alive. It'd happened so quickly. I explored the rest of my body gingerly, finding no breaks, but numerous bruises. The worst of it was the oblique cut across my forehead which still felt sticky when I probed it. At least the feeling of dislocation and nausea had passed. Standing slowly, using a broken and seatless chair-frame for support, I had a moment of dizziness, but nothing like the swimming vertigo from before. I took that as a positive sign.

I was going to be in deep trouble. Part of being a Warder was maintaining a low profile, which I had singularly failed to do. The other part was getting the job done. I didn't even want to think about that. I couldn't go back empty-handed. The safe in Claire's office was long gone. It wasn't my fault, but it would look like it. Perhaps that was the intention. It was not beyond Raffmir to achieve the twin aims of stealing the means to maintain the barrier and discredit me in the process.

Get the job done. That was in the job description.

At least I should find out what happened to Claire.

I let the milky light fade and then stepped gently onto the Way-node, letting it carry me and ignoring its usually exuberant ride, sliding over nodes to loop back on myself and turn back into London without passing back through St Clement's Dane. I'd caused enough excitement there for one day.

The journey left me aching, but brought me out in one of the smaller parks, into the gathering dark – the day had slipped past without me. I shifted my glamour to conceal my blood-stained clothes and the cut on my forehead and hailed a taxi, keeping to myself, sitting huddled in the back while we navigated the streets of West London. We cruised to a halt in front of a row of townhouses converted into flats on a side street and I paid the cab-driver, watching him rumble away as I stood beside the road, suddenly chilled by the freezing wind.

Claire Radisson's mansion flat was rear-facing, but I figured that welcome guests didn't sneak around the back, they knocked at the front door like civilised people. I laid my hand on the street door and felt the lock tumble and click open. Inside, the smell of disinfectant floor-cleaner was overpowering, but at least the hall was warm. I took the stairway up to the flat, listening to the sound of early evening behind closed doors. At Claire's door all was silent, but I couldn't really imagine her watching TV, other than serious current affairs, maybe. I rang the bell, standing back from the door so that she would be able to see me through the security peep. I didn't imagine she had that many visitors. Her role as Chief Clerk to the Queen's Remembrancer and the secrecy about the more esoteric aspects of her role did not invite confidences. I knew that she and Sam Veldon had once been together, but my understanding was that was all in the past. I stood in the hallway while the door remained resolutely unanswered. Perhaps she was out buying groceries, or had gone to dinner with a friend. I re-opened the letter from my pocket, scanning her words. *I hope to God this reaches you.*

I placed my hand on the door, and immediately retracted it. Something was amiss. It felt like unexpectedly touching a snake. I could feel the wrongness in the door. I tried again, feeling for the sense of the door so that I could click the lock open, but as soon as my hand touched the door I was forced to snatch it away.

I tried the bell again and rapped sharply on the door, avoiding touching it for any length of time. "Claire? Are you there? It's Niall." There was no sound from within. I glanced down the corridor. If I made much more noise, I might start attracting attention. The last thing I wanted was someone calling the police.

Blackbird had stayed with Claire for a short while

when she was pregnant and on the run from the Seventh Court. She'd mentioned that Claire had a rear fire escape. If I was not a welcome guest, then maybe I needed another entrance. I walked back to the stairs and descended to the ground floor and the street. Walking along the row, I took the side alley, the wind whipping around the corner and pulling at my jacket, making me wish I'd brought a coat, but I'd only been dropping off my daughter – I had only been going out for an hour or so.

The alley led to a service road that ran behind the rows of houses, populated by dumpsters and networked by fire escapes that climbed the rear of the building. Light spilled from occupied flats, creating more shadow than illumination. I worked my way along the row until I was behind Claire's flat. I could see the fire escape, but her windows were dark. Maybe she was away. That wouldn't be a bad idea if she was feeling nervous. Maybe in the absence of a reply from me she had decided to take a break somewhere warm and leave it all behind, except she didn't strike me as the sort of person to leave when things were in crisis. Intensifying the misdirection around me, I rolled one of the dumpsters under the fire escape. Climbing on top, I leapt upwards to catch the rail of the fire escape, expecting it to lower itself on counterweights so that I could use the steps. Instead, I hung there, swinging from the underside of the rail from the cold steel bars. Shifting my weight between my hands, I felt above me, finding nothing to hold so that I could pull myself upwards.

While I didn't have anything like the reaction to steel that I had to iron, it wasn't the easiest thing to hang from, not helped by the dull throb from my recent encounter with a van. The metal felt intensely cold, and I could feel a spreading ache seeping into my muscles. I dropped back to the dumpster with a booming thud. Perhaps the mechanism had been designed specifically to prevent it being used as an aid to burglary. Perhaps I needed another approach. I jumped down from the dumpster and hauled it out of the way.

Scanning up and down the alley, I listened for signs that I was being observed. I stepped across the alley, putting my back against the wall opposite so that I could see where I wanted to be. I deepened the glamour of concealment, and then opened the well of power within me. The air around me chilled even further and the wind whipped down the alley tumbling empty cardboard coffee cups and discarded carrier bags along. I drew power into me, watching the lights in the surrounding flats dim and flicker. I felt the emptiness within me dilate as more power poured into the well at my core.

Gradually the world took on a papery thinness, as if it were made only of images painted on insubstantial shadows. Walls became translucent, so that I could see the shifting shadows of people moving within. I stared up at Claire's balcony, focusing on that point, and stepped forwards. The world flashed white and then was quiet. I turned and could look down to where I'd been in the service alley. On the walkway above me, a door opened and someone walked along the metal walkway. There was a sharp tapping. A door opened.

"It's only me," said a female voice. "Is your electric all right? Mine is going on and off."

A male voice answered. "No, mine too. It's back on now, though."

"I thought it was gonna go off for good," said the first voice.

"Seems to be OK now," said the man.

"I've got some candles if you need them. They're scented ones, but if you need some I've got plenty."

"I'm fine thanks."

"Am I interrupting something?" said the female voice.

"I was just sitting down to supper," said the male voice. I could hear the blatant lie in that. From the tone, I was surprised she couldn't.

50

"OK then. I'd best be getting back."

"See you, then."

I heard the footsteps padding back to the door above me, and then the door closing. The man's door closed too, but I thought for a moment I could hear the faint sound of giggling coming from the man's flat, though not in a male voice.

I set that aside and peered through the window into Claire's flat. The windows were shut, and there were no lights inside. There was a fire exit off the kitchen and I pressed my hand to the door, wary of booby traps. Claire knew to protect herself from intruders – especially ones with my abilities.

The door clicked and I eased it open slowly, opening my senses to the dim interior. What hit me first was the smell – a stuffy, foetid aroma that jarred with my memory of the flat. It had been spotless when I'd been here last, and I couldn't imagine her leaving it otherwise.

I stepped inside, leaving the door ajar for the fresh air more than anything else. The interior was dim, but I could see marks on the walls that hadn't been there before. I weighed the risk for a moment, and then clicked on the light. I didn't fancy exploring the flat in the dark.

The glow from the energy-saving bulb gradually increased. Now that I could see, my heart sank. There was a long streak down the wall, as if someone had fallen backwards, trailing their hand down the wall while it was covered in brown paint. Except I already knew it wasn't paint.

Now that I knew what to look for I could see the trail along the carpet. I followed it into the living room where I had once spent the night on the sofa. I clicked on another light.

This room had been Claire's sanctuary. It was filled with keepsakes and dark-wood furniture. Some of that furniture had been hacked to pieces. Other pieces were smashed. The sofa I had slept on was slashed so that the stuffing bulged out in white tufts.

Someone had swept blood in spatter-lines up the walls and across the carpet. There were trails of blood everywhere.

Blood spatters onto the glass wall as Raffmir's sword slices the head from the nurse who brought us the key to the cells. Her head bounces down the corridor. Lines of black blood run down the glass leaving a dark smear in their trail. The smell of fear and death is in my nostrils...

I shook myself, trying to push the memory from beneath Porton Down Research Centre back down. It was too much. I turned and ran for the fire escape, bursting through the door onto the balcony and throwing up over the railing into the alley below. There was little enough in my stomach, but that didn't stop the dry heaving.

I already knew I was going to have to go back into the flat.

The kitchen seemed a good place to start. The bedrooms were what I'd been dreading. I'd seen too many bodies in the last year or so, and it never seemed to get any easier. I wondered how policemen coped, which set me thinking about Sam Veldon. Depending on what I found, I would decide whether Sam would have to be told.

I stood in the small galley kitchen and tried to piece together what had happened. Part of the smell was the slowly rotting red peppers on the chopping board and the chopped tomato in the pan on the stove. She had been in the middle of preparing a meal and then... what? Just left it? Heard a noise? There was a knife rack on the worktop. One of the knives was missing. It wasn't on the worktop or in the sink where grease had congealed around the edge of the murky water.

I turned back past the fire exit and looked at the streak down the wall. It was blood – you didn't need to be a forensic scientist to see that. Had she fallen? It looked like she'd pressed her hand to the blood and then collapsed, smearing it down the wall. There was blood soaked into the carpet. That didn't make sense. Surely you fell first and then bled all over the carpet, so how did the blood get on the wall? The living room didn't answer the question. It looked like someone had gone berserk, strewing mayhem around the room. But why attack the sofa? What had it done to deserve being hacked to pieces?

The front door was as I suspected. An iron horseshoe was hanging on a hook on the back of the door. I didn't get too close. It would prevent anyone with fey abilities opening the door, though, which meant that whoever had gained access had come through the back.

I went back through the living room, heading for the bedroom, readying myself for what I might find. An image from my past of a woman lying on a bed with her throat ripped out was at the forefront of my mind. I pushed the door open gingerly. The bedroom looked curiously untouched. The bed was made, the covers pulled over. I checked the far side of the bed, half expecting to find a body. There was only a patterned rug.

That left the bathroom.

I pushed the door open with my foot. There was a shower curtain drawn across the bath, but that wasn't what caught my attention. The sink was stained with blood. The mirror was streaked with it. The tiles had droplets that had run until they dried. There was a facecloth dyed brown with it. I stepped inside, being careful to avoid treading in the bloodspots on the floor and drew the shower curtain back in one fluid motion.

The bath was empty. Not only that, it was clean. I drew the curtain across again and noted the blood spots on it. They had come into the bathroom and sprayed blood across the sink, the floor and across the outside of the shower curtain, and then left. This made no sense at all. Claire wasn't fey, and if she'd died her body should still be here. No one was going to carry her body away. So where was she? My mind drifted back the dumpster in the alley. I had stood on top of it to try and reach the fire escape. Had I been closer than I thought?

I stepped carefully out of the bathroom, retracing my steps and went back to the kitchen passage, polishing the light switch to leave no incriminating fingerprints as I switched it off. The welcoming dark hid the stains and the chaos. I retreated to the fire escape and closed the fire-door behind me, finding the chill, clean air welcome after the cloying smell of the flat. Taking the fire escape downwards, I was able to drop from where I had grabbed on to the rail to the alley below.

Hoisting the lid off the dumpster, I expected to see a set of dead eyes. Instead there were plastic rubbish bags. I pulled them apart looking for something that looked less like a bag and more like a body. In the darkness, a flash of bright metal caught my eye. Amidst the bags there was a kitchen knife.

Angling the knife so it caught the light, I could see brown stains smeared across the blade. She had been cutting peppers and tomato, and this definitely wasn't tomato juice. My assumption was that whoever had found Claire had killed her, but without a body that theory was getting harder to substantiate. This was her knife and it had bloodstains on it.

Maybe she wasn't dead after all?

When I reached the courts, all was quiet. Amber was watching the Ways. As far as she knew, I'd taken my daughter to visit my ex-wife. I'd returned covered in blood, livid bruises across my face, a gash on my forehead, and carrying a blood-stained knife. She took in my appearance and shook her head once, making no further comment. It made me wonder what would be considered worthy of comment in Amber's world.

When I reached our rooms I got more of the reception I'd been expecting.

"Niall! What on earth happened to you? And where did you get that?" Blackbird was referring to the knife. She was no longer dressed up for court and looked more like the Blackbird I knew.

"I found it in a dumpster." It was the truth, but her expression told me it was not sufficient.

"I can't let you out of my sight for two minutes," she said. "Angela, bring me a wet towel – with cold water. For goodness sake, Niall. Where did these bruises come from? I thought you were visiting Katherine." At least she hadn't concluded that I'd murdered them all. She made me sit while she inspected the gash across my forehead.

"I was visiting an old friend." Angela appeared with the towel, handing it to Blackbird, who dabbed it at my forehead. "Ow! That stings."

"Don't be such a baby. You don't want it to get infected, do you?"

"I can't get infections. I'm fey," I pointed out.

"You can still scar, and if I don't close this wound properly you'll have a white gash across your forehead for a long time to come."

"I thought it would make me more handsome... ouch! Do you have to do that so hard?"

She pressed the cloth to the wound on my forehead. "Maybe you'll think twice next time. So what happened?"

Pulling Claire's letter from my pocket, I passed it to Blackbird who passed it to Angela. I explained about what happened at the Royal Courts of Justice. I even admitted to pinning the woman against the wall.

"I didn't have time for twenty questions," I explained, but still earned a frown of disapproval from Blackbird. "And then Raffmir ran me over with the van, or at least he crashed the gates into me. I'm not completely sure what happened after that. I think I staggered down into the crypt of St Clement's Dane. I woke up in a cellar down the Way."

Mentioning the strange dream seemed a bad idea. I didn't want to start sounding crazy after an obvious head injury. Instead I explained why I'd gone to find Claire.

"Why didn't you come back here? We could have got some help, or sent someone else; one of the other Warders."

"If I'd waited and come back here they would have been gone before we got there. I only just caught them as it was."

"For all the good it did you." Blackbird shook her head. "One of these days…" she said, dabbing at the cut.

I told them about the flat and finding the blood stains. I neglected to mention throwing up over the balcony, but I did tell them about the state of the rooms and the absence of a body.

"So you think Raffmir took the body?" asked Blackbird.

"I'm fairly sure it was him in the van. He must have hired someone to steal the safe. By recruiting human help, they were able to remove the safe with all the items inside. They can't do anything with it because they can't open the safe, but now neither can we. They only have to keep it from us."

"We can just make another set of knives, though, can't we? Isn't that what you did before?" asked Angela.

"Perhaps," said Blackbird. "What about the horseshoes?"

"They were only there to protect the knives." I said. "Fat lot of good they did in the end."

"I still don't understand," said Blackbird. "Why take the knives now? We have almost ten months until they're needed again. The ceremony isn't until next October. They've given the game away much too early."

"I don't think Raffmir was expecting to see anyone at the Royal Courts of Justice," I said. "And with Claire Radisson out of the way, who is there to raise the alarm about the missing safe? The woman outside Claire's office clearly thought it was all routine. We wouldn't find out until it was too late."

"But why now?"

"Because no one was expecting it now. We're close to the winter solstice, the time of balance, but they're usually quiet at this time of the year. They can cross between the worlds and lay the foundations for whatever they have planned for next year. We already know they had long-term plans to eliminate the mongrel-fey using biological weapons. Who knows what else they're doing," I pointed out.

"I need to tell the High Court about this," said Blackbird. "They can spread the word that the Raffmir is here. Maybe we can find out what the Seventh Court is up to before it gets any worse."

"I thought we'd finished for today," said Krane, taking his seat. "If I'd realised the Eighth Court would take this much time I'd have never agreed to it in the first place."

"You didn't agree to it," said Teoth.

"No, I didn't. So why are we back here? Is your plan to talk us into submission, Blackbird? An endless debate until you get what you want?"

He had a point. They had already debated for hours, firstly on whether there was precedent for another court, then on whether it could be formed without the agreement of all the other courts, including the Seventh. It seemed like Krane and Teoth would fight her every inch of the way. They had even argued over where she should sit. Krane said that she could not have a seat until they reached a decision on whether there would be an Eighth Court, but then changed his mind when Blackbird went to sit in Altair's vacant seat. Then they had tried to seat her at the end of the row, but as she pointed out, that would place her directly next to Altair, should he return. On the other hand, she didn't want to be in the middle of them all and have to divide her attention between those to the left and right of her. In the end, Kimlesh made a space between her and Yonna. At least there she felt she had some support.

"I have some information which I thought I should share," she said, addressing all of them.

"Perhaps," said Krane, "You have come to inform us that you will no longer be filling the High Court with waifs and strays and you have found some place of your own?"

That was another point of contention. The High Court was supposed to be neutral ground. No one court was supposed to have more claim there than any other, but the Eighth Court had nowhere else. If the Eighth Court were to continue, it would need a home, but unlike the other courts it had no land, property or wealth. It was one more thing on top of all the other things she had to worry about.

"The Seventh Court has stolen the knives and horse-shoes for the Quit Rents ceremony." There was a long silence. There, she thought. That shut them up.

Yonna asked, "How did you come by this information?"

She summarised what Niall had told her. "Raffmir has taken the safe containing the knives and the horseshoes. Niall thinks he recruited human help to steal it. They were in a van. As far as I know, Raffmir can't drive?"

"Who knows what he is capable of," said Barthia.

"I can't see Raffmir driving a vehicle," said Kimlesh. "Can you?"

"You're missing the point," said Yonna. "He's taken the knives. We will need to replace them before the cere-mony is performed again.

"The clerk's also missing," said Blackbird. "There's blood all over her flat."

"If she's dead, that's more of a problem," said Kimlesh. "Will they be able to appoint a new clerk in time for the ceremony? Is there a successor?"

"Your biggest problem is still getting the knives re-made," said Teoth.

"How so?" asked Kimlesh.

"The Highsmiths made one knife for us," said Yonna. "I'm sure they can be persuaded to make another, and

58

while Raffmir may be able to steal the safe with the knives in, he won't be able to steal the hammer or the anvil, even if he has human help."

"He doesn't need to," said Blackbird. "He has the nails. Without the sixty-first nail, we can't reach the hammer either. We can't remake the knives without the hammer."

Teoth smiled. "It's worse than that. While you might be able to get the smiths to make another Quick Knife, you are assuming we will make another Dead Knife."

"Can we not?" asked Yonna. "You are the High Maker, Teoth. You made the original. Can you not make another?"

"If I had the metal, perhaps," he said. "Assuming I was willing to make it."

"Why would you not be willing?" asked Barthia.

"When we put the barrier in place," said Teoth, "we were united in our task to keep the Seventh Court from our world. Our reasons for excluding them have recently become... less compelling." He looked at Blackbird.

"You are surely not holding the Eighth Court to ransom?" said Kimlesh. "That's outrageous!"

Teoth folded his arms. "I am merely pointing out that if you go ahead without consensus, then you cannot expect cooperation when things go badly."

"This isn't a game," said Barthia. "If the Seventh Court return then we will all suffer."

"Not necessarily," said Krane. "Only last year, Altair was willing to enter discussions on the peaceful return of our wraithkin brethren."

"That was just a cover for what Raffmir was doing," said Blackbird. "It was a distraction from his real plan, which was to destroy all the mixed-race fey."

"I thought the discussions were positive," said Krane. "We were making progress until Warder Dogstar tried to destroy half of Wiltshire."

"He saved the mongrel fey, and uncovered systematic torture in violation of our treaty with humanity," said Blackbird.

"Our treaty doesn't cover half-breeds," said Krane.

"That's debatable," said Kimlesh.

"And it only applies to six courts," Krane continued, "not seven... or eight."

"The treaty applies to all of the Feyre," said Yonna.

"But they're not fey, are they?" said Teoth. "How many have you sworn to your court so far, Blackbird?"

"We have pledges from a number of individuals," said Blackbird.

"Pledges? They're not even blood-sworn!" said Teoth. "They could do anything, bring ruin on all of us!"

"Going over this again is getting us nowhere," said Barthia. "Perhaps our efforts would be better focused on finding the original knives. We need to find Raffmir and recover the safe."

"And how do you propose to do that?" asked Kimlesh.

"It could be at the bottom of the Thames by now," said Blackbird. "Or on a container ship out of the London docks, headed for the Far East."

Mellion stood and made a complicated gesture, mimicking the turning of a key in a lock.

"Mellion's right," said Kimlesh. "We should deploy what resources we have and focus on finding Raffmir. If he knows where the safe is, then he holds the key."

"Finding a wraithkin?" said Yonna. "Would you have us turn back time as well? Or move the stars, perhaps? He's probably gone back to their world by now."

"What? And miss the opportunity to gloat?" said Blackbird. "No, Raffmir is here somewhere. We just have to find him."

Kimlesh spoke into the shadows beyond the circle of light around the chairs. "Fionh, would you ask Garvin to step in, please?"

The door opened, spilling light into the room momentarily, and she slipped out silently. Blackbird noticed Niall waiting outside, trying to catch her attention.

"We have time," said Barthia. "It is months until the

ceremony must be performed again. The barrier holds for now. Teoth has a point. we stand united or not at all. His concerns, and those of Lord Krane, must be addressed. We will meet again tomorrow." She rose, as did Kimlesh, and Yonna. Krane and Teoth exchanged glances and rose, then walked out, heads together in low conversation. Blackbird waited until Mellion and Barthia had also left and then joined Kimlesh and Yonna. "I'm sorry to be the bearer of bad news," she said.

"It is worse than you think," said Yonna. "The barrier has been maintained for centuries. This is not the first time that the Seventh Court has tried to bring it down. Always before, though, we have responded together, as one voice. Six against one, Altair knew he couldn't win."

"More than that," said Kimlesh. "Altair knows there is division. That's why he's doing this now. He knew Teoth would block any move to re-forge the knives."

"Which means that Altair is conspiring with Teoth and Krane," said Yonna. They were interrupted by Fionh returning with Garvin. Kimlesh explained the situation and Garvin listened until she'd finished.

"I'll take the Warders," he said, "and walk through the Royal Courts of Justice with Niall. Maybe we can pick up on the trail or find some clue as to who was helping Raffmir. If we can find the van, maybe we can find the safe, or at least discover what they've done with it."

"Thank you Garvin," said Kimlesh.

He held his fist over his heart and backed away. Blackbird made her excuses and followed. When she reached the doorway, Niall was trailing along after Garvin down the corridor. He pointed meaningfully at the ceiling.

"Now, Dogstar!" Garvin's voice carried down the corridor and Niall turned and trotted after him. Blackbird followed after him, the heavy skirts of the dress rustling with her step as she made her way back to the rooms they shared. It was getting late and she was tired, not least of arguing with Krane and Teoth. She was beginning to wonder whether this was all worthwhile.

When she reached the rooms, Angela was there, with Alex.

"Hello," said Blackbird. "I thought you were staying at your mum's."

"I am," said Alex. "Where's Dad?"

Blackbird unhooked the dress and shrugged it from her shoulders, placing it on the waiting hanger. "He had to go out. Warder business."

"He was supposed to fetch you," she said.

"I told you. Garvin took him out. He'll be back in a while."

Alex stood. "This can't wait."

"What can't?" Blackbird changed into comfortable clothes. "I need to check on the baby. I've hardly seen him all day."

"You need to come with me," said Alex, moving towards the door.

"Look," said Blackbird. "I've had a long day, and I'm just about ready to drop. I still have things to do, so I don't need a mystery. Just tell me what the matter is and I'll try and help, OK."

Alex shook her head. "It's you who doesn't understand, and anyway, I promised."

"Promised who?"

Alex looked meaningfully at the mirror on the wall and then went to the desk and found a scrap of paper. She scribbled something on it and handed it to Blackbird. On the piece of paper was a name: *Claire Radisson*.

FOUR

"Are you there?"

The voice whispered from the dark. "Of course."

"They know about the safe. He was there. He nearly caught them doing it."

"He didn't."

"What was he doing there?"

"It doesn't matter. We have them now. There will be no more ceremony," said the whisperer.

"They are talking about re-making the knives."

"What does Teoth say?"

"He's playing hard to get, making them work for it."

"Good," said the voice.

"Do you want me to say anything to him?"

There was no reply, only darkness.

"Fine." After a moment, the shadow slipped away again.

"Very good," said the whisperer, after the shadow had gone.

Alex led the journey down the Way. She wouldn't even tell Blackbird where they were going, though it soon became obvious. The walk to Katherine's house was mostly conducted in silence. When they reached the front door, Katherine opened it and hurried them inside. Claire

Radisson was in Katherine's lounge. There were cups of tea that had been made and left to go cold, and newspapers left open and discarded. Her impatience was written across her face.

"Veronica! Thank goodness you're here." Katherine looked taken aback at the use of the name Veronica, but let it go.

Blackbird took the seat opposite Claire, sinking too far into the upholstery for her liking. "I'm not sure how long I have," she said. "Tell me what happened."

"I'm sorry if I've kept you from something more important," said Claire, taking offence.

"You're not sorry, and I don't have time for games," said Blackbird. "So tell me."

Claire cleared her throat, looking to Katherine for support. Katherine was seeing a side of Blackbird that she hadn't seen before. "It started last week," said Claire. "Jerry, the Remembrancer, you remember from the hospital?" Blackbird gave the slightest of nods. "Jerry has retired – Elizabeth insisted. They have a son, in Australia. Elizabeth said they would go on an extended visit, take Deborah too."

"And get as far away from here as possible?" asked Blackbird.

"Something like that," said Claire.

"Smart move. Go on."

"It's not as simple as that. Jerry is… *was* a senior member of the Queen's Bench Division and there are arrangements to be made. He had lists and dates. All of that had to be rescheduled and–"

"Can we get to the meat of it?" asked Blackbird.

Claire clasped her hands together. "Last week his office was disturbed. There was nothing taken but things had been moved. I've worked with him for, oh, more years than I care to recall, and he has his ways. Things were out of place."

"A potential successor, perhaps, having a look around?" asked Blackbird.

Claire continued. "I was very careful, after what happened. I wanted to know when things were meddled with. You never knew when there might be..." She glanced at Katherine, "whether they might try again. The ceremony this year, it went as planned but there was something missing. We did everything as we should, but it wasn't right. If it goes well... I just know. Is that hard to believe?"

"No," said Blackbird. She could hear a tension between truth and falsehood in Claire's words, but she let it go. "Those are the sorts of feelings you should trust."

"Afterwards Jerry knew too. He told me, after the ceremony. He said, he was on the point of saying, 'Good number!', and it stuck in his throat. He covered it with a sip of water, and the ceremony completed without interruption, but it wasn't perfect. Do you see?"

"Were the nails, the knives, and the horseshoes all there?" asked Blackbird.

"Yes."

"You're sure? Could there have been substitutions? Some sort of switch?"

"How? How could such a thing happen?"

Blackbird could hear something in Claire's tone. She wasn't lying exactly but there was evasion there. "That's a very good question," she said.

"Who has access to the safe?"

"Only Jerry and I do."

"A spare key?"

"Jerry has the spare. I don't think he actually knows what it's for."

"Jerry's in Australia," said Blackbird.

"He is now," said Claire.

"Could a copy have been made?"

"I don't know." Claire was running her fingers repeatedly through her hair.

"Tell me the rest," said Blackbird.

"Would anyone like a cup of tea?" asked Katherine.

No one answered. Even Alex was focused on Claire.

"You'll laugh," said Claire, "I read something in the journals – I tried to summon you by writing your name and Niall's on pieces of paper and burning them. It didn't do any good."

"It wouldn't. You need a talent for that kind of summoning," said Blackbird.

"In the end I contacted Sam – Sam Veldon. It was strange. He didn't even ask me why I wanted to know – he got me an address for Niall, but he said Niall no longer lived here. When I asked him for a more current address he laughed. He said, 'Try behind the mirror, or under the bed.' What did he mean?"

"Niall can be elusive."

"I wrote to Niall, here. That was days ago. I've been on the run, ever since. Katherine said she gave him the letter, but only yesterday – God, it seems like weeks have passed."

"On the run from what?"

"From whom… sorry, old habits." Claire tucked her hair behind her ear. "I'd taken precautions. You know I'm careful. I had a horseshoe on the front door. I had one on the back too, but there's a short-cut. The recycling – you can take it downstairs, walk around the back in the dark and put it in the bins – or you can drop it into the alley and then put it into the bins on the way out in the morning when it's daylight. Everyone does it."

You dropped the recycling over the fire escape?" said Blackbird.

"I was making supper," said Claire. "It was pasta, with peppers and tomato and… anyway, I heard a noise, or maybe just sensed a change. I couldn't put my finger on it. And then I wondered – did I put the horseshoe back after putting the recycling out. I couldn't remember. I knew I should have. I just couldn't remember if I did."

"What did you do?" asked Blackbird.

"I turned and saw the horseshoe, on the counter by the sink. That was where I'd left it. It should be on the back door, but it was in the kitchen. That meant... something could be in the flat."

Blackbird was silent while Claire gathered herself. "I took it with me, intending to put it back, I suppose. I went quietly to where the fire exit is, and he was there."

"Who?"

I don't know!" She calmed herself, lowering her voice. "I don't know. I saw a dark figure. I just reacted. I lashed out."

"You hit him?"

"With the horseshoe," said Claire. "It was in my hand."

"You punched him with it?"

"I don't remember. It was instinctive. He went down – collapsed in the passage like he'd been poleaxed. I panicked. He shouldn't have been there. He was in my flat! I didn't know what to do." She was clasping and unclasping her hands. "I ran into the kitchen. I was in shock. I've never done anything like that before. I was afraid. You must understand."

"Understand what?" asked Blackbird.

"I stabbed him." Her face went white. Her hands started to shake.

"You did what?" said Blackbird.

"He was lying in the passage, out cold." Claire's words were soft, but she was close to breaking. "I took one of the kitchen knives and stabbed him through the heart."

"A kitchen knife?"

"I had this idea. The Feyre, they... when they die they vanish. I don't know how, but it says so in the journals. It crossed my mind – if I killed him he would go back to wherever he came from."

"Not quite the truth," said Blackbird.

"Only he didn't die! He wasn't one of them! He was just a guy who was breaking into my flat. The blood just welled up out of his chest. He was real, and I killed him."

Blackbird sighed. "We're all real, Claire. The Feyre bleed and hurt, just the way you do."

"Only he wasn't fey!" said Claire. "He just lay there, bleeding! I'm going to have to turn myself in," she said. "I can't go on. I can't live like this, not as a fugitive."

"There's no body," said Blackbird.

There was a moment's silence. Then Claire said, "What?"

"Niall was in your flat. There's blood, but no body."

"Niall?"

"He was looking for you. The place has been turned over. The furniture is destroyed. Everything's a mess."

"No body?" said Claire.

"Where's your heart?" asked Blackbird.

"Are you implying that I am without compassion?" said Claire, offended again.

Blackbird shook her head. "Point to it. Show me, on you, where you stabbed him."

Claire took her index finger and pointed to a place just left of her breast bone. "Here, isn't it?"

"You missed," said Blackbird. "You may have grazed it, but it wasn't enough. You have to be right on the mark."

"How do you know?" said Claire. "How can you be certain he wasn't a human burglar faced with a knife-wielding mad woman?"

"A human intruder, having been stabbed through the chest, would not trash your flat, or spray blood all over your bathroom, or go berserk and cut your furniture to pieces. He'd just bleed to death on your carpet."

"That means it's OK," said Claire, clearly relieved. "I didn't kill anyone. I can go home."

"I hate to spoil your illusion," said Blackbird, "but you don't understand. One of the Feyre came for you. You hit him with a horseshoe and then tried to finish him off with a kitchen knife." She paused. "You didn't finish it. You failed to kill him."

"I'm not a murderer," Claire protested. "It's not something I've even thought about before. People don't kill other people. Do they?" She looked to Alex for support. Alex froze, caught on the question, unable to lie directly.

68

"Alex?" said Katherine. "Claire asked you a question."

Alex shook her head. "You don't want to know," she said.

"I think I have a right to know," said Katherine. "Don't you? You've never killed anyone, have you Alex? Not for real?"

"Tracy Welham," said Alex. "Natasha Tolly, Jennifer Longman." Her expression was blank, her eyes cold, meeting her mother's gaze.

"That was an accident," said Katherine. "It was a build up of gas. There was an inquiry..."

"There was a guy called Naylor," she continued. "He drowned – I drowned him." She bit her lip.

"You can't have done," Katherine said. "Is that all of them?"

"Eve, and Chipper..." her hands were balled into fists. "I didn't kill them, but they died because of me."

"How many? How many people have you killed?" demanded Katherine, her voice rising in pitch.

"Not now, Katherine," said Blackbird.

"How many?" Katherine repeated.

"Enough," said Alex sullenly. "No one that didn't deserve it."

"I can't believe you said that," said Katherine. "I can't believe my own daughter... where? Who were these people? What could they possibly have done?"

"Just let it be, Mum," said Alex. "It was them or me, all right?"

"Do you think," said Blackbird, "that you could have this discussion with your daughter at another time?"

"What better time is there to find out that—"

"Enough!" said Blackbird. "Or I will be taking this discussion somewhere else."

Katherine gave her a dark look, but faced with Blackbird's implacable determination, she relented. "We'll talk about this later," she said to Alex.

"I don't think we will," said Alex under her breath.

"Do you have somewhere safe you can go?" said Blackbird, bringing the focus of attention back to Claire.

"I could do with getting some things from my flat...?"

"If you go back there, he'll kill you, if only out of spite. You laid him out and then stabbed him. He has to kill you, or he'll never hear the last of it. He'll be looking for you." She looked at Alex and then at Katherine. "And for anyone else who knows what happened."

"Me?" said Katherine. "I don't know anything."

Alex responded. "Anyone fey can hear the truth, Mum. There's no point in lying." The irony of that statement coming from Alex was not lost on Blackbird, but she kept a straight face for Claire's sake.

"What can I do?" asked Claire.

"You can tell me what really happened at the Quit Rents ceremony," said Blackbird.

Claire's expression became closed. "Nothing happened," she said.

"OK then," Blackbird said. "What didn't happen? Something changed."

"I don't know what you mean," said Claire, but this time there was evasion in her words.

Blackbird shook her head. "It's worse than you think. The safe in your office has been taken, along with the contents. The knives are lost, and the only horseshoes are the one in your flat, and the one in your bag. The rest have gone with the knives."

"That's bad news," said Claire. Again, Blackbird could hear the evasion in her tone.

"Claire has told us the ceremony did not go as it should," sad Blackbird to Alex, "and that the Remembrancer stumbled on his words, and yet she says that everything was as it should be. Even so, the Seventh Court are here, when they should not be able to cross until the solstice, which is still days away."

"They must have come here at the equinox," said Claire. "Maybe they've been here all the time."

70

"That may be true," said Blackbird, "and yet something isn't right here. When I told you the safe had been taken, you barely reacted." She watched Claire closely.

"Jerry and I did everything as we should," said Claire. "You can't blame us."

"For what? What is there to be blamed for?" asked Blackbird.

"I meant for the Seventh Court being here," she answered, but there was that twist of evasion again.

"Very well," said Blackbird, getting to her feet. "Thank you for the warning. We will do what we can. I wish you luck. Keep moving. Don't stay in any place too long. You already know to take precautions." She glanced significantly at Claire's handbag. Even with it tucked out of sight, she could sense the iron of the horseshoe in the bag. It was disrupting her sense of truth and falsehood in the room, but not enough to miss that Claire wasn't being entirely forthcoming.

"What about me?" asked Claire.

"I'd like to help you," said Blackbird, "but you're holding something back. You may have your reasons for that, and I respect your secrecy, but until I know what the problem is, I can't help."

"So what can I do?"

"You can finish it," said Blackbird. "You just need to make a proper job of it this time."

"I can't kill anyone!" said Claire. She glanced again at Alex as if wondering how anyone could do such a thing.

"Then you'd better start setting your affairs in order," said Blackbird, "because whoever came after you won't have any such compunction."

"Why can't she come back with us?" asked Alex. "She could stay at the courts."

"That's not a good idea," said Blackbird.

"Oh, come on," said Alex. It's not like she doesn't know about us, and there are loads of empty rooms still."

"No, Alex," said Blackbird.

71

"I don't want to be an imposition," said Claire.

"It's not safe there," said Blackbird, meeting Claire's gaze, "not for you." Alex sent Blackbird a questioning look, and Blackbird gave the merest shake of her head.

"Where then?" said Claire. "I can't keep living out of motels."

"If you keep moving you'll be harder to trace," Blackbird remarked. "Don't stay in one place more than a day. Never go back to the same place twice. Don't do anything to attract attention – ditch your bank accounts, credit cards, drivers licence – anything that links back to you. You don't want to leave a trail that can be followed."

"They're not in the safe," said Claire.

"What?" said Alex.

"The horseshoes and the knives. They're not kept in the safe all the time – only in the days close to the ceremony," said Claire.

"You understand," said Blackbird, "I am not offering you sanctuary. I am simply offering to help you find a way out."

"I can't live like that." Claire fished into her bag and dabbed at her eyes with a tissue which she proceeded to twist. "You have to help me."

"It may not be enough," said Blackbird.

"It will be something. It's better than sitting in hotel rooms waiting for the money to run out, never trusting anyone, waiting for a knock on the door, or the click of a lock."

"Tell me about the safe," said Blackbird.

"It was supposed to be a secret," said Claire. "We're not supposed to tell anyone."

"Someone knows," said Blackbird, "or you wouldn't be where you are now."

Claire gathered herself, moving her bag, pushing back her hair. She leaned forward in the chair. "You must promise not to tell anyone," she said.

"No," said Blackbird.

"You must!" said Claire.

"I won't make a promise I might break," said Blackbird. "That's not my way. We're beyond that."

Claire, looked first at Alex and then at Katherine.

Blackbird followed her gaze. "They're both in on this, though they may come to wish that they were not... you may as well tell them."

Claire looked from one to the other, then resigned herself. "Since Jerry retired there's been a bit of a hiatus. I had this idea I was going to choose a successor – a new clerk for a new Remembrancer – and semi-retire myself. I've been going through the journals of the past clerks at the National Archives, looking at how previous clerks have chosen their successors. Looking for clues."

"How does this relate to the contents of the safe?" asked Blackbird.

I'm getting to that. This goes back to the beginnings of the ceremony," said Claire. Establishing the barrier took time. There were... incidents. Like Rome, the barrier wasn't built in a day. Sacrifices had to be made."

"What kind of sacrifices?" asked Katherine, moving around to sit at the other end of the sofa.

"The usual kind. You have to understand that as the barrier grew stronger the Seventh Court became aware of it. They took steps to prevent the ceremony being performed. They killed successive Remembrancers – bribed them, threatened them, kidnapped their children, murdered their families. But the crown was committed. One king after another made sure that the ceremony was performed. The first ceremony was in 1067," said Claire. "With just the two knives. The date was kept secret, the venue was changed, people were switched at the last minute. As the barrier got stronger the Seventh Court became more desperate. Still they came. The cost in human lives became difficult to hide. There were... reports."

"Reports?" said Blackbird.

"This was the time of Plantagenet rule. Anything which undermined the King's sovereignty was ruthlessly suppressed. Anything which compromised it was dealt with."

"Only this wasn't dealt with?" said Blackbird.

"Oh, it was. The barrier was established, and for a while there was peace. The Seventh Court could not cross. It held, and the courts and the crown were united. We had succeeded."

"In the year 1244 something went wrong. The Remembrancer didn't perform the ceremony. There were extenuating circumstances – sickness, a bridge collapsed, a servant was compromised. The ceremony failed and the Seventh Court broke through. There was an attack on the King – an all-out assault to remove the figurehead and destroy the barrier forever. They nearly succeeded."

"But they didn't," said Blackbird.

"There were rumours," said Claire. "The Feyre... there was infrequent communication before that time – a dialogue, albeit at diplomatic levels. After that night, nothing was heard from them for years."

"An all-out assault..." said Blackbird.

"Pardon?" said Claire.

Blackbird hesitated, and then relented. "You are sharing secrets, and it is only fair that we should share some of ours. There was a time long ago when the Seventh Court broke through in an effort to eliminate all of the half-breed fey, all those of mixed race, in a single night. I have heard it referred to, but no one talks about it. There are enmities that go back to that time that exist today."

"The King escaped," said Claire, "with the help of a cadre of hand-picked elite knights. They fought with heavy steel and iron. Many of them died, but they saved the King. He was smuggled out in the chaos while those that protected him stood against the Seventh Court. It was a massacre."

"Human knights are no match for wraithkin," said Blackbird.

"They didn't need to defeat them," said Claire. "They only needed to delay them long enough for the King to escape. In that they succeeded, thought the cost was high."

"And they were rewarded?" asked Blackbird.

"Hardly," said Claire. "The knights were Templars – Poor Soldier Knights of Christ and the Order of the Temple of Solomon – it's a misleading title. They were hardly poor, being sons of noble families of vast wealth and power. Neither were they simple soldiers. They were well-equipped, highly trained and exceptionally skilled. If anyone could stop the Seventh Court, they could."

"But they didn't," said Blackbird.

"No, they didn't. But the crown was grateful for what they accomplished. And as crowns will, showed gratitude in ways that were two-handed. They received lands and charters, the gateway to further wealth and power, and they were honoured with certain duties – the assurance that a certain ceremony would be performed, come what may, at sword-point if necessary."

"The Quit Rents…" said Blackbird.

"Six elite knights were chosen, one for each court of the Feyre. Six families were selected to guard the ceremony down the years. One family was too fragile. One dynasty might be subverted, or bribed, or threatened – but six. That was a good number."

"Which families?" asked Blackbird.

"You see now why this is secret," said Claire. "With the knowledge of the families you can find the guardians. You could subvert them, bribe them, eliminate them. But you would have to know who they were, first."

"How do you know?" asked Blackbird.

"Officially, I don't. It is not good for me to know. It is better that I simply know they are there. When the time of the ceremony draws near, they deliver the knives and the nails. I don't know where they're kept at other times, and that's by design. I can't reveal what I don't know."

"We have to find them," said Alex.

"Find them how?" asked Katherine. "We don't even know who they are, do we?"

"I have the journals, so we know one of the names," said Claire. "The horseshoes are rendered in respect of a forge in Tweezers Alley. The forge was on a corner of the Templar's field and was owned by Walter le Brun. He was one of them. That's as much as I'm supposed to know."

"*Supposed* to know?" asked Blackbird.

"Before he went to Australia, Jerry told me something. We were talking about the ceremony, about why it wasn't right."

"Go on…" said Blackbird.

"He said that the ceremony had devolved to the clerks, but that the protection of the ceremony was still the duty of the Queen's Remembrancer. Each year, at the ceremony, they hold up the horseshoes to be counted, but it's not the horseshoes they're counting. There are people in the audience who make themselves known to the Remembrancer as a sign of their continued fidelity and service. If there are enough, the Remembrancer announces *Good Number*, and the ceremony is complete for the year."

"And how many were at this year's ceremony?" asked Blackbird.

"I don't know," said Claire, "but Jerry wasn't happy."

"Can't we just look up le Brun up in the phone book? What about the Internet?"

"That was in 1245," said Claire. "The family lines have merged and divided. There's no guarantee that anyone called Le Brun would know anything about this."

"Then they could all be long dead," said Katherine.

"The point was not that he was the protector," said Claire, "but that the duty devolved to his line. His successors would take on the duty, and their successors, and so on, down the years."

"So where are the Templars now?" asked Alex.

"They don't exist. The order was disbanded in 1307 by Philip IV of France, who seized the assets. A papal bull was issued, dissolving the order. Many of them were killed, a number were tortured. Not in England, though. Edward II disputed the French crown's claim to the assets and the assets in England were gifted to the Order of St John, the Knights Hospitaler. They were succeeded by the Societies of the Inns of Court, which gave us Lincoln's Inn, Gray's Inn, Inner Temple and Middle Temple."

"Temple?" said Alex. "Isn't that the same as Templars?"

"Technically, yes," said Claire, "The Templars were named after the Temple of Solomon in Jerusalem, and Temple in London was named after the order. Nowadays, Inner and Middle Temple are the associations to which court barristers belong. Their idea of a test of strength is to put their case before a judge, and then have a glass of something in a wine bar with the opposition afterwards. There are no Templars in Temple now."

"Are you sure?" asked Blackbird.

"It crossed my mind," said Claire, "But then I would have expected to see them at the ceremony. The odd barrister does turn up, but they generally sit in the upper gallery and watch. Most of the people that come are from the City for the investiture of the Sheriffs of the City of London."

"What about the Remembrancer," said Blackbird. "Does he know who they are?"

"The whole idea is that neither of us know who they are, and then we can't betray them. They protect us, and in return they too are protected."

"I don't get it," said Alex. "What are they for? I mean, they turn up and all that, but why?"

"Why does the testing of two knives, one blunt and

one sharp, create a barrier between the worlds?" said Blackbird. "Claire, in your bag you carry a horseshoe, do you not?"

Claire nodded.

"Would you show it to us?" asked Blackbird.

"I thought it was... impolite," said Claire.

"Just this once," said Blackbird.

Claire reached down and opened her bag, extracting the heavy iron horseshoe which looked massive in her delicate hands. Alex hissed, while Blackbird looked distinctly uncomfortable.

"Alex, what is it?" said Katherine, looking suddenly worried.

"Katherine, would you take the horseshoe from Claire?"

"I wouldn't normally allow..." said Claire.

"As a test," said Blackbird.

Claire handed the heavy shoe to Katherine who took it in both hands. Blackbird watched Alex, whose expression had the look of someone who'd expected wine and found themselves to be drinking vinegar.

"What is it, sweetheart?" said Katherine. "It's heavy, but..."

"Take it from her," Blackbird said to Alex.

"No!" said Alex.

"It's only a horseshoe," said Blackbird.

"You do it then, if that's all it is," Alex challenged.

Blackbird smiled slowly. "It is only a horseshoe. They are only a couple of knives. It is only a hazel rod, and yet there is power in it. Why does the testing of two knives set a barrier between the worlds? As my friend Gregor would tell you, ritual itself is important, method is as important as means. Having the knights at the ceremony is part of the ritual. They are symbols, and symbols are important."

"And if they're not there?" asked Katherine, handing the horseshoe back to Claire with a sidelong look at her daughter's sour expression.

"Then the symbol is absent, and the ritual is incomplete."

"One of them arranged for the delivery of the knives and the nails before the ceremony," said Claire. "And arranged for them to be taken away afterwards. That's all I know."

"How do you know if it's one of them?" asked Blackbird. "What if they were substituted?"

"There are certain forms that must be followed – oaths to be sworn while each of us is holding one of the horseshoes" Claire explained. "No one fey could swear that oath under those circumstance, and no one else knows the oath that's sworn. Someone fey could extract the oath from us, but they'd never be able to swear it holding the horseshoe."

"That still doesn't help us find them," said Blackbird, "but it does mean that the nails and the knives are probably safe for now. The horseshoes are a different matter. You have one, and there's another in your flat."

"The rest were in the safe, wherever that is," said Claire. "We still have no way of contacting the keepers of the nails or the knives, though. We need to warn them or we may yet lose them all, assuming they still exist."

"We'll think about that tomorrow," said Blackbird. "In the meantime I will ask Niall to arrange the recovery of the horseshoe from your flat, and we need to find you somewhere to stay."

"She can stay here," volunteered Katherine.

"Oh, I couldn't possibly," said Claire "It's too dangerous."

"No one knows you're here," said Katherine. "So no one's going to bother us, are they?"

Blackbird was on the point of trying to explain why that didn't necessarily help and then thought better of it. Katherine was right. There was no reason for Claire not to be at Katherine's. The only link between them was Niall, and that was a hard connection to follow.

"She could have my room," said Alex. "I can go back with Blackbird for tonight and come back tomorrow," she said brightly.

Blackbird thought that had more to do with avoiding Katherine's questions than the spirit of generosity, but if it got the job done... "Very well," said Blackbird, "but I want a private word with Claire first, and then I will want to walk around the house and garden. Katherine, when will Barry be back?"

"He's away at the office Christmas party and sales conference," she said. "That was one reason I wanted Alex to stay over. It meant we could spend some time with just us. He won't be back until the day after tomorrow."

That gave them tomorrow to work something out for Claire. It would be a bad idea for her to stay with Katherine for longer than a night or so, in any case.

Before they left, Blackbird spoke quietly with Claire and made her promise to keep the horseshoe close to her to prevent anyone from gaining knowledge of her whereabouts, especially while she was with Katherine. Then she walked the bounds of the property and set a simple warding to turn away curious eyes – it wasn't much but it would do for one night. They would have to come up with something better tomorrow.

When they went to leave, Katherine wanted to call a taxi for them, but Blackbird explained that the fewer people who saw them go the better. In the back of her mind was the thought that she would have to explain to Niall why exposing Katherine to this risk was necessary, but she would cross that bridge when she came to it.

Blackbird and Alex slipped away from the house cloaked in glamour. Despite Alex's complaints that she was shivering and hadn't brought a coat, Blackbird made her wait across the street with her until the curtains were drawn and the house was in darkness. When she was sure there was nothing waiting in the shadows, she took Alex and headed back to the courts.

FIVE

Fionh was in the room where the Way-nodes converged when they returned. "You're late back," she commented dryly.

"Long day," said Blackbird as Fionh removed the stones that opened the Ways into the High Court and closed them off for the night, setting them in their places.

"I thought Alex was staying with her mother?" said Fionh.

"Change of plan," said Alex. "Mum's got an unexpected visitor and there's only the one spare bedroom, so I'm going back tomorrow."

"The house is quiet," said Fionh. "Dogstar said to let you know he's collected the baby from Lesley. I think he's gone to bed."

"Thank you Fionh," said Blackbird. "I won't be long from bed myself."

Blackbird and Alex made their way up through the house, finding the lights dimmed; all was quiet. "It's a nice house when it's quiet," said Alex, as they topped the stairs. "I'd better come and explain to Dad why I'm not staying at Mum's."

"I can tell him," said Blackbird.

Alex smiled. "Probably better if we both tell him, don't you think?"

Blackbird acknowledged her words with a nod and led the way to their rooms. In truth she was grateful for Alex's support. She didn't need a row with Niall about leaving Claire with Katherine and having Alex there to explain would add credence to the tale. There were moments when Alex seemed suddenly more grown up, and this was one of them.

They entered the room quietly, finding the lights turned low and Niall fully dressed on the bed atop the covers with their son sprawled across his chest, both of them fast asleep.

"Awww," said Alex. "Isn't he cute when he's asleep?"

Blackbird assumed she meant the baby, and moved quietly around so that she could lift him into her arms. He grumbled a little but was too asleep to complain. She rested him against her shoulder. "We'll talk to your Dad tomorrow," she said to Alex. "You go and get some rest."

She took the baby through to the next room and laid him in the cot. He grumbled again when she laid him on the cool mattress, but Blackbird covered him with a warm quilt and after a moment he sighed in his sleep. She smiled and watched him for a moment. Then she went back into the bedroom. "Still here?" she asked Alex.

Alex looked up from the side of the bed where she was sat beside her father. "There's something wrong," she said. "I went to kiss him goodnight and he's cold."

"He's probably just been lying outside the quilt too long," she said. "He's been on the go all day, Alex. He must be exhausted."

"No," said Alex. "He won't wake up." There was a tone in Alex's voice that got Blackbird's attention.

Blackbird frowned at Alex. On the one hand, waking up her father when he'd finally managed to get some sleep was a bit mean, but he'd have to wake up to get undressed and into bed anyway. She moved in beside him and shook his shoulder. "Niall, you've fallen asleep in your clothes. Wake up." He didn't stir. "Niall!" She shook him more forcefully.

"Why won't he wake up?" asked Alex, a sense of panic rising in her voice.

"Move out of the way," said Blackbird. Alex moved off the bed and she sat beside him and drew back his eyelids. His eyes were dilated almost to black. "That's not good."

"What's wrong?" asked Alex, her voice rising towards panic.

"This shouldn't happen here," said Blackbird. "The wardings on the house should prevent it."

"He's not..."

"Alex!" That got her attention. "I need you calm and focused. Bring me the bag from the chair." Alex brought the bag and Blackbird rummaged inside it, extracting a long yellow shard of bone.

"What are you going to do with that?" asked Alex.

"Give me your hand."

"No," said Alex, putting her hands behind her back.

"Alex, you want to help your father don't you?"

"What are you going to do?" she asked.

"I need a drop of your blood," said Blackbird. "I need to call your father back. He's got himself lost again and I need you to help me."

"What's so special about my blood? Use some of your own."

"Blood calls to blood, Alex. It always has and it always will. You are his daughter and of his line. Without it I can't call him back."

"There must be another way," said Alex.

Blackbird sighed. "Very well. Bring me the baby."

"What!"

"I said, bring me my son. He is also of Niall's blood. One of you has to help him and if you won't do it, then he'll have to."

Alex stared at the yellow shard in Blackbird's hand. "You can't... you wouldn't."

Blackbird's eyes narrowed. "There are few things indeed, Alex Dobson, that I would not do. I am anchoring your father here. Do you want me to release him and fetch the baby myself?"

Alex hesitated. "Will it hurt?" she asked.

"Yes," said Blackbird. "You were expecting me to lie to you?"

Alex slowly offered her hand. Blackbird reached for it and Alex almost snatched it away. Blackbird watched her. "Yes or no," she said. "Willing is better, but I'll take what I can get."

"You're mean," said Alex, finally giving her hand.

"You don't know the half of it," said Blackbird, releasing her hold on Niall and grasping Alex's hand around the fleshy part of her thumb.

"Hey, you've let go of Dad." Alex protested. "Ah! Fuck, that hurts!"

Blackbird gouged the sharp bone fragment into Alex's thumb. "Don't flinch, girl, or I'll make a mess of it." Blood welled up in the jagged gash in Alex's thumb. Blackbird released her and Alex immediately stuck her thumb in her mouth and sucked, looking resentful.

Blackbird took Niall's limp hand and did the same, gouging a deep hole in Niall's thumb that welled red. "Now mix your blood with his," said Blackbird. "We need to reinforce the connection."

"That's gross," said Alex.

Blackbird unceremoniously seized Alex's wrist and tugged her towards the bed. "Do it," she said.

The expression on Alex's face as she pressed her bleeding thumb to her father's was close to revulsion. Pressing their thumbs together opened the cuts and as she withdrew it left a trail of red spots on the white quilt. Alex's eyes widened and she went pale.

"Bathroom!" said Blackbird, "Quick!"

Alex ran for the bathroom and there was the sound of retching as she threw up noisily in the sink. After a moment there was the sound of running water. She emerged, holding a wet facecloth tight around her wounded thumb.

"Better?" asked Blackbird.

Alex nodded slowly. "You'd think after all I'd seen, a little blood wouldn't bother me."

"Come and sit the other side of him," said Blackbird. "I'd ask you to hold his hand, but I don't want you throwing up on the bed."

"I'm OK now." She sat on the other side of the bed and held her father's other hand, but her eyes avoided the spots on the quilt.

"Ready," said Blackbird. "Once we begin, we're committed. You can't let go, no matter what."

Alex nodded.

Blackbird used the tip of her finger to wipe a fat drop of blood from Niall's thumb. Alex's eyes went so wide that Blackbird could see a ring of white around them. Blackbird lifted the drop carefully and then licked it slowly from her finger. Alex paled – now was not the time to throw up.

A stillness settled in the room. Alex licked her lips unconsciously. The air felt heavy and dense as if it were about to thunder. Blackbird's words sounded slow and thick, even to her own ears.

By his blood I bind him,
By his seed I summon him,
By his flesh I find him,
Niall Petersen, it is time to come home.

The temperature in the room dropped and the atmosphere shifted. There was a sense of opening, as if someone had thrown all the windows wide and let the air in. Niall's eyes opened, but he did not see them.

"Niall?" said Blackbird. "Where are you?"

• • • •

The passage was dark and smelled of damp stone overlaid with wood smoke. Dim light outlined where it ended as I shuffled forwards, stooping to ease under the low arch to where the flares in wall-sconces illuminated a room. The table in the centre had a man standing before it. Six arches formed the dome of the ceiling and five other passages led away into the gloom. At the peak, lantern windows let the smoke from the flares out into the night.

The man stepped back from the table. He wore a heavy cloak against the damp, and his clothes were woollen, though not of a style I recognised. His breeches stopped short at his calves over heavy socks and he wore leather boots which had been in mud up to the laces. His hair was pulled back in a silver clasp. In front of him arranged in a circle on the table were six massive horseshoes. Even from the passage I could feel the presence of the heavy iron. It made my bones ache to be near them.

He glanced at each of the passages nervously. Even though I stood in plain sight at the head of the passage, he did not see me. I looked at my hands. I looked real enough. Was I invisible?

The sound of heavy footsteps approaching drew his attention. He eased back his cloak, revealing a sword pommel, burnished by constant handling.

"Le Brun?" the newcomer called out. "It's me."

Le Brun let his cloak fall forward again, while the newcomer entered the room.

"Montgomerie," said le Brun, "Are the others on their way?" His question was answered by another arrival. "Here's Giffard," said Le Brun. "We're just waiting for Mowbray, FitzRou and De Ferrers."

The other men arrived as one.

"It's a foul night," said FitzRou.

"You're sure you weren't followed?" asked Le Brun.

"You'd be hard pressed to follow a doxy in a dress in that weather," said the man.

"Watch your language, De Ferrers," said Le Brun, darkly. "We'll swear before anything else. Are you set?"

They nodded, moving to stand in a circle around the table. De Ferrers and FitzRou removed their gloves. As one they each picked up a horseshoe from the table, holding it in their bare fists before them where the others could see it. One by one they swore.

"I am Walter Le Brun, Knight and Templar. I serve God and the King."

Each stood with the heavy iron in their hands and swore likewise to his name, his God and his King. Only when they were all sworn did they replace the horseshoes on the table.

"Well and good," said Le Brun. "What news?"

"The ceremony is set," said Montgomerie, "The venue has been moved again. They're nervous – after last year…" He let that sentence trail away.

"What about the knives?" said Le Brun.

"De Ferrers and I will ride them in at the last minute," said FitzRou. "They are well hidden until then."

"What have we here?"

The voice came from one of the passages. As one, the men turned, drawing back their cloaks and reaching for their swords, but within seconds the passages were thundering with boots, and men with short spears held the knights at bay, gleaming points held ready to run them through. Every exit filled with men. I was forced into the room or else be trodden under by them. I stood unnoticed at the side, while the knights stood with their backs to the table.

A tall man in an expensive embroidered cloak entered behind his men. He stood opposite me, surveying the scene. "What treachery is this?" he asked.

"There is no treachery here, Aimery" said Le Brun. "We serve the King's peace."

"And what manner of the King's peace requires you to meet in secret and count horseshoes? Six shoes and six men; it is a pretty number."

"Stand by!" came a new voice. "Stand in the name of the King. Make way for King John." A new man entered the room, pushing aside the soldiers and forcing them into the room. His face was narrow with a deep scar that ran down his cheek into his beard on the left side. He moved with natural authority. He was followed by two other uniformed knights that pushed the soldiers out of the way with little regard, sowing confusion among the men who looked to Aimery for support. The two uniformed knights cleared a space, forcing the men back down the passages. A large, thickset man with a short beard who wore a cloak, black as sable, followed behind them. On his breast were embroidered three gold lions, one above the other. The knights knelt as one, causing a ripple of unrest in the remaining pikemen.

"Order your men to stand down," said the King in a deep voice.

"But, my Liege," said Aimery, "they are…"

"At once," said the King, quietly.

Aimery looked crestfallen. "Stand down," he ordered. The tips of the spears fell. "My Liege, if I have done wrong I beg your pardon. It was done with the best of…"

"Enough," said the King. "Clear the room. Get these men out of here and let in some air, for the love of God."

The two uniformed knights pushed the men back and they reversed with some difficulty back down the passage. It was some time before the noise died away. The King remained silent throughout. No one else dared speak.

When the men had finally gone, the King turned to Aimery. "How did you come here, this night?"

"My Liege, I heard through my own means that these men conspired. I sought only to protect…"

"No, you fool!" said the King. "Did you come by river or road?"

Aimery was taken aback. "I came by river, My Liege."

"Good," said the King, "then you've done something right. Wait outside with my men. I will speak with you later." The uniformed knights escorted Aimery down the passage after his men. The King waited until Aimery was well out of earshot before speaking again. He turned to the scarred man that had come into the room before him.

"When does the tide turn?" asked the King.

"Within the hour, Majesty."

"The river is in flood," said the King. "A man could go overboard on a night like this and no one would ever see him again."

"I will see to it, Majesty," said the man. He bowed and turned to leave.

"And make sure his men understand their fate if word of this should spread," said the King.

The man nodded and followed the path Aimery had taken down the passage, leaving the King with the knights. "Rise," he said.

The men got to their feet stiffly having knelt on the cold stone. It was Le Brun who spoke. "We are in your debt, Majesty," he said.

"You've been careless," said the King. "If Aimery knows of this, then it is possible that others do too."

"We will be more careful," said Le Brun.

The King walked slowly around the room, circling the men. None of them moved. He appeared lost in thought. The only sound in the room was the occasional spit and hiss of the flares and the tap of the King's boots on the stone.

"It's not enough," said the King,"

"I beg your pardon, Majesty?" said Le Brun. "We will do everything in our power…"

"It will never be enough. How much do you love your King?"

"Above my life, Majesty," said Le Brun.

"Above your life…" said the King, continuing to walk around them. "And you?" The King fixed each man with a stare as he circled them. Each man said he would give his life.

"It is the burden of Kings that we must often ask more than those who serve us are prepared to give," said the King. "It was ever thus."

"Niall Petersen?" Blackbird's voice cut across the King, making Niall start where he stood. I looked around nervously wondering whether they too could hear it. But the King continued circling the men.

"It's time to come home," her voice insisted.

"I have something I want you to do for me," said the King to the knights. "It's more than I've asked of you before." The light was dimming, as if the flares were expiring.

"Come home." said Blackbird.

"Anything, Majesty," said Le Brun.

"Come home," repeated Blackbird.

The light faded until only the scent of burning flares was left.

Niall opened his eyes.

"Dad!" said Alex, and threw her arms around his neck, hugging him fiercely.

"What on earth is the matter with you?" said Niall, hugging her back.

There was a sharp rapping on the door. Fionh's voice came through into the room. "Open up!" she called. "What are you doing in there?"

Blackbird stood and went to the door, opening it wide so that Fionh could see inside the room. "It's late, Fionh. To what do we owe this honour?"

Fionh had her weapon drawn and held low. She scanned the room, noting Niall's position on the bed with Alex, the drops of red on the quilt, the flattened area of quilt where Blackbird had been sitting beside Niall. "You've got a nerve, Mistress. You know better than to work blood rituals in this house," she said.

"I was under the impression," said Blackbird, "That the warders were here for our protection. Your wardings have a weakness, Fionh, because something got through and had Niall in its grasp. It took a blood ritual to release him."

"Garvin will hear about this," said Fionh.

"Then I shall look forward to a discussion on improving the protection offered by the courts," said Blackbird. "Unless you're planning to start waving that weapon around?"

Fionh sheathed the blade in one smooth movement, scanning the room again so that she would be able to report every detail. "Tomorrow, then," she said.

"Always a pleasure," said Blackbird, closing the door on her.

"What was that all about?" asked Niall.

"I could ask you the same question," said Blackbird.

Mist was rising over the frosted fields beyond the fence that marked the boundary of the house, drifting like smoke on the night-breeze between the trees. Alex watched it as she walked out from the shadows below the oak tree to lean on the fence. The December night had cleared and the moon had set early, leaving glinting stars. Goosebumps prickled her arms but she was damned if she was going back for a jumper.

Blackbird had made her dad tell them all about the dream, and even made him write down the names of the knights, but just when it was getting interesting Blackbird had declared herself tired and sent Alex off to bed. Alex suspected that she wanted to talk to her dad without her overhearing, but however resentful she felt at being excluded, there was nothing she could do about it.

It was only just past midnight, and her thumb hurt like hell. How was she supposed to sleep when it throbbed like that? It felt twice the size it normally was, though there was little sign of any swelling. Maybe it would get infected and puff up like a balloon – only she didn't get infections, not any more. The magic that ran through her veins was like a possessive disease that left no room for any other, and like a disease, it would claim her in the end.

She turned to face the house. She knew there would be a nightlight in the nursery, but from here the house looked dead and cold, the windows blank against the stars. She tried to picture it as a family home with servants and guests, but it was too big and too empty to fill with her imagination. She'd walked the passages lined with one room after another covered in dust sheets, the curtains drawn to keep out the fading sunlight. Even when they'd had mongrel fey staying, the house had swallowed them with apparent ease.

"What are you doing?"

Alex started at the sudden question, and then forced herself to relax. Of course Fionh had snuck up on her. That was Fionh's way. She couldn't just walk up like any normal person, she had to make you jump.

"I was thinking about the house, and how lonely it must feel," Alex replied, truthfully.

"I'd have thought you'd had enough excitement for one evening," said Fionh.

"I wanted some air."

"Your thumb is bleeding," said Fionh. Alex lifted it, regarding the fat droplet that swelled from the gouge, and then sucked it, tasting once again the metallic tang.

"Be wary where you let the drops fall," Fionh warned. "There are those who will make more of a few drops of blood that you'd have a liking for."

"What are they going to do?" asked Alex. "Snuffle around in the grass for them?"

"You give yourself away too easily, Alex."

"What's that supposed to mean?" asked Alex, regarding Fionh with a cold stare.

"Merely an observation," said Fionh.

"Well cold as it is out here," said Alex, "it not going to bother you, is it, Fionh?"

"Will it not?" she asked.

Alex pushed herself off from the fence. "Nah," she said. "This isn't cold, is it Fionh? We both know you get a lot colder than this." She walked back towards the house, leaving Fionh in the shadow of the oak tree. She didn't look back, but went inside and up to her room, undressing in the dark and pulling the curtains closed, excluding the starlight. She slipped the catches open on the windows, but left them closed, then opened the door and checked the corridor, leaving the door ajar, before she slipped into bed.

She lay in bed with the quilt wrapped round her, shivering and sucking her painful thumb. She tried to think of something restful, but instead was assailed by the images of the drops of blood on the clean covers.

It was some while before sleep claimed her.

Garvin was in one of the empty rooms on the other side of the house, away from the morning sunlight. He'd thrown back the dustsheets on a couple of armchairs and was sat in one, his hands steepled in front of him.

"You wanted to see me?" I said.

He indicated the other chair, and I sat down. He reached forward, and I leaned back warily, but he only wanted to turn my chin so that he could inspect the marks patterned across my face from where the gates outside the Royal Courts of Justice had struck me. "You're going to have a scar," said Garvin.

"Alex has started referring to it as my tattoo," I said.

"That has its own irony," said Garvin.

Alex's arms were wound around with the images of black vines, periodically budding into dark flowers which formed gradually into berries. It'd been like that since her return. It worried me that she wore long-sleeved tops more now, as if she wanted to hide them. When I'd asked her why she was wearing so many long-sleeved tops, she'd simply said, "It's cold."

"Fionh tells me that last night Blackbird was practicing ritual magic inside the courts."

"You'd have to talk to Blackbird about that," I said warily.

"I'm talking to you about it," he said.

"I missed most of it," I said.

Garvin sighed. "It's dangerous, Niall. The wardings of the High Court are there to protect us all. She could have triggered something that would be a threat to everyone."

"I'll tell her," I said.

"What happened?" he asked me.

I shook my head. "Honestly, I'm not sure. I've started having these intense dreams, ever since I was hit by the gates – just fragments of things. It doesn't make any sense. I got lost in one of the dreams last night. Blackbird pulled me out of it, just when it was starting to make sense."

"That's what happens in dreams," said Garvin. "It's an illusion. It's like dreaming of falling – you wake up just before you hit the ground."

"Do you?" I said. "Always?"

He smiled wryly. "Maybe you're reading too much into it."

"Blackbird thinks it might be significant."

That had his interest. "For whom?"

"I wish I knew," I said. "Does Kimlesh speak French?"

Garvin looked surprised. "I've no idea. Do you want me to ask her?"

"No, no." I rested my head in my hands. "I go to sleep and I wake up more tired than I started. I find myself assaulted by images I don't recognise or want. I don't know who most of these people are"

Garvin edge forward in his chair. "Maybe you just need to get some rest."

"I can't rest. I have to find out what this is all about."

"Niall, don't take this the wrong way." He raised his hands as my expression darkened. "You see, your hackles are already up and I haven't said anything."

"What?" I asked, trying to sound calm and reasonable.

Garvin spoke quietly. "I'm already a man down. Fellstamp hasn't stirred and it's been months. We're not sure how long he can last. He's slowly wasting away. If he doesn't come round soon then it may be too late."

"You blame me for that as well?" I asked.

"I'm not blaming anyone," said Garvin, "but I can't afford to lose another man. We've managed on six before and we can do it again, but five? Tired people make mistakes, Niall. Fatal ones."

"What would you have me do?"

"I don't know," he admitted, "I'd recommend rest and relaxation, but there's precious little chance of that with the negotiations on the Eighth Court in session."

"If I rest, I dream," I said. "And it's no rest at all."

"If you were Fellstamp, I'd recommend you get drunk. If you were Tate I'd set you felling trees until exhaustion claimed you. Fionh I'd send to the practice hall to beat seven shades of shit out of whatever she could find."

"And if I were Amber?" I asked.

Garvin gave me an odd look. "Is there something between you and Amber?"

"No, I'm just curious."

"Be careful of curiosity, Niall. It can lead you in odd directions and Blackbird isn't the forgiving kind."

"I'll take your advice on that," I said.

"Seriously, Dogstar. You need to get your head straight. Go for a walk, meditate, jump into a lake – do whatever it takes to clear your head."

"I'll try and think of something," I said, standing.

"And try not to read too much into it," said Garvin.

I shook my head. "How much is too much?" I asked him.

"Are you there?"

"Do you even need to ask?" whispered the voice.

"She was doing blood ritual within the courts. Whatever you're doing to him, they're going to find out."

"I'm not doing anything to him," whispered the voice, calmly.

"Well someone is!"

"Keep your voice down," said the whisperer. "They will hear."

"She only needs to twist it into a divination and they'll know."

"Relax. Divination is not her talent."

"What about the girl? She was there too. She's nosy, hangs about where she shouldn't be."

95

"The girl has power, but not control. That was seen to. Relax. It's all going to plan. Soon we shall see what we shall see."

"Perhaps we can arrange an accident? No one need ever know."

"She's unpredictable," said the whisperer. "Her strength comes and goes. Make a mistake and it could go badly. Leave her alone. Her time will come soon enough."

"That's all very well for you to say. It's not your neck."

"You're too impatient. Nothing is achieved without risk."

"Better when the risk is not yours, though, eh?"

"Do you still want my help?"

"Yes, of course."

"Then stick to the plan. You will get your reward."

"And what then?"

There was no answer.

When I went back upstairs, Blackbird was getting ready to resume discussions with the courts while she discussed tactics with Angela. She stepped into the long dress, threaded her arms into the sleeves and adjusted the bodice.

"You're getting quite good at that," I commented.

"It's practice," she said. "I bless the inventor of the zipper. It's so much easier than all those tiresome buttons. Mullbrook is having another three dresses made for me."

"He's taken a shine to you," I said, "and although he has no official status, he is listened to. You could have worse allies."

"What I need are more numerous allies," she said. "What did Garvin want?"

"He asked me to mention that the use of ritual magic was not permitted at court," I said. "He says it's dangerous."

"For him or me?" she asked.

"He says you could have triggered the wardings. He wasn't specific about who would be harmed."

"Can't be giving too much away. can we?" she ventured. "You can let him know that you've delivered the message."

"He's also worried about me." I admitted.

She stopped fussing with her hair and looked at me, concern in her eyes. "That makes two of us."

I shook my head. "Maybe the incident with the gates did more damage than we realise. Maybe I have concussion."

"Ahem," coughed Angela, politely. "I think I may be able to offer a suggestion, or at least an explanation." We both looked at her.

"Go on," said Blackbird.

Angela looked uncomfortable. "When he... when I was... that is to say..."

"Spit it out," said Blackbird.

"The lemonade," said Angela.

"Spit out the lemonade?" said Blackbird. "What's this nonsense?" She turned to me, only to see from my face that I was having a dawning realisation. "What?" she asked.

Angela continued. "When Niall first came to me, I knew who he was, or at least I knew about him – ever since that night in Porton Down. I was being driven mad by dreams and images and I knew they had something to do with Niall. I didn't know what they meant. I couldn't sleep without dreaming about them. It was driving me crazy."

"Like you're dreaming now," said Blackbird, catching on.

"I wanted him to understand. I needed him to tell me what they were about. So I stirred the memories into a glass of lemonade."

"Oh no," said Blackbird, turning to me, "You idiot! You drank it! You may as well have eaten a shiny red apple with the words 'Eat Me' written on it in dripping poison."

"I think you're getting your stories confused," I suggested.

"Confused?" She was shouting now. "You're the one that's confused. You're supposed to be a Warder. You don't take offerings, bribes or gifts. At all. Ever!"

"It was only lemonade," I pointed out.

"Except it wasn't, was it?" she turned on Angela. "What did you do?"

Angela backed away towards the window, holding out her hands to ward off Blackbirds anger. "It was quite innocent. I never meant any harm."

"I never meant any harm..." said Blackbird. "Those words should be engraved in stone somewhere and used to bash the pair of you into oblivion. Well, you've done it now," she said. "Does Garvin know about this?"

"I don't think so," I said. "I never thought to mention it."

Blackbird paused, folding her arms, thinking. "Don't tell him," she said.

"What? He's my boss. I have to tell him."

"As the Lady of the Eighth Court, I'm asking you not to tell him."

"I'm not a member of the Eighth Court," I pointed out. "I'm a Warder. I work for all the courts."

"Please, Niall. He doesn't need to know."

"He already knows most of it. I told him myself not half an hour ago. I can't start keeping selected bits of information from him. What if he finds out?"

Blackbird chewed her thumbnail. She shook her head. "We have a problem," she said.

"You're right about that," I agreed.

"No, we have another problem. There have been discussions with Yonna, Kimlesh and Mellion. To some extent we see eye to eye on things that matter and we've been trying to work through the issues."

"So?" I said.

"Garvin's been present at some of these discussions, even if only in the background, and remarks made subsequently by Krane and Teoth, especially Krane, lead me to believe that they are aware of the substance of those discussions."

"You're saying that Garvin is spying for Krane? That's not possible. Garvin works for all the courts, not any single court. He's as straight as a die."

"I'm saying that information is getting back," said Blackbird.

"No, that can't be true." I paced in front of the door. "There are all sorts of ways of eavesdropping on conversations. They could be using mirrors, or hidden microphones..."

"Microphones wouldn't work, and there are no mirrors in the High Court. Even the curtains are drawn to prevent reflections from the windows. Discussions in the High Court are limited to the people who are there," she said.

"What about Kimlesh, or Yonna, Mellion – any of them could be feeding back information?"

"In theory, yes," agreed Blackbird, "But the information revealed hasn't helped any of them. What would they have to gain?"

"They could be secretly against the Eighth Court?" I suggested.

"Then why spend so much time and energy fostering it?" she asked. "If any of them changed sides, the balance of power would shift against the Eighth Court. That would be end of any negotiations. There's no reason for secrecy. I'm telling you, someone has been telling tales and it's someone who was there."

I shook my head.

"Niall, I'm asking you not to tell him where the dreams are coming from. If Angela holds the key to this and she's passed it to you, then it has to stay with you. I can't afford for it to get to Krane and Teoth."

"We don't even know what it means," I said.

"But what if Altair does?" she said.

"Then we have to find out before he does," I said.

"The High Court is convening. I have to go," said Blackbird. "The knights, the horseshoes, all of it will have to wait. Take the names to Claire. See if she recognises any of them." She handed me the piece of paper with the names of the knights on it.

"And if she does?"

"Find them."

Six

When I told her I was going to see her mother, Alex volunteered to come along. This time she wore sensible shoes and jeans, but it was still clear to me that she was no longer my little girl. We turned up on Katherine's doorstep for the second time in two days. Katherine hurried us through the door as if we were spies.

"What's all that about?" I asked her.

"We don't want anyone to know that Claire is here," she explained.

"Then just act normal," I told her. "All this cloak and dagger stuff is only going to draw attention."

Katherine hugged Alex, and then cupped her chin in her hands and looked at her. "You have bags under your eyes."

"I didn't sleep well," said Alex.

"Bad dreams?" I asked her.

"N... no," she said. I could hear the lie in that.

Katherine hugged her again and ushered us into the sitting room. The curtains were drawn, even though it was mid-morning. I threw back the drapes without ceremony.

"What are you doing?" said Katherine.

"I'm letting in some light. If you leave the curtains

drawn like that they're going to think someone's died. You'll have the neighbours round."

"Someone will see her," said Katherine. Claire sat on the sofa, blinking in the unaccustomed brightness.

This was nonsense. There were net curtains behind the drapes so no one could see in. "We're going to have to find you somewhere else," I said to Claire.

"Katherine has been very kind," said Claire. "I'm extremely grateful." That was me told.

I sat down on the sofa next to her and handed her the piece of paper with the names on it. "What do you think of these?"

"I recognise that one," she said, pointing to Walter le Brun. "Where did you get these?"

"Let's just say I dreamed them up," I said. "Any of the others?"

"I'm not sure," she said. "These are all Norman names – FitzRou is familiar, but that's not surprising. Fitz means a child of unrecognised parentage."

"A bastard?" I asked, earning a sharp look from Katherine.

"In the original sense," Claire confirmed, "and FitzRou would imply a royal bastard or a bastard with unacknowledged royal connections."

"Any of the others?"

"They're all names I recognise, but not necessarily in this context. De Ferrers is from the Norman French, ferrieres, meaning a farrier or blacksmith."

"That might fit, given the horseshoes," I said.

"This is as a family name," she said. "They weren't necessarily farriers at the time. Montgomerie, that name is familiar…"

"If I told you that these were six knights, who met in secret, would that help?" I asked her.

She looked at me strangely. "It might," she admitted.

"They met in secret and another guy, Aimery, turned up with soldiers, but then the King arrived…"

102

"Whoa, stop right there," said Claire. "Where did you come by this information?"

"I told you, I dreamt it."

She ran her fingers through her hair. "Don't take this the wrong way," she said, "but dreams aren't usually considered reliable as a historical source."

"The King had Aimery killed." I told her. "He had him thrown overboard on the river."

"You saw this?" Claire was incredulous.

"No, but I heard the King give the order. He didn't exactly say that, but his meaning was clear. You must be able to look that up somewhere."

"I'm not sure," she said with measured patience, "that kings kept records of illicit killings. That sort of thing tended to breed unrest."

"Then check one of the other things. Check the names. They met in a hall with six passages leading to it under a domed roof. It must be somewhere."

"I'm flattered that you think my abilities in research are so well-developed," said Claire, "but there could be a hundred places like that, and many of them will have been destroyed by fire, flood, or just fallen down."

"I've given you the names," I told her. "You must be able to do something."

She looked at the list. "I'll go to the National Archive," she said. "It may be that there are references in the journals. I can check, but it will take days."

"I could help," said Alex brightly.

Claire looked pained and shook her head. "Even if you were allowed access, which you are not," she clarified when Alex looked hopeful, "You would need to be able to interpret Norman French, Middle English and be familiar with a number of conventions. No, it is a job I must do alone."

"What if they're waiting for you?" said Katherine. "It's one of the places you might go, isn't it?"

Claire looked from Niall to Katherine, and back to me.

"I can't read Norman French," I said. "But I am willing to stand guard while you do."

"Then that's what we will do," she said.

After four hours I was beginning to regret that offer. Claire sat in the private reading room, requesting one volume after another to be brought up from the vaults while I watched through the glass. She pored through volumes of journals written in tiny script while making notes on a lined notepad. That was as interesting as it got.

I wasn't allowed in the room when the documents were on display. According to the stern lady archivist, that was what *restricted archive* meant.

Most of the people who came to the National Archive were interested in family history, lost in the dream that they were secretly related to the nobility, or simply interested in their ancestor's lives, means and whereabouts. There were a few legal types working their way through ledgers and maps, but other than that it was deathly dull.

Instead, I could sit outside, I could walk up and down, I could even request documents myself, as long as they were not from the restricted archive. I began to wonder whether I should take an interest in my own family history. After all, at least one of my ancestors wasn't human, though I wasn't expecting them to have records of who it was.

There was a rhythm to it: people came, people went, documents arrived, documents were taken away. I found myself lulled by it, until my series of disturbed nights began to wear on me. I felt my eyes droop and shook myself awake to find someone sat across the table. It was Raffmir.

"Late night?" he said. I grabbed for my sword, but he just pursed his lips and leaned back in his chair. "Too late, cousin. Far too late. If I wanted you dead, your blood would be all over that glass by now."

I retracted my hand, realising that he was right, and I couldn't harm him anyway. We had both sworn under Feyre law not to harm the other under the rules of trial by ordeal. He had expected me to die that day. It was a great source of satisfaction to me that I was still here.

He looked through the glass at Claire working her way through another journal. "What's she doing?" he asked.

"None of your business," I told him.

"I see your temper hasn't improved in my absence," he said.

"Pity you came back," I said.

"Nor your manners," he added.

That was also true. With most people I didn't like I could manage to be polite or at worst ignore them. Raffmir brought out the worst in me.

"What do you want?" I asked him.

"Perhaps I was simply worried for your health," he said. "That looks nasty..." he slid his fingertips up the line of his jaw in the place the gates at the Royal Courts of Justice had left their impression on me.

"You took a vow," I pointed out, "not to harm me or allow me to come to harm."

"It wasn't me that harmed you."

"Your driver, then," I said.

"And yet here you are in the peak of health," he said. "A little marred, a little tainted – normal really..."

"What would you have done if it had killed me?" I asked him.

"...still as rude as ever," he finished.

"I'm serious," I said. "It's execution, isn't it, if you'd killed me? I'm quite sure that Blackbird wouldn't have let that go."

"The witch is still with you then?"

"Don't call her that," I warned.

"Shall I not call a goose, a goose? There is power in names, Dogstar, I think you know. And how is your lovely daughter? Such treacherous curls, it makes you want to cut them all off." He made snipping signs with his fingers.

"You swore not to harm her too," I reminded him.

"Unfortunately, she does not seem to have the same attitude to me," he said. "I do my best to preserve her sorry little hide, and how does she repay me?"

"I'll ask you again, Raffmir, what do you want?"

He leaned across the table, clasping his hands together and meeting my gaze with earnest intensity. "I'm meeting the terms of my vow."

"You're *not* harming me? You could have done that back wherever you came from," I pointed out.

"You'd think it would be easier than it is," he said. "You are my burden, and I suppose I must bear you, at least until the end."

"The end of what?" I asked him.

He smiled, long and slow. "Prophesy, it's such a fickle thing, don't you think?"

"I wish you'd just come out and say whatever it is that you came to say," I told him, "and then leave."

"You haven't thanked me for my last gift yet, and once again I find you are ungrateful."

"For what? I have to be grateful because of something you haven't done for me?"

He stood, straightening the lapels of his coat as he moved around the table and looked down his nose at me. "Not long now, Dogstar. The world turns."

"As it always does?"

"Soon," he said, turning. I watched his retreating back as he walked away between the tables. I shook my head, and glanced in at Claire. It looked like she'd had enough too. She was slumped across the books asleep. At least I thought she was until I noticed the dribble of red off the edge of the table.

"Shit!" I grabbed my sword and burst into the room, wary of someone hiding behind the table, under the line of the windows, but there was no one. I lifted Claire by her shoulders and she flopped back in her seat, exposing the long slit across her throat. Blood was soaked into her clothes. Her dead eyes stared up at me.

How? She was OK a moment ago. I'd watched her while Raffmir asked me what she was doing. No one had entered or left since then. Except me. I suddenly realised what this looked like. People were staring at my sudden activity. I stood out in the quiet archive like a food-fight in a convent. I pulled my glamour around me, but they had already seen. When asked later they would make the connection, exactly as Raffmir had wanted.

I pushed the journals away from the growing pool of blood, streaking red across the surface.

Blood running down translucent glass. Watching it form into sticky droplets.

I shook my head. Not now. I had to get a hold on myself. I grabbed the journals from the table, leaned Claire's body forward across the table again, as if she were resting. Pulling the tatters of my glamour around me, I left. With my glamour in full force, no one saw me leave, but that wouldn't matter. They had all seen me arrive, all seen me sat outside the room. The archivist would attest that she had told me that I could not go into the room, and they had all seen me enter it.

Bloody Raffmir.

"You were supposed to be guarding her," said Blackbird.

"You think I don't know that?"

"Now what are we going to do?" said Blackbird. "It was bad enough that we've lost the knives and the horseshoes without losing the Remembrancer's clerk as well. You're sure she was dead?"

"Her throat had been slit."

"Well I suppose it was quick, but hardly what she deserved," said Blackbird. "This goes from bad to worse. I warned her to keep the horseshoe close."

"The horseshoe?" I asked.

"Yes, she was carrying one with her. Don't tell me you left that behind as well?"

I thought for a moment. "She wasn't allowed to keep her bag with her. The archivist wouldn't allow it. She put it in a locker. It's probably still there."

"Or the police have it," said Blackbird.

"Well funnily enough, I didn't stick around to ask them about it," I said.

"Perhaps we could try and keep the discussion constructive?" said Angela, trying to calm things down.

"Perhaps if you hadn't dosed him with your memories," said Blackbird to Angela. "We're in a bind, and no mistake." Angela looked hurt, but Blackbird was in no mood to be sympathetic. "We're up against it, Angela."

"We still have time," I said. "I can go back for it. If I can find some way of transporting them, I could retrieve the one from the flat too."

"We have less time than you think," said Blackbird. "Teoth and Krane are insisting that the Eighth Court moves out of the High Court by the winter solstice."

"But that's only days away," I said.

"Where will we move to?" said Angela. "We won't all fit in my house."

"That might be the only choice we have," said Blackbird, "and I'm truly grateful for the offer."

"It wasn't an offer," said Angela. "I was being sarcastic."

"Do you have a better idea?" asked Blackbird. "Sparky, Alex, Niall, you, me and the baby – that's not so many. The others will just have to stay where they are until we can find something larger. It's not supposed to be a full-time home for everyone – more of a place to gather."

"We'll be camping in the garden," said Angela. "What about Andy and the bees? Julie's about to lose her flat."

"Who's Julie?" I asked.

"She's one of the newcomers," said Blackbird. "She came in last night with a guy called Hathaway – I'm assuming that's his surname. Word is spreading, Niall. They're coming to us because we offer the best hope there is."

"It doesn't say much for the other options," I said. "We need a better plan than Angela's house, with the greatest respect to you, Angela."

"I agree with you," she said, emphatically. "What about Yonna or Kimlesh? Won't they help us?"

"I think they would if they could," said Blackbird, "But they don't own their courts and they have their own dissenters. They can't just give us property as a donation or a loan. Can you imagine how long it would take Teoth or Krane to let slip that the courts were giving their assets away to support a bunch of half-breeds?"

"We can't all go to Tamworth," I said. "How long do you think it would be before the authorities took an interest in us, operating out of semi-detached in a housing estate? How long before one of the new intake loses it and we're attracting entirely the wrong sort of attention. These people need space – room to make mistakes. I give it a week."

Angela picked up one of the journals I'd rescued from the archive office. "Perhaps the knights will help us. They're all old families. Claire said they were wealthy. We might as well go through the journals and see if we can find any reference to them," said Angela.

"Even if you can decipher the text, I'm not sure it'll help," said Blackbird. "We're not supposed to know who they are, let alone ask them for favours."

"By the same token," I pointed out, "If they'd been at the ceremony as they were supposed to have been, perhaps none of this would have happened. They must bear some of the responsibility."

"That's true," said Blackbird, "But what if they didn't come because they're all dead, their throats slit like poor Claire?"

"Then we really are screwed," said Angela.

"What about the Secretariat?" I suggested. "They must have resources. Maybe they can lend us something in the interests of keeping the peace."

"I don't need another set of negotiations," said Blackbird, "and they will want something in return."

"It's in their own interest. Otherwise they have to clean up the mess, and prevention is better than cure, surely?" I saw a shadow pass across Angela's eyes at the mention of a cure. She'd been at Porton Down and knew first hand the sort of cures they'd been developing there. "Sorry," I said to her, "bad turn of phrase".

"If we meet the Secretariat," said Blackbird, "then Garvin will know about it."

"Not necessarily," I said.

"I want him kept out of it, Niall."

"I won't tell him. I promise."

"You won't need to. If the Secretariat is involved then it will get back to him and then he'll have reason to start sticking his nose where it's not wanted. They won't help us anyway. You've said yourself that they're only interested in covering their backs."

"Then we need a better idea," I told her, "and fast."

"Are you all right, Sweetheart? Can I get you something?" It was the tenth time she'd asked that question; well maybe not the tenth, but it was getting on Alex's nerves.

"No, Mum, I don't want anything."

That at least was true. There was nothing Alex wanted and nothing she could do. She couldn't go out, or see her friends, or mooch around the shops, or invite Kayleigh round, or any of the things she might have done. She'd thought twice about inviting Kayleigh, but how did you even begin to explain, and anyway, what would they talk about? She'd stood outside Kayleigh's house one night and watched her. It'd been like time-travel, watching someone from the past. For Kayleigh, nothing had changed. For Alex, everything had changed.

"Are you all right?" asked her Mum.

The question again. "I'm fine."

"It's just... do you mind not doing that with the cushions?"

Alex looked down in her lap at the cushion she had twisted until it was wound tight. She let go and it sprang back into plumpness, though the cover retained the stress lines across it. She smoothed them with her hand.

Katherine sat opposite, waiting for Alex to say something.

"What?" said Alex.

"If there's something on your mind, you can always talk to me about it," said Katherine.

No, she really couldn't. She shook her head. "I'm OK. What's for supper?"

Katherine wasn't put off so easily. "Alex, I've been meaning to talk to you."

"What about? No, don't tell me. I don't want to know."

"You've said some things – I understand. Teenagers make things up all the time. It's part of their narrative – coming to terms with the world. I know you need... attention. But you're home now. You can let all that go."

"All what?" asked Alex, genuinely puzzled.

"All that stuff about killing people, and being on the run. You forget, I was a teenager once." She smiled. "It's all about the drama."

"Drama?"

"You're very creative. You always had an active imagination. It's only natural that you should make up stories."

"I killed three girls," said Alex, coldly, staring at her mother. "I went to school with them, and now they're dead."

"That was an accident," said Katherine. "It was the sewer – there was an explosion. It was a tragedy, of course."

"I drowned them," said Alex, "in sewage."

Katherine laughed nervously. "There you go. Stories. You see?"

"You think this is made up?" said Alex. "You think I'm imagining this shit?"

"There's no need for that language, young lady!"

Alex shook her head. "You have no idea, do you? I've fought for my life, made friends, and enemies, stolen things, taken stuff. I've bargained with ravens, walked unseen through the Houses of Parliament. I've seen the cosmos split apart above me... the universe, opened up – made to take notice."

"You say things I don't think you even understand," said Katherine. "What does that even mean?"

"I've seen Dad, shining in the dark like a..."

"Like a what?" asked Katherine.

"Nothing," said Alex.

"If your father is encouraging this..."

"You still don't get it," said Alex. "This is not about him. It's about me."

Katherine reached forward and grasped Alex's wrist. "What's this?" She pushed Alex's sleeve up her arm revealing the winding pattern of dark vines. "You got a tattoo. It's not even a nice one. What's it supposed to be?" She took hold of her other wrist and looked at that as well. "They don't even match."

"It's not a tattoo," said Alex.

"Is that why you've been sitting in your cardie sweltering while I've got the central heating on? Because you were ashamed to show me? When did you get that done? Did your father let you do that to yourself?"

"I told you it's not a tattoo. It just does that."

"I'll have to talk to him," said Katherine. "This can't go on."

"No!" said Alex. "Don't talk to him about me. Talk to me about me. I'm right here!"

"This is silly," said Katherine, making to stand up.

"Don't walk away," said Alex. "That's what you always do to Dad. You say something and then you make out that it's nothing, but you've already said it by then."

"Leave my relationship with your father out of this."

"Then talk to me," said Alex. "Dad treats me like a grown-up."

"I'll treat you like one, when you act like one."

Alex's eyes narrowed. "You don't believe me," she said. "You think I'm making it all up." She looked around the room. "Central heating pipes, all round the house. How about we make it go backwards?"

"Backwards? What do you mean, backwards?"

Alex opened her hands, took a breath and released it slowly. A draft from the kitchen had a sudden chill to it. The pendant lamp in the centre of the ceiling swung gently.

Katherine narrowed her eyes, but for a moment, nothing happened. "You see?" she said.

The radiator under the window made a ticking noise. The pipes along the wall started to vibrate with a low hum. All around the house, the pipes began to groan and creak. A clanking noise was coming from the boiler in the kitchen. The whole system started banging and clanking as the pressure built.

Katherine stared about her wildly. "Alex! Stop this at once."

"What Mum? I thought I was imagining it? I thought I was making it all up?"

The radiator was making creaking noises. It started rattling against the brackets holding it to the wall. The pressure was building. Any moment and the pressure would blow and then...

Bing bong.

The noise of the doorbell was a signal. Everything

stopped. The vibrations ceased, the clanking fell into silence. The whole system eased as the water started to flow again in its usual direction.

"Who's that?" said Alex.

Katherine looked crossly at Alex. "I don't know," she said. "It might be the postman, he sometimes rings if there's a letter too big for the letterbox."

They waited in silence.

Bing bong.

"I'd better go see," said Katherine.

"No!" said Alex. "Leave it. Let it go." They waited.

Bing bong. Bing bong. It was followed by sharp tapping.

"I'll go and see," said Katherine. "Don't worry," she said to Alex. "I'll get rid of them." She went to answer the door.

Alex stepped up to the window, trying to see who was at the door without moving the net curtains. She hung back behind the drapes, peeking around to view the doorstep. She could hear her mother.

"Yes," said Katherine. "Can I help you?'

The guy on the doorstep was middle-aged with sandy hair and greying temples. He wore a long loose coat.

"Is Niall in?" he said.

Katherine looked taken aback. "Niall doesn't live here any more," she said.

"Only, I have something for him," said the man. Alex didn't recognise him as anyone her Dad had ever mentioned.

"I'm afraid you're out of luck," said her Mum.

"Will he be back later?" asked the man.

"I told you. He doesn't live here. We're divorced, I've recently re-married. Who are you?"

"Just a friend," he said, looking up and down the street. Alex could tell, whoever the man was, he was no friend. "Did you have a caller recently, a lady? About five-six, brown hair, goes by the name of Claire?"

"I'm sure I don't know who you mean," said Katherine.

"She's been missing for a while. I thought she might come here," he said.

"Why would she come here? I don't know anyone by that name."

"Fair enough," said the man. "Well, look, if you see Niall…"

"I won't," said Katherine.

"If… you see him. Would you give him a message for me? Tell him I have something he needs."

"I told you, he doesn't live here," she said.

"Thanks very much," said the man. He walked away down the drive and across the road. Alex watched him as far as she could. He didn't turn, and he didn't look back. Katherine closed the front door and returned to where Alex was watching through the window.

"What a strange man," said Katherine, from the doorway of the sitting room.

"He was lying," said Alex.

"I didn't recognise him," said Katherine, "but I'm not sure that's any reason to assume that…"

"He's lying. I can hear it. We all can."

"We?" asked Katherine. Alex shouldered her bag and went into the kitchen. Katherine followed her. "Where are you going?"

"I'm going to tell Dad," she said.

"Well I expect he'll pop in when he's ready," said Katherine. "We can tell him then."

"He needs to know," she said. "There's stuff going down."

"But what about… you were staying for supper," Katherine said as Alex went to the back door.

"Don't worry, I'll get something later. I can always raid the pantry. The cooks don't mind." Alex opened the door and scanned the garden.

"Alex?" Katherine was stood in the door between the kitchen and the hall watching her daughter as she stood outlined in the doorway. "Be careful."

Alex stepped quickly back inside and kissed her mother's cheek. "Don't worry," she said. "I've dealt with worse than his sort." She slipped back through the door. Katherine didn't hear the back gate, but she stood with the back door open for a long while.

"That," she said, "is what worries me."

SEVEN

The room was at the top of the house. It probably used to be servants' quarters when the house had been in its heyday, only now the stewards lived in the main house and the attic rooms were empty, except for this one.

The bed had been moved to the centre where it dominated the room; the curtains were swept back so that the low late afternoon sun striped the floor. Beside the bed, a stand held a drip that fed transparent solution slowly into Fellstamp's arm. He lay on the bed, eyes closed, looking for all the world like he was taking an afternoon nap – except for the saline drip that had been set up, and for the way his skin sagged from his frame like an oversized suit.

"You don't come up here much, do you?"

Fionh's voice startled me. She was sat back in the shadows in the corner and I wondered if she had deliberately cloaked herself from being noticed.

"How's he doing?" I asked her.

She folded closed the book that was open on her lap and clasped her hands together over it. "How do you think?" she said.

"Has he shown any signs?"

She shook her head slowly.

I walked around the bed slowly, noting how the sheet had been carefully folded back just below his shoulders, how his curly hair fell on the spotless white linen pillow and how thin his frame looked under the sheet.

"Garvin said he's still losing weight."

"He hasn't eaten in months," she said. "It's hardly surprising."

When you looked at his face, he looked older, though the Feyre don't age outwardly, once they reach adulthood. I wondered if that was what happened when you starved to death. You suddenly looked older.

"Is there anything I can do?" I asked her, aware that they had tried everything to wake him.

"You could talk to him?" she said.

"What about?"

"I don't think it matters," she said. "He's not listening anyway."

Fionh stood up and put the book quietly on the side table, as if she didn't want to disturb the sleeper on the bed. "You can say whatever you want," she said, moving to the doorway. "You might start by explaining why the mongrel that did that to him is still alive."

I heard her footsteps as she walked away down the corridor. She was angry, and no wonder. She'd been with Fellstamp when they went in against Eve, Sparky, Chipper and Alex, when they'd been spotted in an abandoned office building in London.

"You know?" I said to Fellstamp, "You misjudged them. You went in hard with the expectation that they would be disorganised and weak." I began to walk around the bed slowly, talking more to myself that to the recumbent figure on the bed. "So you held a blade to Sparky's throat. You made an assumption, that more than anything else he wanted to live, and that the desire to live would give you control. You took him hostage."

As I walked between the bed and the windows, my shadow crossed the bed with me, like a ghostly companion.

118

"You were only half-right. They were disorganised. They weren't trained to act as a team and they hadn't prepared their defence. They winged it.

"Where you misjudged them, though, was in the assumption that more than anything else they wanted to survive, and that they would grasp at any sliver of hope that meant they might live to fight another day. You forgot what had been done to them."

I stopped at the head of the bed. I watched the slow rise and fall of the sheet as he breathed. I almost felt that I could hear his heart's slow beat.

"I think we found out later that, for at least some of them, survival wasn't the objective." I began a slow circuit once again. "I'm not saying they're not to blame – they carry the responsibility for what they did – but you made a mistake. After what had been done to them, there was something worse than death. Whatever happened, they weren't going to be captured again."

My shadow drifted across the bed, following me.

"I've had to learn that. Alex is the same. She can't be contained, not any more. She sleeps with the door open, did you know that? She can handle it by day – but at night, I think there's the thought that if the door once closes, she won't be able to open it again."

I looked down into Fellstamp's face, wondering whether he dreamed, whether he knew anything at all.

"I'm not asking you to forgive them," I told him. "I'm not sure it's your forgiveness they want. The experiments they endured were designed to push them beyond their limits, with no thought for subtlety or finesse. The scientists set out to discover how much they could do. In that, they succeeded. None of them have any real control. It's all, or nothing. Sparky gave you everything he had."

I walked round again, finding that I had said most of what I wanted to say. "Think about it," I told him.

I left him there. I think Fionh was lurking close by

somewhere. I got a sense of her presence, almost like a perfume as I left. I suspect she returned to her reading.

Downstairs, Alex and Angela were talking. "Did Alex find you?" said Blackbird. "She was looking for you."

"I haven't seen her," I said.

"Never mind, come and see this." She indicated one of the journals, which was open on the desk. The journal was open at a series of entries, but there was a loose leaf of paper between the pages.

"Where did this come from?" I asked. Unlike the heavy parchment of the journal, it was written on paper that was so thin it was translucent. The hand was scratchy and the ink was faded in places.

For the manor and the land appertaining to Grey's Court, a red rose, presented in full splendour on midsummer's eve by Robert and Lettice Knollys or their successors in title in full escort and regalia at the foot of the altar of All Hallows of the Keep, unless there be a white rose at midday on the eve of the winter solstice, at the same place, whereupon the manor shall pass to the key-holder in perpetuity.

"It was tucked between the pages of this journal," said Blackbird. "We found it when we were going through them."

"What is it?"

"I'm not sure," said Blackbird. "It's not a contract, or a deed of any kind. We're not even sure what it relates to."

"They're not serious, are they? A manor house in exchange for a rose?"

"It's not beyond precedent," said Blackbird. "In law, a contract must have a consideration, something given and received in order for it to be valid. If you wanted to give something away then you could make the consideration something trivial, like a rose,"

"So it's a gift?"

"What do you mean?" I asked.

"If this is just a copy of another document," said Angela, "then this may all have been resolved years ago. It's just a piece of paper with mild historical value."

"But if this is the only reference to it," said Blackbird, "then it's possible that somewhere there is the contract that this relates to, and by invoking the conditions of that contract we could benefit from it."

"Surely someone must have tried this before?" I said.

"Except for one thing," said Blackbird. "Where would you get a white rose in the middle of winter? This was found in pages dating back five hundred years," said Blackbird, "and at that time there would be no way of producing a pure white rose on the eve of the winter solstice unless you had an awful lot of money."

"Could you do it?" I asked.

"Of course," said Blackbird. "With magic, it's a trivial transformation."

"Then perhaps that's its purpose. It's been left here against some future need."

"Why leave it there, though?" she asked. "The only people who have access to these documents are the clerks and the Remembrancers."

Angela closed the journal carefully. "There are no other inserts. I've been through the other journals. Of course, there are others still in the restricted archive, but they could be hard to access."

"The only way is to try it; present the rose on the solstice eve. Very shortly it will be the shortest day. It's now or never." I went to the dresser and lifted down the sword.

"What are you intending to do with that?" asked Blackbird.

"It's only a precaution," I said.

"Not every problem is solved with a sword," said Blackbird. "We may need subtler skills if we are to make this work for us. Besides, I have another task for you. Without Claire to act as intermediary, even if we find the knights they have no reason to trust us. If we had a token of good faith to offer, though, then perhaps we could establish lines of communication. I want you to recover the horseshoes so that we can return them as a gesture of good faith. Take one of the drivers – you can tell them it's court business. Bring back the horseshoes – the one from the National Archive that Claire had with her, and the one in her flat, if they're still there."

"I won't be able to touch them," I pointed out.

"I'm not asking you to. Take a holdall or something of that nature, and some heavy gloves. I'm sure the gardeners have something you could use. You'll only have to hold them for a moment, and with gloves it shouldn't be too bad.

Alex pushed through the door into the room. "Dad, I need to talk to you."

"Can it wait?" I asked her. "Now is not a good time."

"There was someone at the house," she said, without preamble.

"What house?" said Blackbird.

"At Mum's. A man came to the door, about six foot tall, sandy hair, greying at the temples. Looks like he's had his nose broken – more than once, probably."

"Sam Veldon," I said. Blackbird also appeared to recognise the description. "What did he want?"

"He was looking for you, and he asked after Claire." Alex watched the exchange of looks between me, Angela and Blackbird. "What?"

"Claire's dead, Alex. Someone slit her throat," said Blackbird.

"Oh," said Alex in a small voice.

"We can't have this," I said. "I can't just have people turning up at Katherine's. What does Sam think we're doing, running a consultancy?"

"It's attracting the wrong sort of attention," agreed Blackbird.

"He said he had something for you," said Alex.

"It's not like Sam to volunteer," I said. "Did he say what it was?"

"He just said it was something you need," said Alex.

"Did he say where he'd be? How to contact him?"

"No," said Alex. "He just asked Mum to pass on the message. He seemed to think she'd know where you were. It's what I came back to tell you."

"What about your Mum?" I said. "You've left her on her own?"

"Oh, you know Mum," said Alex. "She'll be all right."

"I'm not happy about Sam sneaking round the house. Maybe you should go back and stay with her, just in case."

"I told her I'm staying here, now," said Alex. "She's not expecting me back."

There was a hint of evasion in that sentence, but then so much of what Alex said was veiled in half-truths.

"As regards the rose, this will either work or it won't," said Blackbird, "but it's too tempting not to give it a try. It could solve a lot of our problems, assuming the manor still exists and hasn't been developed into a housing estate in the intervening years. Even so, I don't want Garvin knowing about this, or the horseshoes" said Blackbird. "Not until we're sure where his loyalties lie."

"I could come with you," Alex suggested.

"I think it would be better if you stayed here," I told her.

"I could watch your back. I wouldn't get in the way. You need someone, and you can't take one of the Warders or they'll tell Garvin," she pointed out.

"Look," I said to Alex. "It'll be a long car drive and there'll be nothing to do. I'm only going to collect the horseshoes and bring them back here. I won't need anyone to watch my back because nothing's going to happen," I said, kissing her forehead. "Blackbird and Angela are going to test a theory. You could do me a really big favour and go and look after your little brother."

"Oh Dad!"

"What? Lesley's looked after him for most of the day. She could do with a break, and besides, he really likes you."

"He pulls my hair," she protested, "when he's not throwing up all over me."

"He's not pulling it, he's playing with it." I told her. "He doesn't mean any harm. I'll be back as soon as I can. Just keep the pair of you out of trouble until I get back."

I left Alex complaining to Blackbird, much good it would do her, and took my sword and headed for the stables to find a driver to take me back into London.

"Why do you always wait for me to speak first?"

"Because I want to hear what you have to say?" whispered the voice.

There was a pause. "Why did you have to kill her? You already had the safe."

"It was necessary. There will be no more ceremonies."

"She was human. It was a very public place. There will be questions. All this invites a level of scrutiny I would rather avoid."

"Deal with it."

"I am dealing with it, but you keep making it harder."

"That's your part of the bargain," the whisperer said.

"Not as I recall."

"It's all the same," said the whisper. "Has the ultimatum been delivered?"

"Yes."

"Have they agreed?"

"She's trying to buy time."

"That must not happen."

"I'm doing what I can to prevent it, but Barthia is inclined to support them. You could apply a little leverage from your end?"

"I'll see what can be done."

"And what about the other part of the bargain? When are you going to deliver on that?"

"Everything comes to those who wait," said the whisperer.

"Seems like there's a lot of waiting and not much delivery."

"You want me to do it now?"

"No. But it has to be soon. He won't last."

"The more she draws it out, the longer it will be," said the whisperer.

"Then do something." The shadow detached itself and withdrew.

"Steady, now," whispered the voice.

Blackbird and Angela left Alex shortly after her Dad. "Fine," Alex said to herself. "I'll hold the fort. Leave it to me."

She went back towards her room, intending to grab the music player she'd acquired in a manner that didn't bear examination, especially from her father. The baby would try and pull the earphones out, if she let him, but as long as he didn't suck them it was probably OK. If she let her hair wind around his stubby little fingers that usually kept him amused until he fell asleep.

"Hey, Alex." Sparky was leaning against the wall outside his room, the slanting lines of the setting sun cutting through his doorway beside him sending slanting lines of light across the corridor.

"Hey you," said Alex, "What's up?"

"Nothing," he said, tucking his hands behind his back and lounging back against the wall, "but that could change."

"Why's that?" she asked, pausing.

"We could do something? Maybe go into town, find one of those clubs you like?"

"You said you don't dance," she said.

"You do," he said, "I could learn. You could teach me."

Alex laughed. "It's not something you learn. You can either do it or you can't."

"OK, then maybe I do dance after all. Maybe I just haven't tried."

Alex sighed. "Not tonight, OK? I have to go and look after the baby. Dad's gone out on an errand, and Blackbird's off doing Blackbird stuff. You know what she's like."

"Yeah. She's cool, though. I like her," said Sparky.

"You fancy her, you mean," said Alex, and then looked away when Sparky blushed. Blimey, she thought. He really does have the hots for her.

"So what about tomorrow?" he asked, covering his embarrassment. "We could make a night of it."

Alex looked back at him. She kinda liked him, but not in that way. He was OK. They'd been through stuff together, and come out closer, but he was always trying to make it into something else. Why couldn't he just accept things the way they were?

"We'll see," she said, and then realised she'd used exactly the tone of voice her Dad used when he meant no, but didn't want to argue with her. Sparky didn't seem to pick up the hint, though.

"I'll come by tomorrow," he said. "I'll bring some boosters, and we can head out."

Alex eased past, "Yeah, maybe," she said. Booster was a combination of energy drink, dark rum and dissolved caffeine tablets. Sparky swore by it, but Alex thought tasted like cough medicine. He was always trying to get her to drink it, claiming it would give her a lift.

"Tomorrow, then?" he called after her.

"We'll see how we are," she repeated.

She reached her room, grabbed her music player and left again, heading further down the hall to the spiral staircase, skipping lightly downwards so she could get back to the main house without having to pass Sparky again. He'd been waiting for her – she knew that. All that nonchalance outside his room was a put-up job.

He was probably just anxious for company, though. She knew how lonely this house could be, and most of the newcomers were older. Sparky was probably just missing people. For a half-second she thought back to the time they'd had together. They'd been a team, Sparky, Chipper, Eve and her. But then she remembered that Eve had tried to kill them all, and Chipper had died. Alex'd killed him, just like the others.

A body lying charred and steaming on the cold grass, its eyes staring out at nothing, the lips pulled back from the teeth in a rictus grin. The gorge-rising smell of burned meat mixes with the stench of sewer water, the choked-off screams echoing back from the tiles as they were dragged under. The swirling brown water in the tiny room, dragging them into the middle…

Staggering at the bottom of the stairs, she was blinded by the onslaught of images in her head, lowering herself to sit on the stairs, feeling for the steps with her fingers while she squeezed her eyes shut, trying to blot out the images. She cloaked herself in glamour, not wanting to be seen like this, trembling and sweating over a memory. Slowing her breathing, one breath at a time, she pushed the memories back down, telling herself that it was done with. It was over.

Using one hand to unclench the other, she massaged her fingers where they cramped and twitched. She couldn't decide whether these attacks were getting better or worse. They were less frequent now, sure, but they were stronger too. She'd thought she was getting better, but maybe they were just getting more extreme. Breathing slowly, she forced herself to relax. She could hear her own heartbeat slowing as she made herself believe it would all be OK.

The calm of the house helped. The ground floor of this wing was deserted: a procession of rooms with dust-covered furniture and closed curtains leaving shadowed interiors. She let herself listen to the peace and the emptiness. As the light faded from the windows down the west side of the house, she welcomed its solitude, the sense of things long past, covered over and forgotten.

If she hadn't been so still and quiet, she would probably never have seen him. The merest suggestion of a shadow crossed the hallway. If you looked directly, there was nothing to see and your eye was constantly drawn away to dusty paintings or the long-silent grandfather clock. It was only when she looked away that her impression of someone moving down the corridor returned. As quietly as she could, she crept after.

She had an idea who it was she was following. His sheer size gave him away, though how anyone that big could move so quietly always amazed her. She was never quite sure how much of that was glamour and how much was just Tate. There was something about the way he walked, as if every step were tested, each pace a measured distance.

She was deliberately looking away while following, trying to keep the sense of him in sight without actually looking at him. Her own glamour was drawn about her, damping her own clumsy footfalls and diverting attention away. They came to the steps down to the Way-nodes and she sensed his presence moving down into the basement room. She hesitated at the head of the steps. If he caught her following him he would be cross, she knew, but her curiosity burned to know why he cloaked himself so, within the bounds of the house. He was up to something, she was sure. How long before she was safe to descend? If she descended too soon then he might still be there and she would have to admit she'd been following him, but if she left it too long his trail would be cold and she would not be able to follow.

Curiosity overruled caution, and she went carefully downwards, trailing her fingers down the cold wall, alert to any sound from within. When she reached the basement room she pushed the door open slowly where it had been left slightly ajar, readying her excuses – *I thought I heard a noise*. No one would ever believe that.

The room looked empty. Even so, she spent a moment standing in the doorway, letting her senses absorb the atmosphere until she was sure he'd gone. The stones were arrayed on the floor. Mostly when the Warders went out they left someone watching the Way-node, but now it was empty. Why didn't Tate want anyone to know where he was going? A sudden pang of jealousy pricked her. Was he going to meet some woman? Is that why he was being so furtive?

She stepped forwards onto the Way-node, suddenly decided, and felt for the Way. It rose beneath her and she was swept away. Sensing the recent passage, the trail through the watery depths was like expanding ripples. She followed in his wake, letting herself glide along after him, barely hesitating as she arced around node after node, only conscious of the trail she followed. She was almost lulled by it, and started when the trail suddenly ended and she found herself in a wooded clearing in the misty darkness. There was a moment of panic as she realised he might be waiting for her, armed with questions as to what she thought she was doing, but there was no one. There wasn't the slightest sign of Tate or anyone else.

Moving off the Way-node, more from habit that any intent, she surveyed the clearing. A tree had fallen across one side of it, half-covered in dark moss. The smell of leaf mould and damp earth surrounded her, while the evening breeze hissed through the high branches above her.

She walked around the clearing slowly until she noticed the path leading out into the wood. He'd been here before then? Maybe there was someone he was meeting. She scrambled up the low bank and wove her way through the trees, her eyes on the ground as she followed the vague outline of a path through the darkening woods. The last remnants of fading daylight filtered down through the leaves and her eyes adjusted until she could see the outlines of trees. Even so, she was slapped in the face by wet leaves more times that she could count. Long strands of bramble snagged in her sweater and her trainers sank into the muddy ground until water seeped into her shoes and made her footsteps squelch.

Listening carefully, there was no sight or sound of Tate, but then she hadn't expected any. If she followed the path, though, that would take her to him and she would see what he was up to. She turned back, looking for the path she had followed, trailing behind her, and seeing none. She shook her head. *Of course* it was there. She was simply seeing it from a different angle.

Walking back along the path she had just followed, she came to the broad trunk of a tree. Had she passed it on the left, or the right? She searched the ground for the signs of her passing, finding only rotting brown leaves, and moss between the stripped-bare shrubs and clumps of undergrowth.

Returning to the place she'd reached, she tried again, but she wasn't sure how far she'd gone. Now that she looked, there seemed to be many paths, though none looked especially used or recently travelled. Nor could she find the path she'd walked. She hugged herself against the night-time chill, wishing that she'd brought warmer clothes. The wood suddenly seemed huge and random, with vague pathways going off in all directions only to end in impassable banks of shrubs or muddy hollows where her trainers sank into the leaves with sucking sounds. Childhood stories echoed in her head and she started at noises in the bushes and imagined large creatures shadowing her movements just beyond her field of view.

She stopped. This was ridiculous. She frowned at her shoes and in a moment they were dry. Likewise, the damp left her clothes, leaving her drier if not especially warmer. She calmed herself down and turned slowly around in a circle, looking for things she recognised. There was a gnarled tree trunk that she was sure she'd passed before. She made her way to that and surveyed her position again. There was nothing she recognised. She had no idea which direction she'd come from or where she was. Somewhere among the wretched trees was a clearing with a trunk laid half across it, and if she could find that, she could at least get home.

Walking in ever-widening circles, she looked for something she'd recognise. The trouble was, the paths she followed weren't circular and they kept leading her in directions she didn't want to go. Within a few minutes she'd lost sight of the gnarled trunk and she couldn't find that again either. Right, she thought, a wood can only be so big, so if she kept walking in one direction she would reach the edge of it, and then she could find civilisation and go home. It might take her longer, but at least she wouldn't be scratched to death, cold and standing in a wet wood.

She picked a direction where the trees appeared to be lighter and set off. She tramped through the brush, her clothes picking up the damp as fast as she could dry them again. She missed her footing jumping over a small stream and ended up half-kneeling in the stream bed. Her temper got worse and the wood went on and on. Was there no end to the trees? After what seemed like half the night, she staggered into a clearing. Her hopes lifted as she thought she recognised something, and then sank when it was the same gnarled trunk she'd left hours ago. There was even the bit of root that she'd scraped the mud off her trainers with, the mud still damp and fresh. All this time she'd been walking in a huge circle. She could have cried. She was tired, frustrated and fed up with sodding trees. Her hands and face were covered in scratches, her knees were bruised and she couldn't remember the last time she'd had anything to eat or drink.

She knew what she'd have to do. There was one person who could get her back to where she needed to be, and it would mean 'fessing up, but she was too exhausted to care. She would wear the consequences and damn the rest. She walked into the clearest space she could find and listed up her chin, ready to shout for help. Tate would be cross at being followed, but anything was better than this.

She emptied her lungs of air and then took a huge breath, lifting her chin to call out far into the woodland.

"Mmmp!" A hand clamped over her mouth and nose, pulling her back against a solid form that dragged her backwards through the undergrowth, clamping her hands to her sides. She squeaked, and kicked, her lungs full to bursting but unable to make more than the tiniest of sounds. They suddenly stopped, backed up to an old tree stump.

There was a whisper, close to her ear. "Not a sound, understand?"

EIGHT

"How do you know where all the Way-nodes are?" asked Angela.

Blackbird walked slightly ahead of her, eager to reach their destination. "Most of the time you find them by trial and error," she said, "but as time goes by you accumulate the knowledge of how to find things, where the nodes are, and how they all relate to each other."

"Like taxi drivers?" said Angela.

"Sorry?" said Blackbird.

"Taxi drivers; they do that thing called the Knowledge, where they ride around London with a clipboard attached to a moped and learn where all the little alleys and shortcuts are. You must have seen them," said Angela.

"Of course," said Blackbird. "I suppose it's similar, though we don't tend to carry passengers."

Angela wasn't sure what to say to that. "It's a strange name, Seething Lane," she said.

"It used to be a threshing ground, where they separated the wheat from the chaff," said Blackbird. "Hence the name. It would have been a noisy, dusty place in those times."

"You didn't see it yourself, then?" asked Angela.

"That was long before my time." said Blackbird.

They reached the bottom of the lane. The Church of All Hallows by the Tower was across the main road and they used the crossing rather than brave the already heavy traffic.

"Have you been in the church before?" asked Angela.

"You ask a lot of questions," said Blackbird, walking towards the church entrance.

Angela stopped until Blackbird had to stop too. "You know many things," said Angela. "You're familiar with codes, and laws, and all manner of lore. You know the correct way to address the Lords and Ladies, and where trolls live, and where the Ways go, but you don't know everything. If you knew what I know, you'd be more scared than you are."

"Would you like to elaborate on that?" asked Blackbird.

"If I could, I would," said Angela. "I can't make sense of it. It scares me just to think about it."

Blackbird regarded her with cold eyes. "I've been scared most of my life – scared of death, scared of life, scared of being noticed. I'm past that. My head is above the parapet and if I get shot at, so be it."

"I don't think it matters whether your head is above the parapet any more."

"It matters to me," said Blackbird. She turned to walk briskly into the Church of All Hallows by the Tower, and Angela had to jog to keep up.

Outside the church, the traffic rumbled and horns sounded. Inside the church it was a distant irritation. Inside was an island of peace in a sea of turmoil. They stepped though a short arcade into the church proper. Fluted stone pillars rose on either side of the aisle forming peaked arches that spanned the dark ranks of wooden pews. Beyond them, light streamed through the plain glass of five vertical panes, which together formed the east window over the altar. A cross was suspended in the space before the window, silhouetted against the fading winter daylight.

As Blackbird approached the altar, a man in a dark suit emerged from the Lady Chapel to the side, intercepting her. "Can I help you?" he asked.

"That depends," said Blackbird, glancing towards the altar and noticing the fresco over the altar depicting a last supper with some seriously anachronous forms of dress.

"We're looking for a rose rent," said Angela. Blackbird gave her a stare that said that she wouldn't be invited on any more of these ventures if she didn't shut up.

The priest smiled ingratiatingly. "You've made a mistake," he said.

"That may be true," said Blackbird, glancing at Angela. "Annually there is a fine presented here. The land in Seething Lane was once owned by the Knollys family and the lady of the house, Letticia, got fed up with the dust and the smells in Seething Lane so she had it made over into a garden. To prevent her boots becoming muddy in the lane when she crossed to her garden, she built a bridged walkway between them, but unfortunately she did not have permission. A red rose from the garden on midsummer's eve was her fine for the bridge. That's presented here at midsummer."

"So there is no rose rent?" asked Blackbird.

"Oh, but there is," said the man. "Henry VIII granted her and Robert Knollys property in Oxfordshire for which the rent is a rose, but that's paid to the crown at the summer solstice, and not the winter solstice. Do you see?" said the priest.

"I understand," said Blackbird. "Will there be anyone here on the eve of the winter solstice – just in case?" she asked. "You never know when others are going to make the same mistake we did."

"The church welcomes visitors at all times of the year, not just for historical events."

"You've got flowers in the church," said Blackbird, "though Advent is traditionally a time of fasting. There are burger bars and sandwich shops all around. Where is the fast? How can there be a feast when no one hungers beforehand?"

He clapped his hand together. "You are right! It is a pleasure to welcome someone who understands Christian doctrine. Will you join me in prayer?"

"I'm not a Christian," said Blackbird.

"We welcome those of all faiths," said the priest, suspiciously.

"I'm a historian. Just because I know what people did, it doesn't mean I think it was right. Is there another ceremony? Another rent paid at the winter solstice?"

"Is this some kind of research?" asked the priest.

"Yes," said Blackbird. "That's exactly what it is – research."

The priest considered her for a moment, glancing at Angela. "I'm sorry. You've come at the wrong time. There is no ceremony at the winter solstice, unless you mean Christmas, which is a little later. We're a Christian church – always have been."

"Thank you, said Blackbird. "Angela?" She turned and walked to the exit.

"I'm sorry if we…" said Angela.

"Angela!" The call was insistent, and Angela shrugged and followed Blackbird to the exit. They walked in silence across the road and back down Seething Lane towards the Way-node.

"Well, that was a waste of time," said Angela.

"What makes you think that?" asked Blackbird.

"The priest said there wasn't another ceremony," said Angela. "You heard him."

"I did indeed hear him," said Blackbird. "But I also heard what he didn't say." To Angela's blank look, Blackbird said, "He didn't say there wasn't another rent, paid at the winter solstice. There are secrets here, I can smell them," she said.

Angela trailed after her. "Let's hope you can tell the difference between secrets and lies," she said.

• • • •

136

Driving down to Kew wasn't the quickest way to travel, but I would not be able to use the Ways once I'd collected the horseshoes. I'd had one bad experience, when I'd tried to use my power to take a hammer across the underground River Fleet. I'd almost drowned proving that magic and iron didn't mix, and I had no wish to repeat the experiment. I was using Blackbird's authority to commandeer the car, and this way I'd been able to wait until we were clear of the courts before expanding on our destination and purpose. Even so, I had simply told Big Dave that I was collecting something for Blackbird and that we needed the car to carry it back. He knew better than to enquire further.

As the daylight faded, I used the time in the back seat of the limo to think things through. I ran my fingers up the side of my cheek, feeling the wheals raised in my skin. Had it been Raffmir I'd seen through the reflection of the glass in the van? He'd made me doubt myself, which was perhaps his intent. Despite everything, I felt sure that he would abide by the letter of the law which bound us both not to harm the other, if not the spirit. Even when Blackbird killed Raffmir's sister, Solandre, he had not broken the oath we all swore before the trial by ordeal that had almost ended my life. That law was enforced by the courts, and even though the Seventh Court was in exile, its members were still bound by it. They were supposed to be held back by the barrier, the construct of fey magic and human ritual that prevented the Seventh Court from crossing from our world whenever they pleased, so how did they get here?

The barrier would stop them crossing between the worlds other than at the equinox and the solstice – the times when the world was in balance; this much Blackbird had told me. Those were the times when the world of exiled Seventh Court and the human world were closest and the barrier was at its weakest and they could cross, either in person, or by taking the thread of power from a newly dead corpse – someone who inherited the thread of dormant power that they could take and use to animate the corpse, using it like a puppet across the barrier. That was what they had tried to do with me when I'd had a heart attack on the London Underground.

Looking back, it was like another life. I'd gone to work, paid my bills, and met my commitments to my ex-wife and the child we shared. I'd done all that was expected of me, and yet it had left me empty, distant and numb. It hadn't been a life, it had been an existence. I'd buried myself in my work because it was too painful to think about anything else. I'd done my duty by my family without ever connecting with who they were. Instead I had walled myself up and felt nothing.

For a moment, I wondered what would have happened if I'd never had the heart attack, had gone to work as normal, had a career, maybe even met someone else. But then Alex's accident would have happened anyway, and I would never have found her without my abilities and Raffmir's help and she would have been drugged up to her eyeballs in a cell at Porton Down for the rest of her unnaturally long life. Perhaps I should thank Raffmir after all, when next I saw him.

Dave eased his way through the traffic, adopting the relaxed approach of the professional driver. We came off the motorway and navigated through West London while I watched the planes climbing out of Heathrow. We made good time through the back streets, but we never appeared to hurry. When we reached the entrance to the National Archive car park, he didn't stop, but rolled past.

"Did we miss the turn?" I asked him.

"There's CCTV on the car park," he said. "If you're not worried about being tracked I can turn around and park, but they'll pick up the registration plate. Otherwise I can drop you in a side street and cruise around the neighbourhood until you're ready. That OK?"

"That would be better, Dave. Thanks. I'm not expecting problems, but it's better if no one knows we were here."

I exited the car on the corner of a network of streets in a permit-only parking zone, taking the black holdall I'd brought to carry the horseshoe, and watched him pull away in the long black car. It was a nice area. so the biggest risk was that he would get stopped on suspicion of casing properties for burglary, not that he would be found cruising for company.

I headed back towards the gates of the National Archive. The entrance was through a large glass atrium and staff were still coming and going. I waited for a few moments and then, cloaking myself in glamour. I tailed one of them inside. The man at the large circular reception desk barely registered my presence. I took a diversion off to the left, heading to where the public lockers were in search of the locker that Claire had used to leave her belongings. The doors to the lockers were transparent, allowing the contents to be viewed while the contents remained securely locked inside. Most of them were empty with the keys hanging from the locks ready to use the next day. I scanned them, looking for one without a key.

It should have been obvious. I should be able to feel the presence of the horseshoe when I got close to it, and the absence of any such sensation was a bad sign. In the end I found the locker – not because of the contents, but because although it was empty it had no key and there was a notice on the inside of the door. *This locker is out of service. Please use another.*

Someone had been there before me.

I checked the rest of the lockers just in case. It could have been for some other reason – a broken lock or a lost key – but although there were lockers that were empty and locked, only one of them had a notice on it. I went back to the locker with the sign, resting my hand over the lock. It gave a satisfying click and I pulled the door open. There was no sign or anything left there, though there were traces of fine dust on the side and base walls. I wiped my finger across it and it came away coated with glossy powder that left a grey sheen across my finger. It was the sort of powder they used to dust for fingerprints. Of course, there had been a murder and they wanted to know who else had used the locker. I searched my memory as to whether I had touched Claire's belongings, whether I had held her bag for a moment, but I could not recall. After all, it hadn't seemed important at the time – I'd not been expecting her to have her throat cut.

Whether they would be able to identify me from my fingerprints, or from the descriptions given by the people who'd seen me with Claire before she was killed was a moot point, in that if I was caught I was unlikely to see trial. Fortunately I was unlikely to be caught and in any case, as a Warder, I had a degree of diplomatic immunity. Like all immunities, though, it had its boundaries, and I suspected that killing people in public places was beyond them.

I crossed the reception and pressed my hand against the keypad, gaining entrance to the staff area. I had a quick walk around the ground floor and then up to each floor in succession, just in case the horseshoe had been collected as an item of curiosity on someone's desk, waiting to be handed over. There was no hint of the iron taint that would have led me to it, though I went through each floor carefully, trying to sense the disruption it would cause.

I retraced my steps and left by the main entrance without anyone knowing I'd been there. The horseshoe had likely been taken as evidence. Perhaps it would appear on someone's inventory: *Horseshoe x 1 – Medieval*. Without access to the investigation, it was impossible to know. I waited for Big Dave to circle round and caught his attention, climbing into the back and driving quietly away.

"Get what you wanted?" he asked.

"Not exactly," I said. "I think someone got there before me."

"Back to the courts, then?"

"Not yet. I have another place to try." I gave him the address.

It was predictable that there would be an investigation into Claire's death with the murder being so public. They would examine the crime scene and follow the evidence. I didn't know enough about police-work to know whether that investigation would extend to her flat, but if there was a chance that the horseshoe would still be there, I had to check. I wasn't looking forward to returning there. The experience last time had been enough to turn my stomach, even though I knew now that she hadn't died there, but somehow I didn't think it would be any easier with the knowledge that she'd had her throat cut.

Dave dropped me at the end of road and I waited until he'd gone before wrapping myself in concealment and making my way to the back of the flats. I could have tried the front, but I already knew the door was warded with the horseshoe I had come to collect. If, on the other hand, it was a crime scene, then I didn't want to be going through the front anyway. The back entrance I had used before would serve me better in either case.

Even so, I waited some time in the shadows across from the fire escape, looking for signs of movement or people showing an interest in the flat. When I was sure it was quiet I began drawing power from the surroundings. Lights flickered in the flats in the row, and a chill wind blew down the alley. As the world faded to parchment thinness, I stepped through the intervening space and was on the balcony. I waited again, hearing the normal sounds return. The flats above me were both occupied, but this time no one crossed the fire escape between them offering candles. Perhaps the hint had been taken.

I waited still, partly out of caution and partly out from the dread of seeing the flat again, knowing this time that Claire was really dead. I steeled myself and tried the door slowly, finding it reassuringly locked. It was a moment's work to trip the lock, step inside and close the door behind me. Light filtering in from outside cast soft shadows into the hall from behind me. Faint noises from neighbours filtered through into the flat, but it was otherwise silent. It was so quiet, I could hear myself breathing. It was then that I realised what was missing.

I stepped forward and clicked on the light. The glow reflected from the white walls and illuminated the passage between kitchen and sitting room. Instead of the smell of dried blood and rotting food, there was the faint aroma of emulsion paint and the smell of bleach. In the kitchen there was washing up dry on the drainer. The sink was empty, the bowl dry. There were no rotting peppers, no half cooked meal. It looked how Claire might have left it if she'd gone to work, or had a weekend away. In the sitting room there was no sign of the blood-spattered walls and mirror, or the hacked up furniture. Instead the mirror reflected back a pleasant living space, with straightened rugs, carefully arranged lamps and strategically placed nick-nacks. The sofa had been replaced with a similar but subtly different one, slightly worn, with cushions plumped up and resting in the corners. The bathroom was similarly clean, and smelled mildly of bleach. The carpets, the walls, even the lamp-shades had been cleaned.

My first thought was that the landlord had cleaned up ready for another tenant, but it was surely too soon for that. Looking around I came to the conclusion that this wasn't for the tenants or the landlord. This had been done for the investigation. Someone had cleaned up, setting everything just so *before* the police got here. Given the timing, it may be that the police hadn't even been to the flat yet – they had no reason to link the murder with her home, though they would probably check here eventually, perhaps once they had informed the next of kin.

Checking the front door, I found that the horseshoe that warded it had also gone, which raised a second question. Who would remove a horseshoe from a door? Where would they take it? Why would they take it? The front door was locked and the lock was deadlocked from the inside. What did that tell me?

I went back through the flat slowly, comparing my memory of what had been here with what I could now see. If I hadn't seen it for myself I would not have believed it. It didn't even smell of paint very much. Yes, there was a vague aroma, but nothing that would prompt you to think it had been recently redecorated. Who had the resources to do that before the police got here, and why would they deploy those resources to cover up the state of Claire's flat? She hadn't even died here. The only blood here, as far as I knew, was from her attacker.

And perhaps there was the clue. The one thing that had been here that should not have been here was the blood. It wasn't even human blood. Was that why it had been cleaned, so that no one would take samples and start analysing it for matches, running its DNA through databases and poking into things which they would rather leave undisturbed?

I stood in the flat and turned slowly, coming gradually to the conclusion that there was nothing for me here. What I had come for had been taken, and the flat had been wiped to remove any trace of me or anyone else. Once again I wiped the light switches, removing any trace of where I had touched. I turned off the lights and opened the door to the fire escape, standing in the open doorway. I couldn't help the nagging feeling that I had missed something. I closed the door and turned the lights back on using the hem of my jacket sleeve, and walked slowly around the flat again. I went into the kitchen and turned around slowly. That was when I saw it. On the fridge was a note attached by a magnet.

Meet Niall on Paddington Green 19/10.

There were no other magnets on the fridge, which was what had been nagging at me. Normally people who put magnets on fridges had loads of them, reminders, mementos, little heart-warming messages, but this was one alone. There was no sign of any other magnets and a quick look around revealed no other notes or reminders. I tried to remember if it had been there when I last came to the flat, but with all the blood and the mess I might easily have missed something that mundane.

There'd been no arrangement between Claire and I to meet in October, assuming that 19/10 was meant to indicate the nineteenth. Paddington Green was an area behind Paddington Station, not far from Edgware Road. It had improved since the modernisation of the station – that whole area had used to be a haven for muggers and low-life. Even now, it wasn't an area a woman alone would care to linger. So why would Claire arrange to meet there? Was she meeting shady characters for some reason connected to her role as clerk? That didn't seem likely, and if she didn't normally leave notes on the fridge, why leave one that was months out of date? Was it there as reminder of something, or did I have a namesake she'd met in October?

But what if the note wasn't left by Claire? What if it had been put there after she'd been murdered by whoever had cleaned up the flat? If so, why did it have my name on it? Was it meant to implicate me? I tried to remember where I'd been on 19th October, but that was months ago. Was there something special about that day? If it was meant as a clue, it was a particularly obscure one. It was odd. There wasn't enough information there, and anyone else finding it might be intrigued by the incongruity of it but they would be hard-pressed to make anything out of it.

Unless that was its purpose. A note left that only the person it was intended for would find or be able to make anything of. Everyone else would walk past it, but the person whose name was on it would look twice. Was it meant for me? If that was the case then it must have been left by someone who knew there was a connection between us. Still, there was no point in leaving a note for me that was months out of date.

So if 19/10 wasn't a date, what was it? A meeting needed a date, a time and a place. It had a place, and it had a date, but no time. What if 19/10 wasn't a date, but a time? What if it was 19:10? If that was true then we had a time but no date. What kind of meeting didn't need a date? Only a meeting that was today. Taking the note carefully from under the magnet, I pocketed it.

I would get Big Dave to drop me at Paddington Green, and this time I would be taking my sword.

As soon as the hand released her, Alex drew a breath to yell for help. The hand clamped back over her mouth. "Mmmmmmm!" she squealed through the hand.

She was running out of oxygen. Spots were beginning to appear before her eyes. She struggled to get an arm free, anything to make release the hand clamped over her mouth and nose. Suddenly it released and air rushed out of her. She took another huge breath and the hand clamped back over her mouth and nose.

"We can carry on like this or you can be quiet," whispered the voice. Alex made some small, whimpering noises. "Can I trust you not to scream?" She nodded again. The hand was gradually removed and she spent a moment just breathing, drawing big gulps of air into her as the luminous dots floating in front of her vision receded.

In the darkness, she gradually became aware of the person still holding her. The size of the hand held ready to silence her was clue enough. "Tate?" she said.

"Shhhh," he warned. "Just breathe."

She gradually caught her breath and relaxed against him. In a strange way it was comforting to be held like that. As she relaxed he eased his grasp until she simply leaned against him, encircled within his arms. "What are you doing here?" His question was whispered close to her ear.

"I saw you sneaking out and I followed you," she admitted.

"Why?" he asked her.

"Why not?" she asked. "I thought you were up to something."

"I'm on Warder business," he said. "You could have got yourself killed."

"I'm perfectly capable of looking after myself," she said, the lie in that obvious to both of them.

"You can't stay here," he said. "Go back to the courts. Wait for me there."

"I can't," she said.

"Why not?"

"I'm lost. I've been trying to find my way back for the last hour." Tate made a noise like a distant steam train. "It's not funny!" she whispered harshly.

"No, unfortunately it's not." They stayed there in the dark. She found herself warming slowly, and he showed no inclination to release her.

"You'll have to guide me back," she said, eventually.

"Shhh," he whispered softly.

"I mean it, people will begin to wonder where I've gone."

"Listen," he whispered.

She listened then, and caught voices carried on the breeze. Someone – no, more than one person, were moving through the wood.

"Who is it?" she whispered softly.

"You don't want to know," he breathed close to her ear.

She pressed herself back in against him, and in response he curled his arms around her tighter. The voices were low and she couldn't make out the words. They

146

passed a little distance away. Gradually the sound receded and they were left alone in the shadow of the tree-trunk again.

"Stay here," whispered Tate, releasing her. "I'll come back for you."

"No!" said Alex.

"I mean it, Alex. We're not playing games." There was urgency in his tone.

She looked up at him in the dark. "What if you don't come back?" Alex tried not to think about the long hours in the dark, but the thought of being left here alone again made her eyes well up.

"Oh, for goodness sake," he said. "Look, it's dangerous. I'll be back in less than an hour."

"An hour! I'll freeze to death in an hour!"

He hushed her again.

"I'll come with you," she volunteered. "I'll be quiet, I promise."

She felt his eyes on her in the dark, and had the sudden impression that he could see her much better than she could see him.

"I'm going to regret this," he said. "I just know."

He beckoned her to follow and mounted the small bank he had dragged her down, offering her a hand when she struggled to climb even that small incline. He moved quickly and silently through the woods, and she followed after, snapping twigs and occasionally exclaiming when a wet branch hit her in the face or bramble caught her hands.

He stopped. "This isn't working," he whispered.

"I'm not hanging round in the dark waiting," she said, determined not to be consigned to the hollow beneath the trunk in the dark for an hour. "I'll make my own way back."

This was clearly so preposterous that it made him smile. She found herself grinning back in the dark. "What?" she said.

147

"You are your father's daughter," he said.

"What does that mean," she asked, offended.

"Never mind. Climb onto my back," he said. "Like a piggy-back."

"I'm too old for piggy-backs," she said, looking at him sceptically.

"It's either that, or I tie you to a tree and gag you," he said.

"You wouldn't dare!" she said, but something in his stance said that he would dare, if that was the only way. "I'm not liking this," she said.

He knelt down, and she climbed on his back the way she used to climb on her Dad's when she was little. Somehow the sheer size of him made her feel small again, as she wrapped her arms round his neck and he gathered her legs under his arms. He rose up, and she clung on tight, wary of being dropped backwards.

"Hold on tight," he said. Instead of the walking pace he'd set before, he immediately broke into a long-legged trot, swerving round bushes and ducking under branches so that her hair brushed through them as they passed. They made surprisingly little noise. There was the rush of the breeze and the whisper of branches as they passed and she found herself on a wild silent ride through the dark, which left her breathless.

They slowed and halted on one side of a high bank, crested with young trees. Tate let her down and she rubbed her legs where he had held her. She was sure she would have bruises tomorrow.

He held his finger to his lips and then slowly and carefully climbed the bank. She found her way up slowly behind him until she reached the crest, where she joined him lying on the damp earth.

Beyond the rise was a clearing, sheltered within an arc of trees that formed a natural barrier. In the clearing was a camp. Now that she could see it, she recognised the scent of wood smoke as it drifted like the thread of a ghost on the breeze. A fire glowed low, without much flame or smoke, inside a ring of stones in the centre of the clearing. Nearby, something between a tent and a shelter was erected around an arch of bendy sticks and covered with a heavy tarpaulin that concealed everything within. They watched in silence for some while, until Alex whispered to Tate. "What are we looking for?"

In answer, Tate hushed her and pointed towards the edge of the clearing. After a while there was the sound of an approach, and four people walked out of the trees. They moved quietly but without stealth. Alex immediately recognised two of them as Lord Krane and Lord Teoth, but the other two were unknown to her. Each appeared to be associated with one of the Feyre Lords – an escort, perhaps. They entered the clearing and a stubby little man emerged from the shelter. He had the look of Teoth's court about him in the same way as Fellstamp did, but he didn't especially acknowledge the Nixine Lord any more than he did Lord Krane. He reminded Alex of an undertaker, and he appeared to be treating the two Lords more like equals, although he greeted both of them courteously, nodded to the escorts, and then returned to the fire to warm his hands. Lord Krane approached the fire, and an animated discussion began.

Though they were too far away to hear what was going on, it appeared to be some sort of exchange – the man appeared to be haggling with Krane over something. Offer and counter-offer was refused until Lord Teoth showed his impatience and demanded whatever it was they were arguing about to be handed over. The man demurred, but then produced a small white cloth, which was stained with something brown. It was passed between Krane and Teoth, and the man questioned about it.

There was a silent exchange between the two Lords and they withdrew a short distance to confer. The discussion then was no less animated, but they kept their voices low. The man at the fire was clearly trying to over-hear, but the two escorts placed them selves between him and their discussion, ensuring a certain amount of privacy. After a while the argument subsided and they returned to the fire. Lord Krane spoke to the undertaker who offered his hand as if to shake on the deal. After a moment, Lord Krane held out the white cloth and dropped it into the fire. The man shouted at this and attempted to grab the cloth from the fire. Meanwhile Lord Teoth pointed to the man, the shelter and the fire, and then walked away with Lord Krane.

Without warning, the two escorts drew weapons and attacked the little man. He wasn't armed, while one of the escorts had an axe, and the other a sword. Alex couldn't bear it. She looked away and covered her ears at the terrible cries from the man as he was brutally cut down. When she looked back, the escorts were taking the shelter apart and tossing it onto the fire piece by piece. The little man's body had been thrown on the fire with everything else. The fire produced thick grey smoke, and for a moment Alex caught the smell of it and nearly threw up. Tate glared at her, and she slid back down the bank away from the sight. She could no longer watch.

She remained at the foot of the bank until Tate joined her. When Alex made to speak, he hushed her, but knelt and let her climb aboard his back. Without a word he set off back through the woods, leaving Alex shocked and confused at what she'd seen. The wild ride through the trees was repeated, but her mind kept returning to the events in the clearing, what she'd witnessed, and why Tate had gone to some trouble to observe the two Feyre Lords unnoticed. By the time they reached the Way-node, she was exhausted, both mentally and physically.

Tate knelt to let her slide from his back. "Can you find your way back?" he asked.

"I'm not sure," she said. "I guess so."

"Then perhaps I'll speak with you tomorrow," he said. "In the meantime, do not discuss what you saw with anyone."

"Not even Dad?" she said.

"Especially your Dad," he said. "If I'd known what was going to happen..."

"Oh shit!" said Alex. "I was supposed to look after the baby. Lesley's been left with him all evening."

"Then you'd better come up with a good excuse," said Tate. "One that doesn't include what you saw."

"What did I see?" asked Alex.

Tate looked at her long and hard. "You don't need to know," he said. "That sort of information can get you killed."

"If you don't tell me, I'll only guess," she pointed out. "Why would they argue about a stained bit of white cloth?"

Tate sighed. "That's the wrong question," he said.

"OK then, what's the right question?" she asked.

"What was on the cloth that they would kill to get rid of it?" said Tate.

"And?" asked Alex.

"If you hadn't been with me," said Tate, "I might have been tempted to go and find out."

NINE

I was beginning to wonder whether asking Dave to take
me to Paddington was a good idea. We had done well
initially, but then the traffic had snarled up and we'd
moved forward twenty yards in as many minutes.

"How far is it?" I asked Dave.

"If we can get through Sussex Square we'll probably be
OK," he said, "Paddington's about half a mile that way,
but a lot of this is the queue to get onto the Westway and
out of London. At this time of day we could be a while."

"OK, you head back. I'll find my own way back when
I've done what I need to do. I can walk from here."

"It'll probably be quicker," he agreed.

Exiting the car, I joined the commuters heading
through the winter streets towards Paddington. It was
already dusk and I hurried through streets flanked with
railway hotels and town houses converted into flats. As
I neared the station I walked alongside commuters heading for their evening trains and reflected briefly that they
used to be me, or more properly I used to be them. They
walked through the streets, talking on mobile phones,
listening to MP3 players, carrying newspapers for the
homeward journey. They didn't acknowledge me, each
other, or their surroundings. The poet John Donne once

wrote that no man is an island, but these men and women were doing a good impression of being cut off at high tide.

As I neared the station entrance the neighbourhood took a turn for the worse and I used my glamour to avoid attention. There's something about railway stations that attracts people who ought to be somewhere else. They get trapped in the ebb and flow and remain in its backwaters, floating around the edges and hoping for... what? Perhaps because such places change constantly they feel that they too could change, or perhaps it's just so noisy and distracting that they never have to hear themselves think.

Behind Paddington Station is an old canal basin. I followed the walkway to a bridge to find that since my last visit it had been redeveloped and was now flanked by glass-fronted office buildings and spanned by steel and cable suspension bridges. Narrow boats and barges were docked in the basin, but these were brightly painted, shiny examples compared to the rusting hulks I remembered.

I crossed the murky water and slipped between the coffee shops and office blocks and headed through the back streets and under the Westway. While couriers on motorbikes weaved through the nose-to-tail traffic above me, I slipped underneath and followed the side roads through to Paddington Green. Where the public side of Paddington Station had been converted houses and seedy hotels, this was rows of flats, one after another. The smell of boiled vegetables overlaid with curry aromas drifted down the side roads, accompanied by a soundtrack of screaming children, teatime TV and distant sirens.

The small park was an island of green in the urban landscape, with the church and its graveyard beside it, the sombre, mossy tombs standing like witnesses to the gradual encroachment of tarmac and concrete. The last light had long faded from the sky to be replaced by the city glow reflected from the underside of the scudding clouds. A group of black youths made their way from Westminster College across the way, huddled against the cold, their heavy bags slung across their chests, heads together in conversation. Like everyone else, they ignored me.

I wandered slowly around the park. A lone figure was sitting on the end of one of the benches, his coat wrapped close. I took my time, looking for watchers, wary of traps.

Having satisfied myself that we were not being observed, I took the path through the park. As I approached, I let the glamour fall away so that the person on the bench would notice me. He sat up straighter as I approached.

As I neared the bench, I realised who had left the note. The sandy hair gave it away, though Sam Veldon could easily have been mistaken for a tramp, sat on the bench, wrapped in his overcoat.

Sam worked for one of the Home Office agencies – anti-terror or against organised crime – Claire had said it was something like that. He and Claire had once been an item, but the relationship had foundered on the secrets between them. Sam had been unable to share his work and unwilling to accept that Claire had her own secrets. Now Claire was dead.

I stopped a few yards away. "Sam? It was you who left the note?"

"We're not on first name terms," he said. "You're not my friend." He steadfastly looked ahead, refusing to acknowledge my presence.

"I'm not your enemy either."

"Sit down," he said. "You draw too much attention."

I looked around the darkened park. "This was your choice, Sam. There are warmer, more private and more welcoming places we could talk."

He took out a stainless steel flask from his jacket and flicked off the top, lifting it to his lips, he took a long swig.

I could smell the whisky from where I stood, and it wasn't the first swig he'd taken. I moved forward and sat on the other end of the bench, leaving enough between for someone else to sit – as if there were a presence between us. "I'm told you have something for me." I reminded him.

"That I do," he said. He tucked the flask back into his coat, struggling for a moment to replace it. There was a sound, like a muted pop, through the fabric of his coat. Something hit me, like punch in the side. It came again. I put my hand down and it came away red. "You bastard." My head was swimming as the shock hit me. He'd shot me.

Sam stood up. "The first one's for Claire," he said, "and the second is for me. You're a hazard, Petersen. Like a mad dog, you have to be put down. They said it would make it slow and painful – and I don't want you to die quickly. I want it slow, so you'd get time to think about what you've done. One in the heart and one in the head may be the professional way, but two in the gut is more satisfying for someone who cuts a defenceless woman's throat and leaves her to bleed."

I was clutching my side where the blood oozed between my fingers. What had started like a kick in the side was twisting in my guts like a serrated knife. "I didn't kill her, Sam. I was trying to save her," I coughed.

"Yeah," he said. "It's funny how people you try to help keep dying. Enjoy the rest of your life, Petersen, for the short time you have left." He turned and walked away towards Edgware Road.

"Sam," I called after him weakly. "You've got to help me." I don't know whether he didn't hear me, or whether he didn't care. Either way he just kept walking.

I tried to stand, but the pain in my guts was excruciating. Sweat dripped from my forehead into my eyes. My lips tasted of salt. My head felt light and I swallowed rising bile. I was losing a lot of blood. If I didn't get help soon, I was going to pass out, and the chances of ever come round were slim. I tried to think what the treatment for gunshot wounds was, but the only thing I could remember were movies where everyone died a quick and clean death. I lifted my hands and they were slick with my own blood. Pressing my jacket to the wounds in my side, I tried to stem the flow of blood, but I had no strength and it hurt like hell. My arms were failing me. I was starting to slump – I simply couldn't hold myself up. My chest was heaving as I tried to get more air. I thought fey were supposed to be hard to kill, but when it came to it, dying didn't seem to be that difficult.

The roughness of the bench rested against my cheek. I was lying there with no idea how I'd got there. I must have passed out. The pain was less acute, but it was spreading through my body until the whole of me ached. My eyelids felt heavy. I had to rest, gather my strength, if only for a moment…

The room was large and dark, but airless. The big stone fireplace holding only embers and the occasional lick of flame, warmed the back of the tall man at the table. He had pushed back the platters and cleared a space so that he could read the curled sheets laid out before him, bringing closer the pewter candelabra so that the light from the candles would fall upon the pages. Another man in a blue surcoat came in and began removing the dishes, moving almost silently so as not to disturb the reader. The man at the table neither acknowledged his presence nor helped him clear.

From my position at the other end of the table I could see the three lions embroidered in gold upon his breast. This was the King, although which King I wasn't sure. I found myself wishing I'd paid more attention in history lessons at school. He looked different from the man I'd seen by torchlight – taller, leaner, and his face had a gaunt look, though there was something of a resemblance there. The meal at the table had been simple bread and cheese with a few apples, and the plain wooden chair on which he sat could never be termed a throne. It hardly seemed a feast for a King.

The servant who'd cleared the table returned and coughed. "Sire. They're here."

The King nodded but continued reading. After a few moments the servant returned with six well-dressed men, who had the look of people who had seen places and done things. Their eyes took in the room, the fire, the servant and the man at the table. They didn't immediately come forward, but hung back in a group until the King, without preamble, said, "Sit."

They moved forward as a group and each found a seat at the table. The King continued reading until he had been through them all, and then sighed. He placed the sheets one on another and rested a small silver knife upon the pile. He regarded each man in turn, until the last acknowledged his gaze, a man I thought I recognised.

"Le Brun," said the King.

"My Liege?" he said.

"Montgomerie, Giffard, Mowbray, Fitzrou, and Ferrers." The King named each of them in turn, as if weighing them up. He cleared his throat. "Your families served my father, and my grandfather, and I hope you will serve my son when the time is come. That may not happen, if we cannot deal with our situation. We are beset on all sides," he said. "There is trouble brewing again in Flanders, and the shipyards have yet more delays. There are reports of riot and insurrection in the north, fuelled by outbreaks of disease only made worse by a terrible harvest and widespread hunger. If there were food to sell, no one could afford to buy it. The coffers are empty and our debts rise faster than we can pay them off. Corruption is rife and there are men taking more in bribes than they deliver in taxes. The people are oppressed and they name me as the cause of it."

"No, My Liege," said Montgomerie. "Your people see you as their saviour."

"In the next life, perhaps," he agreed, "but not in this one. I can sit by and see it fall to ruin, or I can act, but in order to act I need men I can trust. Men who will not be bought, cannot be

157

threatened, and would not be swayed. I need to show strength where it counts and mercy where it matters, but I cannot be everywhere. In short I need each of you to aid me, and bear a measure of this burden.

"We are yours to command, Sire," said Fitzrou.

"Aye," agreed the next.

"My thanks, but if that were not true you would not be here. I need more than that. I need men who can be the King's arm, the King's head, and the King's heart. I need men who can be left to act in trust, who will act in my name, without fail, without expectation of reward other than they do God's will. You will need to use your judgement, use men worthy of trust, and use them wisely. I have chosen you because you stood where no one else would. You are brave, I have no doubt. You cannot be coerced into folly, or bought by those with heavy purses and few scruples. You are intelligent and perceptive. I would have all of this and more."

He took the pile of papers and went through them one by one.

"I have nobles whose sworn purpose is to aid me, but they aid no one but themselves. Those who have sworn to see to our defence milk this country's purse and build private armies funded from my coffers. Some play a double game, fraternising with subversives and traitors. Others plot to replace me with someone more to their liking. Some horde stores, hiking prices until they can swell their purses on the backs of the poor, selling them short loaves made with confiscated grain. This must end."

"Where would you have us start, My Liege?" said Le Brun.

"Understand," said the King. "I am not so careless that I can replace those who undermine my efforts without consequence. I am not offering you their seats. Instead we must lay a double game to match theirs. We work behind the scene, eliminating where we must, bolstering where we can, until the walls are shored up and the gates will hold. Fitzrou, you will be my eyes and ears abroad. The best defence is to head off the attack before it starts. You have the connections, use them.

"Yes, My Liege."

"Le Brun, you have the military expertise. Let anyone who

comes to our shores with evil intent regret their folly. Make us strong, and make us ready."

"Aye, My Liege."

"Mowbray, where Fitzrou protects us abroad, I want you to guard home and hearth. Bring peace to this land. Root out dissent where it cannot be turned to our accord, quell the riots, protect the weak and the helpless. Make it a land worthy of a man's pride and a woman's love."

"I will, My Liege."

"Giffard, I need your unquestioned integrity. When matters are brought before my courts I want them tried openly and fairly. Make the King's justice a deterrent against villainy and the bulwark of the honest man, whoever he may be."

"It will be done, My Liege."

"Montgomerie, your service has long been a source of comfort to me, and your head for numbers is ever a boon. I need a tax regime that works, one that is fair, even-handed and straight. I want every man to know what he owes, and all men to pay only what they must. I need to know who is yet owing and who has already paid, lest any man pay twice while another goes untaxed. I need a man to put me in remembrance of all things owing to the King.

"You have him, My Liege."

The King nodded, and turned to De Ferrers at his right hand. He regarded him long and hard, until De Ferrers asked. "What of me, My Liege? What would you have me do?"

"Your task is simply named, and the least simple of all," said the King. "It is the greatest of burdens since it will eat at the heart of you until you trust no one and give no man but a second glance without wondering what else is in his heart."

"Name it, My Liege," said De Ferrers, "for I am yours to command."

"Your task," said the King, "is to keep the secrets of the kingdom."

I found myself lying on my side on the bench. The pain brought me back from the dark place I'd been hiding, the smell of burning candle wax and damp wool still lingering from my dream. From a distance I was like a wino who'd had too much, just another homeless person, kipping down on a bench. Only when you got close could you see the blood. If I called for help, no one would come. I would lie here until my magic claimed me, and then I would fall into dust and scatter under the night sky. Part of me wanted that – anything to make the pain stop. I drifted again, the welcoming dark claiming me.

What brought me back the second time was having my face slapped. "Come on, stupid. Talk to me."

"Blackbird?" I whispered.

"No, you idiot, it's me." Amber's voice coalesced through the haze of pain,

"Warm Amber," I mumbled.

"You're hallucinating," she said. "You have to help yourself."

"If it's warm... why am I... so cold?" I asked her.

"You'll be a lot colder in a minute if you don't help yourself." She shook me by the lapels. "Reach inside, Dogstar. It's there, waiting. Let it out."

"Waiting?" I sighed. "What for?"

"The power is within you. It can sustain you and heal your wounds. You have to let it out."

"Let me be..." It was too hard. Too difficult.

"What's Blackbird going to say if I let you die? Tell me that?" Amber pinched my ear, trying to get my attention. It was nothing against the pain I was retreating from.

"Let me be..."

"Listen. Reach inside. Open yourself to it. It'll help with the pain. Do it."

"It hurts..." I said.

"Do it now."

Within me there was a flicker, a light that lost its spark. Around it, creeping darkness flared, easing into me, winding its way through my veins. "Light's gone out..." I said.

"What light?" she asked. "Show me."

"The one inside…" The light flickered again, responding to my attention. I focused on it, and it became stronger. "That light…" It flared into life within me, opening the dark well of power that formed the core of my being. I opened my eyes to find Amber's face dappled in moonlight, leaning over me.

"Gently," she said. "Slowly."

"Someone will see…" I said.

"It doesn't matter. I'll deal with that. Let your power extend. Open yourself up to the world and let the pain go. Let your power make you whole."

"I don't know how," I said.

"Yes, you do. Your power knows how. Stop trying to hold the pain inside you. Let it spill out. Let the pain out, and the world in."

If I let the pain go it would consume me, or that's what it felt like. I would be burned up, lost in the intensity of it. Maybe that's what she wanted. Maybe that's what I deserved. And yet, as my magic lay like moonlit velvet around us, I could feel it connecting. It was feeding from the earth and the air that surrounded us, bringing me sustenance, holding back the tide. I let it extend a little and I could feel as it crept out across the grass, as it lent tiny pulses of warmth to my failing body.

Distracted for a moment from the pain, I felt the well of power within me dilate and spill out. It ran out away across the grass like invisible tendrils seeking warmth and life. It crept around Amber, but she slapped it back with a warding. Instead, it spread out through the trees, winding through the gaps in the fences, creeping across roads and under cars, into houses, through the cracks in windows, under the gaps in doors.

All around me there was life. The dense urban landscape was teaming with it, each buzzing with energy, radiating warmth. The threads of power tapped into that energy like roots absorbing ground water. Each tendril took a little of what it could find, pulling back a little of the whole. It travelled back along the threads, building until it was a stream of life, a flood of energy and power.

I felt the pain diminish as the power sang within me. I felt the cold dark power withdraw back into the well inside me as warmth crept back into my veins. My cold, pallid skin warmed and then flushed as it flooded my senses. Inside me, the twisted agony unravelled to be replaced by a tenderness that spoke of healing. The release of not needing to hold back the pain was like a weight taken from me, and I could finally let it go.

I opened my eyes to find Amber looking down at me. "Not too much at once," she said. "Slowly. I think the bleeding is slowing."

"I feel like I've been desiccated," I told her in a hoarse whisper, "my throat is so dry,"

She looked around. "If I leave you here for five minutes are you going to die on me?"

I looked around from my limited position lying on the bench. "I don't see what damage I can do, except perhaps bludgeon myself to death on the bench."

"I'll be back," she said. She walked away into the dark and quickly vanished into the shadows. I closed my eyes for a second – I'm sure it was only a second.

"He's not dead, he's snoring," said a voice. I opened my eyes to find a pale face under a baseball cap looking down at me. "And he's got his eyes open."

I blinked. The voice sounded black and street, but the skin was very definitely pale.

"Look at this, bro?" said another voice. The face over me moved back revealing another in the same style – except this one was brandishing my sword. In my injured state I'd forgotten about it, and my glamour must have slipped enough for it to become visible and obvious.

"I'd leave that alone if I were you," I croaked, but I was in no state to enforce the threat. They both ignored me.

"That's wicked," said the second guy. He sliced at the air experimentally, making his friend step back. To my trained eye, he was more likely to injure himself than anyone else, but the problem of getting it back remained.

"Just give it to me, OK?" I asked, hoarsely.

"Or what?" he said, posturing with the sword.

Amber spoke from behind him. "Or we find out how far you can run without a head." He spun round to find her standing behind him, holding her own blade alongside her leg. As he turned, she stepped in and her blade flashed. She stepped back, with her blade resting by her leg again.

"Missed," he said, grinning broadly at her. Then his trousers began to slowly droop as his belt fell into two pieces and gave way.

"Unless you can use that, you'd better put it down. Slowly and gently," she warned.

He was caught between holding the blade and holding his trousers up. He glanced to his friend.

"You'll never make it," she warned." I'll cut your hamstrings so you can't run and then I'll slice you into little pieces," she said.

"Believe her," I rasped.

He glanced back at me.

"Last warning," she said. "Sword. Ground. Now."

He exchanged glances with this friend and for a moment I thought they were going for it, but he gently lowered the blade to the ground.

"You're wiser than you look." said Amber.

"You're fuckin' crazy carrying stuff like that around. The plod'll have you banged up, well tight."

"We don't bother the police, and they don't bother us. Walk on. Don't come back." He backed away and joined his friend and they both jogged away.

"Fuckin' crazies!" he shouted back when they were far enough away to think they were safe.

Amber stared after them, then collected my sword.

"They're just kids," I said.

"Time was," said Amber, "they'd have more knowledge, and more fear. Here." She passed me a plastic

163

bottle. "It's some kind of sports drink. I found it in the vending machine in the college. The sugar will get you on your feet and you need the liquid."

I sat up slowly and struggled with the top of the bottle. I felt weak as a kitten. She pulled it from me, twisted off the top and handed it back, sitting down beside me with my scabbarded sword resting on her lap.

"You lost a lot of blood. If I hadn't followed you, you'd be dead."

I licked my chapped lips. "You were following me?"

"Someone has to look after you," she said.

"Garvin," I said, tracing my way back through her words.

"He asked me to keep track of you," she said. "Looks like he made the right decision. No, don't sit up. You're going to be light-headed for a bit.

"How did you find me?"

"I saw you leave the courts with one of the drivers, figured that you were going back for the horseshoes. I waited at Claire's flat, saw you enter and then leave."

"Someone cleaned up the mess before I got there," I told her.

"After you left I walked it through. A professional job – very thorough. I thought you would head back to the courts, so I headed back after you, except you didn't arrive."

I took a long drink and sifted through her words.

"That doesn't explain how you found me. I could have gone back with Dave in the car. I would have been on the motorway by now."

"That would have been slow," she remarked. "Why take the long route when you can use the Ways."

"Why are you avoiding my question?" I asked her.

"It's a secret," she said. "If I tell you, I have to kill you."

Was she teasing me? "You've tagged me," I said. "There's something…" A realisation dawned. What did Garvin always tell me to take with me? "My sword.

That's how you found it after I lost it on the Tor. That's how you found me now."

"All the Warders weapons are warded for finding," said Amber. "You never know when you might lose one and need to get it back. If you'd left it behind you'd have been dead. Who shot you?"

"Sam Veldon. He told me he had something for me. He didn't say it was a bullet."

"You'll have to track him down. Give him something in return," she said, with a wry smile.

"The edge of a blade?" I tried to laugh but it emerged as a dry cough. "No, someone put him up to it. Someone guided him to me. I need to know who it was."

"OK. You get what you need from him and then you kill him."

"He thinks I killed Claire. He's just an angry man who lashes out at the nearest target."

"If you don't want to do it, I'll do it for you," she volunteered.

"It's not a matter of... do we have to kill everyone?" I asked.

"It's a challenge. If you don't deal with it, it will only come back and bite you." She was sat on the bench beside me, relaxed and calm, talking about murdering someone.

"He's not fey," I told her. "He's not challenging me. He doesn't even know me. He's just angry because he messed up his relationship with Claire and now she's lying in a morgue somewhere with her throat cut. The only thing he can do to assuage his loss is to lash out. I was nearest, that's all."

"He'll try again, mark my words."

"Then I'll kill him when he does, if it'll make you happy." I said. "Aren't you going to give me a hard time about letting those yobs take my sword?" I asked between swigs. "Garvin would."

"No. I'd give you a hard time about getting shot. But it's too late for that as well."

165

I drank some more. It was sweet, fizzy and tasted like cough mixture, but at that moment it was like nectar. "I'm pretty useless at this, aren't I?" I admitted, shaking my head. "I guess I just don't have the killer instinct.

"There are two kinds of Warders, Niall, dead and alive. We were all useless to start with. We all made mistakes, and we have the scars to prove it. Those that didn't make the grade aren't here to boast about it."

"What about Garvin?"

"Not all scars are on the outside. Fellstamp made a bad decision. He's paying for it now."

That silenced me. I'd fought Fellstamp in my initiation into the Warders, and he'd lost when I'd pierced his shoulders with a long sword. We both knew that I'd won because he was wielding the wrong weapon. If he'd had something lighter he'd have slaughtered me. I gulped some more of the fizzy drink and burped noisily.

"Charmed," said Amber.

"So you would have gone in heavy?" I asked her. "With Sam, I mean?"

"I've already given you that advice and you made excuses for him. Either kill or be killed, that's the rule."

"You have a black and white view of the world, you know?"

"I'm not the one sitting in a pool of his own blood," she pointed out.

I looked down at the congealed stain on the bench. She had a valid point. Maybe the rain that was starting to spot the pathway around us would wash it away. "Drink up," she encouraged. "You need the liquid, and those friends of yours will be back shortly. Paddington Green Police Station is just beyond and they're just the type to break a habit of a lifetime and enter a police station willingly to report us."

"The police won't believe them," I said. "They're more likely to be carrying themselves."

"Nevertheless," said Amber. "I'll escort you back. You need to rest. You can hunt Sam down tomorrow." She stood, and I pushed myself up to my feet. "Can you walk?" she asked.

"I'll manage," I said.

"We'll take the easy route," she said, looking me up and down. "You know what your problem is, Niall?"

"Which one?" I asked. It seemed like I had so many problems.

"You don't accept being fey."

"I thought I was doing quite well," I said. "I've coped with most things so far."

"That's not what I mean," she said. "You call your power when you need it. You summon it when you have a purpose, but most of the time you bury it within you. You hide it, because you're afraid it makes you less than you are."

"And you don't?"

"My power is always with me. It lives and breathes within me and is as much a living part of me as my fingers, or my heart. It's there when I eat, and when I sleep. It's in every breath."

"I'm not sure I'm ready to be like that," I said.

"When you are, and someone tries to shoot you, you'll be able to finish them before they finish you," she said. "Until then, you need someone to watch your back."

She led the way across the grass, waiting when I lagged behind.

TEN

Alex crept along the passage to her room wrapped in glamour designed to turn away curious eyes, checking behind her in case anyone had seen her come in. She went to her door and slipped through, checking the corridor once more before gently closing the door and letting the glamour fall away.

"You're back late."

"Jeez!" Alex spun around to find Blackbird sitting on her bed, her hands folded in her lap. "What are you trying to do, give me a heart attack?" She laid her hand on her heart. She could actually feel it beating. "What are you doing in my room?"

"Waiting for you."

"I was out," said Alex.

"I can see that," said Blackbird, taking in the stains on the knees of Alex's jeans, the mud on her trainers, and the dirt smeared into her sweatshirt. "Your father thinks you were looking after the baby."

"Oh yeah," said Alex, brushing with her hand at the marks on her sweatshirt. "Sorry about that." As Blackbird examined her, the stains began to fade subtly. Her hair became less tangled, her hands cleaner.

Blackbird continued as if she hadn't spoken. "I must

confess that's what I thought too, until I got back and found that the baby's been with Lesley all evening."

"I kinda got side-tracked," said Alex. "I bumped into Sparky and he suggested we go out, and one thing led to another."

"Did it indeed?" Blackbird looked again at the knees of Alex's jeans, which were hardly stained at all by now. "It led to another, did it?"

"What d'you mean?"

"Alex, you are old enough to become a mother in your own right."

"A mother! You're joking, aren't you?"

"When one thing leads, as you say, to another, there can be unforeseen consequences."

"You think I've been having sex?" Alex laughed. "With Sparky? I can't believe you're saying that."

"I'm not accusing you of anything," said Blackbird. "I'm simply making you aware of things that may have escaped your notice."

"I think I know about the birds and the bees," said Alex. "Mum and me had that conversation years ago."

"Did she mention that being a mother has responsibilities?" asked Blackbird.

"I guess that kinda goes unsaid."

"Responsibilities that include being where you said you'll be, doing what you said you would do, and not leaving other people to pick up the pieces for you when you decide to go off and do something else."

"I said I was sorry," said Alex.

"Saying you're sorry isn't the same as being sorry," said Blackbird. "And it's not me you need to apologise to. You may want to find a moment to apologise to Lesley. She ended up looking after the baby in your absence."

"I don't know why I have to look after him anyway," said Alex.

"I'm not your mother, Alex, and I'm not telling you

what to do. However, if you say you will do something, I expect you to do it, or at least try."

"He's your baby," Alex said, resentfully.

"He's your brother," Blackbird reminded her.

"Half-brother," said Alex.

Blackbird stared at her for a moment. "I'm not your wicked stepmother, so I'd prefer that you didn't paint me as one."

"That's OK," said Alex. "Because I'm not Snow White."

Blackbird glanced at Alex's knees again, which showed no signs of the stains that had been evident earlier. "No," she said, "you're not." Alex blushed.

Blackbird stood, and as she did, Alex moved quickly away from the door to the window overlooking the courtyard, leaving a clear exit and staying well out of reach of Blackbird, who smiled slowly. "Since your return to us, your father has asked for you to be given space to come to terms with what happened to you. I think you've had space enough, Alex, and it's time you thought about how you might give something in return."

"I'm not your babysitter," said Alex.

"I never said you were," said Blackbird, "and there are other ways that you could show some gratitude for what you have and some respect for those who provide it, though I can appreciate that a young person might not want to be burdened with a baby," she said. "It would cramp your style somewhat, I think."

"What does that mean?" asked Alex.

"Only what it says," said Blackbird. "Is it your intention to join the Eighth Court, Alex?"

She shrugged. "Not got much choice, have I?"

"There's always a choice, my dear," said Blackbird, "and consequences either way, but if you are to join the Eighth Court then you will have to pledge allegiance, in blood, on oath. That oath will be binding, and if you swear falsely it will trip on your tongue."

"Then maybe I won't swear," she said.

"That's your choice," said Blackbird, "but you will not receive the protection of the court without swearing allegiance."

"Don't need protection, do I? I can look after myself."

"That's easy to say from a room at the centre of the courts, protected by Warders, surrounded by people you trust. But you've been outside, Alex, and I don't think your memory is so poor that you've forgotten what it means to be alone."

"Yeah, well. I survived."

"That's one of the choices," said Blackbird. "Most of us can survive. We find a way because we have to, but if you want more than mere survival then you need help. That's what we're doing, Alex, we're helping each other to build something better. Think about it."

Blackbird went to the door and then hesitated. "If I were you," she said, "I would get myself cleaned up, in bed and at least pretend to be asleep before your father comes back and starts asking the sorts of questions you don't want to answer."

"You're going to tell him?" Alex didn't want to ask, but she had to know.

"That we talked? No, I don't think your father needs to be aware of every conversation we have."

"I meant about coming back late, about not looking after the baby."

"I won't mention it. Alex, but that doesn't mean he won't find out. Sleep well."

The door closed behind Blackbird and Alex was left alone, but even so she counted to a hundred before she finally let the glamour go. She was going to have to find somewhere to stash her ruined clothes until she could get them washed. She stripped and dropped all of them behind the chest of drawers, pushing the soiled trainers under the chest with the edge of her foot so they'd be out of sight. The shower she took was hot and long, and after it she felt as if her limbs had turned to jelly. She turned off the light, cracked the door open so that light from the hallway striped up across the carpet and up the wall and slid into bed.

She was exhausted but somehow too gunned to sleep. She felt wired, as if she'd drunk one of Sparky's boosters and was now so full of caffeine and stimulants that sleep was impossible. Her mind kept turning to the wild ride through the forest, the brutally violent encounter they'd observed, and the promises she'd made to Tate.

But when she slept, her dreams were full of trees flashing past in the dark.

Amber near enough dragged me through the Ways without pause for thought. I was already dreadfully tired and instead of the usual elation, I felt drained and slightly sick. I wondered what happened if you threw up on the Ways. Did it spew vomit out over you when you were finally ejected? That thought held my stomach together until we were back at the courts.

She supported me as far as the door to the rooms that Blackbird and I shared. I leaned against the wall, hatching an ambitious plan to sneak in, grab a shower and change out of my blood-soaked clothes before Blackbird discovered I'd been shot. That plan was rather undermined when I discovered Blackbird and the baby with Angela and Lesley in our rooms.

"You can do the explaining," said Amber, as she helped me inside.

Blackbird almost did a double take. "What on earth happened?" she asked, passing the baby to Lesley and taking in the dark stains spread into my shirt and trousers, almost black against the Warder grey.

"It's not as bad as it looks," I said, the words tripped on my tongue as I tried to play down the situation.

Blackbird pulled open my jacket for a better look. "This is blood! For goodness sakes, Niall, you're covered in it. What happened?"

Now that I was safe, my reserves were suddenly spent. I put an arm out to the door to steady myself and missed my handhold, dropping my sword and stumbling so that Amber half caught me. Instead I slid slowly to the floor, half supported by her. My eyes felt suddenly heavy. "It's OK," I said. "Amber was there."

"You're wounded," said Blackbird. "Angela, get me a towel soaked in cold water. Amber, help me get him out of this jacket." Between them they eased me out of the jacket, and Blackbird inspected the holes where the bullets had entered.

"Amber helped me..." I mumbled.

Blackbird collected some scissors from the desk, addressing Amber. "I suppose you have some explanation for this?" she asked her.

"It's not my doing," she told Blackbird. "This is all his own work."

I roused myself in Amber's defence. "If it hadn't been for Amber, I wouldn't be here."

"What happened to looking out for each other," asked Blackbird, cutting me out of the shirt. "Dump those on the bath, Angela. They're ruined anyway. I need to clean some of this blood off."

"We are looking out for each other," said Amber. "He's here isn't he?"

"This isn't Amber's fault," I said. My words sounded slurred, even to me. "I underestimated Sam. He picked his moment."

"Can you stand?" she asked me, "Walk as far as the bathroom?"

I nodded, though I was far from sure.

Between Blackbird and Amber they manoeuvred me into the bathroom. I had a moment of modesty, but Blackbird overruled me, stripping out of my blood-soaked trousers.

"She's seen it all before," she claimed, but Amber made her excuses and retired gracefully and left Blackbird to

clean me up. She inspected the newly pink skin over the
wounds in my side where Sam had shot me, probing
them gently with her fingers. Taking a wet flannel, she
cleaned off the dried blood while I told her about the
missing horseshoes, the flat, the message left on the fridge
and the rendezvous with Sam.

"I guess Sam knew one side of the story," I said, recovered a little now I was sat down. "I was going to try
and explain the rest."

"It sounds like he's already had an explanation,
reached a conclusion and acted upon it," she said. "Hold
onto the edge of the edge of the sink."

"What for?"

"Just do as you're asked for once."

I did as I was bid and she placed her hands over my
heart and the wound in my side. The air in the bathroom
chilled, the lights dimming as a gentle warmth spread
out under her palms.

"Should you be doing that?" I asked. "You'll upset
Garvin again."

Blackbird explained what Garvin could do with his ob-
jections while the heat in my side intensified. It became
almost painful, and I gripped the side of the sink hard. I
could feel her warmth spreading through me, knitting
together the damage that had been done.

"There," she said, "that will help, but you're going to
be taking it gently for a few days. We're going to have to
rethink a few things. If Amber has been shadowing you
then Garvin probably knows more than we anticipated.
That has implications for whoever he's sharing that information with.

"Amber knows about the horseshoes, but I think that's
as far as it goes," I said.

"Unless she's been spying on us all along," suggested
Blackbird. She helped me sit and then returned to the
bedroom. I could hear her thanking Lesley and ushering
Angela out, telling them that I needed rest and that she

would deal with matters in the morning. When she came back in, she was holding our son, who reached out his hands to me. "He wants you," she said.

I took him from her gingerly, conscious of the tenderness in my newly healed flank. As I took him from her it sent shooting pains down my side, but it was bearable. Whatever Blackbird had done had definitely helped. He was only in a nappy and vest and as I took him he laid his head on my shoulder. It seemed to me that he'd picked up some of his mother's anxiety and wanted to see for himself that I was OK. I held him while Blackbird tossed the rest of my ruined clothes into the bath and soaked the flannels she used to clean me up in a sink of cold water. She shook her head as she watched the water change colour.

"This life…" she said, addressing my reflection in the mirror. "It's not what he needs. He needs stability and love, room to grow."

"We're getting there," I said.

"He needs a father that comes home, preferably not soaked in his own blood," she said, looking down into the spreading cloud of pink water in the sink.

"I'll be more careful in future," I said.

"While you work for Garvin, there will always be risks," she said.

"Everything is a risk. Crossing the road is a risk, taking a taxi is a risk. I could be struck by lightning." She frowned. "OK, that was a bad example."

"Taking a taxi doesn't get you shot, though," she pointed out, not unreasonably. "And while crossing the road may be hazardous, the drivers aren't usually actively trying to kill you."

"Amber says I'm doing better than some," I said. "I can only do what I can do."

"Pity Sam didn't try and shoot Amber instead," she said. "Amber would have killed him."

"He's not himself. He's still torn up about whatever

175

was between him and Claire, and now there's no chance of a getting back together." I said. "He blames me for Claire's death, and there's little I can say to convince him that I didn't kill her."

"And so you let him shoot you. That seems very even-handed, I must say."

"You're not usually so keen on me killing people," I pointed out. My son started shifting and grizzling against my chest. "Now he's upset because you're upset," I said. "He's picking up on your emotions."

"And I'm upset because you could be dead." She lifted him from me and cradled our son against her chest until he subsided into a low grizzle. "He's just tired. I wanted to spend some time with him today, but it feels like it's just slipped by without pause for breath." She rocked him against her, shushing him slowly.

"He's not the only one," I said.

"You're cross with yourself for letting Raffmir get the better of you," she said. "You feel guilty at letting him kill Claire under your nose when you were supposed to be protecting her, but you're forgetting that there were likely two of them and they had the advantage of surprise."

"I'm a Warder, Blackbird. They're not supposed to be able to surprise me."

"Your problem is that you're a good man," she said. "You don't think like they do."

"Then perhaps I should learn to," I said.

"No. It's better that you don't think like them," she said. Our son nuzzled into her breast. "You can't really be hungry," she told him, "It's just comfort you want, isn't it?" She kissed his head and held him close, resting her head next to his and stroking his hair.

I shrugged, making my side twinge again. "I'm not sure any more. This is getting out of hand. People are dying because of us – because of what we're doing."

"And if we do nothing?" she asked. "How will that be better? Should we stand by as the courts select who will live and who will die from the few gifted humans that come forward?

"I don't know," I said. "Why can't they just let them be?"

"Like they let Eve be? Or should we wait until the next angry teenager gets hold of something they shouldn't " she said. "It's got beyond that, Niall, and we both know it."

"Then what?" I asked.

"A sanctuary," she said. "We need somewhere that the gifted can be, away from humanity and away from the Feyre. We need to find our own way," she looked down at our son, "and come to terms with what we are. When we have the Eighth Court, Niall, I want you to think about retiring."

"What?"

"I want you to think about resigning from your post as a Warder. I think Garvin would let you go, and if you have a court of your own then you don't need to be a Warder to receive the protection of the courts."

"You forget, at the moment, as far as the Eighth Court is concerned, I am the protection of the courts."

"Garvin places you in harm's way. One mistake and... I don't want to think about it, Niall. We've come so far together. I can do this alone if I have to, but I don't want to."

I stood, making it as confident a move as I could, and wrapped my arms around her and my son, kissing him, and her. "You won't have to," I said.

She rested her head against me. "I wish I was as confident."

After a moment, she stirred. "Let's put this one to bed. You need to rest or you'll be good for nothing tomorrow. Your body needs rest or you won't heal."

"I feel better than I did," I said.

She gave me a look that implied that wasn't saying much. Taking our son through to the adjoining room, she settled him down while I crawled into bed. I felt wrung out and literally drained. I wondered whether I should drink some more water before I slept, but I was too exhausted to get up and get some. I lay in bed until she turned out the light and crawled in beside me, nestling into the crook of my arm.

I heard her breathing slow, but now that I had the chance to rest, my body resisted. I shifted under her until she turned onto her side away from me. In moments I was too warm and pushed the covers down to get cooler, but seconds later I was shivering. I found myself hunkering down, trying to get warm. I was shaking and my mouth felt dry. My tongue stuck to the roof of my mouth and my throat felt sore. Thinking I would wake Blackbird and ask her to get me some water, I tried to turn over, but the bed was huge and empty. I called for her. My hand twitched with the effort of reaching for her, but wouldn't move. My entire body felt like it was being slowly pressed into the bed, layered in lead, leached of life.

"Why didn't you call me earlier?" It was Garvin's voice and he sounded close. I couldn't see anyone.

"He wasn't like this earlier, ask Amber," said Blackbird. He was injured, yes, and tired, but nothing like this. It must have started after he came to bed. It can't be infection, and he's not being drawn away by someone else. He keeps mumbling things but I can't make them out. Did Amber say anything?"

"Nothing conclusive. She said he'd been shot, and that once she showed him what to do, he healed himself. The injury was purely physical. This is not Sam Veldon's doing – there's something else at work."

"The Seventh Court?" Blackbird asked.

"Not within the wardings of the High Court. They would bring reprisals back on themselves and they know it. No, this isn't magic. Poison?" he suggested.

"It's possible, but his glamour should protect him. One moment he's burning up, the next he's deathly cold. I'm at a loss, Garvin. His wounds were healing, but this…?"

Her voice faded and the dark became a comforting blackness holding me suspended. I drifted between consciousness and oblivion.

After a while I felt something tug at my attention and I found myself being drawn upwards. It was a house – I recognised the style of the study as being from the same sort of era as the High Courts. Was it Georgian, or before that? I wasn't sure. Two men were there, one standing and one kneeling on the floor before him. You could immediately see why, as the standing man had a pistol aimed at the kneeling man's head. The kneeling man was begging for his life. The big desk had been overturned, and the chairs were strewn about as if there'd been a fight.

"Please, Your Lordship, you're not well. We can call a doctor. They'll give you something to calm your nerves."

"You're one of them, aren't you? Admit it!"

"One of whom, Your Lordship? I don't know what you're talking about." The man on the ground was older, dressed in plain clothes with mud on his boots.

"You've been telling them everything!" the standing man accused. The hand with the revolver was trembling.

"I don't know what you mean, Your Lordship. I've served you faithfully, I swear." His voice trembled as he stared up at the pistol pointing down at him.

"Then lie to me properly, dammit. Prove you're not one of them." There was sweat, beaded on his forehead.

"I... don't know what to say. I'm not lying, I'm telling the truth. What do you want me to say?"

"Tell me who you really are," said the standing man.

"I'm Johnson. I collect the rents for you. You know who I am." He reached up suddenly towards the gun and there was a sharp crack. His head snapped backwards, and he toppled sideways onto the ground. The standing man watched him for some time while a coil of smoke rose from the gun to hang in the air before him. "Disappear, dammit!" he shouted at the body. "Vanish! Go wherever you go!" The body remained resolutely present.

After a few moments, the man staggered to a chair and fell heavily into it. He stared at the gun. "My God," he whispered. "What have I done?"

He held the pistol and turned it slowly until it pointed at himself. Opening his mouth, he inserted the muzzle, closing his eyes. His hand was trembling and sweat ran down his face, dripping from his nose. After a while he withdrew the gun and placed it on the floor beside him.

"Oh God, Johnson," he said. "They'll hang me for this."

He sat staring at the body for a long while. It was only then that I noticed the crest on the notepaper scattered across the floor.

On it was a shield, and on the shield were six horseshoes, and underneath them were the words, De Ferrers.

Blackbird's voice was full of concern. "It's getting worse. I've tried bathing him, but these snap fevers are extreme. He was raving about being shot a moment ago. I've sent Alex for some ice and plain towels. If we can wrap him in them, maybe we can hold his temperature down."

"Should I ask Yonna or Kimlesh to come?" asked Garvin. "As a Warder he's entitled to the protection of the Lords and Ladies."

"Will it do any good?" asked Blackbird.

Garvin sighed. "I've no idea. I'd know more if I knew what was wrong."

"Do the wardings for the courts prevent dowsing?" she asked.

"It depends what you're dowsing for," said Garvin. "If you're using it to pry into court business, then yes."

"But not otherwise? It's worth a try," she said. "Get Alex to bring me a pendulum – a rock on a string would do."

"Here, use this," said Garvin.

"What is it?" she asked.

"A keepsake. It has sentimental value."

"It's not been charmed in any way? There's no enhancement?"

"It's just a rock on a chain, Blackbird."

180

"Very well," she said. "It will serve well enough and perhaps it will tell us what we need to know..."

Her voice faded again and I felt myself being pressed down again, consumed by the enveloping darkness. I was wrapped in black velvet, numb to sense or sound, empty of all sensation. I could feel my hold on reality weakening. Something was loosening my grip on life.

I began to hear the slow heartbeat of some great leviathan. Slowly I became aware of a great sea, stretching out to the horizon. The waves lifted, curled high and then crashed, crump, like the beat of a great drum. Then a sigh, as the black water slid over the beach and ebbed back into the deep. Slowly another wave lifted and curled, crump, it came again, and then sigh as it withdrew.

"You shouldn't be here," said a voice I knew well. I turned in the darkness to find a figure outlined in fingers of white light in a nimbus glow, standing a little apart on the black sand of the beach. Now that I looked, there were tiny sparks of light in the black sand, like stars.

"Raffmir. I might have known you'd be behind all this."

"Once again, cousin, you do me disservice. This is none of my doing. Do you even know where you are?"

"Is this like the Glade, but with a beach?"

He laughed, but it had little humour in it. "No one bathes here, Niall. We are on the shores of night, where people come before they die. You have been here before, I think."

"Me? No... I think I'd remember."

"You'd be surprised what you don't remember," he said. "When you had your heart attack on the underground, you would have met my sister here. She would have caught you like a fly in a web as you crossed between life and death. She stranded you here and followed the trail back to your body, hoping to inhabit it, until the witch-woman called you back."

"Don't call her that."

"Shall I not call the prick in my thumb a thorn? If the name sticks, then it must stand."

181

"I don't remember coming here…" I said, looking round. The beach stretched away endlessly in either direction. Further up the beach there was only more sand.

"Few people do. Even fewer come here more than once."

"Why are you here?" I asked him.

"Your gratitude knows no bounds, does it Niall? I stand with you on the shores of night and you ask me why I'm here. For you, cousin. I came for you."

"Why would you come for me? You want me dead."

"That may be true, but I have also sworn to protect you, have I not? Or at least not to allow you to come to harm."

"By your hand. Then you do have something to do with this?"

"You accuse me when you should thank me. You show me no respect, even when I intervene to save your sorry life. No, Niall, I came for you because I have not finished with you yet. You have a role to play and there are things that must yet come to pass. The solstice approaches, the place is appointed, and the time is soon. When you die, it will be at my hand, so I have sworn."

"But you swore not to harm me," I reminded him.

"And therein lies the paradox that we must resolve. Come, Niall. Leave this place. It is not yet your time."

"I must warn Blackbird. The solstice…" I said, as the beach faded and the waves returned to a distant drumbeat.

"You will not remember," said Raffmir's voice, close by.

"I must," I said.

"No more than you did the last time," he said.

ELEVEN

"You'll cut him open?" came Garvin's question.

"You're not serious?" asked Alex.

"The taint must be removed, or it'll kill him. Do you want to do it? Or you, Garvin?" asked Blackbird.

"I'm no surgeon. I wasn't aware you were either," said Garvin.

"There are a lot of things about me you don't know," she said. "Would you rather try and get him to a hospital, assuming there's time for that?"

"And tell them what?" asked Garvin. "He was shot hours ago but the wounds look like they've been healing for weeks? That something inside him is disrupting his ability to heal?"

"Quite," said Blackbird. "He can't get infection, so we're safe on that score. Once the taint is removed he'll be able to heal himself. I just have to make sure I don't pierce anything vital."

"Assuming you can find it. I hope your hand is steadier than it looks."

"Get him down to the kitchen. Alex, bring me as many towels as you can find. Clean ones, preferably. Do you think you can find me something suitably sharp, Garvin? And a needle and thread. It's a while since I've done any needlework, but there's no time now to polish my stitching and I'll need something to pull the wound together."

"I hope you know what you're doing," said Garvin.

"If you have a better plan, Garvin, speak now."

Her voice faded as I slipped back into the dark, but the heat in my blood would not let me rest. It brought me back to the surface where I saw vague shapes and moving patches of colour behind my eyes. The coppery tang of the scent of fresh blood filled my nostrils, underlined by the darker tones of the butcher's shop.

"Hold it steady, Alex. I can't do this if you keep waving it about."

"I'm going to be sick," said Alex.

"Show some spine, girl. Pinch your ear lobe. Make it bleed if you have to, but don't you dare let go. Garvin, pass me that plate."

"Is that the other one?"

There was a thin chink as something dropped onto a china plate. "Two bullets, both forged with iron tips. These were weapons made for a purpose which implies a level of knowledge and intent."

"That leaves me with a simple question," said Garvin.

"A question for which we all have an interest in the answer, Garvin. Hand me the needle."

"Can I throw up now?" said Alex.

"If you do, you will lose the opportunity to tell your father that you helped save his life," said Blackbird. "Now grit your teeth and hold this together."

The voices faded into the gathering darkness once more. This time it consumed me and dragged me down, and as I fell into it, it fell into me. I was held inert in an endless, starless night, and I felt nothing. No light, no warmth, no fear. I could have been buried deep underground, drowned in the deepest well. I felt no pain, and had no hope. Only then, did the voices carry to me, calling me back.

• • • •

The great stone hall must once have been white, but the soot from the candles and the smoke from the fire shaded it into grey. The rays of the afternoon sun cut from the tall windows across the edge of the room, laying stripes of light and dark across the room. Despite the warm day, the fire was banked and crackled with the heat. It shed light upon the throne and the man seated there. Where once he had been lean and strong, now he was wrinkled and despite the grand proportions of the seat, he amply filled it, his belly spilling over his belt. Still, I recognised him well enough. The stubbled jowls and sunken eyes were not enough to disguise that keen stare.

They were arguing: two men standing before him, trying to persuade or perhaps dissuade him from some course. He listened carefully, contributing little, allowing them their say, but at the end he cut them off. The language was beyond me, but his meaning was clear. A decision had been made.

From outside the room, a clamour arose. The door swung open and in walked two people I recognised. Kimlesh, standing tall in a blue flowing gown, was accompanied by Yonna, looking unearthly with her slanted eyes and sharpened features. From behind them came the clash of arms, and then silence. They paused, while the two men before the throne, finding themselves unarmed, took up the fire irons from before the blaze and prepared to defend their lord. They stood before him, regarding the newcomers with suspicion and alarm. Mellion strode in through the doors and closed them quietly after.

From the throne came a curt order, which the men immediately challenged. The big man pushed to his feet, stepped down from the dais and, with a quiet word to each man, took the fire irons from them and put them back beside the fire. They protested and argued, but he silenced them with a look, then ordered them out of the room. Again they protested, but he spoke quietly, warning them and them making promises to assuage their concerns. After a moment, they edged their way around the room and left through a door to the side, leaving the big man with the three visitors.

He asked them a question.

Kimlesh spoke. "King of England, Guillaume, and still you address us in the tongue of Normandy. I have aged every day that you have, though I wear my years the better."

Guillaume spoke again, and it was a harsh and twisted version of the English I knew, but I understood him well enough. "I'll use whichever suits me best," he said. "I know you, and I know that creature you brought with you, but you are a stranger, Lady," he nodded towards Yonna.

"You know me well enough, Guillaume. How is Maude?"

"She's well enough, and far away, as perhaps you know."

Yonna smiled, and the row of teeth she showed were sharp and pointed, putting any sense of humanity further away. Then she shifted, and in a moment the young lass in the shift stood where she had stood. She said something soft in the language of Guillaume's home country and even under the stubble I saw Guillaume blush.

"What witchery is this?" he challenged.

"Be careful of that word," said Kimlesh. "We are guests at your court, but a wrong word will bring your hard won gains down around your ears. We have come to claim our boon. Yonna for bringing you your bride. Were you not wed? You have children, do you not?"

William said something in his own tongue.

"I came to her as I came to you," said Yonna, "and wooed her where you would not. Your marriage was made, and your alliance with Flanders was sealed with my help. Without me you would never have found each other."

Guillaume said something else, and Yonna answered him. "No one denies your love for her, Guillaume, but without my art it would not have happened."

"Nor would your victory over Harald," said Kimlesh. "A single arrow, at just the right moment? It was a shot to make a bowman weep, and it was no accident." She nodded towards Lord Mellion who hung back. The tall figure acknowledged the complement with the slightest of bows.

"And none of that would have come to pass if you'd been caught in the rain and tossed in the river by your pursuers. You promised me a boon that night, Guillaume. You said I could name it. Three is the trick of it, and we will have our due."

"I made no deal of bows and arrows, or wives to woo," said Guillaume, walking up and down in front of the fire.

"And yet here you are," said Yonna. "Now they will call you William the Conqueror instead of William the Bastard, but we can change it back if you would have it otherwise."

Guillaume paced back and forth before them, his step agitated, muttering to himself. Periodically he would look up at them as if he couldn't quite believe they were there. After a while he halted.

"What do you want?" he asked.

"A small thing," said Kimlesh. "We could take what we need but that would eventually lead to conflict. Three things, given freely, to be quit of your debt to us. Three things."

"Name them,"

"The first is the small matter of a ceremony. A ritual which must be performed."

"I'll have no truck with magics," said Guillaume.

"It is ritual, not magic, and as much to protect you as to benefit us. Otherwise your problems will multiply and you will have far worse than our meagre needs to contend with. If you would rather not sully your hands, it would be better handled by those you trust, perhaps?" She glanced towards the door through which the two men had passed.

"What else?" he asked.

"A treaty, if you will. An agreement between our peoples to coexist, without conflict, if not in harmony. We would sue for peace," said Kimlesh.

"That much I can do. And what is the third thing?"

"A portion of what you have gained with our help and aid, Guillaume."

"The kingdom is not as wealthy as some would have you believe," said Guillaume.

The sun faded from the windows and the firelight dimmed as light faded from the room. I held on to hear the last of the bargain being negotiated between the High Court of the Feyre

and the Conqueror. As I slipped down into darkness once more,
I heard Kimlesh's voice confirm the last of their requests.

"It's not money we want," said Kimlesh. "Let me explain…"

Slowly, sounds returned and I became aware of my surroundings. I smelled clean sheets and clean air. The odour of blood and gore had been replaced by clean linen scented with lavender and although I felt as weak as water, the darkness had retreated. I forced my eyes open, though it was an effort requiring force of will, and lay blinking at the pale candlelight from across the room. I turned away to find myself regarded by green eyes. I was rewarded by a slow smile.

"Hello," said Blackbird, quietly.

I tried to say hello back, and found my throat dry and sore. It felt like I'd spent the day shouting at the sea. She sat up beside me and helped me sip some water from a cup. Across the room, Alex was curled into a chair, fast asleep.

When I'd taken some water, I could speak again. "Did I miss something?"

"You could say that," said Blackbird. "You were shot. Do you remember?"

"Yes," I said.

In answer, she turned back the quilt revealing my bare stomach. Down my side, the newly healed bullet wounds were bisected by a long scar. "Your stuffing came out and we had to put some more in," she joked.

"What?"

"When Sam Veldon shot you, he used bullets with iron cores. The iron inside you was disrupting your ability to heal. I had to get the bullets out."

"I like the first explanation better," I said.

"Unfortunately it's the least true of them," said Blackbird. "You're going to have an interesting scar to add to your collection. The kitchen isn't really kitted out for surgery."

"I'll never look at the bread knife in the same way again."

"Fortunately Garvin has no shortage of sharp knives and Mullbrook found me a curved needle. Once we had the iron out, your body could heal itself," she told me.

"I had the strangest dreams," I said.

"The iron was tainting your blood, making you feverish."

"I think they were true," I said. "They certainly seemed real."

"Did they tell you where to find Sam Veldon?" she asked. "I think I'd like to pay him a visit." There was a flash of green fire around the pupil of her eyes that could have been a reflection of the light from the candles, but wasn't.

I found myself defending Sam. "He's only a pawn. He told me he wanted me to die slowly, for killing Claire, but he wouldn't know to use iron. He fired the gun, but the bullets came from somewhere else. Someone wanted me dead."

"If they'd wanted you dead, they could have chopped off your head. No, Niall. This was a message – a warning – not just for you but for all of us. You were sent back to us tainted with iron, so that you would die slowly and painfully, where we could witness."

"Who hates me that much?"

"Raffmir?"

"Raffmir is sworn not to harm me. He'd be breaking his vow if he had me shot."

"Another of the Seventh Court, then."

"Why use iron? That's not their weapon of choice. A length of steel, yes, but iron bullets?"

"Maybe Sam's being doing some research?" she suggested. "Maybe he has some of Claire's journals?"

"Claire's flat had been cleaned – more than that, it had been restored. I'm sure Sam has some shady connections, but he works alone, especially where I'm concerned. He doesn't have the resources to have a flat cleaned and restored so that it looks like nothing happened. That takes manpower, and more people would have to know about it. Sam is all about keeping secrets, not sharing them."

"Then who?" she asked.

"The horseshoes had gone from the locker at the National Archives, and from the flat. Sam didn't have them with him, not that you'd willingly carry them around. Maybe he took them, maybe not, but someone furnished Sam with the bullets, and told him how to find me," I said. "I'd like to know who it was, and why?"

I tried to push myself up, but Blackbird pressed me back down without effort. "Not tonight, Niall. You're still healing. Even Garvin went to bed. Your daughter fell asleep watching you."

"She looks cramped in that chair."

"She's young and she'll sleep better knowing she's with you. She helped save your life, you know." Nestled into the chair, her hair curled and uncurled with her breathing. "Sleep now, and you can decide whether you are ready to be up and around tomorrow. Your body needs rest, so sleep in if you can."

"If I sleep, I'll dream," I said.

"Then dream of healing, and of a better day tomorrow." She stood up. "Angela and I are taking a white rose to All Hallows by the Tower tomorrow, so we'll be able to tell you what happens."

"You want me to come with you?"

She shook her head. "Sleep as long as you can – I'm serious. Only a few hours ago I was up to my arms in your insides. It's a wonder you're still alive. Rest while you can."

"Where will you sleep?"

"For now, I'll sleep with the baby. I'll be close, but I don't want you turning over and pulling the wound open. Close your eyes," she said, "and rest."

She laid her hand upon my forehead, stroking my hair, and despite myself I found my eyelids heavy and her cool hand restful. I drifted easily back into sleep.

• • • •

The dream began more easily, and this time I knew it was a dream. A familiar smell, something of spice, and the familiar prickle of power over my skin.

The sound of conversation drifted to me in snatched phrases. "How many know of this?" A male voice.

A female voice answered. "It will be obvious to anyone who sees the broader picture."

"Mercifully few then," another female voice said.

The light grew and I began to see points of light, flickering in the darkness. These resolved slowly into candle flames arrayed in a broad circle around thrones I recognised. It was not the courts as I knew it, but that was undoubtedly where we were. There was Kimlesh, her hair shorter than I remembered, and Yonna looking somehow less feral, less angular than she now did. Krane lounged in his usual manner, but even he looked leaner. In the seventh throne sat someone I recognised from the one brief meeting we'd had before I'd been sent from the High Court; someone I knew more by reputation than acquaintance: Altair, Lord of the Seventh Court.

"It is a temporary state of affairs," he said, "brought on by the incomers; they breed plague faster than they breed themselves."

"We are immune to plague," said Barthia, her bulky form adorned with heavy bands of gold and silver. "Their malaise cannot affect us. It cannot be the cause."

"And yet here we are," said Teoth.

"This must bring forward our plans," said Kimlesh. "It leaves us no choice."

"There is always a choice," said Altair, "and they are not the plans of all of us."

"Culling the humans will not help us, Altair," said Yonna. "As Barthia pointed out, they are not the cause of our troubles."

"Then it is pure coincidence, I suppose," said Altair, "that their numbers have grown, as ours have diminished?"

"They are stealing something from us, we just don't know what it is," said Teoth.

"How?" asked Yonna. "They have no power, they have no strength. How do they steal from us? This is pure speculation."

"They steal the food from our forests," said Altair, "they pollute our water, cut and burn down the trees, turning abundant wilderness into strip fields and pocket farms. They build on land that is not theirs and call it home."

Mellion made a complex series of hand movements, ending in a bony finger pointed at his open palm.

"I agree with Mellion," said Kimlesh. "All of that may be true, but it does not change our situation one jot."

"How long do we have?" asked Yonna.

There was a long silence, then a crackly voice spoke from the shadows. "Not as long as you think."

Around the thrones indignation broke out. Altair spoke over the others. "Come forward, old one. Don't skulk in the shadows. You may as well come and speak in plain sight, though you are not invited here."

"I need no invitation," said Kareesh, hobbling forward into the smoky light that danced around the candles. "I go where I must, and do what I can."

"I will speak to Garvin on this," said Krane, leaning forward from his throne as if he would pounce.

"Much good may it do you," said Kareesh. "Like all guard dogs, he has his limits."

"What are you doing here, Kareesh?" asked Teoth. "If there is something you wish to discuss, I will hear it, but not now. Perhaps it would be better if I should come to you. You're not as young as you were."

"I don't need you to count my teeth," said Kareesh, "and I came to speak with you assembled. I do not move these old bones lightly or without reason."

"Your reason may be what you left behind," said Altair.

She turned her black almond eyes on him and stared. In the end it was he who looked away. "What has been long apparent to me," she said, "has finally become your concern. We are dying." She looked slowly around the ring of faces.

"Do you say that from foresight, or deduction?" asked Kimlesh.

"Both," said Kareesh. "We have played a trick on ourselves, and now it tricks us in return."

"If this is another one of your bids to mingle the bloodlines of the courts, Kareesh, you can save your breath," said Krane. "There is none other that will live in abomination as you and Gramawl do."

"It is not an abomination to love another," she said. "No matter which court they are from. Sadly. it was too late for us, but there may be others who still have time."

"None of the others wish to indulge in your... practices," said Altair. "They prefer to remain pure."

"Then they prefer extinction," said Kareesh with bitterness. "Deefnir is the last, Altair. There will be no more after him."

"You cannot know that," said Altair.

"Do not tell me what I cannot know." said Kareesh. "You haven't seen it. Would you like to?" Kareesh stretched out her hand, but Altair shook his head, scowling at her.

"Your problem," said Krane, "is that you want everyone to be like you. You cannot conceive of a life unlike your own."

"No," said Kareesh. "The problem is that I cannot conceive at all. Neither can you. Nor can they." She gestured to the wider world. "We have fostered our power down the millennia, using the courts to breed our bloodlines pure but bleeding them dry in the process. There will be no more children."

"The answer is no," said Barthia.

"Unless..." said Kareesh, "there is another way."

"Another way?" asked Kimlesh, leaning forward.

"Each of you knows that there have been occasions... incidents... where the Feyre have mixed their bloodlines with humanity."

"Not in my court," said Altair.

Kareesh nodded. "With the exception of Altair's court then, but the fact remains – the union between humanity and the Feyre is fertile."

"What are you suggesting?" asked Teoth.

"The children of these unions are... unpredictable. Fate rolls her dice and the child may inherit from either parent. Some are more fey than others."

"That's true," said Yonna, "but they are not fey. They are the gifted ones, something in-between."

"And yet there is no barrier against them. The Feyre have long had liaison with humanity. It has become accepted."

"Not as a substitute for our own children," said Teoth.

"There are those that have fostered such children into their homes and presented them to the courts as their heirs, there being none other," she said. Kareesh turned her gaze on Teoth. "How many of your court have children these days, High Maker?" Now it was Teoth's turn to avoid meeting that blank black stare. "When was it last you celebrated a naming day?" The question hung in the air between them. "Any of you?" she asked.

Altair drew himself up in his chair. "Are you suggesting that these children be accepted as fey? On what basis? In which court? Half the time no one even knows what court begat them. Would you have us start taking in waifs and strays and pretending they are ours?"

"Then mix the bloodlines between the courts. We have a last chance, a sliver of opportunity," she pleaded. "Even now it may not be too late. There is reason for hope – we could snatch back our fecundity from the hand of fate and have children once again," said Kareesh.

"Even were we to decree it," said Teoth, "we cannot compel action which goes against the fundamental culture of our people. It's a deeply held taboo, Kareesh, as you knew well when you crossed it. It has set you apart for centuries. Does anyone visit you now?"

She stood there in the candlelight, and did not refute it.

"Enough," said Altair. "We have heard your plea and that is all we are obliged to do, even for you, old one."

"Then humanity is our only hope," she said. "Remember that in your deliberations."

Altair shook his head slowly, but I could see thoughtful expressions in the eyes of the others there: Kimlesh, Yonna, even Barthia. Kareesh turned to leave, and as she did, caught sight of a nod from Altair to the darkness beyond the candlelight. A shadow detached itself.

She paused and then turned back slowly. "There is a chance," she said, "That one of you might think I have become a thorn in your thumb that must be plucked lest it goad you into rash action. I speak to you in particular, Lord Altair."

She made the title sound like an insult.

Her crackly voice continued. "Remember this. I have seen the day of my death and I know what awaits me. I will say this, speaking true and clear. The day of my death is also the day of yours. If I were you, I would have every care for the health of this old one."

She turned again and continued slowly towards the door. Behind her, Altair shook his head minutely and the shadow retreated.

Altair spoke first. "She is old, and she does not see as well as she did."

Mellion opened and closed his fist three times, in response.

"I too acknowledge the debt," said Altair, "but she is not the only one with sight, and she does not see everything. There are others we should listen to."

"Even so," said Kimlesh. "She is right in one thing. We cannot sit here and watch our numbers fade. We have to do something."

"I, for one, will not be mixing my bloodline with humanity," said Altair. "You do not clean the well by adding poisoned water."

"Cleaning the well?" asked Krane. "Is that what we're doing?"

"Are you considering adopting this mad scheme now, Krane?" Altair asked.

"I'm open to all the options, Altair, as we all should be. If you have something new, please share it with us." It was the first time I'd seen Krane say anything against Altair, and the result on the wraithkin Lord's face was worth the wait.

He stood. "Well let me say this, loud and clear. The Seventh Court will not pollute its bloodlines with humanity no matter how fertile they are. Nor will we sully ourselves with the blood of the other courts. We are proud of what we are, as you should be." He strode across the candlelit space, making the candles flutter as he passed. The door opened, and he left. The shadow *dwelling in the darkness beyond the flickering lights followed him, closing the door after.*

"Well," said Kimlesh. "That places us in a difficult position."

"That depends," said Barthia. "Altair has departed, expecting that as we are no longer quorate we must do the same, though I, for one, am not yet minded to leave."

"Nor I," said Yonna.

"Nor I," Kimlesh echoed.

Mellion extended his hand and then placed it on his knee.

Krane said, "I am not leaving if no one else is." He looked at Teoth, who looked from side to side, assessing the situation.

"You understand," said Teoth, "that if we continue, there will be accusations of treachery from Altair?"

"The meeting was not declared closed, Teoth," said Kimlesh. "Are you going to let our brother dictate to you when you may speak and when you may not?"

He looked from one to the other. "Very well then," he said. "I too shall stay."

Even so, they dropped their voices and I leaned forward to hear them better. Their voices became fainter, and the flickering candlelight faded.

The interior of the Church of All Hallows by the Tower received the morning sunrise like a blessing. It streamed through the east window leaving long shadows striped across the altar out into the church. As the morning progressed, the light slid sideways, becoming narrower as the sun rose and the world turned and the sun moved round to the stained glass windows along the south aisle, leaving the altar in shadow.

Into that shadow stepped two men. One wore a long coat, and the other a dark suit.

"Do you know what to do?" asked the one in the coat.

"I do," said the suited man.

"It must be done right," said the man in the coat.

"I know," the suited man replied.

"It's almost noon." The man in the coat glanced down

the central aisle and then nodded to the second man. "Be careful."

"I will," said the suited man. He waited until the first had left the church via the vestry door and then walked quietly into the Lady Chapel and knelt before the image on the wall before him. To one side there was a white sculpture on a stand which was supposed to represent the Madonna, but appeared to have spikes emerging from it. Somehow it seemed appropriate. He bowed his head. He heard Blackbird and Angela when they entered through the door at the far end of the church, but he did not stir. He listened to them approach and only then did he rise and step out into the central aisle.

"There is no service today," he said. "I'm so sorry."

Blackbird started at his sudden appearance. She was holding a white rose in one hand, being careful of the wicked thorns that adorned its stem. "We didn't come for a service," she said.

"Indeed," said the man, noting the rose and glancing from Blackbird to Angela and back to Blackbird. "Is there something else I can do for you?"

"We would like to present this white rose," said Blackbird, "at the foot of the altar of All Hallows by the Keep on the eve of the winter solstice."

"Are you sure you have the right day?" said the man. "And the right church?"

"It is the winter solstice tomorrow," said Blackbird. "Today is the eve."

"I'm sure it is," said the man. His smile was indulgent, as if they were a little stupid, or perhaps confused.

From outside the church, they could hear the chimes of a clock starting to toll out the noon bells. "Do I simply place it on the steps?" she asked the man.

"Do you?" he said. "I won't prevent you, if that's what you wish to do," he said.

"On the cushion before the altar?" she asked, "Is there anything special for it to rest on?"

He smiled. "You're confusing this with the rose rent on the summer solstice," he said. "Do return in the summer and you can see the ceremony then. It's quite a spectacle."

"When you say confusing *this*," said Angela. What is *this*, that you are referring to?"

"That's not for me to say," he answered her, smiling politely.

The chimes ended and there was a slight pause when all was silent. Even the muted rumple of the traffic seemed to pause for a moment. Then the bell started tolling the hour. Blackbird stepped forward and placed the rose on the kneeling cushion at the step of the sanctuary. The man did not move.

"There," she said. "It's done." She turned back to the man.

He waited until the full twelve chimes has rung, then he reached inside his jacket pocket and extracted a large bronze key. "I believe this is what you require," he said, dropping the key into her open hand.

"Is that it? The key to Grey's Court?"

"Isn't that what you were expecting?" he asked them.

"Yes," said Blackbird. "Is that all? There's no deed, no contract?"

"As the key-holder, what else do you require?" he asked. "You are welcome to stay and give thanks." He gestured towards the pews arrayed down the church.

Blackbird looked at Angela and Angela shrugged her shoulders.

"Thank you," said Blackbird.

"You're welcome," said the man.

He watched as Blackbird and Angela walked back down the central aisle, waiting until he heard the outer door close and the sound of the traffic recede. Then he turned and walked slowly to the back of the church and stepped through the arch, turning towards the vestry door. He opened it and stepped through. Inside the man with the coat waited for him.

"Did they take it?" he asked.

"They did," said the suited man.

"What about that?" asked the man in the coat. He gestured towards the floor of the vestry where a man lay dead, his neck at an awkward angle.

"An accident," suggested the suited man. "Hard to prove otherwise. There'll be an investigation, but that needn't concern us."

"Excellent," said the man in the coat. He led the way to the side door and placed his hand on the wood of the door. There was a clunk as the lock tumbled and he pulled open the door, allowing the other man through.

"I would make a good priest," said the suited man.

"Don't be ridiculous," said the man in the coat. "You've just murdered someone."

"Ah, yes," said the suited man. "There is that."

Twelve

"Altair!"

"Do not use that name here," said the whisperer. "I forbid it."

"You were watched."

"When?"

"Whoever it was you sent to put pressure on Kimlesh's Court. They were seen negotiating. Tate followed them."

"It doesn't matter."

"Of course it matters. How could you be so careless?"

"Do not think that because you share my secrets that you can speak to me so. When you chose to throw your lot in with mine, we sealed a bargain, but I am the Lord of the Seventh Court, and you... you are my servant."

"I am not your servant."

"Your loyalty is to none other, not any more. Remember that."

"We did strike a bargain, and I've seen precious little in the way of a return."

"They have taken the bait," he whispered.

There was a pause. "What? You're sure?"

"Of course. I would not say if it were not so."

"Then it could be soon?"

"The solstice. There will be a window of opportunity," said the whisper.

"And then you will deliver on your side of our bargain?"

There was only silence.

When I awoke, I was in bed alone. I tried to sit up, and then regretted the attempt as the skin at my side tightened, making me gasp. Looking down at my side, the wound was already scarring over. Blackbird's skill was healing them even faster than I would normally heal, but they were still tender to touch.

Sunlight edged through the gap in the curtains, and I rolled out of bed in an ungainly but less painful manner and went to draw them back, revealing a crisp day where the frost still lay wherever the winter sun had not yet touched. The sun was as near high as it was going to get – Blackbird must have already left to keep the appointment at the church with her white rose, leaving me here asleep. Perhaps she thought I would be more trouble than help, or perhaps she thought I needed the rest. Checking in the nursery, I found the cot also deserted. I found it hard to believe I had slept through my son's awakening, but it had been the sleep of exhaustion, and hopefully of healing.

Then it came back to me – the dream of the courts. I felt sure it was a true dream, but how long ago had that happened? If I asked any member of the High Court, they would want to know where I came by such information, and I was not ready to show my hand. Some of the memories that Angela had given me were coming to the surface and I was slowly discovering things that no one outside the High Court knew. I wondered if even Garvin was aware – or had that been him skulking in the shadows at the edge of the court?

I showered, cleaning the pink skin on my side where Sam's bullet had left a puckered scar, now bisected by a newer scar running down my side. The water allowed me to clean off the patches of dried blood. I was healing impressively fast now that the iron bullets were removed. I probed the new skin with my finger, finding it still tender.

I washed the rest of me, then dried and shaved, being careful to avoid the pattern of red marks that still covered one side of my face like a livid tattoo. I had to admit that I was starting to look like a patchwork – too many injuries, too quickly. Still, I was alive.

I rinsed my face and inspected the damage. With a shake of my head, my glamour concealed the mark, but almost invisibly slowly it began to creep back, rising like a pale shadow across my face. Was that because it had been caused by iron? I found myself rubbing the palm of my hand where I had once grasped a set of iron gates. The scars there had healed eventually, but in that case I had barely touched them. Resigning myself to the fact that there was nothing I could do about it either way, I pulled on my Warders greys, and went in search of my son and something to eat. I was suddenly ravenous.

I found him in his favourite place, in the high chair at the end of the big table in the old kitchen, a bread stick in one hand and his other hand in his mouth. There was a bowl of greenish goo in front of him, some of which he appeared to eaten while the rest was smeared across his face.

"Good morning," said Lesley. "We were beginning to wonder if you'd sleep all day, weren't we?" My son grinned at me – not a pretty sight with a mouth full of green goo. I attempted to take the bread stick from him, but he would not relinquish it. His grip was firm and his determination was greater than mine, so I let him keep it. He used his hand to scoop up some more from the bowl, pressing it against his lips so that the goo squeezed between his fingers.

"You're enjoying that aren't you?" I said to him.

"It's one of his favourites," said Lesley, "though what there is in peas, potato and sprouts that he likes is hard to fathom. Still, he shows his appreciation, don't you, Sweet Pea?" She kissed him on the top of his head, and he craned his neck around to see what she was doing.

"How are you feeling? I understand it was a busy night?" she said.

"I missed most of it, but I'm doing OK, thanks. Surprisingly well, given that I was shot."

"Are you up to breakfast?"

"I'd love some," I said.

"I meant for him, rather than you, but I can arrange some for you too." She passed me a plastic spoon so that my son and I could engage in the well-tried game of me trying to get the food inside him while he tried to spread it onto me.

"I don't know which of us should have a bib," I said. "Him or me."

"I can get you one if you want," said Lesley. "I have one that says Cute when Asleep."

"It wouldn't suit me," I said.

"I'm not sure Blackbird would agree with that," she said.

"Did she say anything this morning?" I asked.

"She said something about a theoretical rose," said Lesley. "By the way, I wanted to ask you, have you thought about Stewards for the Eighth Court?"

"Sorry?" I was taken aback by this change in tack.

"All the courts have their own Stewards, but there isn't a precedent for a new court. I wondered if you'd spoken with Blackbird about it?"

"I can't say I have," I said. "It's not really my responsibility."

"I took the liberty of mentioning it to Mullbrook, and he suggested I should talk to you."

"To me?"

"You do have Blackbird's ear," she said, "and if you go and live somewhere else then I'd hardly ever see Sweet

Pea here, and I get on so well with Blackbird, and you wouldn't hardly know I was there…"

"Are you asking me for a job?" I asked her. She looked uncomfortable, busying herself with some paperwork spread across the other end of the big table. "Well, I'm flattered that you think I have that much influence, but I'm not even part of the Eighth Court. I'm a Warder. Next week I could be assigned some other duty."

"Realistically, that's not going to happen, though, is it?" she said, looking up from the papers.

"I'm not sure I can predict what will happen, Lesley, but for my part I would be honoured if you were to join the Eighth Court. Our son thinks the world of you, and he has few enough friends in the world that he can afford to lose any of them, can you son?" He grinned at me, which would have been more endearing without the green smears. "It really is up to Blackbird, though. I can speak to her about it if you want me to, but why don't you just ask her?"

"It seems a little forward?" she said.

My son waved his breadstick at Lesley. "Eh! Eh!" She rose and went to take it from him, at which point he stuck it back in his mouth, grinning at her.

"Tease," she admonished him.

One of the reasons he liked the old kitchen so much was that it was a centre for operations for the Stewards. People came and went, delivery drivers arrived with trays of vegetables or orders of meat. The High Court had to be ready to accommodate whoever arrived, at whatever time of day, and this room acted as an informal hub for the staff. Deliveries were signed for and stored away, while my son sat like a lord at his table and watched everyone with interest. I gave up trying to spoon-feed him and wiped his hands and face with a damp cloth that Lesley had passed to me. He settled into chewing the end of the breadstick. Once he was happy, she found me some fresh bread and golden yellow butter, and a jar

204

of pale honey. I sat and ate, trying to avoid my son getting his fingers into any of it while I was not paying attention.

As Stewards came and went, many of them stopped to say hello to him or ask Lesley how he was. He rewarded those he favoured with a bread-covered smile. It pricked me slightly; they didn't ask me, they asked her. I realised that I needed to spend more time with him, and resolved to do so as soon as the present crisis was over. The trouble was, there always seemed to be another crisis around the corner.

"Did Blackbird mention when she would be back?" I asked Lesley.

"She just said she hoped to return with good news. I don't know any more than that. Angela was with her, if that helps?"

"I have something I need to do," I said, pulling my side as I rose and earning a worried look from Lesley.

"Should you be going out so soon?" she asked.

"I promise I'll take it gently," I said. "Is it OK to leave him with you?" I was only too aware that I was prevailing upon Lesley's good will once again to look after our son.

She just smiled. "We'll be fine, won't we, Sweet Pea? I'll give him his bath in a while, but I need to make a few calls and check some things first."

"You know," I said, "It's time that boy had a name, before he starts to believe he's called Sweet Pea."

Lesley looked hurt, "I have to call him something," she said.

"That wasn't a criticism," I said. "Six months is a long time to wait for a name, and I think we've waited long enough. I'll speak to Blackbird about naming him. I heard somewhere that they used to have name-days – a ceremony to welcome new children into the court. Maybe we should have some sort of get-together and make a thing of it?" I suggested.

"I think that's a lovely idea," said Lesley. "I'll speak to Mullbrook and see what we can come up with."

"Well, maybe I better speak with Blackbird about it first," I said, in a moment of hesitation.

"Nonsense. She'll be delighted that someone else has organised it, and you're right, I can't call him Sweet Pea all his life." She ruffled his downy hair affectionately.

I left them there, jealous of the time Lesley would spend with my son, but knowing I had other things I needed to do so that he could have a home where he could grow up in safety.

I went to my room and collected my sword and a small torch. There was someone who knew more about this than anyone realised, and I was beginning to see a pattern. I needed to talk to Kareesh, and I needed to do it while Blackbird wasn't around, being protective. I left before Blackbird came back and either insisted on coming with me, or dissuaded me from going at all. Down in the room under the courts where the Way-nodes were, Amber was leaning against a wall when I entered.

"Are you guarding the room, or waiting for me?" I asked.

"Both?" she said.

"Are you going to be following me today?"

"No," said Amber. "I'm coming with you."

"Oh?" I said.

"Blackbird said I wasn't to let you out of the courts alone."

"Ah," I said, thinking that maybe she was ahead of me on that one.

"I think she's gained the impression that since I didn't let you die I might be able to keep you out of trouble," said Amber.

"She might be right," I admitted.

Amber's expression said otherwise. "Where are we going?"

"To visit an old friend. I need to see Kareesh, but I want to see her alone."

Amber looked sceptical again. "Are you sure you're up to seeing an ancient frail fey without an armed escort?"

I was obliged to take the rebuke in good humour, given my success rate, but insisted that I had to see Kareesh alone. "I need to ask her something, and if you're there, she won't give me the answer I need," I explained.

"Just as long as you don't get hurt," said Amber. "I'm not delivering you to Blackbird again like last night. It's not good for my career prospects."

"You're looking for promotion?" I asked.

"I'm looking for survival," she said.

We left the courts and headed out on the Ways towards London, skipping across the nodes until we emerged in a gym in central London. The pumping bass emitted by the sound system and the movement of the people exercising was good cover. No one saw us in the exercise room, and when we emerged we were just another couple leaving the gym club.

We walked together up St Martin's Lane and onto New Row, the small boutique shops displaying designer shoes, jewellery or framed photos of London with touched-up skylines. Slipping past the Metro supermarket we made our way across the road into Covent Garden proper. Here restaurants offering lunchtime specials were nestled between clothes stores and souvenir shops selling plastic Union flags. The streets were paved in cobbles and pedestrians wandered in the road, heedless of the occasional delivery van.

The entertainers were out in force, competing for the lunchtime crowd, and on the breeze I could hear the high, pure tones of an opera singer, warming up for the evening's performance by singing to the tourists in the covered market. As we strode up the rise to the tube station, we passed hawkers selling balloons to bright-eyed youngsters, and entertainers who had painted themselves to resemble bronze statues, looking even more frozen than usual. The winter sunshine had tempted out the tourists and the opportunists were determined to make the best of it, no matter the cold.

The wind whistling down Long Acre cut through the pedestrians, making them turn up their collars against the cold. I reached the underground station and we strolled through the ticket gate unheeded, the metal gates flipping open despite the lack of any Oyster card. The lifts were ferrying people up from the tunnels below like workers coming off shift. They spilled out of the station on one side before the doors opened to allow us in for the downward journey.

In the warm air of the tunnels, the air smelled faintly of machine oil and electric sparks. It was easy to hang back and let the other passengers disperse. They marched along down to the platforms while we drifted into the service tunnel between the lift entrances. There was a door there that said Staff Only, and it was a moment's work to unlock it and let myself through onto the top of the stairway leading down to the service access for the lifts.

"Wait here for me?" I asked Amber.

"Don't be too long," she said. "Or I'll be forced to come and get you."

I took that as a serious threat, and began to wonder what Blackbird had said to her. The door swung closed and darkness reasserted itself.

The last time I visited here, I was unwelcome. The tunnels had been blank with no stairway rising to a private chamber filled with scented hanging lamps and old rugs. I had been forced to follow the phantom sounds of the person leading me through the tunnels. This time I was hoping for a warmer reception, and an explanation. I was certain now that Kareesh knew more than she was letting on. I also dared to speculate that when Blackbird brought me here, it wasn't my first visit. The memories from Angela hinted that I'd been here before that, though my own memory of that visit had been wiped from my mind. Kareesh was old, that was obvious, but old didn't mean weak. The Feyre trod around her as if on eggshells and, if my dreams were correct, that was despite her flouting certain taboos.

I remembered, at my first encounter when Blackbird brought me here, wondering at the difference between Kareesh and Gramawl, and trying to reconcile the huge troll who dedicated himself to guarding and keeping Kareesh in her nest, against the fragile form he guarded. I'd asked Blackbird why he stayed with her and she'd told me that he stayed with her because he loved her. She'd never mentioned that their love was outside the norm, or that others of the Feyre might not approve of a cross-courts relationship, but then she'd grown up with them, an outcast herself. It was something I meant to ask her about when I saw her next.

Conscious that using the shifting light shed by gallow-fyre to light my way might be interpreted as a hostile approach, I used my torch, and I made my way down by its beam to the tunnels at the base of the stairs. It struck me then that I'd not noticed before that the rounded arch with its flat floor made the shape of a horseshoe. Was there significance in that or was I starting to see patterns everywhere I looked? I listened intently, aware that I was the visitor here.

"Gramawl?" My voice echoed back from the tunnel. "Gramawl, it's Niall. I need to talk to Kareesh. Can I see her?" There was no sound in the tunnel except the faded echoes of my voice. "Gramawl?"

Edging into the tunnel, I expected at any moment to see a looming figure emerge from the shadows. My hand drifted unconsciously to the hilt of my sword and I had to will myself to withdraw it. I wasn't here for a fight, and didn't want to give that impression. I entered the tunnel one slow step at a time, using the torch to push back the darkness until the turn in the tunnel revealed the side passage with the stairs heading upwards. The entrance to Kareesh's domain was normally hidden, but perhaps I was welcome here after all.

As soon as I reached the opening I knew something was wrong. When I was here before, the steps had been illuminated by the softest light from above, mixed with the aroma of spices and scented candles. Now the stairs upwards were lit only by the beam of my torch. I took the stairs slowly, my hand now firmly on the hilt of my sword. There was something wrong, I could taste it.

I reached the place where the stairs turned back on themselves and rose to Kareesh's lair, but there was no light from above. Instead the questing beam of my torch illuminated only the dangling hangings strung from the ceilings in the room above. This room had been like a grotto, with Kareesh at its focus. As I topped the stairs I already knew it was empty. I pushed through the limp hangings, tapping my head against a copper lantern as I ducked through, the darkened lamp gonged dull and soft within the confines of that space. It was immediately apparent to me that it smelled different. Where before there had been musk over new-turned earth, now it smelled stale, lifeless and old. Under the beam of my torch, the hangings were threadbare, and the lanterns mottled with corrosion. I found the nest of cushions where Kareesh had held court. They were scattered listlessly, with no sign of occupation. Kareesh had gone.

I scanned the pile of cushions, looking for evidence of dust. Had she died, finally? Was there sign of her passing? The Feyre live a long time, but when they finally reach death, they are consumed by the power that they hold at bay with their life force, and Kareesh's power had been formidable. If there was a trace of her, I didn't find it. In amongst the cushions I found a bag of boiled sweets – Kareesh's favourite. It was hard to think of her leaving them there.

What hit me then was that I would have to tell Blackbird. I couldn't leave her to find out from someone else. Kareesh and Gramawl had taken her in when she was helpless and alone. Blackbird had told me once that Kareesh had initiated her in the ways of power, teaching her how to wield the magic she'd inherited. She had grown up with Gramawl and Kareesh when no one else would shelter her. It was going to be hard to explain what I'd found.

I turned away from the nest of cushions and went back to the stairway, descending the steps to the tunnel in torchlight and remembering how Kareesh had granted me the sight of a future where my daughter and I could survive. It had been her gift to me, and following that path had kept both Alex and me alive long enough to begin to learn the ways of the Feyre, and try to find a place in their society. I wondered whether her intention all along had been to ensure that Blackbird was not left entirely alone after she'd gone.

I reached the bottom of the steps and turned to retrace my steps. As I did, the light of my torch flickered, as if the batteries were giving out. I tapped it, trying to improve the contact.

As my tapping faded into the dark, something enormous cannoned into me, sweeping me off my feet and ramming me into the arc of the ceiling. I dangled there, held by a huge paw, pressed against the tiles, winded and coughing, the wrench having pulled the newly healed skin at my side. A sound rumbled through me, echoing off the tiles and making my guts reverberate.

"Gramawl," I coughed, "it's me, Niall. Remember me? Rabbit?" Looking down from where I was pressed against the roof, I could see the light from where the torch had fallen, outlining the huge shadow in the dark and revealing only two huge golden eyes staring malevolently up at me. "Gramawl, you're crushing me…" He was pressing me so hard against the roof, I couldn't

211

breathe. I coughed weakly, trying to summon the thought of power. I needed to do something. My hand flailed out, trying to work out where my sword was. As it did, Gramawl vanished from under me and I fell flat onto the floor like a sack of wet sand.

"Oof!" I sprawled on the floor, winded and aware that I should be rolling to me feet ready for the next attack, but my body was still weak and I had no fight left in me. My bones felt like jelly, and my face was numb on one side from the impact. I raised myself up onto my elbows, trying to focus. The torch was a few feet away, pointing down the tunnel, illuminating the exit, if only I could get to my feet and make a run for it.

Ha! The way I felt at that moment, I might as well have wished to fly.

I pulled myself forward on my forearms, edging towards where the torch lay. My sword was in the light, just beyond it. As the torch came almost into reach, I felt my ankle snag and I began sliding backwards away from the torch. As I did, a pair of boots walked into my limited view and stopped.

She stood in the torchlight where she could be seen and spoke. "OK, Gramawl, how do you want to do this?"

"Amber," I said. "Kareesh has gone. Don't hurt him."

"Don't hurt him? Have you seen yourself?"

"We don't need any more violence. It won't help anyone – least of all Kareesh."

"No, wait," she grinned. "Your plan was to lull him into a false sense of security and then... what? Tickle him to death?"

"Gramawl?" I gasped. "I need to talk to you. This isn't helping. It won't bring her back."

The air filled with shivering subsonics which bypassed my ears and made my teeth ache. I took a breath. If he was going to kill me he could have done it already. There was clearly something wrong, and I had to find out what. "Gramawl, I need to know what happened."

My leg was released and I collapsed back onto the cold floor. Rolling over, I could see a pair of pale golden orbs watching me from beyond the light.

"Amber?"

"I'm here," she said from behind me.

"Would you wait for me upstairs?"

"You're joking, right?"

"I need Gramawl to understand that I haven't come to hurt anyone. I came to see Kareesh, but she's not here. I want to know what happened, but he's not going to tell me while you're standing there with a sword."

"And what do I tell Blackbird if he tears your arms and legs off?" she asked.

I watched the eye watching me. "He's not going to hurt me," I said, "but if by some chance he does, you can tell her that she should ask Gramawl for an explanation. He can explain it to her himself."

"You're sure you know what you're doing?" she asked.

"No, but I don't know how to do anything else. I'll join you upstairs in a few minutes."

The torch skittered across the tiles to where I was kneeling. My hands closed around it and pulled it near, setting it on end on the floor so it shone up the tiled wall, illuminating without dazzling. The golden orbs flicked to the light and back to me. "Can we talk?" I asked.

The sound reverberating through the tunnels faded to a low hum.

"Is Kareesh...?" I let the question hang. The figure in the dark blinked and then edged further into the torch-lit area where I could see him more clearly. I was struck again by the silence of his movement. I could not guess his mood from his face, but from his posture I would say miserable, angry; frustrated. He shook his head slowly, an obvious no.

"She's not dead?" I asked. He shook his head again.

"That's good news isn't it? Where is she then?" He

shrugged his massive shoulders, opening his gnarled hands in a gesture of helplessness.

"You don't know? She can't have gone far. Where could she...?" His paw slammed into the floor, making the entire passage reverberate with the impact. "OK, OK. I'm sorry. I was only trying to help. I guess you've already looked for her and didn't find her."

He nodded slowly. I watched his face, noting how his nose twitched. "You're very good at finding people, aren't you?" I said, hazarding a guess. He nodded again. "But you didn't find her, so..." I suddenly understood the problem, "she didn't want to be found. She's hidden herself from you. But why?"

Gramawl let out a long, mournful sound. It echoed down the passages, and faded slowly from the tunnels. It was the sound of loss and heartache.

"She must have used magic to hide herself," I said, speaking out loud, "but she's not left these tunnels in years, Blackbird told me that. When did she last go outside?" I asked him.

Gramawl shook his head and his fingers flickered in complex sign language.

"I'm sorry Gramawl, I never learned to sign. Blackbird knows, but she never taught me."

He clenched his fists in frustration and tried again. Pointing to the stairs, he made a sign like someone walking with his fingers.

"Kareesh is leaving? Has left?" I suggested.

He nodded, then made a sign holding his hands together under his cheek and tilting his head, closing his eyes to indicate sleep.

"She's sleeping somewhere?" I guessed.

He waved his hand to indicate not, but then mimed waking and sleeping, waking and sleeping...

"A day?" I suggested.

He nodded enthusiastically, then motioned that he meant bigger.

"A week?" I asked. He did it again. "A month? A year?"
With this last he clapped his hand together. "A year."
I said.

He held up his paw, counting along his fingers. He
counted five, then closed his hand and raised one finger
on the other hand. "Six years?" I asked. Then he did it
again, only this time he raised two fingers.

He was counting, but in base six instead of base ten.
As soon as he realised I'd got it he held up all his fingers.

"That's…" I struggled with the calculation, "Thirty-five
years?"

He nodded, and then flashed his open hands at me,
time after time.

"That's… no wait, that's too many. That's hundreds."

He clapped his hands together.

"Hundreds of years. She hasn't been outside on her
own for hundreds of years? That's what you're trying to
tell me?"

He nodded slowly.

"Then why leave now?" I asked.

Again, the anguished moan filled the tunnels.

"You don't know, do you?" I asked him. "She didn't
tell you?"

He shook his head, the moan trailing off mournfully.

"She waited until you weren't here, and then left. She
must have been planning this for some time. Where
would she go without you? Is there somewhere only she
could go? Somewhere she couldn't take you?"

Gramawl's massive shoulders sagged, as if under a
great weight.

"Or she's gone to do something that she has to do alone?"

Again the mournful wail, haunted the tunnels. I
looked at Gramawl and understood him at last. He
thought she'd taken herself somewhere else to die. It was
a journey on which he could not accompany her, and it
was the only thing he could not protect her from. She'd
waited for him to go outside and then left him behind

215

because she didn't want him following her. I already knew Gramawl was much younger than she was. It was obvious in the way he moved and in the lustre of his fur, the pale whiteness of his tusk-like teeth. She must have known that she would not survive him, as must he. I reached out my hand to him, offering comfort.

Sensing that I had finally understood him, he took my hand and squeezed it gently in his. I had expected it to be rough and course, but it was warm and soft, like old leather. "I'm sorry Gramawl." I said. "What will you do now?"

He shook his head and sat back, his eyes glowing in the dark. He folded his hands into his lap and settled himself.

"You'll wait?" I asked. "What if she doesn't return?" He shrugged.

"How long will you wait?" I asked. Again, the shrug.

I stood up, testing where I was bruised. I was sore, and the wound in my side ached, but I was whole. "Do you want me to tell Blackbird?" I asked.

He hesitated, then nodded slowly. "Then I'll tell her." I said. "She will want to see you."

He simply raised his hand and pressed the tip of his finger to the floor. He would be here.

"Yeah, I guess so," I said, picking up my sword and collecting the torch.

I backed away and then walked to the bend in the tunnel and looked back into the dark. There were the faint glimmers from two golden eyes in the dark. There was a question I hadn't asked – one that I'd intended for Kareesh, but maybe Gramawl could help me with it.

"Gramawl? I was here before wasn't I?" My voice echoed strangely in the darkened corridor, illuminated only by the ring of torchlight around my feet. The eyes blinked at me from the dark. "Before all of this, before Blackbird introduced me to you and Kareesh, before I even knew the Feyre existed, I was here, with you and Kareesh, wasn't I?"

The eyes blinked again, but this time they did not re-open. I went back, shining the torch down the corridor. He had vanished silently into the dark. There were only the cold tiles and the empty stairway leading upwards.

Amber was waiting in the dark at the head of the stairway. We went through the door into the access tunnels below Covent Garden station and she looked me up and down.

"I'm OK," I said. "A little bruised, but..."

She shrugged, and led the way out of station and back to the Way-node in silence. It gave me time to think about Gramawl, Kareesh and what they were doing. This was Kareesh's doing, I knew that now, but what was it she had planned? In order to discover that, I needed to find her, but if Gramawl couldn't find her, then what chance did I have? She'd vanished, after all those years sequestered in the tunnels below the Underground Station. I was not looking forward to telling Blackbird that Kareesh had disappeared.

Arriving back at the courts, I left Amber to her duties and went up into the house. With Kareesh unavailable, there was one other person who could help me figure out what this was all about. I went to see if Angela was back.

Thirteen

"Altair?"

"I have warned you not to use that name," said the whisperer.

"It has to be now. He's fading. If we don't reach him soon, it will be too late."

"After the solstice."

"Now. He needs you now. You promised. After all I've done for you."

"Done? Anything you've done has been for your own reasons."

"Help him, or I'll tell them everything." Her voice was a low threat.

"By all means, tell them. Your part in it will be obvious. You'll be executed on the spot. It won't help him."

"You have to help him. You promised me."

"I said I would help Fellstamp, and I am helping him. He's about to embrace the void that claimed him."

"You said you would bring him back."

"No, I said I would help him return. We all come from the void, and we all return to it. It's inevitable," said Altair.

"That's not true – only the wraithkin return to the void," she said.

"Ultimately we all come from the void, and we will all return to it," he said. "Everything else is transitory illusion. It's simply a matter of time."

"You lying wraithkin bastard! You lied to me! You've betrayed me and Fellstamp!"

"You're the one who's been doing the betraying, Fionh, and if I were you I'd keep very quiet about it. Fellstamp must find his own peace with the void. I can't bring him back, but I can give you revenge on the ones that placed him there. In a few days they will be at your mercy."

"I don't need you to deliver revenge," she said. "I can do that for myself." She walked away, no longer caring whether anyone saw her.

"Shall I follow her?" said a low voice.

"Only as far as the edge of the wardings," said the whisperer.

"What if she tells Garvin?"

"She won't. She's too proud."

"You're sure?"

"I'm sure."

When I reached Angela's door it was closed and I wondered if she was still out with Blackbird, but when I tapped lightly on the door there was a noise from within, and Angela opened the door.

"Blackbird's downstairs somewhere," she said. "She went to speak to Mullbrook."

"I wasn't looking for Blackbird. I came to see you," I told her.

She opened the door a little wider as if she were wondering who was with me, and seeing I was alone, opened the door further. "You'd better come in then."

I couldn't recall being in Angela's room before, but I could see that she'd made it her own. She must have been being bringing items from her house, since there were trinkets that were nothing to do with the courts, and she had an ancient mechanical typewriter set up on the bureau. The rest of the space was covered in typewritten drafts and documents that she'd been working on. I looked around for somewhere to sit.

"There isn't much room," she said, clearing a space on the bed. "I don't get many visitors." I sat in the space she cleared, and she sat on the chair at the bureau. She waited until I got the hint.

"I came to see you because I dreamed again," I said.

"That's hardly a surprise."

"I have a lot of the pieces now, and I know how some of it came to be. I just don't know how to fit them together. I wanted to ask if you would help me."

"Help you how?" she asked.

I paused for a moment to think how to put this to her. "I think you were right, this is important. Whatever this is that I've become involved in has an impact on all of us – it's affected us all along. This isn't new, it's been going on for years. There are clues... some of this has been planned."

"I don't see what I can do," she said.

"You can help me piece it together," I said. "You're the only other person that knows all this stuff. You gave me these memories – help me make sense of them."

"I can't," she said.

"You must."

"You don't understand," she said, shaking her head. "I gave you the memories I had, but none of it made any sense to me. You say that you have pieces, and that's good. I never had more than a jumble of tattered fragments with no order or sequence. You saw what I had; it was all over the walls of my office."

"But you have the rest," I said. "You have the missing pieces. Between the two of us we could put it all together."

"You're wrong. I don't have anything. I only got any of this when I touched you in the cells under Porton Down." She sounded angry now, and I couldn't really understand why. "You infected me in a second with images I didn't recognise, messages I couldn't decipher, and memories that weren't mine. None of this came from me, Niall. It came from you. Before I touched you I was fine. Afterwards... I couldn't get any relief from it."

"That's how I feel," I told her. "There must be more. Maybe if you stirred something into a drink?"

"I gave you everything. Your brain... it's making the connections, do you see? All of this is related, and it comes back to you as a dream or a memory. You have all you need; you just need to tease it out."

"No. There are things missing, I'm sure of it."

"Then maybe those things were meant to be missing, or maybe they were never there in the first place. I don't have anything else for you. You took it all."

"So you won't even try."

"I can't help you, Niall." Her mouth was set in a determined line.

I stood up, disappointed by her reaction. "You did this to me," I reminded her. "You share some of the responsibility."

"You did it to yourself," she said. "And to me."

On an instinct, I reached out and grabbed her. The contact should have been shocking – an instant flash of mind-crushing recollection and foreign memories. Instead I felt my hand, tight around her arm. The muscle was warm under my hand, where I held her firmly. She looked at my hand, surprised by my sudden rush to touch her and then resentful at the liberty I'd taken.

"It would have served you right if you'd been a gibbering wreck on the floor," she said.

"I'm not, though, am I?"

She plucked at my grip with her free hand and I released her. "What happened?" I asked her.

"Nothing," she said. "Nothing happened. You have everything I can give you, there's nothing else to take. I'd like you to leave now."

"You know more than you're letting on," I accused her.

"What I know and what I feel are separate things," she said. "You know what I know, but what I feel I'll keep to myself. It can't be taken from me, not even by you."

I went to the door. "I'm sorry," I said. "I had to try. You should understand that, at least."

She stared at me for a long while. "It is by our choices that we know ourselves," she said. "You could have asked."

"You would have said no," I said.

"Yes," she agreed. "But that doesn't give you the right to take that choice from me."

I left her then, feeling that I'd made a mistake. I felt like I was being backed into a corner and that the choices that remained to me were limited and none of them were ideal. I went back towards the suite that Blackbird and I shared, wondering if there was some way I could make amends. Angela was right, I'd taken a liberty that was not mine to take, and it had got me nowhere.

As I emerged into the head of the stairs, Alex was coming the other way. "Dad! I've been looking for you everywhere. She's going to kill him!"

"Who is? Kill who?" I asked.

"Fionh!" said Alex, as if I were stupid. "She's going to kill Sparky." She turned and headed through the door and down the corridor. Running after Alex, slowed down by the healing wound in my side, I followed Alex as she raced ahead. Sure now that I would follow, she guided me up through the house until we reached the room where Fellstamp lay.

Alex stepped into the room warily. "You'd better let him go now. Dad's here."

I moved into the doorway, unsure of what to expect. Fellstamp was as I'd left him, draped up to his shoulders with a white sheet. Towards the back of the room, the big French doors had been thrown open. Fionh stood, her back to the sky, outlined against the light. Beside her,

Sparky was held by the hair, throat exposed while Fionh held a wickedly sharp blade under his chin. They were both standing on the balustrade over the three storey drop to the paving below.

"What's going on, Fionh? What's he done?" I asked her.

"Done?" she asked, as if it were a joke. "He doesn't have to *do* anything." There was a frayed edge to her voice that I didn't like. Fionh was normally an island of still calm in a sea of trouble – this was not the Fionh I knew.

"Something's happened," I said. It was a statement, not a question.

"You're not wrong," she said. "Look at him."

"I am looking at him. What's he done?" I repeated.

"Not him, you idiot! Look at Fellstamp!"

I looked at the body on the table. His face was pinched. He didn't look like he was in pain but he was even paler than before. It couldn't last much longer. In its comatose state, his body was slowly consuming itself.

"What's this about, Fionh?" I asked, stepping forward into the room.

"Stay there!" she warned. "You're only bringing the inevitable closer."

"What's inevitable about it?" I asked. Alex moved to the other side.

"Stay back!" said Fionh. The edge of the blade held at Sparky's throat left a red line at her warning. I could see his Adam's apple bobbing as he tried to resist the urge to swallow. Behind them both, the sky darkened as the clouds gathered above the courts.

"I only want to help," I said.

"Help yourself, you mean," said Fionh. "You're no better than the rest of them, stealing scraps from the plates of your betters. Pretending you're part of something."

"I don't know what you mean," I said.

"You don't even know not to lie," said Fionh. "You're like all the rest of them."

"I don't understand," I said. "The rest of what?"

"The rest of the mongrels," said Garvin, standing in the doorway behind me. "That's what you mean, isn't it Fionh?" I glanced at him, taking my eyes momentarily off Fionh. He was entirely focused on her.

"You betrayed us," said Fionh to Garvin.

Garvin shook his head. "I haven't betrayed anyone," he said.

"You led us down this path and now there's no way back," she accused.

"I'm not the one doing the betraying, though, am I?" he said. "I couldn't figure it out. Our loyalty has never been in question – until now."

"And it would have stayed that way," she said.

"It would, except things started leaking out. Small things at first – a word here, a nod there. The obvious suspect was Niall. He's the newcomer. It only started happening after he joined the Warders."

"He's not a Warder," her scornful glance barely registered my presence. "Where was he when we needed him? Changing nappies? Chasing his daughter? He's been more trouble than he's worth since the beginning."

"I couldn't figure out where they were getting their information from," said Garvin, continuing his train of thought. "That was the problem. Where were his sources? Who was feeding him? Did he have some hold over one of the Lords and Ladies? One of the other Warders? I was looking in the wrong place, wasn't I, Fionh?"

"It doesn't matter." She glanced at the form lying draped in the sheet. "Nothing matters now."

"And then it got worse," said Garvin, "Just when Blackbird was chosen as head of the Eighth Court, the leak went from a trickle to a stream. All of a sudden Altair knew where we were going to be, when we were going to be there, what we intended to do." He laughed. "In some ways I'm as guilty – I'd already made the connection. I figured that Blackbird was telling Niall, and Niall…"

I was having trouble believing what I was hearing. "How could you think that?" I asked him. "I've shown you nothing but loyalty, right from the beginning. I've done everything you've asked."

"And more beside," said Garvin, "which is what I expect. But a little thought nagged at me. The wraithkin have always been close. What if they'd overcome their prejudice and offered you something in return for information. What if the fact that you were one of them made the difference? What if they'd cut you a deal?"

"That would mean betraying Alex, Blackbird... My son..."

"Blood calls to blood, Niall. It always has and it always will."

"What are you saying? They are my blood." I nodded towards Alex.

"I'm saying sorry, Niall. I should have trusted you, but I didn't. Instead I kept you busy, trying to minimise the damage until I could figure out who your source was. It didn't do me any good, did it Fionh?"

"You should have killed him when you had the chance," said Fionh. "Then none of this would have happened."

"Always just at the edge of things," said Garvin. "Always there when she's needed, always listening attentively. That alone should have been a clue."

"That's not how it was," she said.

"Wasn't it? What did they offer you? What was the price?"

"You've got it all wrong," she said. "They didn't buy me. They didn't have to. You sold us all, Garvin. You mortgaged our future against what... a bunch of no hope, half-fey, helpless, graceless nonentities? How could you?"

"It's simple," said Garvin, "and as obvious to me as I thought it was to you."

"Obvious? The only thing obvious about them is that they are a poor substitute for the real thing."

Behind Fionh, lightning flickered in the clouds outside. There was a low rumble, a warning of what was coming.

"You hear that?" said Fionh. "He thinks he can do to me what he did to Fellstamp." She shook him, making him lift his chin even higher to avoid the knife and wobble precariously over the edge. "Take a good look down, lightning boy," said Fionh. "It's your future down there."

"Just let him go, Fionh. We can talk this through."

There was a bright flash. Fionh was outlined against the white. In my peripheral vision I saw Alex backing away. The thunder followed close this time, rattling the windows. Fionh didn't waver.

"You can't control it, can you boy?" she said. "It's beyond you. I'll tell you what, though. I can feel it building, and just before it strikes, your head is coming clean off."

"It's not me," said Sparky through gritted teeth. "I'm not doing it."

"You don't see it, do you? None of you do," said Fionh. "You wanted the Feyre to have children, but what you got was human children with power. He doesn't even know he's doing it. They're not fey! They're not anything!"

"They will be," said Garvin.

"No they won't! Look at Fellstamp. Look at him! That's what they do. That's what they are. They leech the life out of people until there's nothing left. What do we call it when a creature lives off another? Parasites! That's what they are. Parasites!" She pulled Sparky's hair, so that he was forced to arch his body backwards, stretching his throat against the blade as he leaned back to keep his balance.

"How long, Fionh?" asked Garvin.

"Any moment now," she said.

"No, I meant how long have you been in love with Fellstamp?" he said.

"What?" she said.

"It must have hurt, seeing him bed everyone but you. He never saw you like that did he? Fionh the ice queen was untouchable, and that's the problem."

"Shut up!"

"It must have twisted in your gut like a barb every time he charmed some girl under his covers. Every time, a betrayal."

"You don't know what you're talking about," said Fionh, but everyone in the room heard the lie.

"It won't bring him back, Fionh."

"I don't want to bring him back!" The words hung in the air. This time it was the truth. They words were torn out of her, and tears ran down her face. "I don't want him back," she said. "It's too late. I just want him to die."

The clouds behind them were luminous, bruised purple and black. The hairs on my arms stood up. I found myself stepping back, involuntarily, away from the window.

Garvin stepped forward. "Let him go, Fionh, and we'll say goodbye to Fellstamp together."

Her face distorted with anguish. Her hand was shaking under Sparky's chin. Sparky's eyes were wide with fear.

"Let him go," said Garvin.

When it came, the flash was brilliant. My eyes registered colours I'd never seen before. I didn't hear the blast or the thunder that came with it. Instead, I felt it; the shockwave tearing through my body as if I were insubstantial mist. Even with my eyes tight shut, I saw the outline of Fionh against the window, her hair standing out from her head like rays from a sun. Even with my eyes screwed shut, I saw the look on her face.

Strangely, she looked peaceful.

My hearing came back slowly. My ears were buzzing, and at first all I could hear were what sounded like squeaks and chirps. My eyes showed blotches of green and pink colour, obscuring my vision. Then I realised that Alex was screaming. As the spots cleared from my eyes I could see that Garvin had leapt forward and was lying over the parapet, reaching down. Alex was screaming at me, but I couldn't understand her. Then I realised she was screaming at me to help Garvin.

I ran forward and grabbed hold of Garvin as he slid a few inches more over the balustrade. By holding onto his clothes, I could stop him sliding forward any more. I leaned forward, one part of me expecting to see Fionh dangling from his outstretched hand, the Warders loyal to each other at the last, but instead it was Sparky's terrified face I saw staring up at me. On the paving below, I could see the outline of a body, slowly drifting into dust.

"Get help," Garvin spoke through gritted teeth. "I'll hold him."

"If I let go of you, you're both going over the edge." I told him.

"If you don't let go, I'm going to have to release him, assuming we don't get another strike first." Above the courts the clouds roiled in purple and dark grey, lightning flickering in its heart. I glanced backwards and Alex was behind me, chewing her knuckles in distress.

"Alex!" I shouted. "Get Amber. She's down with the Ways. Hurry!"

Alex disappeared behind me, while the thunder cracked and rumbled over our heads.

"If you start to feel it building, let go," said Garvin, through gritted teeth.

"How can I let go?" I asked him.

"You have to, or we'll all fry. Just do what you're told for once, Niall."

I glanced upwards. I could already feel the static rising in the air, taste the ozone tang. "Can you hold him for two seconds?" I asked Garvin.

"Probably," he said, clamping his hand on the balustrade. In truth there was little to hold on to.

I released my grip hesitantly, expecting any moment for Garvin to start slithering forwards over the edge. In a panicked moment I darted backwards, grabbing the edge of the sheet that was draped over Fellstamp, dragging it from him while grabbing the leg of Garvin's trousers, just as he started sliding forward again. I heard him grunt with effort as he reinforced his grip. Below him, Sparky wailed as he swung back and forth, buffeted by the sudden breeze rising under the clouds.

I whipped the sheet around in my hand, whirling it into a twisted strand and then leaned forward, half lying on Garvin to dangle the sheet over to Sparky. He flailed his arm out for it and missed, swinging from Garvin's grip, then caught it on the second swing. I took the strain, feeling the fine cotton strands' tension as some of Sparky's weight transferred to the sheet. Garvin was able push himself back momentarily, gaining a better grip.

There was a flash as lightning stabbed down from the clouds, striking somewhere on the roof above us with a heart-stopping crack. Thunder reverberated through us, drowning out all sound and making my bones ache. I tried to ignore the prospect of another strike closer to home and started drawing in the sheet. Garvin pulled too, gaining a better grip on the parapet. The sheet was stretched tight over the lichen covered stone, and I leaned back to take the strain better. There was a tearing sound and I fell backwards as the sheet ripped in two across the edge of the stone. Sprawled in the doorway, I expected any second to hear the soft thud of another body hitting the paving. Instead, I looked up to see Garvin hauling Sparky over the balustrade, reaching forward to grab his waistband to drag him to safety. He was dumped unceremoniously into the rain gutter, while Garvin collapsed back breathing hard.

"I thought I'd dropped him," I gasped, lying on my back, winded by the effort and the strain of holding on.

"I've got him," said Garvin, lying in an ungainly sprawl. "If it hadn't been for the sheet, I wouldn't have held him. You owe Niall your life, boy."

Sparky lay looking up at the bruised clouds as the rain started spattering down in huge drops. In a moment, it was a downpour, hammering on the balustrade, streaming into the gutters that ran along the edge of the roof.

"I'm alive," he said, in a tone of wonder as the rain soaked into his clothes and ran down his face. Where the knife had broken the skin across his throat and the blood was diluted by the rain, it soaked into his white tee-shirt in a pink stain.

"I'm alive."

By the time Alex brought Amber, it was all over. Garvin and I pulled Sparky in out of the rain and he lay on the floor, marvelling to himself.

Garvin and Amber went down to stand in the rain and pay their respects over the place where Fionh had fallen. It didn't matter to them that she had betrayed us all, they still went. I went out onto the balcony and peered over the balustrade at the place and in truth there was nothing there. The torrent of water overflowing the gutters had washed all traces of her away. I couldn't find it in me to feel sad. All this time she'd been betraying us to the Seventh Court. All this time, Garvin had thought it was me.

After a while they reappeared.

Garvin spoke. "The Warders are a team," he said, "but we are also individuals. When you put on the greys, you take on the mantle and you make decisions of life and death. That's what we do." He looked in turn at Amber and me. "When I give you Warder's discretion, I ask you to use your head, and follow your heart. I place my trust in your judgement and I leave you to decide. I did the same with Fionh. She made her decision, and I cannot blame her if she decided as I would not."

"She betrayed us all," I said.

"She followed her heart, as you follow yours" said Garvin, "and perhaps she was a fool for it, but that was her choice. As a Warder she made difficult judgements all the time. As a Warder, if you make a mistake, it's your life on the line. That was as much true of Fionh as it is of any of us. If her judgement was clouded, then that is between me and her. I gave her Warder's discretion. It was my responsibility. I should have seen the signs, and I did not."

I remained silent. This wasn't the time and the place to point out that she'd deceived all of us.

"She was a Warder," said Garvin. "And she will be remembered for her spirit, her intelligence, and her courage, not for the mistakes she may have made. I would say the same of any of you, and hope you would say the same of me."

He looked at me, long and hard, and it was me who looked away. I glanced sideways at Fellstamp, and I thought I saw him move.

"Garvin...?"

"We will all need time to think through the implications of what we have learned," he said. "This is not perhaps the time—"

"Garvin, it's Fellstamp..." There was definitely movement. The others moved forward.

Alex spoke. "Is he waking up?"

Garvin stepped forward, leaning over Fellstamp to place his ear over Fellstamp's mouth. After a moment, he withdrew. "It's time," he said.

Garvin took his place at Fellstamp's head. We placed ourselves around him, Amber and I on either side of him, Sparky and Alex at his feet.

"Should Sparky and Alex be here?" I asked Garvin quietly.

"Why not?" said Garvin. "Let them be witness."

No more words were said. I expected Garvin to give a speech, or at least eulogise his friend and comrade, but he was still and silent. The room that was host to such a recent drama was so quiet you could hear Fellstamp's ragged breath – in and out, pause, in and out. There was labour in it now, an effort to draw in air and release it. His skin hung from him like the sheet which had draped him, in folds.

"Not long now," said Garvin quietly.

When it came it was as a sigh. He released his breath and did not claim another. His body neither tensed, nor showed any sign of pain. He simply left, and his absent shell collapsed in on itself, the magic that had been held at his core, finally consuming his remains. Within moments there was only dust.

Garvin looked at each of us in turn. "It's done," he said. "Fionh was right about the end being close, at least."

"I'm sorry," I said to him, holding back the emotion that threatened to overwhelm me. "About both of them."

Garvin sighed. "Not your doing, Niall," he said. "We make our choices and we wear the consequences, for better or worse."

"That's an epitaph for all of us," said Amber.

Alex and Sparky left quietly, leaving the Warders present to their thoughts. I nodded to Garvin and took my leave, leaving him with Amber. Fellstamp was my comrade too, but even so I felt like an intruder at a private party. They had known and worked with him for many more years than I, and had shared both victories and defeats with him. I had no such claim and left them to their thoughts.

Making my way through the house, I made my way down to one of the empty rooms and found a quiet space to think in an abandoned sheet-covered armchair. I didn't bother to remove the sheet – the shrouded furniture suited my mood.

Had Fellstamp shared Fionh's secret hatred of the mongrel fey? I found that hard to believe and preferred to think that was what had kept the distance between them. I'd once fought Fellstamp in a duel, to earn my place as a Warder, and Garvin had hampered him with a broadsword, a slow, heavy, brutal weapon. Even so he had fought skilfully and with courage, until I'd pierced his shoulder with my sword. I remembered that it was Fionh who'd fallen to her knees beside him and pressed a pad to the open wound. We were supposed to be fighting to first blood – a scratch with the tip of the blade, not running him through. He'd pressed me with the broadsword until I had no choice but to use the lighter, faster blade with full force. I'd been lucky not to make a real mess of it, and pierce his heart.

Fionh had objected to my being tested in the first place, claiming that I was not ready for a Warder's greys. Frankly, I had agreed with her, and said so, but it was not my decision or hers. It was Garvin's.

I'd felt the cooling in my relationship with Garvin. I'd let him pressure me into action, sometimes for reasons I could not fathom, because I thought he had my best interests at heart. As it turned out, he'd been thinking I was betraying him at every turn, and intent on discovering why and how. Blackbird had said not to trust him, interpreting the wariness to some treachery on his part. Now that we knew who the traitor was, it made obvious sense. Fionh had been the Warder the courts trusted most. She had been present for more of their discussions – more even than Garvin. She was their conduit, their confidante, and had been given access to all their secrets.

There was a bitter irony in that betrayal, not just because she'd been the most trusted, but because she had maintained her loyalty in her own twisted way while secretly betraying the mongrel fey to the Seventh Court.

"I thought I might find you here." Garvin stood in the open doorway.

"I just needed a little space to think," I said.

"Can I disturb you?"

"Sure."

He came and sat facing me across the fireplace, and for a while he said nothing.

"I was thinking about Fellstamp, and about Fionh," I said.

"They are foremost in all our thoughts," said Garvin.

"It seems that at least some of this can be laid at my door – mine and Blackbird's."

"I'm not blaming anyone," said Garvin, "Except perhaps Fionh. If I'd known that she felt that way then perhaps I would have been able to accommodate her elsewhere." He sighed heavily. "No, I'm kidding myself. If I'd have known, then I would have been forced to strip her of Warder status. I can't have Warders choosing their own sides and playing one off against another – she knew that."

"She was right about one thing. We've brought you nothing but trouble," I said.

"If that's true, and I'm not saying it is, then it is trouble of our own making. We set off down this road because it was what we had to do. I came to apologise."

"What for?"

"For not trusting you. For failing to recognise the treachery where it lay. For assuming that you were the traitor."

"It was an obvious conclusion," I said.

"And one exploited by Fionh to sow the seeds of doubt in my mind. When I think back… she used my own prejudice against me."

"It's where we are most vulnerable," I acknowledged, "and she was ever one to exploit a weakness."

"So she was."

"What are you going to do?" I asked him.

"Now? I'm going to go and tell the Lords and Ladies that the Warders are down to five. I'm going to tell them that their confidences may not be as secret as they would wish, and that the fault is mine. I'm going to offer my resignation."

"Resign? Why?"

"In these circumstances, it's the right thing to do. The Warders have failed them, and it's my responsibility. I was blind-sided and I should have known. That has led to the Warders going from seven to five. We are weakened and our enemies are all around us."

"Perhaps that was our enemy's intent. You don't think they'll accept your resignation, do you?"

"I don't know what they'll do," he admitted. "These are strange times, Niall."

"If you go, I'll go too," I said.

He shook his head. "I'm offering my resignation, but it's up to them to decide, Niall. I swore an oath to serve until they release me from service, as did you. It's not up to me whether I go. The same applies to you. You can't resign."

"What will the Warders be without you, Garvin?"

"That," he said, "is not for me to say." He stood and offered his hand, which is a gesture of profound trust amongst the Feyre where a touch can be an opportunity to exercise power over another.

I took his hand and held it for a moment. "I'm sorry about Fellstamp – about both of them."

"Me too," he said, releasing my hand and straightening his jacket.

As he left the room, I called after him, "Good luck."

The problem was, I thought luck had very little to do with it.

Fourteen

I was waiting for Blackbird when she returned from the meeting of the High Court. "I have something to tell you," I told her.

"Garvin just explained," she said. "We all need time to think through the implications. None of us openly suspected Fionh, and we're now all wondering who knew and who didn't. It was a surprise, I think, for most of us." She unzipped her dress and stepped out of it, hanging it carefully on the waiting hanger. "I wish I believed it was a surprise for all of us."

"Is Garvin still Head of the Warders?" I asked.

"For now. He's offered his resignation, but the High Court hasn't accepted it. They've asked for time to consider the matter, which would probably be the right thing to do if we had time. The trouble is, I don't think we do."

"So what happens in the meantime?" I asked.

"Nothing. That's the problem. Garvin asked the same question, and the answer was far from clear. They've asked for time, and he has no choice but to grant them all they want."

"Without Garvin, the Warders are leaderless," I pointed out.

"I never thought I'd hear myself say this," said Blackbird, "but we need Garvin. There isn't anyone else who can ensure the safety of the courts, and the idea of choosing a successor is ludicrous. Who will take his place? Amber? Slimgrin? Tate's a great Warder, but he's a follower, not a leader, and you're just not ready for that kind of role."

She didn't say it unkindly, but she saw my face fall. "I'm only stating facts, Niall. You are coming to terms with life as a Warder, but you're not ready to lead. You don't have the experience, or the confidence of the other Warders or the High Court, and you know it. The trouble is, I don't think anyone else does either."

She slipped into her skirt and top, and used the mirror to reorganise the tangled curls of her hair.

"Anyway," I said. "That wasn't what I meant when I said I had something to tell you."

"There's something else? I think I've had my share of surprises for one day, don't you? What now?" she asked. "Alex has disappeared again? More new arrivals? Another disaster to clean up?"

"I went to see Kareesh."

She put the dress away. "Did you take her anything? Not boiled sweets, I hope."

"She wasn't there."

"If she doesn't want to see you Niall, you mustn't take it personally. What did you want from her anyway?"

"You're missing the point. I went to see her and she'd gone."

"Gone? Gone where?"

"I don't know. Neither does Gramawl."

That got her attention. "I don't understand. She never goes anywhere without Gramawl. I don't think she's capable of going anywhere without him."

"It seems that may be a misconception," I pointed out gently.

She shook her head. "You've made a mistake. She

probably in one of her moods. She's being difficult. She can be like that for days."

"She's not there. It's deserted. Gramawl is waiting in the tunnels waiting for her return. I don't think he knows what else to do." I told her what I'd found at the top of the stairway, and my limited conversation with Gramawl.

She sat down on the bed heavily. "But where could she go?" asked Blackbird. "There isn't anywhere."

"She's gone somewhere," I said. "Maybe we can send out a message, you know, ask around, get people to look out for her?"

"It won't do any good," said Blackbird. "If Gramawl can't find her then no one else is going to be able to. I can't understand why she'd do that to him."

I sat down on the bed next to her. "Gramawl seems to think that she's going somewhere he can't follow." I said it as gently as I could. "He's so much younger than she is – more vital."

"She wouldn't leave him, would she?" she said. "Not like that."

I held her against me and she passed her arms around my waist and rested her head against my shoulder as if the world were heavy on her shoulders. I stroked her hair and tried to ease the burden, knowing that whatever I could do would not be enough.

After a while, we went down and collected the baby from Lesley, who was talking with Mullbrook in the Kitchen. The baby held his arms out to Blackbird to be picked up and then sat on her lap and played with her hair while she explained what had happened with Fionh. I think Mullbrook already knew, but he listened patiently, perhaps gaining some insight from Blackbird's own perspective. Then Mullbrook asked her about the naming ceremony, which I hadn't had chance to mention to her, and it came out that Lesley and I had been discussing it. I thought she would be cross with me for planning something without her, but she was OK about it, making suggestions and acknowledging that it was time our son had a name.

"You've chosen a name?" Lesley asked me. "Don't tell me what it is, but you have chosen one, yes?"

"We haven't really thought about it," I said. Blackbird looked strangely shifty, suddenly, for reasons I couldn't fathom.

"You do know it's your choice?" said Lesley, glancing at Blackbird.

"Traditionally, a daughter is named by the mother," said Mullbrook, "and a son is named by the father. You may choose not to follow such traditions…" His tone said he would much rather we did.

"You didn't tell me it was my choice," I said to Blackbird.

"I'm sure I must have mentioned it at some point," she said, her words jarring to my sensitive ear. "I'm sure I told you that we don't name our children until they reach six months," she said. "I possibly neglected to mention who gets to choose the name."

I gave her a long look.

"I would have told you," she said. "I've been busy."

I sat down. "So I get to choose? Can I ask around for ideas, or does it have to be done by me alone?"

"You may consult with whomever you choose," said Mullbrook, "but the final say is yours alone. Perhaps a family name might be nice?" he suggested.

"My Dad's name is Marcus," I said.

"I went to bed with a Marcus, once," said Blackbird. "He had golden hair all the way down to…"

"Maybe not Marcus, then." I said, giving her a stern look. I tried to figure out whether she was winding me up, but her words at least were true.

"Stephen's a nice name," Lesley suggested.

"I'm not keen on Stephen." I said.

"I think what Lesley was trying to tell you," said Blackbird, "is that Stephen is Mullbrook's name."

239

"Ah," I said. "I didn't mean…"

"No matter," said Mullbrook. "As I said, the choice is yours, but also the responsibility. You must choose a name that will suit your son, that he will carry with pride and honour, and that he will thank you for in years to come."

"No pressure, then?" I said. Lesley and Blackbird exchanged a look that was too brief to interpret. "Are you two plotting something?"

Blackbird shook her head innocently, while Lesley shared a smile with Mullbrook.

"I quite fancy something different," I said, "something distinguished. What about Julius?"

"A fine idea," said Blackbird. "Then we can call him Julie for short."

"Are you intending to torpedo every suggestion I make?" I asked her.

"If we don't call him Julie," she said, "the other children will."

"What other children?" I asked her.

Again, there was a look that passed between Lesley and Blackbird. What was going on between these two? "You're not pregnant again, are you?" I asked Blackbird. She shook her head, but it wasn't quite a no. "Is there something you're not telling me?" I asked her.

"I am," said Lesley.

"You are what?" I asked her.

"Pregnant," she said.

For a moment my mouth fell open, and then I recovered and kissed her cheek and told her what delightful news that was.

"Dave and I have been keeping it a secret, but as soon as it starts to show, everyone will know, I suppose."

"Dave?" I said. I felt a kick under the table while Blackbird looked entirely innocent. "He's a lovely guy," I said, realising I had strayed into potentially hazardous territory. "I'm delighted for both of you."

My son stretched out his arms to me, wanting to be part of whatever was happening, and it gave me an excuse to recover myself and lift him from Blackbird, sitting him in my arms where he could see what was going on. "So Lesley was suggesting we might need stewards for the Eighth Court," I remarked to Mullbrook, "though we're a little ahead of ourselves perhaps?"

"It often pays to plan ahead," said Mullbrook. In the periphery of my vision, Lesley was giving me meaningful looks while trying to avoid catching Mullbrook's eye.

"It's up to Blackbird, of course," I said to Mullbrook, "but I wondered if there was anyone you might recommend we should talk to?" I felt another kick on my ankle, but from the opposite direction. In this case I ignored it.

The faintest of smiles crossed Mullbrook's lips, and vanished so quickly that I wondered if it had been there at all. "Well," he said, "there are one or two names that come to mind, but you must understand that it would be a great loss to the courts. That kind of person would be very difficult to replace. We might need to go through a long selection and appointment process, and then there would be a handover, and maybe after five or six years…"

"Years?" said Lesley.

"Unless there's someone who would be willing to take on such duties who happened to be willing – someone I trust implicitly who has both the confidence of the courts and of Blackbird herself?" The smile played across his lips again.

She glanced between Blackbird and Mullbrook. "You're teasing me," she said to him.

"In part," he agreed, "but that doesn't mean I'm not serious too. It is a big commitment, and you have a baby on the way. You may want to consider whether this is the right time?"

"There'll never be another chance like this," she said.

"I find that at my age, Lesley, never is a word I hardly use at all," he said. "Take some time to consider it carefully. There will be other opportunities in due course, I'm sure, and if you decide that it's too much to take on at once then that can be accommodated. The important thing is to make the right decision." He laid his hand over hers and gave her a warm smile and a nod. "There's no rush."

"I think I've already decided," she said, glancing between Blackbird and Mullbrook. "I've been thinking about this a lot, but I didn't know how to ask."

"Let's take that as a statement of intent," said Blackbird, "and sleep on it. In the morning we will go to Grey's Court and see what we can see." She took out a large bronze key and held it up, turning it so that it caught the light in a dull gleam. "If you would like to come with me, Lesley, I would value your thoughts?"

She smiled. "I'd be delighted."

"I'll come too," I said.

"I was thinking you might do a spot of baby-sitting," said Blackbird. "Spend some quality time with your son?"

"I will spend some time with him," I said, "but I think it would be a good idea if someone went with you to Grey's Court. I can't put my finger on it, but there's something…"

"We are not in a position to look gift horses in the mouth," said Blackbird.

"Yes," I agreed, "but gift horses do have a habit of kicking you just when you least expect it, don't they?"

"I'm not taking the baby with us," said Blackbird. "We don't know what sort of state it's in. It could be a ruin."

"Don't worry. I'll ask Alex to look after him for a few hours. She'll be OK with that."

"Ah, yes," said Blackbird

"Did I miss something?" I asked.

"She's actually been very helpful," said Lesley. "I didn't even have to ask."

"There you are then," I said to Blackbird. The look she gave me said she was sceptical as to whether it would continue.

Alex was quite pleased with herself. It had been surprisingly easy to find out which room was Tate's. A few offers to help here, a bit of assistance there, and with a little gentle prompting, people would chatter away to you about all sorts of things. It had all been so easy. Now she was approaching his room, she could feel her resolve faltering. This had been a great idea when she'd been back in her own space, but outside his door it was a different matter.

All she had to do was talk to him about it. It was probably accidental – he probably didn't even know he was doing it. All she had to do was fix things between them, and she would be gone – no hurt, no foul. She could be grown up about it, and she was sure he could too. Even so, she stepped lightly, knowing it would do her no good because he would hear her anyway.

She tapped lightly on the door, her stomach squirming into knots. She mustn't be tongue-tied. She must be confident, assertive and straight. At the same time she prayed there would be no answer. She tapped again louder. No one answered. OK, if he wasn't there she couldn't talk to him. She turned away, but then hesitated. What if it wasn't accidental? What if he had some charm, or talisman that was doing this to her?

Her hand rested on the door handle. What if he was asleep in there? What if he had someone with him? What if it was someone female? That thought was particularly unwelcome. No, Tate wasn't like Fellstamp. If he was there then she would speak to him. If he wasn't, then it would be wise to find out what she was up against. As her hand turned the handle, she could hear the heartbeat thumping in her ears. The door opened with a light click.

"Tate? It's only me, Alex." The door swung open. "Tate?" The room was empty.

She slipped inside, placing her back against the closed door. She might not have long, and it would not do to get caught in here. The butterflies in her stomach were like an alarm.

She wasn't sure what she'd been expecting. Something grand and imposing perhaps? Instead there were soft muslin drapes hanging from a wooden rail at the window, filtering the daylight into a soft glow. The furniture was of very dark wood, deeply polished and burnished to a lighter chestnut shine in spots where it had seen long use. There was a half-height wardrobe over a set of drawers against the wall, and a wide chest against the opposite wall over which a long-handled axe was mounted on the wall. The room was dominated by the huge bed. She would avoid the bed.

"Is there something here?" she asked herself softly, wandering around the room, looking for some trace of herself – a lost trinket, a scarf or bangle, something that could be used against her. Beyond the wardrobe was a door to a bathroom. There was a shower that was easily twice as big as hers. Over the rail were soft white towels and on the back of the door was a linen robe which would cover her like a tent. When you were close to him you could forget how big he was. Another unbidden thought came into her head and she left the bathroom more quickly than she'd entered.

Back in the bedroom, she went to the stand by the bed, opening drawers and finding cufflinks and a pen and notepad, along with other small personal items. There was nothing of hers. She went to the chest, opening the lid and finding stacks of clothes, some weapons, clean towels. The chest smelled as he smelled – earthy, scented with something herbal and exotic with the slightest hint of musk. Was it a cologne; an aftershave, perhaps?

She closed the chest and climbed on top of it to run the tips of her fingers along the long handle of the axe, noting how the wood was worn where his grip held it. Then she realised what was doing and snatched her hand away.

"There must be something," she said. "It can't be nothing."

She went to the wardrobe and opened each drawer in turn, finding spare clothing, piles of underwear, and some leather-bound books that looked about a hundred years old. She wondered if one of them was a spellbook, and started leafing through them, only to discover they were history books, full of dates and events that were long since forgotten. There was no book of charms, and no secret diary that would give her a clue to what was going on. She closed the drawers and turned around.

It was a very big bed, but then it would have to be. He was a very big guy. Her hand rested on the quilted coverlet that was carefully turned down. Maybe this was just somewhere he slept? Maybe he had another house somewhere else and that was where he kept his secrets? There was nothing here that made it look like home – no personal clutter, no trinkets or mementos.

A distant noise brought her back to reality. She had failed to find anything but that didn't mean there wasn't anything to find. She quickly looked under the wardrobe and beneath the bed, finding not so much as a missing cufflink, or a lost pen. Why was it all so tidy? What was he hiding? She went back around the room, replacing everything just as she'd found it. When she was satisfied that no one would know of her visit, especially Tate, she cracked the door and listened for the sounds of anyone in the corridor outside. When she was sure she was unobserved, she stepped out, closing the door carefully and quietly behind her, and headed back to her side of the house.

"Score one to you," she muttered to herself, "but the game's not over yet."

After a while, Lesley left and then rejoined us, bringing Dave with her. Mullbrook produced a bottle of champagne from which Lesley would only accept the tiniest glass. Dave looked uncomfortable until we explained that he didn't have to make a speech, at which point he cheered up considerably, kissed Lesley to rowdy cheers from around the table and accepted our toasted congratulations.

I excused myself and took the baby upstairs to his bed, changing him and then spending a while reading stories to him while he settled down. The excitement of the day must have worn him out, because despite his effort to stay awake, his eyes drooped and he was quickly asleep. I continued reading until I was sure he was settled and then pulled the door to his room almost closed. There was something else I wanted to do, while I had a moment alone.

Taking revenge was not something I was generally given to. I didn't make a habit of bearing grudges – my view was that every grudge had to be carried, and it was you that ended up with the burden. In one case I would make an exception, though.

I placed my hand upon the mirror in my bedroom, and felt for the connection with the stillness behind the mirror. I'd asked Blackbird about mirrors once, and why I seemed to have a particular affinity with them. She didn't exactly know but speculated that perhaps all mirrors were subtly connected and that my affinity was not with the mirrors themselves, but with the space between them. As I felt the connection grow, I could feel the tension inherent in the connection, and I spoke two words.

"Sam Veldon?"

The surface of the mirror cooled, and around my hand the faintest mist of condensation clouded the surface. To me it felt like dropping a stone into a still pool, waiting for the ripples to return from some distant object. A buzzing emerged from within the mirror, and then a ringing tone. It rang five or six times and then was answered.

"Hello? Who's this?" There was background noise – a pub perhaps, or a busy restaurant.

I removed my hand without saying anything, withdrawing my intention from the mirror, and the connection faltered and collapsed. That was all I wanted for the moment, so I went back down to the kitchen to rejoin the conversation around the table.

After a while I went back upstairs to check on my son. I reached down into his cot and rested my hand on his forehead, stroking his hair. He sighed softly, content in the sleep of the innocent. Then I went back into the bedroom and used the mirror again. This time there was no mobile phone signal, only the rattle and squeal of a tube train running down the tracks. I waited for a lull in the noise, perhaps when the train slowed for signals or before a station, and then said, "Sam?"

"Huh?" A voice, questioning, as if he were half asleep, or drunk maybe. "Who's there?"

I took my hand away, and went to find Alex. I found her in her room, alone. "Are you OK?" I asked.

She looked momentarily as if I'd asked her some searching and incisive question, but then she relaxed. "Yeah, I'm OK."

"Come and join us," I said. "Mullbrook's telling stories in the kitchen."

"I don't know," she said. "Maybe I'll come down in a while." She sighed as if the weight of the world bore down on her.

"You always say that when you mean no," I said, echoing her words to me.

She looked at me curiously for a moment, and then relented. "OK," she said. "Are they good stories?"

"It's Mullbrook," I said. "When I left he was telling us how he stopped the cheese being stolen from the fridges by painting it with green food colouring."

We went together down to the kitchen and Amber had slipped in, standing against the back wall. I smiled at her, but she ignored me, continuing to rest against the wall near the door.

"You can come and sit down," I said, in low tones.

"On duty," she said. "But I can listen from here."

I sat Alex between Blackbird and I, and we were drawn into the storytelling. It had evolved into taking turns, where each would tell a story and then defer to the next. When it came to my turn, I hesitated. "I don't really have any stories," I said.

"What about the fishing village?" said Blackbird. "Tell them about Ravensby." So I told them about Greg, the vicar of Ravensby, and how he'd discovered his calling riding bikes at breakneck speed down the hills of East Yorkshire, and helped me find the missing girls. I missed out exactly what happened on the fishing boat, as perhaps that was a story for a different audience.

Then it was Alex's turn, and I thought she would be like me and have nothing to say, but almost immediately she began with what had happened at the top of Glastonbury Tor. The way she told it made it vivid for me. She described the universe torn open and laid out above her in such lucid detail that it was like being there. I could feel the piercing cold, hear the crunch of the frozen grass under my feet. It seemed more real when she told it than my memory of it, though I had been there, outside the protective barrier thrown up around the Tor. After she had finished there was silence for a short while. I think everyone felt as I did, in awe of what had she had seen.

Then it was Blackbird's turn and she told a story of two brothers who fought over the possession of a magical talisman. Each of the brothers thought it was meant for them and no other, and the lengths they went to in order to prevent the other getting it left me wondering how much of the tale was true and how much fiction. She never did say what the nature of the talisman was.

There were more stories, and when it came time to withdraw I was glad to see that Alex was reluctant to retire. It was the first time I'd seen her enjoying company for a while, and it left me hopeful and optimistic. She bade us good night, and went to her room in a better frame of mind than I'd seen her in for some time.

While Blackbird went to check on the baby, I placed my hand on the mirror once more. The connection was quick and easy. I could hear snoring through the mirror, a rhythmic rasp punctuating each breath.

"Sam?" I said.

"Wha–? What is it?" The voice sounded panicky.

I released my hand and let the connection fall away.

"What are you doing?" asked Blackbird from the doorway to the nursery.

"I'm preparing my ground," I told her.

"Who was that?" she asked.

"An old friend," I told her. "Someone who owes me a big favour."

"If he was a friend, why didn't you speak to him?" she asked.

"It was Sam Veldon," I said.

"Oh, was it? Perhaps I could speak to him. I have one or two things to say that would set his ears ringing."

"I have plans for Sam," I told her. "At the moment he thinks I'm dead, though there is a growing realisation that I might not be. I intend to capitalise on that."

"Just don't get shot again," she warned me. "Next time he might choose to shoot you through the head."

"I don't intend to give him that opportunity," I told her.

My intention was to stay awake for a while and wait until Blackbird slept, but I was more tired than I thought and slipped quickly into a deep sleep. It wasn't until the baby grizzled in his sleep in the small hours that I came awake again. I padded across into the adjoining room and stroked his hair in the red light from the night-lamp until he slept more peacefully. The more I could persuade him to skip his night-time feeds, the better. No doubt he would wake early and protest his hunger, but that was a fair trade if he would get into the habit of sleeping through.

When I was sure he was asleep again, I slipped into the bathroom, leaving the lights off, and placed my hand on the mirror, whispering into the glass, "Sam?" I felt the glass cool under my hand and heard the characteristic change in background noise as the space on the other side of the mirror opened up. I could feel a presence beyond the glass.

"I know you're there," said a voice. "Where are you?"

"Soon," I whispered softly, almost beyond the level of hearing. The words were swallowed by the mirror as I pulled my hand away and released the connection. I had what I wanted. Sam was awake, waiting for a word, living off nervous energy, wondering what would happen next. I had him where I wanted him. With a smile I went back to bed, and was soon asleep.

FIFTEEN

The next morning Blackbird was getting ready to visit Grey's Court. She was dressed practically, without the finery of the courts, in a plain skirt and loose top with a woollen coat over the top.

"You don't need to come, Niall. You can rest, here. It'll be fine," she told me.

"I want to come. I want to see what it's like."

"If you come, leave your sword here," she said.

"Why? If I don't need it, you won't even know it's there. I left the baby with Alex a few moments ago. She seemed happy enough to look after him, and it'll do her good. We won't be that long, will we?"

She started at me. "If you bring the sword, you'll draw it. We're not trying to intimidate anyone, just find out what the situation is and make a decision. It's as simple as that. There'll be no fighting."

"What if it's not what it appears to be?"

"Nothing's ever what it appears to be," she said, "but we'll deal with that when we come to it. It doesn't mean we have to start a war."

I met her gaze, and for once it was her that looked away. "OK, have it your own way, but you don't start waving it around without my say-so."

"Yes, Lady," I agreed.

"And you can stop that as well," she said.

"Yes, Lady."

Lesley had been sent ahead with Big Dave in the car, and the plan was to join them in the village near the house and arrive together. Angela met us in the room where the Ways converged. Blackbird had already found a route which would lead us directly to the village, and she led us down the Ways. Angela went after her and I followed them to a clearing in a wood, just outside the village of Rotherfield Greys in Oxfordshire.

We arrived on a cold, clear morning with mist still drifting through the trees like pale shadows and walked to the edge of the woods where the fields were still edged with frost from the clear night. We crossed a field to the road and walked into the village, finding the car waiting in the car park of the *Maltsters Arms*, just on the corner. We climbed into the back, while Lesley stayed in the front with Dave.

"Have you had a look yet?" asked Blackbird.

"We cruised past the house," said Dave. "It's set back from the road, but there was no obvious activity. There are a few working farms around it, but it was quiet."

"There's something else," said Lesley.

"Yes?" said Blackbird.

"Grey's Court is advertised as a National Trust property," said Lesley.

"National Trust?" said Angela.

"It's open for visitors for at least part of the year," said Dave. "You don't think this could all be some kind of weird prank?" he asked.

"I don't understand," said Angela.

"I think we have to go and look," said Blackbird. "Dave, if you would be so kind?"

The car pulled away and travelled through the lanes at a stately pace. We turned down a side road and travelled down a lane with the winter sun striping across the road through the trees. As we approached a sign, Dave slowed so that we could read it.

Grey's Court – National Trust, said the sign. Visitors welcome from March until October. Limited opening at other times.

"It's not open at the moment," I pointed out.

"So we're OK until March," said Angela, "and then what?"

"I'm sure something can be arranged," said Blackbird. "Let's go on and see the house."

The car followed the lane until Dave slowed at the entrance to the house and turned in, following the drive through more trees until it opened out into a broad meadow through which the drive turned in a long crescent. There was a signpost diverting the public off to a separate car park, but Dave ignored this and drove on to the house.

Leading off the crescent was a gravelled drive circling a raised lawn with flower beds in quadrants. The tightly pruned skeletons of roses were stark against the mulch and straw spread around them. In the summer, with the blooms full and heavy, it would be impressive but in the winter sunlight it looked stark and bare. The house behind them had a terraced garden stepping up to a bold frontage which overlooked the meadows and the woods beyond.

"Not bad for the price of a single white rose," said Angela.

Dave pulled up at a large front door which was sheltered by a stone porch supported by grey stone columns wound around with tendrils of ivy that spread out like questing fingers across the stone and brick frontage of the house. Everyone got out and stood by the car, looking up at the house as if any moment we expected some crusty old gent to storm out of the house waving a shotgun and demand we left the premises immediately.

Stone mullioned windows looked out over the meadows below three matching gable ends, each with a small square window. Red bricks formed horizontal stripes in the walls, a style characteristic of Tudor buildings, while tall brick chimneys topped each end of the building. It was clear that at some stage someone had decided to add additional features in pale Cotswold stone, which neither matched nor enhanced the original building. In my experience, few structures survived as long as this one had without someone "improving" them. I just hoped it hadn't been internally modernised by the Victorians.

Blackbird looked around our little group and then said, "Shall we go inside?"

I was first to reach the door, earning a disapproving look from Blackbird. Testing the brass door handle, I found it was locked. Blackbird held up a large bronze key and I stood aside while she inserted it into the keyhole slotted into the heavy oak door. The lock gave a heavy clunk as she turned the key, and the door swung ajar.

There was no sound from within. I stepped forward and said, "Shall we see if there's anyone home?" She nodded her assent and I pushed the great door back.

Within was an entrance hallway with stairs rising from one side to a gallery above. The floor was stone flags, and the stairway was dark wood, heavily grained and black at the edges. The odour of old stone and wax polish permeated the atmosphere. In the light filtering down from above, I could see there was a door set immediately to the left and double doors to the right under a gallery walkway. Around the doors, the wood had been carved into an elaborate pattern of heart-shaped ivy leaves, echoing the columns at the front.

I pushed the double doors open and entered a great hall with a massive stone fireplace which would not have looked out of place in one of my dreams, the grate dressed with dried flowers in red and gold.

"Hello?" I called. "Anyone here?" My words were swallowed as I walked slowly around the edge of the room. Light flooded in from the front windows, setting the edge of the fireplace, carved with flowers and vines under a stone lintel, into shadowed relief. In the centre of the room was a huge dark wood table set with benches along either side. The inner walls were decorated with rectangular wood panels to shoulder height, and then white plaster to the ceiling cornices. I drew the curtains back from the wall beside the fireplace, allowing daylight from a bay to flood into the room. The stone of the annex was yellower than the grey stone of the windows and the light was warmer as a result. I found myself approving of the change, the warm light lifting the rest of the room.

There were further double doors at the back which led into a large semi-circular space with a glass dome skylight – a garden room. Facing south, it captured the best of the winter sun but the room itself was bare. Through the windows I could see a formal rear garden laid out in ordered rows of carefully cultivated order, like a maze but more symmetrical, with a stone fountain at the centre. I went back past Angela and Blackbird and across the hallway to the other side.

"Hello? Is anyone home?" I called. The words sounded flat and dull in the space. There was a furnished sitting room around another stone fireplace, but again there was no sign of occupation. The cushions were plumped and showed no indication that anyone ever sat in the chairs or on the sofa. The tables were empty, the bookcases complete, with no empty spaces where books had been borrowed to browse and read.

I went through another door, finding a short corridor, and then doors to a kitchen and a storeroom. Everything looked ordered. Even the brooms looked as if they'd never swept the floors. The range cooker was cold, no food in the cupboards, no water in the pots. It looked like a home, but it was only a facsimile. No one actually lived here.

I banged open doors, calling for someone to answer, finding a boot room, complete with clean and completely unworn boots, a washroom with a dry jug and wash-bowl with a locked rear door.

Retracing my steps, I went quickly up the staircase and around the gallery. There were bedrooms large and small, the biggest with a great bed, curtains drawn back around a mound of covers. The pillows were all neatly placed, the beds carefully made. I found a bathroom, rel-atively modern compared to the washroom downstairs, and an ancient but serviceable toilet. I couldn't imagine that the house had been built with indoor plumbing, so I assumed that this, like the additions downstairs, had been added later.

I met Blackbird and Lesley coming upstairs.

"Is there sign of anyone?" Blackbird asked me.

"Nothing," I said. "No one lives here. There are no per-sonal effects, no shampoo or soap in the bathrooms, no clothes in the wardrobes. It's empty."

"That could be to our advantage," said Lesley, "though it's a bit spooky. It makes you wonder what happened to everyone."

I left them exploring the upstairs and went back down, thinking there must be somewhere that people actually spent time, and wondering whether there was a potting shed somewhere with people hiding in it.

I went back past the kitchen, through a maze of passages, into the store and found another door to the back. The door opened onto a different scene. I stood in the doorway, held back by instinct, and surveyed the room. Then I carefully closed the door and went back for the others.

I stood in the hallway and called. "Blackbird? Lesley? You better come and see this."

Angela appeared from the great hall, Dave behind her. Blackbird and Lesley came downstairs, and I led them though to the room at the back of the house. I opened the door and went inside, standing away from the desks, careful not to disturb anything.

There were two offices, modern in style, built into what

must have been an outbuilding. It was warmer than the rest of the house, probably due to better insulation. There were modern desks and office chairs, a couple of desktop computers, a small kitchen area, a notice board with leaflets and notices pinned to it – but no people.

More than that, the area showed signs of recent human presence. There were two coffee mugs on a desk, both part-full with coffee. I touched them and they were stone cold. Under a desk I pointed out a pair of men's brown shoes that had been placed carefully and left with no sign of the owner. I jogged the mouse on a computer and the screen flashed into life, showing a spreadsheet program that had been left open. On the counter in the kitchen area there was a mug with a dry teabag in it, as if someone had been making tea, and then been called away. There was even milk in the fridge – I sniffed it, finding it on the edge of going sour.

"I thought it was spooky before," said Lesley.

"Where are they?" I asked Blackbird. "It's like they just vanished."

"Maybe there was an emergency," said Blackbird.

"Or an accident," said Angela.

"Wouldn't they come back to use the phone," I suggested, pointing out the land-line on the desk. "Or just to get their shoes?"

"They might have been called away," said Dave. "Maybe they all went outside and left the key inside – locked themselves out, maybe."

"I don't like it," said Lesley, shuffling closer to Dave who placed his arm protectively around Lesley's shoulders.

"What's that?" asked Blackbird, pointing to the desk in the corner.

I turned to where she motioned and saw a white envelope on the desk. The words, *To the New Occupier*, were written on the envelope in looping script.

I picked up the envelope and passed it to Blackbird. "I guess that means you?" I said.

She smelled the envelope, then weighed it in her hand and shook it gently next to her ear, listening for what was inside. When she was satisfied, she tore one end off the envelope and extracted a piece of white paper, which she read loud.

Dear Occupier,

We are given to understand that you are the new occupier of Grey's Court and that the lease for the Trust has been revoked. This is unprecedented in our experience, but we have been assured that this is the case and that the effect is immediate. You will appreciate that these are highly unusual circumstances, and as a result we have been unable to make any preparations, especially with it being so close to Christmas. We never anticipated that the conditions in the lease would be invoked so suddenly.

We have been told that the house and everything in it is yours, and although we feel this may be open to legal challenge we are obliged to abide by the conditions of the lease, at least for the meantime. As a result, the staff have been asked to leave everything. We would also be grateful if you would look after the property the Trust has left in your care until the legal ownership of the items can be confirmed.

The house is a national treasure and I am sure you are aware that any deterioration in the condition of the property would be a loss, not only to the Trust, but to the nation as a whole. We would ask therefore that you treat it carefully and considerately.

Yours,
Cynthia Burgess
Legal Advisor, National Trust

"Does that mean the house is ours?" asked Angela.

"Perhaps," said Blackbird. "At least they believe it. They can challenge it, and we'd need a copy of the lease to know whether there is any basis for a challenge, but it sounds like they've accepted the situation, at least for the meantime. We can appoint lawyers to look at it if necessary, but for now, it's ours."

"It explains why it's so creepy," said Lesley. "I was beginning to think they'd all disappeared – like a house version of the Marie Celeste."

I wandered around the office, finding a newspaper left open, the crossword half-completed, a half-written note, an uncapped pen lying next to it. It was time to mention what was bothering me. "There is something," I said. They all focused on me. "Do you feel it?"

They all looked at each other. Blackbird nodded slowly, "I feel it too."

"I can't place it," I told her. "To begin with I thought there was a Way-node here, and maybe there is, but I can't find it. I've been all around the ground floor, and I can't see any signs of a cellar or a door leading down. Is it just me?"

"No, she said. Whatever is here is very faint. It's like a residue, or an echo of something."

"Do you think it is actually haunted?" asked Lesley.

Blackbird shook her head. "No. There are no ghosts, but Niall's right. Something was here, long ago. It might explain the strange business with the lease."

"You think that's part of it?" I asked her.

"You have to admit, it's an odd arrangement. I know the National Trust doesn't own all the properties they operate, that's not so unusual, but the business with the rose – that must be unique."

"So what was here?" I asked.

She looked around the deserted office. "Originally? A shrine, perhaps, or maybe there was a weak Way-node here that we haven't found. If the house is mentioned in the Domesday Book, then it's over ten centuries old – predating the Norman conquest." She gestured around her. "The house you see now would have been built later – it's mainly Tudor with some late additions, but there would have been a structure prior to that, probably a smaller house. It could have been destroyed in a fire, or fell into ruin, and later rebuilt in a Tudor style. Who knows?"

"And if there's a legal challenge?" asked Angela. "We don't have any money for lawyers and court fees."

"Perhaps we can get legal aid?" I suggested.

Blackbird frowned at me. "Once the Eighth Court is established, we have an income," she said. "That's part of the reason for our search for a home. The income of the courts is divided equally between the courts, and once we are established within the courts we qualify for a share of that. Teoth and Krane tried to challenge that, but their own share of the income is based on the same principle. If they cut us off then they leave their own sources of income open to challenge."

"I don't understand," I said. "Where do the courts get money from? They don't make anything – none of them do any work that I'm aware of."

"You forget," said Blackbird. "The courts are very old. They've had land since ownership became possible: farms, houses, property, tied up in trusts and held by proxies. There are investment funds, charitable trusts – they own houses like this one, all over the place. This may have been leased by the National Trust, but you have to ask, who did they lease it from? If you work hard enough and pursue it long enough, you could probably trace the lease back to something that links to the courts. That would explain the arrangement with the rose rent. I know for a fact that they are the ultimate owners of some very exclusive property in London. The income exceeds the outgoings, so year on year, it just accumulates."

"So why don't we simply use the money we get from that to buy a place?" asked Angela.

"We have income, but no capital," explained Blackbird. "In order to receive an income, we need to establish the court. Without capital we can't buy a place, and without a place we can't establish a court. What do you suggest, we take out a mortgage?"

"It's a thought," Angela said.

"You're not thinking this through. We'd have to prove our identity, and enter into financial debt with a bank based on income for which we are not able to disclose the source. That's not going to work, is it? We'd be better off declaring your semi in Tamworth as a court, though I doubt you're quite ready to donate your house to the cause."

Angela's silence confirmed Blackbird's assessment.

"If we had this place for a while, though," said Dave, "we could build up a reserve, and once we have a reserve we can find somewhere else if we need to."

"We, Dave?" said Blackbird.

Dave suddenly looked embarrassed at his verbal slip. "I thought... you know... if Lesley is going to be Steward...?"

"She hasn't decided yet," said Blackbird. "It's a big commitment," she said, "for both of you."

Dave and Lesley shared a hesitant smile. "So are we moving in?" asked Lesley. "Is this the home of the Eighth Court?"

Blackbird looked around her slowly. "I think it will do for now. We'll have to resolve any dispute about legal ownership. We could start by returning the possessions of the people that worked here, as a gesture of good faith."

"So we inherit the contents?" I asked.

"They will certainly challenge that," said Blackbird, "but yes, in part. We might have to purchase our own furniture, but that's only to be expected. Once we have an income it all becomes easier."

"That's not going to happen until the New Year, though," I pointed out. "None of this will be sorted out before Christmas. What do we do in the meantime?"

"I will return to the High Court and inform them that we have an establishment and that the Eighth Court will leave the High Court by the solstice, as agreed. They will want to see the new court for themselves, no doubt, but that can happen in due course. Before we can accept visitors we need to start acting like a court. We need to take down the National Trust signs, and make it look like someone lives here. We need to secure the bounds of the estate and set wardings in place. For that we need the court to have members."

"I can bring people in," said Angela, "provided we can accommodate them."

"Actually that's something I meant to speak with you about," said Lesley to Blackbird. "Niall was suggesting a celebration."

"I was?" I said.

"It was your idea," said Lesley, "and once Mullbrook heard about it he was very supportive. With your permission, Lady, we'd like to throw a party."

"What kind of party?" asked Blackbird, looking between me and Lesley.

"A naming celebration," said Lesley. "At the same time it will give us an opportunity to bring everyone together for the first time under one roof. We certainly have room – the great hall would be ideal, and I think we could accommodate everyone as long as they're willing to share."

Blackbird looked at me, and I shrugged, "I was thinking of a few friends and family. It's rather gone out of my hands," I said.

"Very well, she said. "How long will it take to bring everyone together?"

"For a party?" said Angela. "If you're inviting them, they'll come."

"We're inviting them," said Blackbird, "by ancient custom, we are summoning the court. Anyone who has pledged allegiance and wishes to take blood oath and become part of the Eighth Court must attend. It's less of an invitation and more of a summons," she said. "Do you still think they'll come?"

"They have nowhere else to go," said Angela. "They'll come."

"Tomorrow is the winter solstice," said Blackbird. "It's the shortest day followed by the longest night of the year, the best possible night for a celebration. Lesley, can it be done?"

She nodded. "I think so, provided people are prepared to muck in. Mullbrook will help."

"That could be problematic," said Blackbird. "We cannot be seen to use the resources of the High Court for our own purposes. Teoth and Krane will undoubtedly object."

"Lady, you don't understand. I don't think I could stop Mullbrook helping, even if I wanted to," said Lesley.

Blackbird smiled. "You're probably right," she said, "but you might make him aware of the sensitivities and ask him to be discreet."

"Discretion is his default position, Lady," said Lesley.

"And if you are going to start calling me Lady," said Blackbird, "then I am going to start referring to you as my steward."

At that Lesley smiled, and Dave hugged Lesley.

"Very well," Blackbird said, "Angela, summon the court." She turned to me. "Niall, you have until tomorrow to decide what name our son shall have."

"I was thinking," I said. "We don't have a Tarquin in the family."

"Don't you dare," she said.

While Lesley and Dave made their way back from Grey's Court to begin making arrangements for the following evening, I travelled back with Blackbird and Angela.

"You should arrange for people to arrive an hour before dusk," said Blackbird to Angela. "We will walk the bounds of the Eighth Court together, so you'd better tell them that we'll be outside – bring boots and outdoor clothes if that's appropriate. They'll have opportunity to explore the house a little and find a bed for the night after that. Lesley will be setting up in the great hall, and we'll begin receiving people at eight."

"Have you done this before?" I asked her.

"It's not hard to see that this could turn into chaos if it's not organised properly. It's no worse than directing students at college, and frankly easier than organising an academic conference. The trouble with academics," she said, "is that they can never agree on anything, least of all arrangements. Niall, I will need you in the great hall before eight. Bring your sword."

"My sword? Are we expecting trouble?"

"We will be swearing blood oaths," she reminded me. "And that requires blood. Bring your sword and something to wipe the blade that won't show the stains. You don't want people fainting when you pick up a blood-soaked rag."

"We could ask Garvin to do it," I suggested. "He's done it before."

"No, I want you to do it. It's a symbolic moment and it needs to be done well. I trust you." She rested her hand on my arm. "You'll be fine. Just don't lop anyone's hand off."

"No pressure then," I said.

"We'll let people meet each other, and then when everyone's had chance to socialise, I'll say something to the assembly. I don't know what, yet, but I'll think of something."

"A welcome address, perhaps," suggested Angela.

"Something of that nature. After that, we'll name the baby, which means it's your turn to stand up and say something, Niall. It'll be the first naming ceremony in a fey court for hundreds of years, so you'd better come up with something good."

"This gets better and better," I said.

"Apparently this was all your idea," said Blackbird, smiling, "so you can't complain about it now. You keep telling me that's it's time our son had a name, and now's your chance. It's your choice, so choose well."

She didn't say, *or else*, after that, but I felt that it was implied.

"Speaking of our son, you could relieve Alex from looking after him. Lesley will have her hands full with the arrangements for tomorrow, but you could bring him back here. I need to find him something to wear when he's presented to the court. What are you going to wear?" She asked me.

"Just Warder grey," I suggested. "I don't really have anything else.

"As good as anything, and it emphasises your neutrality. Angela, can you ask Mullbrook if he can have one of the new dresses ready for tomorrow? I'll need to be presentable, and I'll need something to wear when we beat the bounds – I can't do that in a court dress..."

I left them to their discussions and went to find Alex. She was in her room, headphones plugged into her ears while the baby sat in her lap. I had to wave at her to get her attention. She didn't look very happy at being left with the baby all morning.

"Are you OK?" I asked her.

"Yeah," she sighed. "I'm fine." That was clearly not the truth.

"I'll take him off your hands now," I said. "Thanks for looking after him. We couldn't have done what we did this morning and taken him along."

"That's OK," she said. "He's been no trouble at all." This time her words rang true.

"Is something the matter?" I asked her.

"No," she said. She must have heard the lie in her own words, because she added, "Nothing you can do anything about."

I sat on the bed, gathering up my son, who kicked his legs furiously as soon as he was lifted up.

"You can tell me anything," I told her. "You know that, don't you?"

"I guess," she said. "If there was anything to tell."

"You should see the new place," I said, trying to find

something that would lift her spirits. "It's quite some-thing."

"I s'pose I'll get to see it eventually," she said, refusing the bait.

"Sooner than you think. You're being invited to attend a gathering at the new court, along with all the others. There's going to be a party. I have to make a speech." I tried to make it sound impressive.

"You're not going to be embarrassing are you?" she asked.

"That depends whether you cheer up or not," I told her, smiling. "I might have to tell everyone how you're my best girl, my own little angel."

That was usually enough to get her going, but instead she just shrugged. "If you want," she said. "Sorry, I'm just a bit down, that's all."

I held out my arm and she gave me a brief hug. The baby reached out a hand for her, and she gave him her finger which he promptly stuck in his mouth. "You could give Blackbird and Lesley a hand," I said. "They're going to be running around like mad things for the next day or so. I'm sure they'd appreciate it."

"Yeah, maybe I will," she said, reclaiming her finger from being gummed and wiping it on the bedclothes.

"Well don't sit up here moping all day. It won't make you feel any better, trust me," I said, standing up. "If you're helping, at least you can be miserable in good company. Blackbird's choosing something to wear, and I guess you'll be needing something too?" I prompted. Usually the mention of shopping opportunities was enough to cheer her up.

"Who's going to be there?" she asked.

"Everyone who's anyone," I said. "In the Eighth Court, at least. There are more of us than you might think these days."

"Is anyone else going? Garvin or anyone?"

"Garvin? No I don't think Garvin will be there. Why do you ask?"

"Just wondering," she said. "It's not everyone, then?"

"It's for the new court," I told her. "We'll be moving to the new place, you'll have a new room and everything."

"Leaving?" she said. "But I was just getting used to it."

"We can't stay here," I told her. "We've only been able to be here as guests of the High Court. Now that we have our own court we need our own place."

"I s'pose," she said again. Somehow the news seemed to depress her even further.

"Once you have a room that's properly your own, you'll be able to have your own things around you. Won't that be nice?"

"Yeah," she said. "Nice."

Unable to penetrate into whatever it was that was bothering her, I left her to it. She was a teenage girl and maybe she was just having the blues that day. It happened. At least she wasn't shouting or bothering the plumbing. Maybe she'd cheer up in a bit and join in.

I took the baby back to Blackbird and then made my excuses on the pretext of Warder duties. The next couple of days were likely to be busy ones and I had some outstanding business with a certain Sam Veldon that I wanted to deal with before I got embroiled into Eighth Court business. I found an empty room on the ground floor with a mirror in it.

"Sam Veldon," I said into the mirror. It misted slightly and then cleared to the sound of low snoring. "Sam!" I shouted into the mirror.

"Wha–?" said a voice. "Who's there?"

"You know who this is," I said, "don't you."

"You're dead," he said. "I shot you. You're dead." He sounded only half awake, as if he were wondering whether he was dreaming.

"If that's true, then I won't be able to meet you on Westminster Bridge at midday, will I?"

"Westminster? What's that gonna do?" He wasn't

making a lot of sense, but then he'd had a disturbed night, and had just been wrenched from the limited sleep I'd allowed him.

"Midday – don't be late." I released the mirror, sure now that he would be there. I had one or two preparations to make and then I would go and meet him, and this time I would be the one who was waiting.

Sixteen

On a December afternoon on Westminster Bridge, even when the low winter sun is at its strongest, no one stops to admire the view. It was bitterly cold. People huddled past wrapped in scarves with coats buttoned tight, eager to escape the freezing wind off the river.

I waited in full view for Sam, knowing he would watch for me. I took a risk. It was possible he could be in one of the buildings overlooking the bridge with a rifle, taking a bead on my head, but I didn't think so. That was the reason I'd chosen this spot. It had a good view of the Houses of Parliament and the security services tended to take a dim view of people with sniper rifles and telescopic sights so close to the seat of government – something Sam would be aware of. He'd almost succeeded once in killing me by getting in close. I wasn't sure whether he'd worked out that I could avoid the glassy stare of the CCTV cameras that were undoubtedly trained on the bridge, tracking everyone who crossed. Maybe he was relying on that.

People hurried past me, eager to reach the relative shelter of the buildings on each bank, their breath clouding in the chill air before it was whipped away upstream. Sam stood out as he approached. He didn't huddle and he didn't rush. His coat was loosely wrapped around him, giving him easy access to the inside pockets.

You bastard, I thought. You're planning to shoot me again.

He looked grim. The stubble was raised on his cheeks where he hadn't shaved for days. There were loose pockets of saggy skin under his eyes and dark smudges that spoke of too much whisky and not enough sleep. He paused and checked behind him, timing his walk so he would reach me while no one else was passing. I could see him weighing it up – one to the chest, one to the head, then over the parapet into the Thames.

He walked up to me. "Peterson," he said. "Last time I saw you, you were dying."

"I'd love to say there were no hard feelings," I told him.

He turned as if to glance back and went for the inside pocket of his coat. That's when Amber kicked his legs out from under him. He landed badly with a dull crump from his shoulder. "Aaagh!" he shouted.

Amber stood on his wrist and placed the tip of her blade on his neck, pulling out a wallet, a mobile phone, a card wallet and an automatic pistol from his coat and jacket pockets. I caught them one by one, tossing the pistol over the parapet into the Thames.

"Sam," I said. "I do believe your intentions were less than honourable."

"Fuck off!" he said, trying to pull his wrist out from under Amber's boots.

"Be polite," I advised him. "You don't want to upset her."

"Go and f–" He got as far as that when Amber hauled him up by the front of his coat and swung him round, and tossed him straight over the parapet. He screamed as he went over, flailing his arms in desperation. I waited a moment, and then leaned over the parapet. Sam was dangling by one ankle from Amber's grip. His free leg and arms were flailing around wildly.

"I warned you," I told him. "I tried to tell you. You're just not very good at accepting advice."

"You bastard," he shouted. "For fuck's sake!"

"If I were you," I said. "I'd stop struggling. You might loosen her grip and that would leave you with two choices. You'd hit the water hard, and you might go unconscious if you were lucky." I stared down at the brown water heading towards the sea. "You might just drown."

Sam started shouting. "Help! Heeeeelp!"

"On the other hand, I'm not sure how good a swimmer you are. If you hit the water right, you could make it to the surface. Of course, at this time of year in these conditions you have about a minute. Hypothermia will be nicer than drowning. It'll be like going to sleep. Do they teach you survival in your line of work?"

"Heeeeeelp!" he shouted. Amber raised one eyebrow, as if she were considering letting go.

"No one can hear you," I told him. "You have just one chance, though Amber thinks that's one chance too many. I'm going to have to convince her not to let go."

"I hate you, Petersen!"

"Who gave you the bullets?" I asked him.

"Fuck off!"

Amber's grip slipped an inch up his ankle. He screamed like a girl.

"Who?" I asked.

"I can't tell you," he said. "I don't know anything."

"OK," I said. "You're probably right. Even as a policeman trained in undercover work, your powers of observation were probably off that day. I understand. I'm just sorry we couldn't make this last longer. Amber, drop him."

"Noooooooooo! Wait! Wait!" He swung from her grip, his fingers scrabbling upside down against the base of the parapet searching for some grip, some handhold.

"What for?" I asked. "I already told you that I didn't kill Claire. You don't believe me. I think I know who did, but your chances of catching him are approaching zero about as rapidly as you'll be approaching that river in a moment. I don't kill people who don't try and kill me, whereas my colleague Amber here has no such scruples. To her you're just a dead weight, shortly to have the emphasis on dead."

Sam started kicking again, "For God's sake. It'll be cold-blooded murder."

"I don't kill people who don't try to kill me, but you're not on that list, are you Sam? You're the sort of guy who shoots someone through a coat. You leave them to bleed to death. We have nothing left to say. Amber's right, the only thing left between us is a loose end. One that can easily be severed."

"Wait! Wait! I can tell you something. I can."

"What?"

"Not from down here. Haul me up. I'll tell you if you get me up."

"Naah," I said. "You're bluffing." Amber's grip slipped another inch. He screamed. She had hold of his foot now. I noticed the way the hairs on his legs were caught in her grip. That must be quite painful.

"No! They were spooks. They knew who you were. They told me about you. They said you'd killed her."

"Who did, Sam? Who did?"

"They didn't give names. Their type never do. For Christ's sake, I'll tell you everything, just get me up!"

"What do you think?" I asked Amber.

"I think he'd say anything right now," she said. "He doesn't yet realise that if he's lying I'm going to toss him over again, and this time I'm not catching him."

"I swear," he said. "I'll tell you it all. For God's sake."

"God won't help you now," I said. "Not in this world." I could hear that he was telling the truth, though. He would tell us everything, and I needed to know.

"Get him up," I said.

When Amber brought him up, I pulled off his coat and threw it over the parapet into the Thames. He watched it float out on the stiff breeze and then vanish.

"That's you if you don't tell me everything I want to know," I said.

"For fuck's sake," he said. He was shaking, and it wasn't from cold.

"Watch your mouth," I said, glancing at Amber. "You'd better learn to keep a civil tongue in your head if you want to live."

Sam held the glass of whisky to his lips, his hands still shaking. We had adjourned to a pub, the Slug and Lettuce, part of a chain conveniently situated just near the old County Hall. We had followed Sam to the place, making it clear that he could run, but then Amber would have to hamstring him and carry him back to the bridge.

He was seated opposite me, nursing a triple scotch cupped between his hands.

"The meter's running," I reminded him.

He visibly tried to stem the trembling in his hands. "There were two of them," he said. "There are always bloody two of them." He looked between Amber and me. I waited for more.

"They came to me at work, arranged an interview room. It was official," he said.

"Officially what?" I asked.

"They came to give me the news. They'd brought photos and everything – her face, lying in a pool of blood. The initial forensic analysis, before the autopsy. The death certificate – it said cause of death was loss of blood."

"What did they want?" I asked him.

"They showed me a picture. It was a photo of you just outside the crime scene. You looked panicky, desperate. They asked me if I knew who you were."

"And you told them you did."

"You don't tell that sort anything if you don't have to. They told me what had happened, that there was no

273

family, few friends. They asked me if I wanted to arrange a funeral. I didn't see the point. They left me to it."

"So how did you get the bullets?" I asked him.

"After they'd gone I started going through the files. I knew there was stuff on you. If I could find you then we could settle it for good. I went through everything I was cleared for."

"And?"

"And then they came back. They knew I'd been through your files. They knew what I knew, and a lot more besides."

"Did they say where they got that information?"

"Don't be daft. They said you were a problem. They said you were a loose cannon and that sooner or later, someone would have to deal with you. I volunteered. They gave me the bullets. They were issued for the firearm I already had, so they'd done their research. I didn't care. I just wanted you dead." He stared at me, and there was hate in his eyes.

"I didn't kill her," I repeated, shaking my head.

"I don't fucking care!" he shouted. "Ever since you arrived it's all gone pear-shaped. Everything is screwed up and fucked over. If you didn't kill her, then you made it happen, I just know it."

I didn't challenge that view. I wasn't sure I could. "She knew it was risky," I told him. "She was braver than you are."

"Too fucking right," he said, taking a good mouthful of scotch.

"What were their names?" I asked him.

"They didn't introduce themselves. You learn not to ask too many questions."

"So you have no idea who they were."

"They knew what they were looking for, they had clearance to see what I was checking on the system, they had the authority to commandeer a meeting room. They were spooks. That's all I needed to know."

That didn't sound quite as true as the rest of it. "If you

start holding out on me, Sam, I'm going to leave you to Amber." Amber smiled sweetly at him.

He sighed. "I overheard something between them. They were talking between themselves. They mentioned a couple of names."

"What names."

"A codename, and his secretary."

Amber and I exchanged a glance. "Tell me."

"I can't remember. It wasn't important."

"Try and remember."

"As I said, at the time it wasn't important. An odd name, obviously a codeword, and some woman."

"Was it Secretary Carler?" I asked him.

He looked up over the glass. "Yeah," he said. "That was her. Carla, that was her name. You know her?"

Amber caught my eye and shook her head very slightly. I wasn't ready to let it go, though.

"The other name, what was it?"

He shrugged. "I only remembered it because it was odd. It sounded like 'deference' – something like that. These guys love their codes and ciphers."

"You're going to do me a favour," I told Sam.

"Like hell I am," he said.

"The choice is simple. You can do what I ask and you walk. Either that, or I'm leaving you to Amber, and I won't look back. Which is it?"

"You wouldn't," he said.

I stood up. "I can find him myself if I have to. It will take me longer, but I'll do it."

"Find who?" said Sam.

"Secretary Carler," I told him. "It's a he, not a she, and I think he and I need to chat."

"Find him yourself; it's nothing to do with me."

"Fair enough. Amber, I've finished with him. He's all yours."

"Hey," he said. "I told you everything I know. That was the deal."

"No, Sam. The deal was that you get to live as long as you're useful to me. You shot me. Twice. Now you find out the true cost of those two bullets."

Amber took out a long knife. The edge glinted in the dim light of the bar.

"Hey!" he called. "You can't leave me with her. She's psychotic."

"What did you say to me, Sam?" I called over my shoulder as I reached the door. "Enjoy the rest of your life, for the short time you have left."

I left the pub and a moment later, Sam was dragged out of the door by Amber. He was swearing and kicking, but Amber was calm and relentless. Everyone in the bar carried on as if nothing was happening. They simply didn't notice that someone was about to be murdered on their doorstep, even though he was screaming for help. She had his arm pinned behind his back and painfully twisted, and the long knife held up against his throat, restricting his ability to twist out of her grip without cutting his own throat. She marched him past me.

"Bye," I called after him. I'm not normally cruel, but maybe Amber was right.

"Wait, wait! I'll do it!" he shouted.

Amber paused. "He'll turn on you as soon as you let him go," she said.

I walked up to him slowly. "Is that right, Sam? Will you turn on me?"

"No, I swear," he said, through gritted teeth. His words rang with falsehood.

"I want you to remember something," I told him. "I can find you, wherever you hide, no matter who you pretend to be. I don't even have to be there. I can creep into your dreams and kill you in your sleep. You know it's true. The only reason I'm letting you go is because I want to know who Secretary Carler is, where he works, where he lives, who he works for. Do you understand?"

Amber pressed the edge of the knife in tighter. "Yes," said Sam.

"The other name I want information on is De Ferrers," I spelled it for him. "That's what you thought you heard, isn't it?"

"Could have been," he admitted.

"Find me that information and meet me back here in an hour."

"An hour?"

"Either that or start running, and you better not stop. Ever."

Amber released him and threw him forward onto the ground. He sprawled out like a drunken derelict.

"I can't get that sort of information in an hour," he said. "You have to give me more time."

I shook my head, and tossed him back his wallet, mobile phone and the card wallet. "No Sam, time's up. You have an hour."

Amber and I walked away into the winter sunshine and the Embankment. I threw a glamour around us, and to Sam's eyes it must have looked like we'd just vanished.

"Would you like a hand?" Alex asked from the doorway.

Blackbird, who had the baby naked on the bed, a wipe in one hand and a clean nappy in the other, wasn't really in a position to refuse. "You could put that dirty one in a sack and put it in the bathroom for now. I'll take it down to the bins later.

"They're very un-ecological, you know," said Alex. "They just end up in landfill in the end." She put the heavy nappy in the disposal sack and tossed it into the bathroom.

"I'm not in a position to wash terry nappies myself, said Blackbird, "and it seems a poor reward for the care and comfort that we receive from the court staff to present them with a pile of dirty nappies to wash every day, don't you think?"

"I s'pose," said Alex. "Mum used disposables with me, too, when I was little, but we didn't think so much about the planet in those days."

"It's a very recent phenomenon for people to be concerned about their environment," agreed Blackbird. "And not a moment too soon, in my opinion. Is that what you came to see me about – to remind me to be conscious of the socio-environmental impact of our lifestyle?"

"I came to see if you needed any help," said Alex, looking slightly hurt but sounding disingenuous.

"I see," said Blackbird. "Well that's very thoughtful."

"And to ask you a question," said Alex, almost as an afterthought.

"What kind of question?"

"About magic. I was wondering," she mused, "whether you would you be able to tell if someone was casting a spell on you?"

"Casting a spell?" said Blackbird. "What a quaint idea. We don't cast spells, Alex. We exercise power over ourselves, our environment, and others. Is that what you mean?"

"Kind of," she said.

"Would you like to be more specific?" asked Blackbird.

"What if someone laid a glamour on you, or on themselves, so they would appear... different?"

"The Feyre can appear how they wish to appear," said Blackbird, popping together the vest and tickling the baby's stomach so he gurgled at her and tried to grab her fingers.

"More than appearance," said Alex. "What if they made you like them more? Made you think about them, even when they weren't there?"

"It's a simple enough glamour," said Blackbird, "but like most simple things it's easy enough to unravel. A simple warding should do it. If you ward yourself against them then they have no power against you."

"Even if they touched you?" she asked.

278

"If they were touching you at the time," said Blackbird, "then that would be more difficult. You would have to break the hold of their power. You could do that with magic, or you could do it physically. What's this in relation to, Alex?"

"Nothin' much," said Alex, clearly lying.

Blackbird held out the baby to her. "Here, hold onto him for a moment while I put all this away." She busied herself putting away changing mats and nappy cream while Alex held her baby brother. The baby liked Alex because her hair would play with him even if she wouldn't. When Blackbird looked up, the baby was trying to catch hold of a curl that was doing its best to evade his grasping fingers, while at the same time he was trying to swat away another curl from tickling his ear.

Blackbird finished putting things away and sat at the desk, turning the chair out to face Alex. "This is all theoretical?" she asked.

"Potentially," said Alex.

"You need to be careful who you allow to touch you. Touch is for people you trust – that's true for humans and even more so for the Feyre. Is there someone who has touched you against your will?" asked Blackbird.

"No," said Alex, a little sulkily.

"Is this to do with Sparky?" asked Blackbird, remembering the mud-smeared sweatshirt and the grass-stained jeans.

"No," said Alex. "Sparky's just a friend. We're mates."

"Then why do you look so unhappy?" asked Blackbird.

"I… I was touching, as in physical contact with someone…" Alex read Blackbird's expression. "Not like that. It wasn't… you know. It was something else. I can't talk about it, but we touched, and now… now I can't stop thinking about him. I think about him when I'm reading a book, listening to music, having a shower…" Her colour deepened slightly and she covered it quickly, "Even when I'm doing something else like talking to you, or helping Lesley. I think he might have, you know, accidentally maybe, used his power on me? I don't think he meant any harm, but I can't sleep without thinking about him, and when I do sleep, he's in my dreams..." She trailed off.

"And this is making you feel bad?" said Blackbird.

"Kind of," agreed Alex. She smoothed the downy hair on the baby's head while the baby tried to get one of the curls in his mouth.

"Have you tried warding this person from you?" asked Blackbird.

"Yeah. It didn't make any difference."

"Then I don't think the problem is magical," said Blackbird.

"I thought maybe if he'd got something of mine, he could be using it, like a voodoo charm, or a talisman to focus his power?"

"I think it's much worse than that, Alex."

"You do?"

"Yes," said Blackbird. "I think you're in love."

"You think I'm what?" she said.

"Does your tummy jump when you hear his name? Do you get tongue-tied when he's near? Does the thought of him touching you send prickles across your skin?"

Alex's look was one of growing horror.

"It doesn't take magic to do that," said Blackbird, "and there's no defence in the universe against it. Wardings are useless, power will not serve you and even though you may deny it, it will find its own way into your heart."

"It can't be," said Alex.

"May I ask who the object of your affection is?" asked Blackbird. "If it's not Sparky, then who?"

"I'm not sure I should say," she said.

"Alex, if you want me to help you, you need to tell me who it is. Is it someone I know?"

"Tate," said Alex. "I can't believe I just said that. You mustn't tell anyone. You have to swear to me."

Blackbird found herself grinning. "Tate? Tate the Warder?"

"It's not funny," said Alex. "Yes, Tate. There can't be two of them, surely?"

"No," said Blackbird, "I think there's just the one, though that one is large enough for two. And has he expressed any affection towards you?" she asked.

"No," said Alex, sulkily. "I don't think so. I don't know, I think he likes me, but not... you know, in that way." She handed the baby back to Blackbird who took him from her and settled him in to her lap. "What am I going to do?" she asked, sitting back in the chair and wrapping her arms around her knees.

"I have to ask this," said Blackbird, suddenly serious, "and I don't want to sound prudish, but you said he touched you. Did he force himself on you in any way?"

"No!" said Alex. "He's been very kind."

"Have you had sex with him?"

"No! It's not like that. You don't understand."

"Would you like to?" asked Blackbird, frankly.

"No," said Alex, but the words squirmed on her tongue. "I don't know," she admitted.

"I see," said Blackbird. "So, one thing I don't understand. How did you come into physical contact with a Warder?"

Alex looked evasive, but then sighed. "I followed him. I know it was wrong, but I wanted to see where he was going. We ended up in a wood and there was no sign of him. I got lost and tramped around in the brambles for hours before he found me. I was scratched, and sore, and cold, and wet."

"You do know how dangerous it is to follow one of the Warders?" said Blackbird.

"I didn't mean any harm," Alex protested. "If there'd been any danger I'd have just hopped back on to the Ways – left him to it."

"Promise me you won't do anything that reckless again," said Blackbird.

"Anyway, he found me and carried me back," she said, carefully skipping over both the promise and what she'd seen in the woods.

"He carried you back," repeated Blackbird, "and since then you've been thinking about him a lot?"

Alex sniffed. "I guess. You won't tell Dad will you?"

"We've already established that not every conversation we have is shared with your father," said Blackbird, "though if he knew you were following the Warders around he'd be horrified."

"Don't tell him," Alex pleaded. "He doesn't need to know."

Blackbird shook her head. "He may find out anyway, Alex. Your father is also a Warder and Tate may tell him."

"What am I going to do?" asked Alex.

"About your father?"

"No, about Tate."

"Well you have the usual options. You can declare your heart to Tate and find out if he reciprocates your feelings," said Blackbird

"What if he doesn't? What will I do then?"

"Or you can keep your feelings to yourself, and remain as wretched as you are now," she said.

"Oh, God," said Alex.

"Or you can take a hot bath, eat chocolate and get over it."

"I can't," wailed Alex. "Don't you understand?"

"Or there's the fourth option," said Blackbird.

"What's the fourth option?" asked Alex, miserably.

"Among the Feyre, Alex, it is the custom and practice for the females to choose a mate. The males can register a protest if they are not happy with the choice, but it is not their choice. I chose your father, though he has not been unhappy with that choice, I think."

"A mate?" asked Alex.

"With the intention of becoming pregnant and having a child," said Blackbird. "It's not a commitment to be entered into lightly, and if you are not ready I do not advise you take that course, but if you were to choose Tate as a mate, he could be yours."

"Oh," said Alex.

"Perhaps," said Blackbird, "you are not ready for that commitment just yet. Why not consider one of the other options. All of them are less complicated than the last."

"Oh God," said Alex.

"Quite," said Blackbird.

SEVENTEEN

An hour later I was standing watching the London Eye turn in slow cycles. The wardings I had set made sure I was conscious of Sam's approach, though I did not turn. He approached quietly, moving on the balls of his feet.

"What do you have for me?" I asked, without taking my eyes off the Eye.

"Is she around?" he asked.

"She could be right behind you and you'd never know," I said, truthfully. I turned and watched him scanning the crowds for Amber. "What have you got?"

He took a deep breath. "There is no Secretary Carler. There's no one in Whitehall by that name – not a private secretary, not even a receptionist. The name, by any spelling, does not exist. It's another codename, probably, and it's locked up tighter than a duck's arse."

"If you're telling me you've wasted my time, Sam…"

"The second name, De Ferrers, sparked a reaction, though," he said. "We got a phone call within minutes of me typing it into the system. I was immediately suspended, pending an investigation into my conduct. My access is revoked and I am on indefinite leave. You've trashed my career," he said.

He didn't sound that upset about it. Maybe it was trashed already. "You want an apology?"

"There's no loyalty any more," he said. "Not in this new lot. They all hate each other."

"New lot?" I asked.

"The old guard, we look after each other. We've been through it together. We know it takes trust to succeed."

"Spare me the pep talk," I said.

"I got a call before the interview. They told me the word had come through that I was for the high jump. The short of it was that I was poking my nose into things that didn't concern me."

"Interesting," I said, "but not enough."

"It came from Cheltenham."

"What did?" I asked.

"The call. It routed internally, over secure lines. It was encrypted to buggery and scrambled to hell because it came from the one place that cares more about secrets than anywhere else."

"And where's that?" I asked him.

"GCHQ," he said. "And if they're interested in you, they'll know everything. Your inside leg, where you buy fuel, who you text, what you say, what you had for lunch. They'll know what's in your Christmas presents before you do."

"They don't know everything," I said.

"I wouldn't bet on it," he said.

He hugged himself, beating his jacket in an attempt to stay warm. "So that's it. I don't have access to anything any more. I couldn't get you information if I wanted to."

"You don't understand, Sam. You're mine now. The only reason you get to walk around is because I think you might be useful. If I were you I'd try and stay as helpful as possible."

On cue, Amber appeared at his shoulder. She grinned at his reaction.

"I'll be in touch," I told him.

Amber and I walked away.

"I don't have anything any more. They're not going to let me back in after this," he called after me.

We vanished into the crowds.

GCHQ is not exactly a secret. It was established as a listening and intelligence agency after the code-breaking work that went on at Bletchley Park in the Second World War. It persisted as a result of cold war paranoia when some countries, including ours, started building nuclear bombs. That was about as much as anyone outside the intelligence community knew about it, including me. There was much speculation as to what else it did – it was a favourite of conspiracy theorists who alleged that it sifted through all our communications, cherry picking the streams of voice, text and email for indications of criminal, immoral or unpatriotic activity.

For an organisation based on secrecy, it's not hard to find. There is a large building at the edge of Cheltenham in Gloucestershire with clear signposting to the entries and exits. It has car parks around it for employees and visitors, and entry gates at various points around the perimeter. It's only when you start looking closely at it that you begin to see that careful thought has gone into its construction.

The car parks have pedestrian turnstiles which require an access card and a code to enter or exit, the implication being that people are counted in, and counted out again. Once inside the perimeter, you have to go through security to reach the building itself. There are more gates, each monitored. The building itself is a giant ring – toroidal is the term, like a doughnut, a nickname used by local people for the place. The roof of the building has a curved shield on it, it's not clear from outside what that's hiding, but it makes entry via the roof nigh impossible. There is an inner courtyard, within the ring, but that's only visible from above. All this we could see from the top of the hill about a mile away, using the powerful binoculars we'd brought with us.

"What do you think?" I asked Garvin.

I'd expected him to object when Amber reported my intention of going to Cheltenham to discover who it was that was trying to kill me. Instead he'd volunteered to come along.

"Interesting," he said. "It's smooth, clean and has very limited points of entry. The frontage is glass, but I would expect that to be reinforced, possibly bomb-proof. It's a literal interpretation of circles of secrecy. You see the buildings around the outside? They'll be administration, accounts, facilities, that sort of thing. On the outward facing side of the main building will be the public areas – meeting rooms, canteen, and anything else which isn't privileged. Raw information will arrive and will travel further inwards the more it's analysed and correlated. In the centre, possibly underground, you would find the clever bits – the really secret stuff."

"I think I can get inside the building," I said. I can get past the fences and the perimeter, and once I'm there I can walk in with everyone else."

"This is not the same as gaining free access to the Underground," said Garvin. "There will be multiple security systems monitoring each other. As soon as you use one of the gates it will look for a record of your movements. When it finds you've just arrived in the middle of the building, it will raise the alarm, quietly and efficiently. The building will be locked down before you know it."

"I can get out if I have to."

"I believe you, but at what cost? Even if you get inside, what are you intending to do?" he asked.

"Find out who tried to kill me, and why?"

"You think they're just going to tell you? Maybe it's posted on a noticeboard somewhere? The information you gained from Sam has led you here," said Garvin. "But that's all you have. Hundreds of people work here, possibly thousands. Most of them will know about their bit, and nothing else. That's what secret organisations are like."

"So your real reason for coming was to dissuade me from doing anything."

"Rash or careless action is counter-productive. I came to offer my advice, and to see if I could help. I also came because someone tried to kill one of my Warders, and I take exception to that."

"So what should I do?"

"If you break in, you'll only provoke them, and to what end? It'll prompt them into action and they will see themselves as the aggrieved party. At the moment, all you have is a link between two iron-tainted bullets, Sam's attempt to kill you, and a couple of names, plus the mention of GCHQ. It's enough to ask some questions, but be careful about jumping to conclusions."

From the top of the hill we could see the winter sun sinking below the horizon, and as it did, the car-park floodlights around the complex below came on. The offices facing the outside were brightly lit against the failing light. It all spoke of an organisation that operated twenty-four hours a day and seven days a week.

"At the moment you have a legitimate grievance, which they should answer. Make them come to you," suggested Garvin

"And how do I do that?

He grinned, "It's time to request a meeting with Secretary Carler."

"In that case," I told him. "There's somewhere else I want to visit before we do that."

On the eve of the solstice, the High Court of the Feyre was in session for the last time before the turn of the year.

"We've been locked in disagreement for too long," said Krane to the assembled High Court. "We all acknowledge the situation, but we can't continue like this indefinitely.

In the interests of moving things forward, I would like to propose that we shelve this issue for the foreseeable future and move on to other matters."

"To what end?" asked Kimlesh. "The issue of the mixed-race fey remains unresolved."

"We have other business apart from the mongrels," said Teoth. "It's taken too much time already. We're almost at the solstice and it's time we moved forward."

"I agree," said Blackbird.

A murmur went around the arc of the chairs.

"You do?" said Krane.

"I would like to discuss finance," said Blackbird.

"You don't understand," said Krane. "Without the establishment of the Eighth Court, you are no longer part of these discussions. We will not be discussing anything with you, let alone finance."

"I have an established court," she said, "or I will by tomorrow. It was the solstice tomorrow, you said, Lord Teoth?"

Teoth blustered. "Impossible," he said. "You need a home for the court, members sworn in. You don't even have a room of your own, never mind a court."

"I have one now," Blackbird said. "We are moving to Grey's Court in Oxfordshire tomorrow. Court members will be blood-sworn on the solstice night. By the turn of the year there will be eight courts, not seven."

"Grey's Court? I've never heard of it," said Krane.

"Is that a requirement, now, that you have heard of it?" asked Blackbird. "If it is, you have not mentioned it previously."

"This is extremely timely," said Barthia.

"Are you implying that I am being less than truthful?" asked Blackbird. "I would have thought my words were enough?"

"It's not that," said Barthia. "This is all very sudden, to be reprieved on the eve of the deadline."

"My Lords Teoth and Krane gave me very little time

to meet their stringent requirements," said Blackbird. "It has been a challenge, as they intended, but we have risen to it and we have our court. We will celebrate the solstice as the Eighth Court of the Feyre."

"That's preposterous," said Teoth. "How can they swear a blood oath if they're not even fey?"

Kimlesh leaned forward. "You raised that point some time ago, before the issue of establishment came up. We dealt with it then."

"Not to my satisfaction," said Teoth.

"You agreed, Lord Teoth, did you not?" said Yonna. "Which was why we moved on to the issue of establishment. There would have been little point in discussing establishment if the members of the court were unable to swear fealty."

Mellion made a complex gesture involving placing the tips of his fingers in and then flicking them out of his palm.

"Mellion's right," said Kimlesh. "You cannot scatter pigeons and eat them."

"Or eat cake and have it," agreed Blackbird. "Can we discuss finance now?"

Krane stood. "This is a trick!" he said. "They seek to dupe us with hollow words and hidden meanings."

"I mean what I say," said Blackbird. "I will have my court. Tomorrow."

"I want to see it," said Teoth. "I want to touch it."

"Is my word not good enough?" asked Blackbird. "Are we to distrust each other's words now?" She looked around the room. "For if that is the nature of things then I would want to visit each of your courts, so that I may establish that they are more or less than my own."

"You are welcome at mine," said Kimlesh.

"You've seen mine," said Yonna.

Teoth pointed a finger at Blackbird. "You will set foot in the Nixine Court over my dead body."

"Then how do I know the Nixine Court exists?" asked

Blackbird. She appealed to those around her. "How do any of us?"

"Of course it exists," said Teoth. "Unlike your fabrication, the Nixine Court has been an integral part of the Courts of the Feyre for generations uncounted."

"Has anyone in living memory seen it," asked Blackbird. "Apart from you, my Lord?" Once again she looked around the faces. Even Krane had to admit with a shake of his head that he hadn't.

"I invite you, all of you." said Blackbird. "Once the solstice is past and we have our court, you must come and be welcome there. We will have a celebration that the High Court will remember for centuries to come, providing of course that we have some money," said Blackbird.

"Very clever," said Krane. "By giving you money for your feast, we acknowledge the court, but we can't see it until you have your money, and it's acknowledged."

"You don't expect to be fed on air and magic, do you?" said Blackbird. "That kind of feast tends to leave one hungry."

"There's a sleight of hand here," said Krane. "I can taste it."

"There is a sleight of hand," said Blackbird. "It's called moving the target. I have met your requirements and your immediate response is to question my veracity. Then to place new requirements in my way. If this were any other member of this court, there would be uproar."

"You're not a member of this court," said Teoth.

"I am tomorrow," said Blackbird.

"Be careful," said Krane, standing. "Tomorrow is yet a day away. Much can change between sunrises."

"Is that a threat?" asked Blackbird.

"It's an observation," said Krane. "Come, Teoth. We have much to discuss. Will you join us, Barthia?" He met Barthia's gaze and for a moment something unspoken passed between them.

"No," she said. "I will stay."

"Very well," said Krane. "Teoth?"

They marched from the court, opening the great doors for themselves for once, and slamming them shut behind them.

"Well, that was unexpected," said Kimlesh.

"Was it?" said Blackbird, breathing out. "I've been looking forward to that for a long time."

Alex stood in the darkness. The moon was approaching fullness and it lent a hazy softness to the view across the fields. The temperature was dropping fast, and the mist was rising, adding a further soft-focus to the view and yet she didn't go inside for a coat. She'd made a habit of coming here, watching how the seasons stripped the trees of leaves and then coated them in white. She would go inside when she got too cold to stay.

She ought to be tired. She'd worked all day, helping Lesley shift stuff into vans so that they could move it in the morning. Alex watched carefully, knowing Lesley was pregnant, and wondering whether she ought to take it easier. Shouldn't pregnancy be lots of lying around having your feet rubbed, or was it this mad burst of activity? Is that what it made you do?

She'd been to the new place now. She'd wandered around it, touching the surfaces, drawing lines in the dust, getting the feel of the place. It was strange, as if there were someone waiting in the wings to enter, like a stage-play. You felt like the lights had gone up, but no cast had appeared. She'd found the article about Lettice, like a misspelled salad vegetable, and thought it was funny until Blackbird explained that it was an old spelling of Letticia, and the Letticia Knollys had been the lady of the house long ago. Personally she preferred Lettice.

"Aren't you cold?" The voice was behind her, and it made her jump, but she hid it as well as she could.

"Hello Tate," she said. "Do you enjoy creeping up on people?"

"Professional habit," he said, leaning on the fence to look over the fields. "Pretty, isn't it?"

"It has its charms," she said. "I should be going in." She stood back from the fence.

"Someone was in my room," he said.

She froze. "Were they?"

"While I wasn't there, someone went in and moved things."

"Did they?"

"Why?" he asked.

She waited, but he didn't say anything else. He was like a rock or a tree – just there, still, waiting.

"I thought... I thought I'd lost something," she said.

"So it was you," he said.

"You didn't know?"

"I do now," he said. "What did you lose?"

"I'm not sure," she said, too quickly.

"Did you lose anything, or were you just taking a look around?"

"I told you," she said. "I'm not sure."

He was stillness again.

"Sorry," she apologised.

"What were you looking for?" he asked again.

"I don't know. I didn't take anything, I promise. I thought maybe..."

"What?"

"Nothing. I shouldn't have done it. I'm sorry." Now she felt like shit. "I should go."

He returned to the state of stillness. It was like looking at a photograph of someone. It didn't look natural. "Tate?" It was just the instinct to make him move, make him come alive again.

"Yes?"

"Have you ever been in love?" As soon as she asked, she regretted it. What was she thinking? Even to have mentioned it was stupid. What was she thinking?

"Yes," he said.

It was not the answer she was expecting. The one she was expecting was, *why do you ask?*

What she wanted to say was, *who with*, but came out was, "What was it like?"

He stared at the fields for a long time. She thought he wouldn't answer, but after a while he did. "It was like drinking honey and finding ground glass in it."

"Did she hurt you?" she asked.

"Not intentionally," he said. "But the effect was the same."

"I would never…" but then she swallowed her words. "Sorry," she said. "I've really got to go."

"Where?" he asked.

"What do you mean, where?"

"Where have you got to go?"

Alex looked at him. "To my room, I suppose. It's cold. I'll catch my death."

"No you won't," he said. "Why do you run away?"

"I'm not running," she said, anger tinting her words.

"Then, what are you doing?" he asked.

"I'm going inside. I can't stay out here all night."

"No," he said.

She waited for something else, some clue, some tiny indication, but it was like he'd merged with the fence and become part of the scenery. "How do you do that?" she asked.

"Do what?" he said.

"Disappear in front of me while I'm watching you. Where do you go?"

"Professional habit," he repeated. "You want me to show you how?"

"Sure," she said.

He leaned back, shrugging his shoulders as if he was loosening part of a cliff in a landslide. "Rest your hands on the fence," he said.

She did as he said, looking at the fields laid out before her. He moved around behind her, resting his hands either side of hers. She could feel the warmth radiating from him on her back, though he did not touch her. "Watch the moonlight," he said. "Let it seep into your bones, slow your heart."

Her heart was anything but slow. "I'm not sure this is a good idea," she said, listening to her heart thump in her ears.

"Just relax," he said. "Let it seep into you."

She was more than conscious of the man behind her. His arms encircled hers, inches apart. She felt the heat of him behind her. She flushed, no longer cold. She twisted around, "I'd really better go..." And there he was, facing her. His long hair draped around his shoulders, the gleam of moonlight as it caught the reflection in his eyes. "Oh God," she said.

"What's wrong?" he asked.

Her eyes searched his for some sign, some indication. She wanted to reach up and touch his face, to see if felt the way her dreams told her it would.

"Tate?" she said.

"Yes?" he answered. She could feel his warm breath. There was a scent of musk and earth rising from him.

"Will you kiss me?"

He looked down at her for a moment. *Oh shit!* She thought. What did I have to say that for?

And then his lips touched hers. He was unexpectedly warm and soft, and she leaned into him, not wanting it to end. After a moment, he withdrew. "Like that?" he asked.

"Uh huh," she said. "Again."

He kissed her again, this time enfolding her in his arms and pressing her against him. She felt her knees give way, but he held her up. Her hands were searching for a way under his shirt, searching for skin. She slipped them under his shirt and found warmth and a gentle roughness. He released her, but she could not let go.

"Alex?"

"Uh huh?"

"Are you sure you want this?"

She pressed her lips to his again. "Yes," she said, breaking away for a moment. She could feel his body responding to hers. The rush in her was impossible to defy. It was like the tide. She was incapable of resisting.

"Oh God! You're going to have to take me somewhere."

"Where?" His breath tingled across her neck.

"Anywhere," she breathed. "But now."

EIGHTEEN

When I opened my eyes, I knew something was different. I was lying on my side, and the dawn light was just starting to brighten the room from behind the curtains, which in these shortest of days meant that I'd slept in. Still, there was something else. I rolled over to find myself being observed by two pale eyes.

"What are you doing there?" I asked my son, who was lying where Blackbird would normally be. She must have risen without waking me, and then popped him into bed with me while the bed was still warm.

His answer was to wriggle, waving his arms until he got one under himself and turned over so he could lift himself up on his hands.

"That's a new trick," I told him. He grinned at his achievement.

I sat up and stuffed some pillows behind me so I could lift him onto my lap.

"Where's your mum gone, then?" I asked him.

"Mmmmmmmmmm," he said, trying to tangle his fingers into the hair on my chest.

"Mum mum mum mum mum," I said, encouraging him to repeat it.

"Ghrammugharghle," he said, not helped by trying

to get his fist into his mouth.

"One of us smells," I told him. "And one of us needs a shower. Can you guess which one is which?"

That was enough to get me out of bed. I took him into the bathroom and changed his nappy. A small bit of tickling may have been involved. I tried to put him back in his cot so that I could shower, but he wasn't having any of that, so I settled him into a nest of towels on the floor so he could watch me while I showered. He was quite amused by the splashing water, and it meant I was clean.

Once we were dressed and presentable I thought I would wake Alex and see if she would join us for breakfast. We had a busy day ahead of us and her help would be appreciated. With the baby in one arm I tapped on her door.

"Alex, it's Dad. Are you awake?"

There was no response, so I tapped a bit louder. "Come on, Babe, it's time to be up and about."

There we still no answer. "Shall we see if she's awake?" I asked the baby.

"Lalalalalal," he said.

It was then that I noticed that the door was shut. She normally slept with the door open, but it was closed. I knocked more loudly this time and opened the door. "Alex, it's getting up ti…"

Her room was empty, the curtains were open and her bed was made. There was no sign of her.

"How odd," I said.

"Labalabalaba," said the baby.

I closed her door again and went downstairs to find the baby his breakfast, wondering at the same time whether Alex had slept at all last night. Maybe she'd pulled an all-nighter – not the best idea with the celebrations this evening, which she would be expected to attend.

I went into the kitchen, looking for Lesley, and found my daughter instead.

"Morning, Dad," she said brightly. "Morning, precious,"

she said to the baby, ruffling her hand through his fine hair.

"Good morning," I said. "Are you OK?"

"I'm fine," she said, kissing my cheek while the baby tried unsuccessfully to snag one of her curls in his grasp. "Breakfast has been cleared, but if you're OK with toast I can do some for you?" She went to the big larder fridge, extracting a fruit-flavoured rice, then the cutlery drawer for a plastic spoon. "Are you OK feeding him that while I make you some toast?"

"Yeah," I said. "Are you sure you're all right?"

"Yes," she said. "Why? What's up?"

"Nothing," I said, settling the baby into his high chair and strapping him in. He could see the rice pot now, and was getting impatient.

She warmed up milk for the baby in a pan of water. "Do you want tea?" she said. "Coffee?"

"I think coffee," I said, stripping the top off the rice pot.

The baby stuck his tongue out. "Labalabalaba." I wiped the sticky bit from the lid on his tongue and he grinned at me, then spread the goo around his chops with his fingers.

"Lesley tells me off if I do that," Alex told me, placing a coffee out of the baby's reach.

"Lesley's not here," I reminded her. "Thank you for the coffee."

"I'm going for a shower," she said. "You can drop him with me when you've finished, if you like?"

"That's very kind of you," I told her.

"Garvin was looking for you. I said I'd wake you but he thought you needed the sleep."

"Did he say what about?"

"Something about a meeting? He said you'd want to be there."

"Ah," I said. "I may not have time for breakfast," I pushed the chair back.

"Sit down and finish that while I make you some

toast," she insisted. "He won't go without you, and any-way, he said it would do them good to wait, for once."

"Are you sure you're OK?" I asked her. "You look different."

"I'm growing my hair," she said. "Do you like it?"

"It's lovely," I said, unsure I could tell the difference.

She placed toast in front of me along with a pot of honey and some butter, and the milk for the baby. "Don't let him have any honey until he's eaten the rice," she advised. "Or he won't eat the rice, and then he'll scream blue murder until he gets more honey."

"I'm not a complete novice," I told her. "I managed with you."

She kissed the top of my head. "I'm going for a shower," she said, "but I'll be back before you've finished, and I'll take over while you go and do Garvin things."

"Did I ever tell you were a wonderful daughter?" I asked her.

"Don't be soppy," she told me, and headed off for a shower.

"Ah," I said to my son. "So that was Alex after all. I was beginning to think she's been replaced by an alien."

"Labalabalabalaba," said the baby.

Garvin was waiting for me in the basement room where the Way-nodes were. Tate was with him. He nodded to me in greeting, but said nothing.

"They're already set up," Garvin said. "I've sent Slim-grin ahead to keep an eye on them. Are you ready?"

"I have everything I need," I said. My sword was held scabbarded in my left hand.

"Do I need to remind you that this is a diplomatic meeting?" asked Garvin.

"I don't think so," I said.

"Good. Tate, you take the lead. We'll be two minutes behind you."

Tate stepped onto the Way-node and vanished into a

twist of air. "I'm not expecting trouble," said Garvin. Let's not leap to conclusions. We're simply there to establish the facts and see what their reaction is."

"And if they deny all knowledge of it?" I asked him.

"All I'm saying is that we can't allow ourselves to be deceived by our own assumptions. It's a difficult time for us. We're down two people, the courts are in flux; we can't afford to sour our relationships with humanity as well."

"Even if they're trying to kill us?" I said. I didn't get an answer. I hadn't expected one.

He gestured to the Way-node and I stepped forward, reaching down into the flow of power beneath me. It rose in response, carrying me through an endless blackness streaked with whorls of silver as I veered around Way-nodes following the trail left by Tate. Voices that sounded like the calls of the lost echoed through the void, until I began to wonder who was more lost – me or them. I forced myself to focus on the traces of Tate's passing.

Stepping out onto the frosted grass, I moved away from the Way-node, wrapping the area in a cloak of glamour. Tate had already moved away, probably scoping out the area with Slimgrin. I waited for Garvin to step out of the air beside me and then we both crossed the grass towards the great hall, letting the glamour fall away as we did.

Oakham Castle was never particularly large or grand and all that remains of it now are the outer walls and the great hall with its tall leaded windows. I had been here before twice – once with Lord Krane after we discovered the experiments being conducted on fey-humans at Porton Down Research Facility and once after Alex's image was captured by a remote camera as she left the Tower of London having stolen a raven's feather from one of the Tower birds. They say the third time is the charm.

It was used as a neutral meeting place for the High Court and The Secretariat – the government agency charged with handling relations with the Feyre. It was used because the walls inside the great hall were decorated with horseshoes. The proximity of the iron shoes made it impossible to hear the truth or lies in the words of the people there. Something in the iron, or the shape of the shoes, disrupted that ability and meant that in that space humans and fey were equally unable to hear the truth in each other's words. It was supposed to level the playing fields, but actually it worked against us. The Feyre didn't usually tell lies – something about truth and power makes lies uncomfortable for us. They twist on our tongues, and the presence of the iron does not help with that. We are obliged to tell truth, while our human opposite numbers can lie all they like. There are other ways of revealing the truth, though, as they were about to discover.

The guy in charge of security was a gruff Scotsman we'd met previously. He was standing on the roadway, wearing a dark suit and smoking. He was flanked by two policemen armed with short-muzzled sub-machine guns. He was the one who'd showed me the video footage of my daughter being carried by the Thames current under Tower Bridge after she'd escaped the Tower. At the time he'd pointed at the pictures of my daughter and told me she resembled nothing human. I'd disliked him before he said that.

"You're late," he said, as we approached. He flicked the end of the cigarette into the bushes.

"We were finishing our breakfast," said Garvin, calmly. "Are we ready to start?"

"Petersen." The Scot acknowledged my presence. I don't think he liked me any more than I liked him.

"I'd like to return the greeting," I told him, "but I don't think I know your name?"

He grinned at me. "Do I look stupid?" he said.

"Ah, already the difficult questions," I said.

His smile faded. "You'll be laughing on the other side of your face by the time all this is done," he said.

"I'm not laughing," I said.

"Shall we go in?" said Garvin.

We entered the great hall and the, by now familiar, taint of the horseshoes enveloped us. To my sharpened senses it was like having everything muffled, a dulling of the sensation of sound. It made the room feel uncomfortable and unnatural.

Secretary Carler stood to greet us. We did not shake hands. He was flanked by two men in dark suits. The Scot filed in behind us and closed the door, standing with his back to it so he could listen in on the meeting.

There were three high-backed chairs arrayed along each side of the table, and Garvin and I took two of them.

The secretary sat in his grey suit in the central chair opposite Garvin and shuffled a small stack of papers before him – expenses claims, perhaps, or maybe his tax return. The two men behind him remained standing. "You called our meeting, today," he said without preamble. "Would you care to explain the urgency? It's a busy time of the year and we would have preferred more notice."

"Something came up," I said.

Garvin frowned at me and turned back to Secretary Carler. "It's good to see you well," said Garvin. "We were a little concerned when you were absent at our last meeting."

"I was detained elsewhere," said the secretary. "Your concern is appreciated," he said, without smiling. "If we could move on the matter at hand?"

"It concerns a potential treaty violation," said Garvin.

"Indeed?" said Carler. "In what respect? I am not aware of any violations, and I would normally expect to discuss such matters with one of the Lords and Ladies. That's normally the protocol," he reminded us.

"It's a security violation," said Garvin. "One of my Warders was injured." While Garvin talked I was extending my senses into the room. It was extremely difficult when surrounded by so much iron. I was trying to pinpoint something, but the sense of it was being smothered by all the iron.

"Injuries happen all the time," said Carler. "It's a dangerous business."

"That's true," said Garvin, "and made more dangerous when someone is providing one side with access to weapons they would not normally have."

"What kind of weapons?"

"It's well understood that our kind have a susceptibility to iron," said Garvin, looking around at the walls of the great hall. "Someone supplied an assassin with iron tainted bullets." He dipped into his pocket. The two dark suits behind Carler reached under their jackets.

"Steady," said Garvin. "We don't want anyone to get hurt."

He slowly brought out his hand, revealing a small leather pouch. The dark suits didn't remove their hands. He upturned it over the table and two small slugs dropped onto the table. He dropped the pouch on the table and the dark suits removed the hands from their jackets.

Carler reached forwards and picked up one of the slugs. "Where did you get these?" he asked.

"They were given to a man named Sam Veldon," said Garvin. "They've been fired since then," he explained.

"Interesting," said Carler. "Who gave them to him?"

"We're not sure – we thought you might know," suggested Garvin lightly.

Carler dropped them back on the table. "Can't help you there, I'm afraid. They could have come from anywhere."

My hands were in my lap, with my sword resting between them. I grasped the scabbard and the hilt. "I was shot with them," I told him.

"How unfortunate," he said. "I'm pleased to see that it did no lasting damage." The edge of his mouth twisted when he said it, and his eyes were too steady, they lingered on mine too long. Did he know something?

Garvin glanced sideways and realised where my hands were. It was now or never.

I burst upwards from the chair, hefting the edge of the table upwards and throwing it into Secretary Carler's face. Garvin, half-expecting something, launched himself backwards in a graceful somersault. The table hit Secretary Carler as he went backwards and collided with the two suits behind him, knocking them backwards. I grabbed Carler's legs and hauled him towards me under the table so that he was laid on the floor where the table had been. By the time the dark suits had their weapons drawn, the tip of my sword was at Carler's throat. A glance at Garvin behind me showed me the Scot, his hands held high, one holding the pistol he'd managed to draw, but unable to bring it to bear with Garvin's sword-point over his heart.

"If the policemen outside start shooting through this door," he reminded the Scot, you're going to be riddled with bullets."

"Hold your fire!" he shouted. There were shouts outside, a short burst of machine-gun fire, and then silence.

"Niall, it's your show," said Garvin.

"Let him go," said the closest dark suit, his pistol aimed at my head. The furthest one had it aimed at my body.

"On the contrary," I told him. "I just went to a lot of trouble to get him where I want him. Now, slowly and carefully put the guns onto the floor," I told him.

Carler went to say something, but it was choked off when I pressed the point home. "Two things can happen," I told them. "I've already survived being shot – maybe you already know that. You might just get lucky – I may get shot again, but I guarantee that you'll all be dead. So will the officers outside. You'll have a massacre on your hands and there'll be a lot of explaining to do back at head office." I let that sink in. "Alternatively, you can both place your guns where I can see them and we can all take a step back."

I waited, counting to thirty in my head. The man on the ground was unarmed at present, so the priority went with the closest armed man. I readied myself and my power. I'd been trained for this. I could take them.

Slowly the second dark suit lifted his pistol and placed it on the stone floor. The second one waited and then did the same. I regarded Carler, who looked less like a bank manager with a sword at his throat. I moved slowly around, putting him between me and the suits, reached down and flipped open his jacket. There was a similar pistol in a holster under his arm. I lifted it out with the tips of my fingers.

"Garvin?"

"We're clear," he told me. "I have the gun." He backed the Scot around until he was joining his colleagues behind the upturned table.

I stepped back and let Carler get to his feet. "This is an outrage," he said. "The Lords and Ladies shall hear of this."

I passed the gun from Secretary Carler to Garvin while I watched the Scot and the suits. Garvin removed the clip and neatly ejected the chambered round, holding it carefully up to the light by the brass case. "Not this one," he said.

He took the pistols from the floor and did the same with those. "Not these either. I hope we've not gone to a lot of trouble for nothing," he mused, casually.

"What about him?" I said, nodding towards the Scot.

Garvin popped the clip from the Scots weapon and ejected a round onto the floor. I knew immediately when he picked it up that we'd found what we had come for.

"This one," he said, carefully holding up the round from the gun. "It's a pistol round with an iron core. I couldn't swear it's identical, but it's a good enough match for me. You're aware, Secretary Carler, that the hoarding of weapons specifically aimed at the Feyre is prohibited under the treaty. I think iron-cored rounds count. What's your man doing with them?"

"Think very carefully," I told Carler. "I want an answer to this, but if I don't get one I like, I'm going to drag all of you outside, hang you by your feet from a tree and start asking questions away from these horseshoes. I'm quite tempted to do that anyway."

"We do not respond to threats," said Secretary Carler.

I shook my head. "If only that were true," I said. "Someone supplied bullets similar to these to a man called Sam Veldon with instructions to shoot me with them. If he'd done what he was told and shot me in the head, I'd be dead, but he shot me in the gut. If that wasn't a response, what was it?"

"You're only proving we were right," said the Scot. "You're a loose cannon, Petersen. You're putting us all in danger."

"Ah, I said. "Now we come to it. What exactly am I supposed to have done?"

"You're a murdering bastard," said the Scot, "and we all know it." Carler shot him a warning look, but he ignored it.

"And who am I supposed to have murdered?" I asked him.

"Where do you want to start?" asked the Scot. "The body count at Porton Down alone would justify any action we cared to take."

"Porton Down was in violation of every treaty we have," said Garvin to Carler. "I thought Lord Krane made our position clear on that when we were here last. If we're going to start a score-settling exercise, I think we have a few of our own."

"This isn't about score-settling," said the Scot.

"Then what is it about?" I asked.

"A rogue. Someone upsetting the status quo," the Scot answered. "Whenever the body count starts to rise, we just have to look for you and you'll be lurking somewhere. Like a bad penny, you always turn up."

"That's like accusing firemen of always turning up at a fire," I said. "It's nonsense."

"Were either of you involved in this?" asked Secretary Carler of the two dark suits. They both shook their heads. "Very well," he said. "This is an internal matter," he said. "I can only apologise for my colleague's ill-advised actions."

"Hey now," said the Scot. "You're not burning me for him, surely? He needs taking down."

"We would like to restore the meeting to some order," said Carler. "You," he addressed the dark suits. "Arrest that man. Take him into custody. Hold him until I tell you otherwise. If he has accomplices I want them held as well." They stood watching him. "Now!" he barked.

"Are you nuts?" shouted the Scot. "Do you know how many deaths this guy has caused? Take your scabby hands off me, you moron."

We watched as they manhandled him out of the room. There was a difficult moment when they tried to take him outside. Apparently there was a stand-off outside between the Warders and the police. It wasn't resolved until Garvin went outside with Secretary Carler and together they ordered everyone to stand down.

While they were busy I collected all the weapons and put them safely out of reach, ejecting the rounds from each gun and paying special attention to the pistol used by the Scot.

"I can only apologise," said Secretary Carler when they returned, "and assure you that such an operation was not authorised."

"I'd like to believe that," I told him, looking around at the broken chairs and scattered furniture.

"I wish I could say something to reassure you," said Carler.

"There is no Secretary Carler, is there?" I asked him.

"I'm sorry," he said calmly. "I'm not sure I understand you."

"I checked. There is no Secretary Carler anywhere in Whitehall."

"What makes you think I work in Whitehall?" he said.

"Then where?" I asked.

"Better not to go into too much detail. It only makes things more difficult."

"Let me guess," I said. "Cheltenham, a big building, locally known as the 'doughnut'. How am I doing?"

"I really couldn't say," he said. His face was studiously blank.

"The way I see it, you owe me," I told him. "After all, you've been spying on me and my family and you ran an operation to try and kill me."

"I don't think I want to comment on any of that," he said, "but if you want to trade information, I'd like to know what you did with the safe that was taken from the Royal Courts of Justice."

"You think I took it?" I asked him.

He smiled. "Now who's being evasive?"

"OK," I said. "I did not steal anything from the Royal Courts of Justice, especially not a safe or what was in it. If you know anything about us at all, you'd know we'd find it difficult to lie about something like that."

"You were seen," he said. "You attacked one of the staff on the same day the safe went missing."

"I was asked by the Remembrancer's clerk to go there," I told him. "I went to protect the safe and the clerk."

"So why did you kill the clerk?" he asked.

"I didn't," I said. "Now it's my turn. Who is De Ferrers?"

He went suddenly still. "I can't say I know what you're speaking of," he said.

"Which is an interesting way of phrasing it," said Garvin.

We were rejoined by one of the dark suits who nodded confirmation to Carler and stood waiting at the door.

"I came here last night after dark," I told Carler. "I was looking for a link between this place and GCHQ at Cheltenham."

He was better at hiding it this time. "You didn't find anything," he said.

"Instead, I found that this castle was owned by the De Ferrers family." I looked around slowly. "A castle hall lined with horseshoes, used by you and your predecessors for meetings with the Feyre, all arranged under the name, De Ferrers."

"What does that have to do with Cheltenham?" he said.

"A very good question," I told him "How would you describe the purpose of GCHQ?"

"I'm not sure I would," he said.

"To keep the secrets of the Kingdom, perhaps?"

"What an odd phrase," he said, his face carefully neutral. "Quite archaic, don't you think? If you didn't kill Ms Radisson, then who did?"

"Honestly, I didn't see," I said, thinking back to the events in the National Archive. "I thought I knew who took the safe, and who killed Claire, but now I'm not certain. You need to ask yourself, though, in whose interest is it that the safe and the clerk are out of the way? Who stands to gain? Then you can answer your own question." I watched him absorb that information. "Was it your lot that redecorated Claire's flat?" I asked.

"From time to time it is necessary to ensure that peace is maintained," he said. "It doesn't do to leave too many loose ends."

"So you took the horseshoe," I said. "Did you also take the one from the National Archive as well?"

"The horseshoes are not your concern," he said.

"Did you know the family crest of the De Ferrers family has horseshoes on it?" I asked him.

"What an interesting coincidence. As you pointed out,"

he said, "no one will ever stand trial for Ms Radisson's murder. It serves no purpose to leave a host of confusing evidence that goes nowhere and leads to nothing. Better for the police to spend resources on problems they can solve. Speaking of which, do you know the whereabouts of the missing journals from the National Archive?"

"I believe I do," I admitted.

"We would like them returned," he said, "sooner rather than later."

"What about the two knives," I asked him, "one blunt, one sharp."

"The knives are not your concern," he told me. "Neither are the nails or the horseshoes. Those things will be taken care of."

"But you lost the safe," I told him. "What was inside it?"

"That would be another matter that is not your concern," he said. "Omnia praesumuntur rite essa acta."

"Latin," said Garvin to me. "Roughly translated it means, it is presumed until proved otherwise that what should have been done, has been done."

"Quite so," said Secretary Carler.

"And if you can't do it?" I asked.

"We try not to give ourselves airs and graces," he said. "We only do what we can."

"We have what we came for," said Garvin. "I assume you will take appropriate action regarding our Scottish friend?"

"An internal matter," said the secretary. "Please give my regards to the Lords and Ladies and tell them that we value our continued accord on all matters. I'm glad we were able to clear up a few matters. We hold to the treaty.

"As do we," said Garvin. "You'll excuse us."

"Of course," said the secretary.

When we got outside, there were a lot of nervous policemen. Instead of holding their weapons across their chests, as before, they were now held ready, pointing at the ground. Opposite them stood Tate. In his hand was a sword, the blade naked. It looked like a toy in his hand. Slimgrin was nowhere to be seen, but then that was to be expected. Garvin smiled at the policemen. They exchanged glances, but did not respond.

He walked across the grass towards the Way-node. Tate didn't move. "Next time you plan something like that, tell me first," he said to me.

"I didn't plan it," I said, "and you would have left me back at the courts if I'd voiced my suspicions."

"You're making assumptions about what I will or will not decide," he said. "We can be deceived by our assumptions, I said that to you before."

"I'll try to remember that," I said.

"Good."

"What would you have done?" I asked him.

"If I'd been in your place? Probably much the same. I liked the move with the table. It was worthy of a Warder."

"Thanks," I said. Compliments from Garvin were rare.

"Don't get over-confident," he said.

"I'll try not to get carried away."

Nineteen

When I returned to the courts I went to find Blackbird. She was in the kitchen with Lesley, discussing arrangements for the evening while Lesley laid out plates ready to be carried to Grey's Court. I told her what had happened with the meeting with Secretary Carler.

"And you say that after all that he still claimed to be Secretary Carler?" she asked.

"He was evasive on the matter."

"Hmm," she said. "It may be the truth."

"I had Sam check the records. There is no government department with a Secretary Carler, male or female."

"Secretary," said Blackbird. "Literally *one who keeps secrets*. Carler – from the word *carl*, a loyal bondsman."

"So Secretary Carler is...?"

"A title, most likely, or a codename. It's appropriate, don't you think?"

"I wonder if his real name is De Ferrers?" I asked her.

"Why?"

"There are links to the De Ferrers family. Oakham Castle was owned by the De Ferrers.

"One of the Knights in your dream was called De Ferrers – it is a Norman name," said Blackbird, "Probably from Ferrier, a Blacksmith, but it could also mean simply *of iron*."

"An iron keeper of secrets?" I commented. "That seems a hell of a coincidence.

"Or it is no coincidence at all," she said. "It's a powerful combination and may offer some protection to the holder of that role. Still, it was resolved peacefully. A death today would be an inauspicious event, Niall. If you'd asked me, I would have recommended any other day than this. Such things leave a taint, which is not something I want to carry into the founding rituals of the Eighth Court."

"I'd rather go into the founding ceremony knowing that the person who was trying to kill me is not still out there waiting for an opportunity," I told her.

"There are always dangers," she reminded me. "At dusk we will beat the bounds of the court to establish a boundary. It is an ancient ritual both among humanity and the Feyre, which in our case will place a warding around the court. We will finally have the beginnings of a secure future."

"Do you think someone might try and prevent us?" I asked.

"It's possible," she said. "But we must establish our boundary for ourselves. No one can do it for us."

"As a Warder, I'm bound to all the courts," I said.

"I know. In time I hope you will join us, but until then you may not join in. It is only for the members of the new court. You may accompany me as my escort, but you may not join in."

"I shall be pleased to escort you, Lady."

"Just keep your eyes sharp," she said. "There are those who would not see this come to pass."

"I shall bring my sword."

"And your wits," she said.

They came in ones and twos, looking nervous and furtive. Some arrived in cars, complaining that sat-nav never worked for them. Others came down the Ways, tramping up from the village. No curtains twitched as they passed.

There wasn't even a face at the window of the house with Neighbourhood Watch stickers in the window. No one in the village saw them arrive. Alex surprised me by offering to direct them from the Way-node. I went into the village and hung around near the *Maltsters Arms*, the only pub in the village, so that I could offer directions to the lost. My directions to the couple looking for the road to Henley-on-Thames were probably less than accurate, but I expect they found their way eventually.

As the afternoon grew late and the light started to fade, I headed back to the house. Angela was at the door most of the afternoon, greeting those she knew and welcoming those she didn't. Word had gone out, and the response was larger than anyone had expected. I joined Lesley and Blackbird in the sitting room as they watched the latest batch of arrivals climb out of a battered Citroen 2CV.

"I hope we'll have enough food," Lesley said to Blackbird.

"They're still unloading round the back, and if there's a problem, we'll send out for takeaway," said Blackbird.

Lesley looked horrified.

"It's a joke," Blackbird explained.

"Do you normally make jokes?" asked Lesley.

"Not really," said Blackbird. "I never got the hang of it."

"That explains it," said Lesley.

Somehow, through a combination of cajoling and threats, Angela managed to find them all places. Yes, some were sleeping on the floor, or in the servant's quarters in the loft-space, and some were cosier with their colleagues than they would like, but they did it. The converted office became Angela's hub, and messengers were appointed to relay information back and forth. There was a buzz of excitement, an air of expectation. People were introducing themselves to each other, hesitantly and awkwardly. I heard Andy explaining to a bald guy from the North East with his hand stuck out expectantly that the Feyre didn't shake hands, and why.

"That's just rude, that is," the guy said.

I left them to it.

Angela sent out a call to assemble before dusk at the front of the house, suitably attired for a walk. It mostly worked apart from the young woman in the yellow miniskirt who swore she only had heels. She had to manage in black knee-high boots, which were made her look very sixties. I was guessing that she was a city girl. There was a dark-eyed teenager all in black standing at the edge of the crowd. I watched Sparky sidle up to her and offer her a swig of whatever brew it was he had concocted.

"Long time, no see." The voice came from behind me. It was low and soft but definitely female. I turned and faced a face I knew. "Megan?" I said.

"And a memory for names, too," she said. "You'll go far." She looked exactly as I'd first met her in Covent Garden when I'd been on my way to Kareesh with Blackbird. She still wore the long hippy skirts and loose top, and her neck and waist were decorated with strings of small stones.

"How's the jewellery business?" I asked her.

"Same as always," she said. "Not been a great year for the market. Too many other things going on. I told you she'd find you," she said, nodding towards Blackbird who was marshalling people with Angela.

"And you were right," I said, "though that's a story in itself."

"And I understand you have a son," she said. "I'm jealous." It was said without any malicious intent, but in the way that the Feyre sometimes have of saying something completely true.

"Perhaps that proves it's not too late for any of us," I said.

"Maybe," she agreed. "Isn't that what this is all about?" She looked around the faces of the people gathered before the house. "We're all looking for something."

"If that something is a home – somewhere to be accepted for who you are, and what you are, without anyone judging you for not being something else, then yes," I said, and I found myself believing it.

"You've changed," she said, looking up at me. "The guy following Blackbird around in the market would never have said that."

"Maybe I was looking for something too," I said.

At that moment we set off, straggling into a long line, following each other into the dusk. I excused myself and headed up the line to join Blackbird. "We're going to need sticks," said Blackbird.

"I wish you'd mentioned that earlier," I said.

"No, they must cut them for themselves." It's part of the ritual.

Angela walked down the line, handing out wooden handled hatchets and billhooks she'd found in the outbuildings to random people in the line. "Is that wise?" I asked her. What if one of them is an assassin?"

"If they're an assassin," she said, "they'll have brought their own weapons."

I watched as the tools were dished out. The woman in the miniskirt held a billhook as if it might bite her. No one held it easily and professionally, which was a cause of some solace to me. If they couldn't hold a bill hook they'd make awful assassins. Blackbird led us across a field with brown stubble waiting to be ploughed under to a hedge along the back of the estate.

"I want each of you to select and cut a stick," she said to the assembly. "It doesn't have to be a big one, but you have to be able to beat with it, so choose something you can handle. Pass the tools between you until you all have something."

There was a degree of hesitancy and then someone stepped forward and started hacking at the hedge. I walked down the line, helping out where people were unfamiliar with the tools. I saw Andy neatly sever a rod and tip and tail it with the billhook before gracefully presenting it to the women in the miniskirt. She took it from him as if it were a snake.

As an ice-breaker it was working, though. The challenge of equipping everyone with a stick to beat with meant that they had to speak with one another. At the back of the line I found Alex with a pole, almost as tall as she was.

"Where did you get that?" I asked her.

"It fell off a tree," she said, lifting her eyes to the sky.

"Isn't it a bit big?" I asked her.

"It's fine." She smiled, and I wondered what the joke was. "I'll be able to walk with it."

She seemed happy enough, and Blackbird was about to speak to them again, so I left her to it.

"We are beating the bounds of a new court," said Blackbird. "In practice that means we are touching every inch of the boundary around the court. This is to protect us, both symbolically and with power. As a symbol it shows us as a united force, and as a warding it divides the court from the surrounding land. This will be the extent of the court that we form tonight. Each time we do this it will get stronger.

"You don't have to know how to set a warding to join in, just touch your stick with everyone else and that will join your power to theirs. Those who can set wardings, add your strength to mine and we will forge a warding that will turn away those who are unwanted, warn us against those who would harm us, and protect us against the power of others."

With that she set out, trailing her stick along the hedge so that the bushes rattled with dry leaves. The sound echoed down the line as others joined in, a low hum of chatter mixed with the clatter of sticks and the tramp of many feet. I waited while people filed past, watching Andy show the woman in the miniskirt how to set a warding as they went along.

When the back reached me, I found Sparky, the dark-eyed girl and Alex trailing from the end of the line. "You're the back marker," I told Alex. "Don't let anyone get behind you and if you need help, shout."

"We'll be fine," she said, shooting a conspiratorial smile to the dark-eyed girl.

"If anyone twists an ankle or trips over and hurts themselves, send someone up to the front and we can get them taken back to the house."

"Stop fussing," she said. I stopped fussing and went back to the head of the line.

Blackbird led the procession, guided by Angela who'd apparently been out and scoped the route earlier in the day. We startled a pheasant or two, and surprised a dog-walker who watched for a while as the procession of strangers walked down the edge of one field and then turned and went through a gate. He didn't follow, and the dog stayed with him.

At least it didn't start howling.

By the time we had completed the full circle and were back at the house it was dark. The evening was turning into one of those winter evenings where the sky clears, the temperature drops fast and by morning everything will have a layer of frost. A three-quarter moon edged in a halo of silver climbed over the horizon.

Everyone was frozen. Having been warned to take warm clothing, most people had still been unprepared. Megan passed me, her fleece zipped up and her scarf wrapped around her ears.

"At least we'll have an appetite," she said.

I waited until Alex and the other youngsters wandered in at the last.

"I'm freezing my rocks off," said the dark-eyed girl in a broad Bristol accent.

"Nah," said Sparky. "We've seen colder than this, haven't we, Alex?"

Alex let them continue into the house. She was

319

wearing a blue cardigan which barely covered her shoulders. "You must be frozen," I told her.

"Like Sparky says, once you've been really cold..."

"Get yourself inside. Lesley has mulled wine to warm everyone up. There'll be some time to get changed afterwards, if you want to."

"Damn," she said, glancing back into the darkness. "I've left my outfit back at the courts. What with all the fuss this afternoon, I didn't bring it." There was something evasive in that. The way she said it was a little too easy, almost as if she'd planned it.

"What are you up to?" I asked her.

"A girl's got to look nice," she said, eyes wide. She looked down at her clothes "I can't wear this, I have mud all over my jeans. Besides, all my hair stuff is back at the courts and the bathrooms here are going to be crazy busy."

"You can use the one in our room," I said, but the look she gave me told me that was not going to satisfy her.

"I don't have my outfit," she said.

I knew I was being conned, but I wasn't quite sure in what way. Sometimes, however it pays to give in gracefully. "You'll be back in time for the swearing-in," I said. "Promise?"

"I'll be back," she said.

"Promise," I insisted.

"I'll be back in time for the party, and you can give me a hard time if I'm not," she said.

It was as good as it was going to get.

There was a knock on Tate's door.

"Yes?" he said.

"It's me," said Alex in a hoarse whisper. She opened the door enough to peer around the edge. "Are you busy?"

Tate was lying across the top of his bed, reading a book. "You'd better come in," he said. She could see his hair was draped forward around his face, the waves in it catching the light from the lamp. He closed the book gently and placed it on the bed. The leather cover was worn where it had been handled, as if he'd read it many times. "What's up?" he asked.

"The shower's not working in my room," she said. "I wondered if I could come and use yours."

"Yours is not working?" he said.

"I need to get changed. The big party starts in a while and I've got a lovely dress to wear. Would you like to see?"

"See?" he said.

"You keep repeating things I say," she said to him.

"Repeating..." he said. "Yes, I do."

"Well?" she said, getting a little bit annoyed with him now. This was not the reception she was expecting.

"There's nothing wrong with your shower, is there Alex?"

"It's not working," she protested.

"Why isn't it working?" he watched her struggle to come to an explanation he would accept.

"It was working yesterday," she said.

"You don't have to lie to me," he said.

"I'm not lying," she said. "It was."

"Alex, you have an ability with water. If you wanted a shower to work, it would work."

"OK," she said, flushing with anger. "I'll go and try it again." She turned to the door.

"Where are you going?" he asked her.

"I'm going back to my room to see if I can get the frickin' shower to work." Now she sounded sulky and resentful.

"I thought you were going to show me your dress," he said.

"I need to get changed. I'll come back later, maybe."

Her hand was on the door handle. "Alex?" She stopped, but she didn't turn around. "What did you really come for?" He thought she would bolt, back to her room. She stood there, hand on door handle, clothes draped over her arm. He waited, allowing her time to think.

"I thought..." she said, still facing the door. "I thought, we haven't seen each other all day, and you've been busy and me too, to be honest, and I have to go to this party tonight cause my Dad will kill me if I don't go, so I won't see you until tomorrow at least and I thought..."

"Yes?" said Tate.

"Never mind," she said, tugging on the door handle, which seemed stuck all of a sudden.

"Alex?" said Tate.

"Ugh! Wretched thing. It's stuck."

"I don't want you to go," his voice was quiet, barely more than a whisper.

"You don't?" she said.

He scooted across the bed, so that he could sit in the edge. "Put your clothes down on the bed."

She placed the bundle on the bed next to him. He reached for her hand and guided her in front of him. Even sitting he was almost as tall as she was standing up. "If you use my shower, you'll be naked in my room," he said.

Her tummy was doing tumbles. "I can lock the bathroom door, if you want."

"It doesn't have a lock," he said, reaching for the buttons on her shirt. He started undoing each one. They looked tiny in his fingers. He untucked the shirt from her waist. His hand slipped under her shirt and around her back and he drew her forward so that he could kiss her neck. She slipped the shirt from her shoulders and it fell on the floor.

"Oh, God," she said. "I'm going to be late for the party."

"We have plenty of time," said Tate, undoing the button of her jeans.

"No," she said, kissing him full on the mouth. "I am definitely going to be late."

• • • •

322

"What are you looking so nervous about," asked Blackbird. She was wearing a teal shot-silk dress which made her look every inch the Lady of the Eighth Court.

"Alex was supposed to be back by now," I said

"Alex? I thought she was getting changed."

"She left her outfit at the courts and she went back for it. She promised me she'd be back in time for this evening's events."

"She went back to the courts?" said Blackbird, eyebrow lifting.

"What?" I asked her. "Is something wrong?"

"No, I'm sure it's nothing," said Blackbird. "We need to be downstairs in three minutes. Angela will be waiting for us. Put your jacket on. Have you checked your sword?"

I slipped into my best jacket, one without bullet holes. "Yes. I even polished the edge."

"Then you may escort me," said Blackbird. I held open the door and as she passed she held out her arm so that I could entwine mine in hers. As we went down the stairs, keeping step, I could hear the gathering of people in the great hall. Snatches of conversation drifted to us.

"...like some sort of demon..."

"...all that is achieved by insects the size of your thumbnail..."

"...he can't have done that before, surely...?"

The double doors were pulled back allowing us to see the newly decorated great hall. The room fell into silence. The fire crackled in the great hearth, warming the room, and I saw that Lesley had adapted some generic Christmas decorations to our purposes. The room was garlanded in green and gold, with gold baubles hanging from the ceilings and strings of white lights over the pictures and the hangings.

There was a burst of applause from somewhere near the back, and then everyone was clapping.

"Smile," said Blackbird through her teeth.

"Why are they clapping?" I murmured to her.

"It doesn't matter. Just smile."

We entered the room slowly and a corridor opened up for us. We were guided around until we reached the back of the room where the double doors into the garden room had been shut to prevent the chill from the night cooling the room, though a little cool air would have been nice. We stood with our backs against the doors until the applause died down.

I looked around, and there was a sea of faces. I tried to avoid catching anyone's eye, but I could see Andy, the stubble from his face gone and his hair pulled back. He was wearing a lounge suit and looked handsome next to the woman who'd been wearing the miniskirt, who was now in a bright orange full-length dress and high heeled sandals. Megan wore a simple layered dress of muslin over gold silk. Even Sparky had dressed up, wearing a shirt and pencil-thin tie, standing next to the dark-eyed girl, who looked waiflike in a little black dress and kitten heels.

"Tonight," said Blackbird, "is a special night. It is the end of the year, and the beginning of a new year. The sun dips its lowest and returns tomorrow with new vigour. This is the longest night, and that renewal will take time, but it will come, as we all know."

She paused, looking around the room.

"I have summoned you here tonight because you are special, each of you. You carry with you the hope of a race whose vitality is fading like the dipping sun. It is my fervent and abiding hope that we will bring renewal to the Feyre as the sun brings spring to the earth."

The applause broke out again, and it was a short while before she could be heard.

"That hope, like the first shoots of spring, must be fostered. It must be nurtured and brought to fruition. This court – the Gifted Court – the Eighth Court of the Feyre, begins tonight with the express purpose of fostering that hope and all who embody it. It is a night of rebirth, of transformation and renewal, and therefore I would ask each of you – if you wish to become part of that renewal, to step forward now and swear your allegiance to the Gifted Court in a blood oath."

Twenty

Garvin found the Dragon Hall in darkness. He'd been expecting some gathering, some celebration of the end of the old year and the beginning of the new. Instead the hall was empty and hollow. There was no music, no gathering of friends. In the dim light from the windows, the beams and struts across the high ceiling looked like the inside ribcage of some great beast – perhaps the dragon after which the hall was named. He went to the light switch and flicked it on and off. The electricity was out. It must have tripped.

"Lord Krane? Lord Teoth?" Garvin moved into the pool of light where the moonlight slanted in from the side window, where he could be seen.

"It was good of you to come," said Krane stepping into the space before the opposite window so that he was outlined against the light.

"And at such short notice," said Teoth, moving out against the next window. "I appreciate that this is a difficult time for you – things are so… fluid."

"It is no more difficult than at any other time," said Garvin. "My loyalty is to the High Court, and always has been. What is this about, my Lords?"

"The High Court, ah yes," said Krane. "It's so much

easier when we are united in our purpose. At the moment you must feel pulled in all directions."

"I will not take sides," my Lords. "If you're intending to ask me for my support, then you will be disappointed. I serve the whole court."

"You weren't always so dispassionate, though, were you Garvin?" said Krane.

"What do you mean?"

"Once you did take sides," said Teoth. "You stood against the Seventh Court on the side of the mongrel fey. You murdered our brethren while protecting those who are less than fey."

"I defended the High Court," said Garvin. "And those whom the High Court sheltered. I would remind you that some of my own Warders were among the gifted, and that they fought and died to protect you and the other Lords and Ladies that night."

A figure moved across the next window from Teoth. "You weren't serving the whole court, though, were you Garvin?" said a soft voice.

"Lord Altair," said Garvin. What an unexpected...."

"Pleasure?" asked the soft voice.

"Indeed," said Garvin, measuring the distance between the windows and the door. It was a long time since he'd been here. The building had been remodelled several times, extended, then partitioned, and finally restored to something resembling the original. He tried to remember where the exits had been.

"I lost people that night, Garvin," said Altair. "Good people."

"As did I," said Garvin.

"Your divided loyalty cost me greatly," said Altair.

"It was a night I will not forget," said Garvin.

"No," said Altair. "You won't."

"What do you want?" asked Garvin. "I take it this is not a social call. My Lords, you keep interesting company on solstice night."

"Unlike you," said Altair, "they have chosen the side on which they prefer to be."

"We're choosing sides are we?" asked Garvin. Around him he could feel the prickle of power building in the room. His first thought was for escape to warn the others, but the door would be blocked, obviously. The windows, then. Behind him a shadow inserted itself into the space before the window, blocking that exit.

All around the room, ghostly figures flickered into being, first one, then another. They were blacker than the shadows in which they stood, and outlined in numinous fox-fire that flickered like fingers of light. The circle of figures tightened around Garvin and the mouth of the trap closed.

There was a hiss as Garvin's staff separated into a blade and a silver shod scabbard. "I would remind you, Lord Krane, Lord Teoth, of the duty of protection owed to the Warders. You invited me here."

"So we did," said Krane. "Unfortunately, things appear to have changed."

"The High Court is still the High Court," said Garvin, warily watching the circling wraithkin. "The Warders are still the Warders."

"The High Court is one of the things that have changed," said Altair. "Everything must die, and it has reached the end of its usefulness. It's been dissolved."

"You can't dissolve the High Court," said Garvin. "You don't have that authority."

"Do I not?" said Altair. "Krane? Teoth? What say you?"

"I say aye," said Teoth.

"As do I," said Krane.

"You are not quorate," said Garvin. "It's a minority decision."

"No," said Altair. "Kimlesh was stabbed through the heart with Yonna's own bone-handled knife. It is a sweet irony, is it not?"

"Yonna and Kimlesh are allies," said Garvin. "Yonna would never do that."

"I never said she did it," said Altair. "Kimlesh was killed by one of her own, though that fact was lost on her court who took their revenge on Yonna and drowned her in her own blood."

"Impossible," said Garvin. "No one from Kimlesh's court could harm her. It would violate the oath of allegiance to their court. It would be suicide."

"True," said Altair. "But some debts must be paid. There are many ways to die, and some are worse than others. It is a privilege denied to most to choose the manner of your own death. Some would rather flee, it seems. Mellion is nowhere to be found. The Goblin Court has vanished."

"Vanished?" said Garvin.

Altair continued. "At their solstice feast, Barthia and many of her court died in a tragic fire – a terrible way to go, especially with the windows and doors all sealed. I'm told that sand turned to glass, the heat was so intense."

"Why?" asked Garvin. "You're destroying everything. Why?"

"Sometimes there must be death in order for there to be renewal," said Altair. "You cannot always succeed with negotiation, and so must turn instead to the sword, speaking of which, it's time you were finally repaid for the lives you took."

They moved in as one. Garvin's sword flashed in the darkness, and blades rang together. A shadow darted in, and the silver end of Garvin's staff found an eye. There was a scream and a sound of crunching bone. One of the shadows fell back into darkness. Without breaking step his blade swept around, clearing space, opening up the fight as he moved across the circle, forcing his opponents back. If he was going to break out, it had to be quick. He could not win a long fight against so many. The circle of ghostly figures distorted into an oval. He carved diagonal arcs of glinting light as he worked his way towards the door. His sword rang each time he parried a cut, the long staff clattering against steel as he pushed to break the circle, which now tightened and bunched as he neared the door. With blades stabbing in from all sides, he whirled to deflect each attack, but with so many, it was inevitable something would get through. An initial stab drew a gasp of pain, a slice across the arm another. The circle turned with slow menace around him, slicing, stabbing; wearing him down.

In a desperate attempt to break the circle he pushed away from the door. An upward slice produced a satisfying cry and he pressed the advantage into creating an opening, but it was all taking too long. The advantage was short-lived as another moved to take their place, and he was forced back into the ring. Now, one after another beat forwards to cut at him. It was a ring of slicing, cutting blades each falling in different time or stabbing in to catch him out. He cried out in anger as an opponent's sword found its mark in his side, roaring at them in defiance, finding enough space to whirl around and take the head clean off one of the stabbing shadows. It was a reckless move – others lunged in, piercing his undefended flank. Relentlessly the circle closed, the blades hacking down, until it was a ring of rising and falling steel with only silence at the centre.

After a few moments, they subsided and the circle opened, leaving the pile of tattered grey cloth and the weapons, where they fell.

"It is done," said one from the circle, now arrayed in a semi-circle around the three remaining members of the High Court.

"Finally," said Altair.

"What about the rest of them?" asked Krane.

"The Warders are no more," said Altair. "Fionh and Fellstamp are gone. Slimgrin is missing, along with Mellion. Amber and Mishla are all that remain and they are not enough to stand against us. Without Garvin to lead them they will fall."

"Then the day is ours," said Krane.

"Ours?" said Altair. "There is still much to do, but the day will never be ours."

"What do you mean?" asked Teoth.

Altair walked forward through the semi-circle of ghostly figures outlined in a nimbus of white fire. "Your record does not serve you well," he said.

"But we delivered Garvin to you," protested Teoth.

"Yes," said Altair. "You betrayed him, just as you betrayed me long ago. Just as you would betray me as soon as I turn my back."

"But we trusted you!" said Krane.

"As I trusted you," said Altair, "even while you were planning my downfall. You know what to do," he said.

Even as the semi-circle started to close, the ground beneath the hall began to tremble as Teoth reached down with fingers outstretched to the ground. Krane's form shifted, becoming more feral, with elongated eyebrows, fingers more like claws, teeth lengthening into fangs.

Four new figures stepped forward into the ring around the two. Their clothes were the colour of ash, their eyes cold grey. From them, a darkness deeper than any shadow spread forward, initially slowly and then running across the floor like water.

Eager to escape the spreading blackness, Krane leapt at one from the ring of shadows, half-man, half-beast, and twice the size with claws extended and long fangs bared. The figure went down under that onslaught but the others moved in and the were-creature was unceremoniously hacked, stabbed and sliced by the swords gathered around.

Teoth watched in horror and shrank back. The foundations of the building vibrated to his summons. From the earth below the hall a huge figure burst upwards through the floor, rising with ponderous implacability, splintering floorboards and crashing its blunt head into beams. Vaguely man-shaped with a blank earthen face, its maw opened with a gravelly roar, sand spilling from its open mouth while its mighty arm swept at the ring of shadows, the swordsmen falling back before the assault of mud and stone.

Not so the grey shades, who stood their ground and shifted into insubstantial mist. The huge stone fist passed right through them while the blackness reaching for Teoth advanced as he tried to climb the wall away from it. The blackness spread up his legs and thighs, chest and head, enveloping him.

Teoth screamed and crashed to the floor, thrashing blindly and choking as the darkness entered his mouth, nose and eyes, He thrashed briefly, kicking out at nothing. The huge earthen shape wavered back and forth, flailing its arms, staggering blind, then fell apart, tumbling into crashing mounds, crumbling into rubble, slipping back into the hole it had risen from, even as Teoth spasmed on the floor and was still. The four figures watched as Teoth's body collapsed into dust no different from that drifting in the air. Then they kicked what was left into the hole after the rest of the dirt.

Outside, figures emerged into the moonlight, patting their clothes and spitting grit and sand. "Is it done?" asked Altair.

"Who would have thought the old bastard still had the power to raise an elemental?" asked Deefnir.

"It didn't help him," said Altair.

"Shame about the hall," said Raffmir, looking back. "I rather liked what they'd done with it." The roof sagged where it had been weakened and tiles slipped from the roof to clatter noisily into the yard below.

"Don't get too attached to anything," said Altair. "By the time we're finished they'll be burning anything they can find just to hold back the dark."

"Ah," said Raffmir, with a sigh. "Just like old times."

There was a stillness in the room. For a moment I thought no one would step forward. Then Andy moved forward out of the crowd. "It is my wish to be first," he said. "Though I do not know what is expected."

"Come forward," said Blackbird, "and bare your wrist."

A space cleared in front of Blackbird as people drew back. I stepped forward into that space and drew my sword. Andy looked worried then, but slipped out of his jacket and passed it to the woman in the orange dress to hold. As he stepped forward he unbuttoned his cuff and pulled back the cuff.

"Hold out your wrist," said Blackbird.

"You'll be able to sew it back on afterwards, right?" said Andy to me, joking. A murmur of nervous laughter rippled through the room.

"You can close your eyes if it helps," I told him. His eyes met mine and held them.

It was with a moment of trepidation that I readied myself. A mistake at this point would be a bad moment, and no one else would volunteer after Andy. In a single fluid movement, I lift the sword and cut swiftly downwards, stopping the blade over Andy's bare wrist. He looked momentarily relieved and then paled as a line of red welled across his wrist. It was the moment when I acknowledged that all those hours of sword practice had been worth it.

"Taste it," said Blackbird, "and stand before me."

Andy turned and lifted his wrist and pressed it to his lips, sucking the blood from the long cut.

"By your blood do you swear to serve the Gifted Court until released of your bond?" asked Blackbird.

"I do," said Andy. I could feel the power building in the room.

"By your heart, will you abide by the rulings of the Gifted Court, for better or worse, even until life or death?" she asked.

"I will." My own mouth watered at the memory of the taste of blood.

"By your mind, will you become an embodiment of the honour of the Gifted Court, always remembering your place in it, and its place in you?"

"I will," he said."

"By your power, will you seek to protect the Gifted Court, its Lady, and all its members, even unto the cost of your own life?" said Blackbird.

"I will," said Andy.

Blackbird offered her hand and Andy gave the hand with the cut on the wrist to her. She pressed her other hand over the wound and when she removed it there was no trace of the cut, or the blood.

"Be welcome into the Gifted Court, The Eighth Court of the Feyre," she said.

Applause broke out around the room, and Andy turned around and beamed at everyone, relieved that I hadn't accidentally chopped his hand off at the wrist. After that they came forward, initially in ones and twos, but then a line formed. Each of them was sworn into the court, one after another. Each tasted their own blood, and with each taste, the sense of power in the room built.

At one point I briefly looked for Alex in the line, but she was not there. I found myself angry and disappointed after what she had said, but then had to push all those thoughts to one side when the next cut was a little strong and that much deeper. A gasp went down the line, and there was a degree of hesitancy in the next in line. After that I centred myself completely in the moment, focusing, as in a battle, only on what was in front of me.

Alex regarded herself in the mirror. It kept trying to steam up, but Alex wasn't quite finished. Her make-up was a flawless fusion of glamour and art, her dress fitted OK, and her hair – well it was behaving itself. That was the best that could be said.

Her only problem was her tattoos. She'd become used to the black vines that normally twined around her wrists, but at some point the black flowers had receded and now she was adorned with tiny pale blossoms. She'd tried to make them vanish, but they persistently grew back. Each white four-petal bloom had a tiny red centre that didn't go with the dress, but she was damned if she could make them go away. She was just going to have to live with it.

She smoothed down the dress and turned to the bathroom door. "How do I look?" asked Alex from the doorway.

Tate looked up from the book he was reading and regarded her for a long time.

"Well say something," she said, smiling hesitantly.

"I was trying to find the right word," he said, still appraising her.

"You don't like it? You think it's over the top? Too long? Too tight?" she drew the skirt sideways in a slither of material and plucked at the neckline of the royal blue dress. "The back's quite low as well," she said, turning slowly in her high heels.

"Beautiful," said Tate, as he closed the book and shifted across to sit on the edge. "Simply beautiful."

"Now you're teasing me," she said, approaching him. "Tell me what you were really thinking." She stood next to him, looking down into his eyes. They were very dark. He didn't need to say anything and she knew. The honestly in his eyes made her blush, but she smiled. "I really have to go," she said. Her tummy was tight again and she knew she was already late. If she stayed any longer then she was going to be in so much trouble.

"Then I will escort you," he said, taking her hand.

"You don't have to," she said, brushing her lips against his in a way that made her want to change her mind. "I know the way."

"How are you getting there?" he asked.

"Down the Ways, like always."

"And you're going to walk from the Ways to the house in those shoes, are you?" he asked.

She looked down. "Maybe I can take my trainers and change when I get there?"

"Or I could carry you?" he offered.

Grinning at him, she said, "We are not doing piggy-backs again. No way. Not in this dress."

She found herself swept up into his arms as he stood, cradling her against him. "Like this?" he said.

"Tate?" she said. Her ear was against his chest and she could hear the slow thump of his heart.

"Yes?"

"We could go back to bed."

He shook his head. "Duty calls. You promised, and you must keep your promise. But I will come with you as far as the house." Without difficulty he carried her out the door and down through the house.

"What if someone sees us," she said.

"No one will see," he said. In moments they were slipping down the Ways.

When Tate travelled the Ways it was like being carried along by an avalanche. They slid around the nodes at a pace that left her breathless, arriving in the darkened wood at the edge of the village. Without breaking stride he carried her through the trees to the road.

"How far to the house?" he said.

She looked up and down the road, getting her bearings. "The pub is just down there, so the house is that way. It's about half a mile.

He carried her until they reached the driveway where he set her down.

"I can manage from here," she said.

"I'll walk you up to the house, and then head back to the courts." He strolled along beside her as she tripped along in her heels until they cleared the trees. The drive circled around to where the house stood, lights shining through every window.

"Looks like the party's already started," she said.

"Where are we?" asked Tate, halting on the drive.

"I told you. Grey's Court. It's the house where the Eighth Court is having its gathering. It's OK, I expect they'll all be too busy to worry about us."

"I've been here before," said Tate.

She stopped and looked back. Something about his expression had changed. Suddenly she felt cold and exposed. "What is it, Tate?"

"This isn't Grey's Court," he said. "I've been here before. It's changed a bit, and they've done things to it, but I'd recognise it anywhere. It's not a place you'd forget."

"If it's not Grey's Court," said Alex, "then what is it?"

"It's the Court of the Wraithkin," said Tate. "This is the Seventh Court."

"It can't be," said Alex. "Blackbird paid for it with a rose. It's ours."

"You have to warn them," said Tate. "Get everyone out." He turned and started running back towards the village, his pace increasing with every step.

"Where are you going?" Alex shouted after him.

"Get them out of there," he called back. "I have to get help."

He disappeared into the dark. Alex slipped her shoes off, then turned and ran across the meadow to where the house stood illuminated against the dark.

At the end of the line of people was Angela. No one else waited after her.

"Are you the last to swear allegiance?" I asked her.

She nodded, bearing her wrist.

"Where's Alex?" I asked her.

"I could ask you the same question," she said, quietly. "Is it her intention to join the court?"

"As far as I know," I said. "I haven't seen her since we came back from beating the bounds."

We had to concentrate then, since it would be a shame to spoil an otherwise almost unblemished record by severing a limb. Angela tasted blood, as had those before her, and in a moment it was done – we had formed a court. There was another spontaneous outbreak of applause. My suspicion was that the applause was being orchestrated by Angela, but she looked as surprised and nonplussed as I did.

I wiped my sword for the last time, carefully stowing the cloth in a pocket out of sight less the sight of blood spoil someone's appetite. Having stood for over an hour, I was ready to sit and eat, but Blackbird had other ideas. Lesley brought forward our son, dressed in an outfit of teal silk to match her own. It was a measure of my experience with fatherhood that my first thought was – if he throws up on that we'll never get it clean.

She approached me and, as she did, he reached out for me. I took him from her and she turned to the assembled people. "Members of the Gifted Court, if I may have your attention for just one moment more." She waited until the hubbub of conversation died away. "There is a tradition among the Feyre that children are not named for the first six months of their life, but are simply referred to as 'baby'. It harks back to a time when children were more prevalent, a time which I hope will come again, but we are in the happy circumstance that tonight the son I share with Niall will receive his name."

There was a scattering of applause and she waited while it died away.

"Amongst the Feyre, a male baby's name is traditionally chosen by the father, and so Niall would like to say a few words." She turned to me.

I stepped forward, and there was another bout of scattered clapping. My son clung to me, nervous at being the sudden focus of attention. I couldn't blame him. I could see Lesley, passing among the members of the new court, handing out glasses of champagne, and I took that as a cue.

"Like me," I said, "many of you have grown up with the traditions and rituals of humanity. You would have been looking forward to Christmas, some of you with mixed feelings, and your New Year celebrations would have been not long after. It seems strange, then, to be celebrating the New Year on the solstice, when Christmas is not yet come. Indeed, Christmas is not a festival celebrated by the Feyre."

There was a murmur of *shame* from somewhere at the back.

"Nor are christenings, and the tradition of Godparents, with all that entails. Instead we have a naming ceremony, something that will be strange and new to many of us, me included."

I looked around the faces, seeing many I did not recognise.

"All of you have just participated in a ritual of power. You are the new members of a new court, formed tonight on the solstice, sealed in blood, bound with power. That's one ritual completed. Now we have a different ritual, which is no less powerful, when we give my son the name by which he will be known. Names have power, which I think you all know, and by giving him his name we acknowledge him as a member of this court, even before he goes through the ritual you have all been through. He will be the first child of this court, but not, I think, the last." I smiled then, at Lesley, who smiled as she handed out champagne.

"Names are important," I said, "not just because they give us a measure of identity, but because they are symbolic. When we say the name, *Blackbird*, we invoke the symbol of the Lady of this court, and in doing so we acknowledge her power and influence. When I came to choose a name for our son, I wanted it therefore to symbolise something for him, and for us. Our court stands between the human world and the fey world, and each of us straddles that divide. We all know, some of us to our cost, what that means." I glanced at Angela.

"I could have chosen a fey name – there are some I admire, some I find inspiring, but everyone else in this court has a human name, some of us more than one." I nodded to Blackbird. "At the same time I wanted to choose a name that recognised the spanning of these worlds and acknowledged the dual nature of all of us here.

"There was a man who spanned those worlds. He connected the human world to the world of the Feyre, though whether he truly knew what he was doing, I do not know. He chose to weld the fate of fey and humanity together and the choices he made hundreds of years ago are the reason we are here tonight. He rose from being a no one, hunted and persecuted, to being a king. He was born a bastard, and he became known as the Conqueror. It's a strong name, and my son will need to be strong. He had enemies, as does our son. The difference was the people around him. I hope you will be the friends and supporters that our son needs as he grows." I held the baby up high, so that they all could see him. "I give you..."

Through the crowd gathered around the long table, someone was moving forwards. There was a flash of blue as she pushed her way forwards, her mass of curls wild and unruly. She pushed through the gathered rank at the front and stopped in front of them all, breathless. She was holding a pair of high-heeled shoes in her hand, swinging from the straps, and her feet were bare and dirty. When you looked at her dress, the bottom of it was stained dark where it had soaked up water.

"You're late," I told her in a low voice. "I will speak to you later."

"You don't understand," she said, leaning forward to put her hand on her thighs and catch her breath. "You've got to get out."

I sighed. "No amount of dramatics is going to get you out of this one, Alex. You're in deep trouble." I lifted the baby high and called out to the assembled court. "I give you, William, first son of the Court of the Gifted, may he live in happiness and peace."

340

"To William!" they shouted, raising their glasses, trying to ignore the theatrics from my daughter.

"You have to leave!" Alex shouted at them. "Go now!" The room fell into an uneasy silence.

"Alex, that's enough," I said to her.

She ignored me. "You've all got to get out!" she said. "While you still can."

"Alex!" I shouted.

She turned to me. "It's a trick, don't you see? This isn't Grey's Court, it's a trick to get you all here. You've got to get out, while there's still time."

"What are you talking about?" asked Blackbird.

Another figure pushed forward through the crowd, slowly this time. They parted around her, and there were murmurs of unease as she advanced through them. Finally she stood beside Alex, looking up into her face. Alex looked down on her with a mixture of revulsion and fascination.

"So this is the girl," said the spindly figure in her crackly voice. She reached up with her oddly formed hands – no thumb but a little finger at each side articulated inwards. The wispy material of her sleeve fell back revealing alabaster skin so thin it was as if you could see the bones beneath. Alex stepped back to avoid her touch.

"Kareesh," said Blackbird. "What are you doing here?"

TWENTY-ONE

"I thought you'd be taller," said Kareesh to Alex. "So many of the young ones are tall these days."

"Who the hell are you?" said Alex, staying out of reach.

"Pretty, though," said Kareesh. She spoke to me. "She has your eyes."

"I came to see you," I said quietly to Kareesh. "Gramawl is looking everywhere for you. We need to talk."

"Too late for talk," said Kareesh, hobbling towards Alex who backed steadily away into the people behind her. "The girl has it right. You should listen to her."

"What is this about?" asked Blackbird.

Kareesh turned her glass-black stare on Blackbird. "Ah, girl, a Lady at last and so beautiful. So sorry it has to be like this."

"Like what?" said Blackbird.

Kareesh turned her gaze back on Alex. "Tell them," she said.

Alex stared at her, mute.

"Tell them," she insisted.

"I was with Tate. He recognised the house. It's not what it appears to be."

"What were you doing with Tate?" I asked her.

342

"Not now, Niall," said Blackbird.

"What do you mean, not now?" I asked Blackbird. "What do you know about this?"

"You have to listen!" Alex shouted over us. "It's called Grey's Court now, but it was the Wraithkin Court. The National Trust doesn't own it. It belongs to the wraithkin. It is the home of the Seventh Court!"

Murmurs spread throughout the crowd, between those who didn't know what the Seventh Court was, and those who did.

"It can't be," said Blackbird. "We beat the bounds. The wardings – I'd know."

Kareesh spoke. "Not for centuries have they been here, not since they were exiled – nigh a thousand years. In all that time it has lain fallow and empty. No one renewed their wardings, no one beat the bounds of the court. It has all but been forgotten, but for a few of us who remember."

"I knew I felt something," said Blackbird in disbelief. "I didn't know what it was."

"It was a trick," said Alex, "to bring you here. Can't you see?"

"We have to get everyone out," I said to the assembled company. "Everyone down to the Way-node in the village," I told them. "Go now! It doesn't matter where you go, just get out! We'll find you later."

The doors behind us that led to the garden room drew back and opened wide. I caught Blackbird's hand and drew her away as the doors drew back into the darkness beyond and figures emerged. We pressed back into the crowd behind us, facing the doorway.

"I think you'll find," said a voice I knew well, "that the Way-node in the village is not the safe, happy place it once was. Anyone who wants to leave is going to have to run, and keep running."

"Raffmir," I said.

He moved to one side of the door, another wraithkin

343

I did not recognise moving to the other side. In between them was someone I had only ever seen once before once, at the High Court of the Feyre.

"It's been a long time since the Wraithkin Court had visitors," said Lord Altair.

"You..." said Blackbird. "You should not be here."

"Why so?" asked Altair. I was struck again at the rich musical tone of his voice. It had timbre and lightness where you would have expected something harsh and mean.

"You are banned from this world," she reminded him.

"You forget yourself,' he said, letting his eyes wander around the room, taking in the decor. "I do believe the old place has had a lick and a promise," he said. "It's almost as if we were expected."

"You cannot be here," Blackbird said.

"Cannot?" said Altair. "Do not presume to tell me what I can and cannot do."

"The barrier..." said Blackbird.

"You forget," said Altair, "assuming you ever knew in the first place. The barrier was created after we left. We were not sent away, we took ourselves apart. We crossed the void so that we might have peace and safety." He looked around at the gathered faces. "What we could once cross, we can cross again."

Kareesh hobbled forward. "Always the tricksy one," said Kareesh in her crackly voice. "Never to be trusted."

"Why is it, Kareesh?" asked Altair, "that wherever trouble is, you turn up? Somehow I knew you'd be here."

"I came to plead," said Kareesh.

"For their lives?" said Altair. "They were never meant to be. This is your doing, old one. Their pain is your burden. Their blood is on your hands."

"Not to plead for them," said Kareesh. "For you. It doesn't have to be this way."

"Oh, please," said Altair. "Not this again? Surely we are beyond that at least."

"Long ago, I saw the future of the Feyre," said Kareesh. "Long ago, I knew that without change they would stagnate and eventually die. It was as inevitable as the tide."

"Spare us," said Altair, looking at the ceiling.

"I knew my time was near, my last chance to save them all. It began with you, Altair. You had your chance," said Kareesh. "You could have mixed the blood of the courts and all would have been well again."

"You wish to justify your own perversions," said Altair. "Purity will out."

"And there's none more pure than you, is there Altair?" she said, her voice wavering.

"You cannot sway me with compliments," he said.

"And so there was another path," said Kareesh. "By mixing the bloodlines with humanity the Feyre could endure."

"Half-breeds," said Altair. "Mongrels. Neither one thing nor the other. A dilution of the noble quality of the courts to be replaced by charlatans." He looked around the faces, "Fakery, frauds and dog-witches, begging a seat at the hearth for a handful of herbs and a tin whistle."

"You would have killed them all, but the barrier kept you apart. In time those children bore their own offspring, each generation renewing the pattern," said Kareesh. "Now that pattern emerges again." She searched the faces around her, looking for something she recognised.

"We tried to cleanse them," said Altair. "But the High Court would not listen. The Warders stepped in, and we were beaten back. Well, not this time."

"Why not?" I asked. "Why not this time?" I looked between Kareesh and Altair, but they were focused only on each other.

Kareesh ignored me. "When the barrier fell, you would have wiped them away, but it did not fall."

"Your meddling will be your undoing, old one," said Altair.

"How you must have raged," she said, "to find yourself denied by a stripling girl and an untutored novice."

"We will be denied no longer," said Altair. "Tonight it all ends."

"So it does," said Kareesh. "The sun will rise and they shall fall. So say I."

"...they shall fall," echoed Angela.

I looked between Angela and Kareesh. "What?" I asked them. "What does it mean?"

Kareesh looked up at me with those unblinking black eyes. "I am so sorry," she said, "that the burden must be yours, but you would have died in any case, had I not despatched her to the platform at Leicester Square to save you."

"...so much brightness," said Angela.

"What is it?" I shouted at them. "What are you telling me?"

"They are telling you that tonight is your last," said Altair. "It is the winter solstice and tonight the sun has reached its nadir. From tonight it will rise, each day a little higher in the sky."

"And tonight," said Raffmir to me, "I will finally have my revenge. You will die by my hand."

"You can't kill me," I told him. "You are sworn not to harm me or mine. If you do then under fey law your own life is forfeit."

"There is no fey law," said Altair. "The courts have fallen. They are dissolved. There is only one law, and it is mine."

"But Kimlesh, Yonna, Mellion?" said Blackbird. "If you do this they will stand against you."

"Kimlesh is dead," said Altair. "So is Yonna. Mellion has fled, and Barthia is fuel for her own pyre. Krane is a ragged pile of fur and dust, and Teoth? Teoth is buried in his own earth."

"They have fallen," said Kareesh sadly. "The sun is at its darkest. There is no night longer than this."

A shadow emerged behind Kareesh. Altair saw it and called out, "No, don't...!"

There was a soft punching sound, and the tip of a blade emerged from the front of Kareesh's shift. She looked down, not in surprise, but in recognition. The blood welled around the blade, soaking into the soft grey cloth. "So it begins," she said, and slumped forward, her body crumpling into a heap at Deefnir's feet.

"Enough words," said Deefnir from behind her, wiping the knife and returning it to the sheath at his side. "She talks too much."

Altair looked on in shock. "Deefnir, you do not know what you've done," he whispered. Then he shouted. "Kill them! Kill all of them!"

"Run! Hide! Get away if you can!" I shouted, passing the baby to Blackbird and drawing my sword, as the people behind her scrambled past each other to get away. I backed towards the door.

"This ends tonight," said Altair. "I want them all, no matter where they run, wherever they hide."

Raffmir stepped forward, baring his sword in one smooth movement. He extended his free hand and the lights died. In a second he was outlined in cold fire. "Hide and seek," he said. "My favourite game."

I turned and ran through the door, looking for Blackbird, Alex, and William.

Sparky grabbed the wrist of the dark-eyed girl and pulled her out of the press heading for the main door. "Vicky, this way!"

"Let me go," she said, pulling back resentfully, trying to rejoin the outward flow.

"Where are you going?" asked Sparky in a hoarse whisper.

"We have to get out. Didn't you hear?"

"Yeah," said Sparky. "They'll be waiting out there in the dark, you mark my words."

"You think so?" she said, watching people pushing through the main doors in their rush to get away.

"Course they will," he said. "Stands to reason doesn't it? First you cause panic, then you divert everyone straight into the mouth of the trap." He clasped his hands together like the teeth of a beast, and she flinched and looked away.

"What are you going to do then?" she said. "They'll be here in a minute and then it won't make any difference."

"We've got to use our heads," said Sparky, tapping the side of his. "Come on, follow me."

"Where are we going?" she whispered after him.

"Where we're not expected to be. We'll hide out somewhere quiet and emerge when all the fuss is over. We can slip away when no one's the wiser." He ducked into a door under the stairs which she hadn't seen before. Inside, he pressed the door closed until it gave a light click.

"It'd be better if we could lock it, but there's no lock so that'll have to do," he whispered. "I daren't put a light on in case it draws attention." In the darkness they felt around.

"Oi! Pack that in," said Vicky.

"Sorry," said Sparky. I can't see a damned thing. I was exploring with my hands."

"Well explore somewhere else," she said firmly.

She didn't sound too cross, though, and Sparky was beginning to think he might have fallen on his feet. There were coats hanging from pegs along the wall. They smelled musty and faintly of wet woodland walks and stale dog. Sparky started going through the coats one by one.

"What are you looking for?" asked the girl.

"You never know what you might find and I figure anything useful is good news. It's all gone a bit pear-shaped, you know?"

"You're not kidding," she said. "How long do you think we need to stay in here?"

From beyond the door, there was a long shriek which ceased quite suddenly. "We're not out of the woods yet," said Sparky.

"Is it me, or is it getting lighter?" said the girl.

"It's your eyes, getting used to the dark," said Sparky. "No, hang on a minute, it is getting light."

A voice spoke from the darkness at the end of the row of coats. "Perhaps your search would be more productive if you had a little more illumination." The tiny room chilled sharply, and the room filled with dappled moonlight.

"Aw crap!" said Sparky.

"Where are you?" called Raffmir softly into the dark. "Come out, come out."

He could hear distant screams already in the house, echoing down the stairs. Perhaps they thought he wouldn't be able to find them in the dark? Perhaps they simply imagined that if they couldn't see him, he wouldn't be able to see them either. Of course, if he absorbed enough power he'd be able to see them behind furniture and through walls, but where was the fun in that? He would find them all eventually. They were like rats in a barrel, they had nowhere to go.

Walking slowly through the parlour, he checked behind the sofa and upturned the chairs. "Hmm," he said. "Not here."

Moving quietly through the passages, he left the public part of the house and entered the area reserved for servants and underlings. It amused him that any of them would choose to hide here – he found it strangely appropriate. The door to the kitchen and scullery was beyond. They forgot, he already knew the layout. He knew where all the hiding holes were. He'd scoured the hallway niches. He'd checked the space under the stairs. Disappointingly he'd found nothing yet, but there was plenty of time.

Stepping gently into the darkened kitchen, he could hear the copper pans hanging from a battery above the table clinking gently as if disturbed by a night breeze. He lifted his sword and then ducked sharply just as the skillet whooshed past where his head had been.

Clang! It crashed into the battery, sending pots and pans tumbling noisily across the floor.

He stepped sideways. *Clong!* The skillet swished back and hit the wall.

He stepped in, grabbed the handle and wrenched it from his assailant's hand, tossing it aside. He twisted her around; he had his arm around her throat, her hand pinned against her side. Instead of struggling, she reached upwards and touched his face.

"I saw you before," she said, breathing hard. "You were wreathed in white fire beneath the labs at Porton Down. "I wanted to touch you then, but instead I touched Niall."

"Now you have your chance," he said. "What do you see?"

"Death."

He palmed the long kitchen knife from the worktop behind her where it had scattered with the cutlery.

"It's Angela, isn't it? Whose death do you see, Angela?" he asked.

"Yours," she said. "Uh!"

The knife slipped between her ribs. "Wrong again."

Her knees went first and she slumped to the floor.

He went to the sink and ran some cold water over his hands, carefully dipping the edge of the frilled cuff from his white shirt in the cold water where it had soaked up some of the blood. "I'll never get the stains out of this," he said. "Might even have to have a new shirt."

Collecting his sword he regarded the body on the floor. "Shame, we were just getting to know one another."

He went to the kitchen door. "This is too easy. Now

where's my delightful cousin? There are a few things we need to settle between us."

He walked back towards the parlour.

Two people crashed through the scrub and brush. "It's here somewhere," said the first.

"For God's sake, Hathaway, I'm not kitted out for tramping around in the woods. We did that earlier." The woman struggled after, sliding on the mud as she tried to keep up.

"I could find it in the light," he said, "but it all looks different in the dark."

"Yeah," she muttered. "It's usually the other way around."

"That way," he said, suddenly. "It's over here. I told you I could find it."

She caught up with him. "At last," she said. "Let's get out of here." She slid down the bank, staggering as her she missed her foothold.

"Wait," he said. "It's supposed to be guarded."

"You see anyone, Hathaway? I'm not hanging around for anyone. Let's get out of here."

She heard him scramble down after her to the dip where the leaves had gathered in deep piles. "I know it's here," she said. "We just have to locate the spot under all these leaves. You try over there." She looked up. "Hathaway?" She was the only person in the dip. She could have sworn she heard Hathaway follow her down. "Stop messing about," she said. "This isn't funny."

There was a sound – a soft thud. She looked down to see blood welling out from the blade protruding from her chest. "Oh fuck," she said, and toppled forward.

A dark figure outlined in a nimbus of white stood where she had been. Retrieving the sword, he wiped the blade carefully on a kerchief and returned the blade to its scabbard.

There was a rustling from the Way-node. The trees shivered and the cold wind turned, catching twigs and whipping the whispering dry leaves into a spiral of flut-tering movement. He moved forward to see what was causing the disturbance and something dived out of the Way-node, rolled and sprinted away up the bank. He chased it for a short distance, but having quickly lost sight of whoever it was in the shadows between the trees, he returned to the Way-node. Anyone heading to-wards the house was in for a nasty surprise in any case. He needn't worry.

He returned to the Way-node, looking for shadows and keeping a close eye out for any other disturbance between the wood. All was quiet.

Thumph! His head rolled away into the leaves, dead eyes staring until they fell into dust.

Amber strolled back through the trees. "There's only one left on guard," she said. "They always were an arro-gant bunch."

Tate shook his head. "We're spread too thin not to do the same."

"I'll stay," she said. "Let them know I'm keeping the Way open. We'll get as many clear as we can."

"Assuming there are any left," said Tate.

He strode into the trees, while Amber melted into the shadows.

"Hey, is someone there?" The figure climbed up the loft stairs. "We're getting people out." There was si-lence. "It's only me," she said. Her heels clacked on the wooden stairs as she rose into what was once the servants' quarters. The orange dress glowed in the moonlight coming through the windows set in the gable ends.

"Here," said a voice. Andy stepped out from behind some packing cases. "Where's everyone else?"

"We're getting them out," said the woman in the or-ange dress. "It's clear at the moment but we have to be quick. Is there anyone with you?"

"There was someone," said Andy, "but I'm not sure where they've gone."

"That's OK," said the woman in the orange dress. "We'll try and find them on the way down."

"You lead the way," said Andy.

"It's dark," she said. "Take my hand."

"How do I know you are who you say you are?" he asked.

"Don't be silly. Who else would I be? Now take my hand and we'll go down together."

"I'm OK, I don't need help," he said.

"Not for you, silly," she said. "For me. You think it's easy in these heels?"

"They're not that high" said another voice. The woman in the orange dress spun around to find herself faced with another woman, also in an orange dress and similar heels. "You know, that colour really doesn't suit you as much as it suits me."

There was a crash. A chair splintered as Andy swung it across the back of the impostor, where it exploding into dusty fragments. "Shit! It's full of woodworm," shouted Andy. "Save yourself, Julie. Get out while you still can."

The orange dress of the impostor lost its colour and faded into grey. "Too bad for you," it said, transforming into a tall grey woman and reaching towards Andy. Her voice took on a breathy whisper as her body drifted into insubstantial spectral form. "Much too bad."

The loft area was already cold, but now it took on a bone-chilling intensity. The ghostly form turned on Andy who was retreating back from her, throwing oddments of chamber pots, broken picture frames and long discarded toys in her direction. None of them had any effect. "Time up," she said.

"Too true," said Julie. Heat was radiating from her. The dress started smoking and turning brown where it touched her skin.

"No!" said the impostor. "You don't understand." She started condensing inwards, visibly pulling herself together, but she was already extended towards Andy.

Long licks of flame started travelling up Julie's arms. As soon as they did, the flame flashed across the gap and the impostor exploded. Julie and Andy were flung backwards in the blast. The whole roof buckled and shook, fragments of tiles raining on them like shrapnel. The fire caught across the loft area, the flames flickering on all manner of things. In moments, old curtains, abandoned teddy bears, cardboard suitcases – everything caught. It was like a giant tinder box.

"We have to get you out!" shouted Julie to Andy who was sprawled across the floor. She was no longer wreathed in flame, but seemed unaffected by the heat that was rapidly building.

"The smoke," coughed Andy. "I can't deal with the smoke."

"Come on," she said. "I'll help you downstairs."

"The window," choked Andy. "You have to open it."

"If I let the air in here it'll go up like a furnace. You'll die in the heat or be killed by the fall."

"Do it!" Andy insisted.

She picked up a wooden baby cot and hurled it at the gable window. It crashed through, toppling on the rim and then fell two stories to the ground below where it smashed on the paving. The air rushed in and the heat intensified. Fire started jumping from one thing to the next like it was a living entity.

"Help me out," said Andy.

"You have to be kidding," said the woman.

"Do it," wheezed Andy.

She leaned down and grasped under his arm, heedless of the heat and the roiling smoke.

"Air," Andy gasped.

She helped him to the broken window, smoke rolling upwards into the night air. He thrust his head and shoulders out and took a huge breath. "Now," he coughed. He toppled forward and fell out, twisting in the air as he fell. She screamed, but as he fell he dissolved and became a thousand tiny particles which swirled and swarmed, turning in the night air, buzzing with the thrum of thousands of tiny wings, streaming out over the drive to form a twisting column of turning, angry bees. Andy's coat fell, a flapping discarded remnant, onto the broken shards of the baby cot.

"OK," she said. "Now I just have to get myself out before the roof collapses."

"Not that way, that's the cloakrooms," said Alex. She went to the next door and listened, trying to blot out the sounds of screaming behind her.

"Maybe we should hide in there," said Debbie, wishing she's worn something more practical than a pale trouser suit and ballet shoes. "If we turn the lights out, they won't know we're in there."

"Yeah, cause no one ever hides in the toilets," said Alex. "It's the first place they'll look. Haven't you seen any movies?"

"There's no need to be mean," said Charles. His father was something in the city, apparently, though that meant little enough to Alex. "She's only trying to help," he told Alex.

"And they can see in the dark," said Alex, ignoring him. "Through here,"

"Where does this go?" asked Megan, following Alex through a maze of passages at the back of the house.

"Those are sculleries, and that's the gun room. There are stables at the back, converted into offices. There must be another exit here somewhere." She led the way through.

"Why don't we go to the gun room?" asked Charles. "We can at least arm ourselves. I can use a shotgun."

"Do you know how to work a matchlock?" asked Alex.

"No, I thought not. Besides they don't leave working guns lying around in National Trust properties. It's not the done thing. Shut the doors behind you," said Alex.

"Why?" asked Debbie. "What if there is something down here and we need to get out this way?"

"You hear that sound?" said Alex. The screaming from behind them was suddenly choked off. "That's you, if you go back that way. Close the door, it might slow them down."

"Can we lock it?" asked Megan.

"There's no locks on the internal doors. My dad said you can seal a door if you know how. Anyone know how?" One after another they shook their heads. "Keep moving," said Alex, "and hope they're not coming around the outside and waiting at the back to intercept us."

"You think that's likely?" asked Megan.

"You have a better idea?" asked Alex.

When she reached the office, she pulled them through and shut the door behind them. The door had a Yale lock, which she clicked shut and latched closed. "It won't hold them," she said. "Help me move this." She stood one side of a low bookcase and she and Charles manoeuvred it across the door. "This isn't heavy enough," she said, pulling out an A4 file with loose paper in it. "Find something bigger."

"Like what?" said Charles, exasperated.

"Did you find the exit door?" Alex said to Megan as she emerged from the other room.

"It's locked," said Megan.

"So unlock it," said Alex. "It's not hard." She pushed past Megan into the adjoining office. At the end of the office was a single door labelled *Fire Exit*. It had one of those quick release bars. She pressed it and the lock flipped open but the door didn't move. "It's a fire exit," said Alex. "It's not supposed to be locked.

"Tell me something I don't know," said Megan in an irritated voice from behind her.

Alex pressed her hand on the door and concentrated. The lock flipped open on its own, but the door stayed resolutely shut.

"Break it down," said Alex to Charles, pointing at the door.

"What?" said Charles.

"You're a man!" said Alex. "Do manly things. Break it down."

Charles exchanged glances with Debbie and Megan, and then took a few paces back and shoulder-charged the door. He met it with a solid thump and the door shuddered but remained closed.

"Again," said Alex. Charles hit the door again, but with no greater effect. "Keep going," said Alex.

"It's not your shoulder," said Charles.

"It'll be more than your shoulder if we don't get that door open," said Alex.

"I read somewhere you're not supposed to shoulder charged doors. You're supposed to kick them down," said Debbie.

"You want to try?" said Charles to her.

"I was just thinking of you," said Debbie, resentfully.

Nevertheless, Charles changed tactic and stood in front of the door and kicked it with all his might. There was a bigger bang but no greater effect. "There's something on the other side of it," said Charles.

"Hold the lock open while he kicks it," said Alex. A dull thump came from the other room. "Shit!" said Alex. "Get that door open. I don't care how."

Back in the first office, the door thumped again. The bookcase shook, and files fell out onto the floor. Splits appeared in the wood around the lock. Alex rushed to the door, putting both hands on it. "You're a wall, not a door. You don't open, you hear me!" The door thumped again, and this time it held.

"That was timely," said Megan, trying to pull a desk across to bolster the bookcase. They watched the door

357

lock flip open and closed, open and closed. Alex put her hand over it, and it stopped.

"It won't be enough," said Alex, helping her. She looked around the room. There were no ground level windows, but the stable had high angled roof-windows set between the black beams of the slanted ceiling to let daylight in. "Can you get up there?" asked Alex.

"How?" said Megan. "You want me to fly?"

"Can you?" asked Alex, hopefully.

"Don't be ridiculous," said Megan. "You think if I could fly I'd be trapped in here?"

"Good point," said Alex. She flinched as the door thumped again.

"How long?" asked Megan.

"Not long enough," said Alex. "Is that door open yet?" She went back to where Charles was repeatedly kicking the door.

"It's not just the door," he said. "There's something blocking it."

"We already know that," said Alex. "Find a way to re-move the block. Burn it down, I don't care."

"We can't" said Debbie. "None of us is that strong. Are you?"

"Wrong element," said Alex. There was a sudden sour smell, sharp and distinct. "Oh fuck!" She went back into the first room to find a spreading black stain on the door. "Don't touch it," she said to them. "We have three min-utes. Think of something."

"You got us in here," said Debbie.

"That's not helping," said Megan, but Alex knew she was right.

There was another thump, this time from the wall. "Oh now they're coming from both directions," said Charles. "It's just a matter of which lot gets us first."

"We fight," said Alex, looking at each of them in turn. "I don't care what you can do, but do it. Throw every-thing you've got at them."

"It's not going to be enough," said Megan.

"I know," said Alex softly. "I know."

The plaster in the wall began to crack. There was another thump and grit particles and chunks of plaster rained onto the carpet. At the same time, the smell of fungus and rot from the door intensified. Another thump from the wall sent clouds of dust into the room. They all stood back. Charles picked up an office chair to hurl at their attackers. In Debbie's hand a paper knife glinted dull. Her knuckles were white on the handle.

A loud thump came from the door. A hand reached through the gaping hole, feeling for the lock. Charles whirled the chair into the door and it crashed through leaving a gaping hole.

The wall erupted in a blast of stone, plaster and wood, a huge figure burst through. Charles went for another office chair. "Wait!" said Alex.

Tate finally burst through into the room, bits of wall collapsing around him.

"Out!" he called, spitting grit and stones. "Everyone out!" He grabbed Charles and propelled him through the gaping hole in the wall. The others scrambled through after him. Behind them the bookcase was being pushed aside and eager hands were reaching through. Tate grabbed a large stone from the pile of rubble, weighed it in his hand and threw it through the hole in the door. There was a satisfying crunch and a scream from the other side. He guided Alex through the hole and then followed.

Outside Alex threw herself at him, her hands around his neck. "I knew you'd come back for me."

"That was too close," he said.

"We were trying to get out the back door," said Alex. "We couldn't get it open."

"They will have sealed the windows and doors that weren't guarded," said Tate, "which is why I came through the wall. Come on, we'll get you and the others to the Way-node and I'll come back for more."

"I'm not leaving you," said Alex, following Tate as he trotted through the arranged beds of the formal garden.

"It wasn't a suggestion," said Tate.

They reached the hedge at the bottom of the garden. Beyond the hedge, Megan, Charles and Debbie were clustered into a tight group. Around them were arrayed a wide semi-circle of figures holding swords, outlined in ghostly white fire.

"Houston," said Charles. "We have a problem."

TWENTY-TWO

They could hear the commotion behind them as those in the stables pushed through the gaping hole in the wall. There was no going back.

"Behind me," said Tate, adjusting the grip on his axe and moving out onto the clear grass sloping down towards the pond.

"Which direction is behind?" asked Charles as the wraithkin circled around them. Tate turned slowly to face the ghostly silhouettes, while the four of them stumbled around to remain roughly at his back. From back at the house there was a dull boom. Somewhere up on the roof, an explosion sent fragments of tiles tumbling and pattering into the flower beds. The smell of smoke drifted on the breeze.

The flickering fingers of light faded around one of the figures who returned to a more normal aspect, illuminated by the cold moonlight. He spoke, "Finally it comes to this."

"Deefnir," said Tate. "I might have known you'd be hanging around here somewhere."

"Like fish in a trap," he said, "we simply wait and they come to us. Why engage in all that tiresome running around?"

"You've caught more than you bargained for this time," said Tate.

"What's this?" said Deefnir. "A threat? An opening bid? Will you bargain for your skin, their lives for yours?" From the gap in the hedge, the other wraithkin joined them. The circle extended to accommodate the newcomers, so that interspersed with the dark figures outlined in pale fire were the Shades, grey women, their hair falling around their faces, their hands outstretched as if they would leech the warmth from their victims.

"I'm not leaving without all of them," said Tate.

"You're not leaving at all," said Deefnir. "Oh, I'm sure you'd love to roar, and sweat, and swing that great axe of yours, but I don't think there'll be a need for that kind of histrionics." The moonlight dimmed and dappled shade filtered across the grass, even though there was nothing shading the moonlight.

"What's going on?" said Debbie.

"What's happened to the moon?" said Charles.

"Gallowfyre," said Alex. "They're not going to stab us to death."

"That's good?" said Debbie.

"They're going to drain our life from our bodies where we stand," said Alex.

"Not so good, then," said Charles.

Around the circle, each of them dimmed, spilling out shade onto the grass. Where the gallowfyre met between them, shimmering walls came into being where one wraith's power pressed against another, flaring into a purple so deep it was barely visible. From around the woman a dark pool of blackness crept across the moonlit grass.

"Your time is at an end," said Deefnir. "A new age dawns, and it is the age of the wraithkin."

"Ready?" said Tate.

"What are you going to do?" asked Alex. "You can't fight them."

"I'll die trying," said Tate.

362

There was a sound. It was like a mosquito, or a night moth, flying swift through the darkness. It stopped with a sudden, *thup*. Alex turned around and one of the wraithkin who had joined the circle behind her stood with the pale shaft of an arrow emerging from his chest. He looked down in surprise, and then slowly toppled backwards onto the grass.

"Down!" said Tate. He caught Alex by the neck and pulled her down to the ground, lying across her.

"Ow!" she cried, "Get off! You're hurting."

Charles looked around. "What the…?" Tate kicked the legs out from under him and he went down on his back, the air whooshed out of him.

Then the air was filled with buzzing, fluttering death. The arrows came from everywhere, whizzing over them, disappearing into the hedge or sailing into the night where they missed. The wraithkin were peppered with them, whirling around, trying to see where they were coming from, but where wraithkin stood, the arrows found them. Alex watched as one found an eye and the figure staggered blindly away into the dark before falling on the grass.

The Shades fell back from the circle, dissolving into thin mist, vague outlines in the moonlight. The arrows whizzed and buzzed, but could not touch them. Across the grass, Deefnir crawled on his belly, an arrow protruding from the back of his shoulder. He reached for Tate across the grass. "Too late for you," he said, the dappled shade extending across the grass between them.

Tate's arm swung the across his body. The blade of the axe was an arc of light in the dappled shade. It flew across the gap between them and sank with a satisfying *thock* into Deefnir's head. Figures ran up the slope towards them, carrying burning brands and long spears with glinting points. At the sight of the flames, the Shades drifted back, merging with the shadows, drifting insubstantially in the night breeze, leaving the still bodies of their brethren scattered across the grass, slowly turning to ash.

"Slimgrin, here!" shouted Tate, holding up an arm. In seconds they were surrounded by tall, long-limbed figures covered in golden fur, the glint of many white teeth showing in the moonlight. Each carried a long spear. They fell on the figures scattered on the grass, using the long spears to make death a certainty.

Tate rolled off Alex and pushed to his feet, helping her up. For once she didn't complain. The circle widened as new warriors joined, holding pale bows that curved back on themselves in organic symmetry, pale arrows nocked at the ready, each with a glinting silver tip and pale feather fletches. There was a sense of wrongness around her and she shifted uneasily. It was then that she noticed the black metal tips on the arrows, gleaming dull in the moonlight. The arrows were tipped with iron. The warriors with spears knelt, forming a barrier of spears while the archers took up places behind them, watching the dark for signs of movement. If they were discomforted by the metal-tipped arrows then they did not show it. Tate retrieved his axe.

Into the defensive circle walked two figures, almost identical to the warriors. One had a silver chain around his neck, and Alex immediately recognised Lord Mellion. The other held out his free hand to Tate, who clasped it firmly in his.

"I've never been so glad to see you, old friend," said Tate.

Slimgrin held his fist over his heart, then touched his forehead.

"We stand together," said Tate, holding his fist over his heart.

Slimgrin made a complex gesture that Alex couldn't see.

"Any help is welcome," said Tate. "Amber has the Way-node secure, but we're not fighting a battle, we're just trying to save as many as we can."

"They're using iron," said Alex to Tate. "Iron-tipped arrows against their own kind."

Lord Mellion considered her for a moment and then made a series of complex gestures, ending with a fluttering gesture over his heart.

"What did he say?" asked Alex.

"He says that we are no longer fighting for honour," said Tate. "We're fighting for survival."

They started talking about numbers, how many wraithkin they'd seen, how many they'd killed, and how many of the gifted they'd been able to save. As they tried to evaluate the situation, Alex looked back towards the house. The rooftop was now ablaze and she could see columns of flame rising into piles of smoke above the house.

"If we don't get people out soon," she said. "There won't be anything left. Where's Dad? Where's Blackbird and the baby? Where are they?"

Tate stood beside her. "Let's hope they got out," said Tate. "Even with Mellion's warriors we don't have a big enough force to take the house, and that's if it wasn't burning. We're going to try and secure the exits and help people out if we can."

Alex turned away. The smoke from the house was making her eyes sting. She blinked. "What's that?"

"It's all we can do," said Tate. "We don't have enough…"

"No," said Alex, pointing at the sky. "What's that?" She pointed at a light in the sky that was getting steadily stronger. They watched as the light became intense and a heavy thumping filled the air. In a moment a big helicopter banked away in a long curve to the left of the house. They could see an open door in the side and green lights inside. There were figures in the doorway looking down at them.

"Do the fire service have helicopters around here then?" said Charles.

"You are such a city boy," said Debbie.

The helicopter banked away in a long arc and then circled around until it slowed and hovered, a way off beyond the pond at the bottom of the slope.

"What are they doing?" asked Alex.

"I think they're waiting to see who wins," said Tate.

Blackbird guided Lesley out of the great hall ahead of her while Big Dave tagged along behind, leaving Niall to watch their backs and keep people moving. Strangely, neither Altair nor his cronies seemed in a hurry. They must have been planning this for a while.

Blackbird shook her head – they were bottled up, they'd never get everyone out. "Up," said Blackbird to Lesley.

"How will that help?" asked Lesley.

Blackbird's mind was racing. They'd been seriously wrong-footed and they had to regain the initiative. "Up will give us time," she said. "They're expecting us to run, and they'll be waiting for us if we do."

"Do I have to remind you that there are no exits up here?" said Lesley, ascending the stairs up to the gallery above.

"I'm aware of that," said Blackbird. "Do you have a better idea?"

"It doesn't leave us with many alternatives," Lesley said.

"There are always alternatives," said Blackbird, "you just may not like them very much."

"I already don't like them very much," said Lesley.

They reached the top of the darkened stairs and Blackbird pushed through the door into the main bedroom, carrying the baby on one hip and holding the door open with the other while Lesley and Dave came through. The baby stared around wide-eyed at this sudden change of mood, but at least he wasn't yelling. Maybe even he knew how serious their situation was.

"Find something to block the door," said Blackbird to Dave, pushing the door closed behind them.

"Will it stop them?" asked Dave.

"No," said Blackbird.

"Then why bother?" said Lesley.

"Because it'll give you something to do, and me time to think," said Blackbird.

She stared around the room in the limited light coming in through the tall leaded windows. There was a large tallboy, and a wardrobe, but not big enough to hide any of them. Hiding wouldn't work in any case. The fireplace was cold, there wasn't even any kindling. How anyone was supposed to have lit a fire in here, she couldn't imagine, but that was the National Trust for you. History could freeze to death as long as it looked pretty. The curtains were all very nice, but they looked too heavy to make a decent rope, even assuming there would be no one at the bottom waiting for them to climb down.

"Damn!" she said.

The bed was large, but not much use as a weapon. The chandelier looked substantial enough for someone to swing on it, assuming they were cavalier enough to try.

"We should have gone to the kitchen," she said. "At least there would be knives in the kitchen."

Lesley and Dave moved a chest of drawers in front of the door. Blackbird put the baby on the bed and went to the door. As soon as she put the baby down, he started crying, initially a hesitant whimpering, but rapidly ramping up to a full-blown yell. Concentrating for a moment, she sealed the door. That would give them a little time.

Lesley picked up the baby and started rocking him, but he would not be placated. Blackbird took him back, and he quietened a little, sobbing into her shoulder.

"There, there, little one." She wanted to assure him it would all be OK, but she really wasn't sure it would. Above them there was a dull boom that shook the house, followed by a noise which sounded like rats running through the walls. Her senses told her that fire was blossoming above them.

"What the hell was that?" asked Dave.

"Nothing good, you can be assured," said Blackbird, looking up.

The door handle rattled, followed by a heavy thump as something hit it hard.

"Dave," said Blackbird. "Pull the curtains down, Use them to climb down the outside and get Lesley away."

Dave went to the window and started furiously tugging at the curtains.

"What about you?" said Lesley.

"I'm the reason they're here," said Blackbird. "They're not going to allow me to leave."

"But the baby," said Lesley. "What about little William?"

"Get yourself out," said Blackbird. "When you're safe, I'll follow you down." What she didn't say was, *if you can get down.*

Dave rattled the window open, and pushed it wide to the night air. The cold rushed into the room, chilling it further. He'd got the curtain loose but was now having trouble finding anything to secure it to.

"This is not going to make very good rope," he said.

"Use the bed to anchor it," said Blackbird. "It's heavy enough." The door thumped again, and then again, as whoever was on the other side became more determined.

"This doesn't work," said Dave.

"I know," said Blackbird. "It's the wrong sort of material. Can you smell smoke? Is that coming from outside?"

"Then why the f…" said Dave.

At that moment the doorframe split from the wood panelling of the wall and the edge of the door splintered inwards. "Knock, knock!" said Raffmir, from beyond the door.

"Step out of the way," said Blackbird.

"What are you talking about?" said Lesley. "What do you think you are doing?"

"I'm doing what I must," said Blackbird. "I'm ordering

you as Steward of the Eighth Court to stand aside." She stood up straight, lifted her chin, and patted the baby's back gently. "There, there, honey," she said.

"But Blackbird..." said Lesley.

"Dave, move her out of the way. It's me he wants." Blackbird flinched as the door crunched and split under the force of his blows.

"At least give me the baby," said Lesley. "At least give me little William." Dave was drawing her back towards the window, but she pulled against him.

"He wants William too," said Blackbird. "It's what they're here for."

Raffmir grabbed the edge of the splintered door and wrenched it, breaking it in two and tossing the pieces over the gallery banister into the hall below where they clattered. "They don't make them like they used to," he said. He kicked the chest aside, and it lurched, the leg buckling so it collapsed. He pushed it aside with his foot.

"Have you any idea how difficult all this is going to be to replace?" he said. "Still, out with the old." He drew his sword. The edge glittered in the dim light.

"I demand that you leave this place immediately," said Blackbird. "You are not wanted here."

"You demand?" said Raffmir. "You have a nerve."

"I invoke the wardings of this place. Begone!"

Raffmir laughed softly. "I was setting wardings here before you were born. This was our court long before it was ever yours."

"Then we would request your leave to vacate and leave you to it," said Blackbird.

"We are a little beyond that, do you not think?" said Raffmir.

"As the Lady of the Eighth Court, I demand the right for me and my people to withdraw peacefully."

She said it with all the dignity she could, but Raffmir simply chuckled to himself. "There are so many things wrong with that, I can hardly count them. There is no

Eighth Court. You are not a Lady of the High Court of the Feyre. There is no High Court – it's gone… dissolved… ended."

"Some of us still hold to our laws. Did you not swear that you would do me and mine no harm? Is your word worth nothing, Cartillian, Son of the Void, Star of the Moon's Darkness?"

"You invoke my name? Very well, Velladore Rainbow Wings, daughter of Fire and Air, I remind you how you came by that name. You bought my name with the life of my sister. You killed her with your own hand."

"She broke the law."

"She did nothing! She would have drawn back. She would have remembered herself, if you hadn't killed her first."

"No," said Blackbird. "She wouldn't, and you know it."

"Well, now there is no law, there are no courts, and there is nothing between you and the edge of my blade."

"Oath-breaker," said Blackbird.

"A badge I shall wear with pride," said Raffmir. He stepped forward, and as he did a shadow materialised behind him. There was the flash of a blade. He twisted on the spot, and parried the cut on the edge of his blade about six inches from his neck.

"Cousin," he said, as he used his sword to push mine away. "I was beginning to think that you had disappointed me and fled." He twisted the blade so that his slid free and sliced into the space where I stood so that I was forced to jump backwards out of reach.

Amber finished dragging the pieces of fallen timber into the loose horseshoe she had formed around the Way-node. The broken branches wouldn't prevent anyone reaching the Way-node, but the wardings she'd placed on them would give her warning.

She stopped again and listened to the sounds of the woodland around her. The night was still, and the trees reached frozen fingers up into the night air. She shrugged and returned to the small mound in the centre of the hollow where the Way-node was, placing her feet above the node. She breathed in slowly, and when she exhaled, a few of the fallen leaves around her lifted from the ground, floating on the air in a gentle dance, circling around the inside of the barrier she'd made. More joined them, until a silent column of floating leaves, brown, orange and gold, circled slowly around her. She stood at the centre, sword in hand, eyes half-closed, feeling the drift of the air, sensing each fluttering leaf, searching for disturbances that shouldn't be there.

After a while she opened her eyes. "If I were you," Amber said quietly, "I'd find another way."

Where the hollow had been cold, now it chilled further, as three grey shadows coalesced into being beyond the barrier of branches.

"You are the one who is in the wrong place," hissed one.

"We are three," said another.

"And you are one alone," said the third. The leaves continued to circle as the three shadows formed a triangle around the column on leaves. "You can try and escape down the Way, but we will follow you wherever you go."

"I'm not going anywhere," said Amber, quietly.

The three figures hissed as one. Around the barrier, the twigs began to crackle and the sticks to rattle against each other as a blackness deeper than the night spread over them. The sharp smell of decay crept through the undergrowth, reaching inwards for the figure at the centre of the whirling column. As it did, the column of leaves expanded, until it encompassed not just the barrier, but the insubstantial grey shadows at the edge. The leaves didn't touch them, but passed over and around them, until they were shadows within the column. The blackness raced across the leaf-litter towards her.

"And now you're committed," said Amber.

In response she lifted her arms, sword held out. She turned swiftly, scribing a circle in the air around her with the tip of her sword. Into the hollow came a different smell, the smell of bonfires and autumn. There was a hiss and crackle from the barrier, and all at once it flashed into fire, the flames rising through the floating ring to the screams of the Shades caught there. The centre of the ring was a column of orange flame with Amber at the core. There was a low, *whump* expanding outwards, and a ball of smoke rose from the hollow into the night air, extinguishing the flames.

When it dissipated, all was silent. Amber walked naked from the mound at the centre of the hollow, holding only her sword, and regarded the charred ground. She shimmered and her glamour re-clothed her. She shook her head and her dark hair fell back into the short feathered style it had always had.

"You were warned," she said.

"Your quarrel is with me, not with her," I told Raffmir.

"I will settle it with both of you," he said. "Give me a moment, Blackbird, and I will bloody this blade and return to finish our conversation."

"Lesley, take Dave and run. Get free while you can," I heard Blackbird say as I retreated.

"We won't leave you," said Lesley.

Raffmir launched a series of diagonal cuts so that I was forced to retreat along the gallery above the stairs. I parried each so that I could draw him away from Blackbird and the others. He swirled and spun his sword in tight arcs, each aimed at testing my defence, each seeking the weakness that would give him the opportunity to deliver a killing blow.

"Do as she says," I called to them.

"There is no need," said another voice, materialising from the shadows. "While Raffmir plucks one thorn from our side, I shall pluck the other."

Altair moved into the doorway, blocking their exit. I tried to warn them, but Raffmir was harrying me, forcing me back around the gallery and into the rooms beyond. He used the momentum of his blade to drive me, making each cut flow neatly from the last. I was forced into a series of jarring parries.

"Good to see that you've been practicing while I've been gone," said Raffmir. "Still slow, though, and a little sloppy, I might add."

I didn't tell him that the place in my side where I'd been shot was still stiff and healing, and that it was making me favour my left side rather than my right. Instead I used the distraction of his words to launch a counter-attack, pushing him back towards the doorway where he would have less room to manoeuvre.

He spun in front of me, a lightning move, whirling the blade around his body so that my attack glanced off his blade. The hard end of the pommel on the hilt of his sword punched into my side where I'd been wounded. "Oof!" I staggered back.

"Do I detect a weak spot?" he said.

My side flared into pain where he'd punched me. I rolled backwards and came to my feet in time to sweep his downward cut to one side. It would have split my head open, but it was slow and he'd meant me to parry it.

He was playing with me.

Twenty-Three

Altair stood in the doorway, outlined in a white nimbus. "No need for any further delay," said Altair. "We can settle this now, just between us."

"There is nothing to settle," said Blackbird.

"Oh, come now," said Altair. "This is no time for false modesty. You have been a thorn in my side for some time, recently more so."

"It seems only fitting, given that you've been persecuting me and mine for most of my life," she reminded him.

Altair stepped into the room, avoiding the wreckage of the furniture Raffmir had demolished. As he did, Dave moved around, shielding Lesley.

"I have merely held to the traditions and values of the Feyre, something I do not expect you to comprehend. It is as beyond you as flying is beyond a dog." He edged forward.

Blackbird backed towards the fireplace and reached behind her with her free hand, feeling tentatively with her fingers for the fire irons hanging on the stand beside the cold grate. She gritted her teeth. She could feel the ache in her palm as her hand neared the dark metal. Her timing would have to be perfect.

Altair moved forward again. "I would offer you the

374

boon of a quick death," said Altair. "But that would deprive me of the pleasure of delivering what is justly yours." He reached for her.

"What I don't understand," said Blackbird, "is why? If all you wanted to do was destroy the courts then you could have achieved that a hundred times before now. I can't make sense of a strategy that leads to your own extinction."

"You forget, Kareesh's perverted vision is only one version of the possible future – the only one she was prepared to contemplate. There is another way, even though it is not the way I would have chosen, had I been free to negotiate a settlement. I tried, I truly did. You forced my hand. All of this would not have happened if you hadn't formed a mongrel court and threatened the very purity of the Feyre. That is why this fate is rightly yours."

"What other way?" asked Blackbird.

"The Wraithkin possess the power to draw the life from others. This is what sets us apart. Using that lifeforce we can renew ourselves and become what we once were. We have sacrificed our brethren to renew them. We will build a new Court of the Feyre, filled with the life of all who sacrificed themselves. From death will come life, and renewal." He sounded triumphant.

"You chose genocide?" said Blackbird. "You'd destroy everything just to save your own sorry skins."

"I did not expect you to comprehend our vision of the future," said Altair.

"I comprehend it perfectly," said Blackbird. "I'm just stunned by the myopic, selfish, stupidity of a bid to save a race by consuming its people. It has all the sophistication of trying to turn yourself into a cow by eating beef."

"You are not fey enough to understand," said Altair.

"You mad bastard," said Blackbird, shaking with anger. "You deserve the extinction that will certainly achieve. So say I! Lesley!" She launched William at Lesley. Squealing in surprise, William flailed his chubby arms as he sailed through the air to be half-caught by Lesley, who broke his fall and rolled with him back onto the bed, her relief at catching him written plainly on her face.

Blackbird reached behind her.

At that moment, Big Dave launched himself into a flying tackle at Altair. Altair caught the movement in the corner of his eye and swept the sword around, using his fist on the hilt to backhand the attack. He connected with Dave's chest and Dave flew backwards as if hit by a truck, crashing into the wall so hard it cracked the plaster, showering everyone with fine dust.

"Pathetic," said Altair, "and pointless."

As Lesley screamed, Blackbird seized the iron poker from the stand, ignoring the burning shock travelling up her arm and swung at Altair's head. Altair ducked and it swished through the space where his head had been. Altair swatted the back of Blackbird's hand and she could no longer keep hold of the bitingly cold, nerve-jangling metal. It flew from her hand, bounced off the wall and landed on the floor behind him. Altair had hold of her wrist.

"Normally," he said, eyes narrowing, "I would not pollute myself by drawing the life from a mongrel like you, but in this one case I will make an exception." Blackbird felt the room chill as the room filled with limpid, swirling moonlight. She gasped as he twisted her arm cruelly, feeling the bite of Altair's magic sinking into her skin where he gripped her. She swatted at his head with her free hand but he evaded her easily. She was weak. She could feel the fight draining from her.

"At last," said Altair, "you will get what you deserve."

There was a sound like an impact on a wet melon. Altair's eyes rolled up until only the whites showed and then closed. For a moment he looked beatifically peaceful, and then he let go of Blackbird and sank to his knees. Behind him, Lesley was standing with the fire poker, held two handed. It was dripping blood. "I hit him," she said, and dropped the poker.

376

Altair's eyes opened. For a moment he had trouble focusing.

"You wanted my magic," said Blackbird. "So take it!"

She pressed her hands to either side of his head. He tried to pull away, but she had him firm. A vague scent of cooking meat came into the room, and steam rose from Altair's kneeling body.

"No!" he screamed. "Noooo!" He grasped her wrists, trying to seize control of both her and her power, but Blackbird's magic was in the ascendant. She had her power and she was determined to use it.

"Take it," she said. "Take it all!"

The kneeling form burst into flame, the heat forcing Lesley back. The front of Blackbird's dress started to blacken as she held onto him, the column of flame rising around her face. Her hair was a crown of copper flames, and her eyes were filled with the reflection of fire. She held him until there were only charred, hollow remnants, and then she let go. The smoking corpse toppled sideways and fell into ashes.

Blackbird staggered, toppled sideways, and fell.

When she came to she was looking up into Lesley's face. "William. The baby…" she said. "Is he…?"

Lesley passed William to her, and she wrapped herself around him. She stank of smoke, and reeked of the foul smell of burned flesh, but she had her son. He cried in her arms while she rocked him, whispering small words of comfort.

"Dave?" Blackbird asked.

Lesley shook her head. "Something broke when he hit the wall," she said. "I tried to move him, to make him more comfortable, but… no." Her eyes filled with tears.

"I'm so sorry," said Blackbird, reaching for her hand. She winced where the wheals left by the iron poker had blistered her hand, but held on anyway. "If he hadn't distracted Altair…"

"I know," said Lesley. "I can't think about it. It hurts…"

"He was protecting us," said Blackbird. "Both of us." She let go of Lesley's hand and reached around her shoulder, pulling her close.

There was a low sound, like a rhythmic thumping. It built until they could hear the wine of the helicopter's motors as it banked over the house.

"What now?" said Blackbird.

"I just want to curl up," said Lesley. "I want it to stop."

"We have to get out," said Blackbird. "Come on, help me up."

They reached the doorway. Lesley couldn't look at the broken body of Dave where it sagged against the wall. His eyes were open but they no longer saw. When they reached the door it became obvious the house was alight. Flames ran down the curtains, and smoke was pouring from the other rooms.

"Where's Niall?" asked Blackbird.

"I don't know," said Lesley. Maybe he got out?" She didn't sound as if she believed it.

Blackbird handed William to Lesley, who immediately started yelling. "Take him outside. Get him away from the fire and the smoke."

"You have to come with us," said Lesley. "We can't make it alone."

"Do it!" ordered Blackbird. "I can walk through the flames and survive, but you can't and neither can William."

"Then come with us," said Lesley.

"I have to find Niall," said Blackbird.

"I've looked forward to this for so long," said Raffmir as he drove me back through the house, away from Blackbird and Altair. He moved in fast, ringing blows onto my guard, then drifted through the hanging coils of smoke like a phantom. Somewhere the house had caught fire. I could hear pops and bangs above me as it spread.

Raffmir's magic blossomed out around me, only to be met by my own. Purple light flared in the smoke where our power met, illuminating the room with unearthly light. Flickering moonlight rippled in the smoke.

"You're forgetting," I goaded him. "You've already tried to kill me once, and you failed. So did your sister."

He launched into a series of punishing strikes, putting pressure on my weak side, making me parry his blows in painful repetition. The concentration of meeting his attacks while holding back his power was telling on me. I whirled aside and spun back on him, trying to push him back, but he danced lightly away into the smoke, laughing at my clumsiness.

"You can't provoke me, I'm in too good a mood," he said. "I don't know what I'm going to do with myself after you're gone. No one is as much fun to taunt as you are. You really should avoid gambling games," he said. "Your face is too open, too readable."

"What makes you think I'm going anywhere?" I asked him.

He stepped into my next cut, whirled around and struck me again, exploiting the same spot as before. "Ooof!"

He skipped backwards as I made a clumsy sweep to try and catch him out. He grinned at me, actually waiting until I recovered.

"I'll give you this," he said. "You have been practicing and you're better than you were, but you'll never be a great swordsman. You lack the willpower, the grace, the poise." He gestured expansively.

I regained my feet, wishing that I hadn't had two of Sam Veldon's bullets dug out of my side. Immediately, his power pressed against mine and he resumed hammering at my defences, testing the strength in my arms until the muscles burned with effort, and using light swift blows to force me into positions that made me unbalanced and vulnerable. That wasn't what worried me, though.

Raffmir's favourite technique was like a flourish at the end of a signature, a whirling motion where his sword arced around him in a spiral, protecting him from incoming blows, but somehow the blade emerged in a low thrust designed to punch straight through the opponent's defences. He'd used the same move twice, now, but only with the pommel of his sword, and each time I'd seen it coming and not been able to do a damned thing about it. He knew he could have me any time he wanted.

He forced me back into the moment by raining cuts on my head, making me lift my sword to deflect them away. I skipped backwards and came back at him with a horizontal slice that would have parted his head from his shoulders if it had been there. Instead he laughed at me.

"You're such a bore," he said. "That's your problem. Everything's life and death with you. You never have any fun."

"It's only life and death when you're around," I told him. "Have you considered that you may be part of the problem?"

He swept in again, testing my guard, making me sweat. The air was getting bad, filled with acrid smoke, but it didn't seem to bother Raffmir.

"I'm doing you a favour," he said. "You should thank me for lifting the burden from your shoulders."

Somewhere in the house, something collapsed, and there was a *whoosh* as the flames caught and spread. I could hear the fire now. We didn't have long before Raffmir wouldn't need to skewer me on his sword, I would be roasted instead. I edged back towards the doorway.

"Oh, no," said Raffmir. He danced in, stepping in with rapid thrusts and short sharp cuts, so that I was driven back from the doorway. "You're not leaving me, the party's only just started."

Over the whistle and pop of the fire, another sound came. There was a rhythmic thumping and then a whine as a helicopter banked over the house.

Raffmir listened attentively. "Do you hear that?" he said.

"A chopper," I said. "Military by the sound of it." I was getting tired, and I knew it. I didn't have the stamina he had. He was rested and prepared. I wasn't.

"It's the sound of the cavalry arriving too late," said Raffmir. "It would be great if they would help you, but they won't. That's what you fail to understand. I told you before, they will never accept you. No one will. You're a misfit."

"No," I told him. "You're the ones who don't fit. You tried to pull this off before and you messed up. You got your arses kicked and you had to run. That's what really gets to you isn't it? Then you and your mad sister failed to kill me. Then I stopped you infecting the world with your mad diseases. Every time you've failed."

"You know, I tire of the whiny tone of your voice." He slowly circled me.

"Niall?" said Blackbird from the doorway. I could see her outline through the smoke.

"Hasn't Altair shut you up yet?" asked Raffmir.

"Altair's dead," said Blackbird. "I killed him."

"Ah, then it's all to play for," said Raffmir. "There will be a new Lord of the Seventh Court, and I fancy I may be up for the part."

"Get out while you can," I told her. "Get people out."

"I'm not leaving you," she said.

"You hear that?" said Raffmir. "She's not leaving you. That means that when I've killed you I can kill her too. That should be enough to secure my position on its own."

"You?" I said. "You're not capable. It's just one failure after another. You know what? You couldn't even best my daughter. A fifteen year-old girl and she had the better of you."

"That's an argument we can settle, right now," he said. He danced in, rattling blows off my guard. He moved in, and I saw it coming.

"Niall!" screamed Blackbird.

He whirled in front of me and I did the only thing I could think of. I did exactly the same. I spun on the spot, twisting my sword in an elaborate spiral, just as he'd demonstrated for me. I heard a *tang*, as his blade rang off mine, and then felt a *thump* which travelled down the blade.

I opened my eyes. I wasn't even aware I'd closed them. In front of me was Raffmir, close enough for a kiss. He looked down at my hands wrapped around the hilt, the blade of my sword piercing his chest. The blade fell from his hand and clattered on the floor.

"No," he coughed. "That's too rare, too special."

I jerked the blade in and up. He spasmed.

"You're enjoying this," he gasped. "We're alike, you and I."

"No we're not." I told him. "I'm not dying."

"Here," he said, lifting his hand. "If I must go…" he laughed a hollow laugh. "A parting gift. Something for… old… times." He opened his hand and there was a tiny light there, like a minute star.

I pulled the blade. It slid with a sucking sound from his chest, and in a move which would make Garvin proud I arced the blade around and struck his head clean from his body. It sailed into the corner of the room where it bounced once and rolled into the corner. His body folded in on itself and crumpled to the floor.

"It's done," I said, stepping back, the smoke coiling about me.

"Niall?" said Blackbird. "What's that?" Above Raffmir's remains, the tiny star floated in the air. Now I looked more closely it seemed to be shimmering.

"I don't know," I said. "Raffmir made it."

"It's still there," she pointed out.

"I can see that'" I said.

"It should have disappeared when he died," she said. "You're sure he's dead?"

"His head's over there," I pointed out.

382

I put my hand out and the star floated gently over to it, hovering over my palm. It was bright white, like an intense spark, but persistent. I passed my hand around it. It followed my hands, almost as if it liked me.

"It's strange," I said. "Almost as if it has a life of its own."

"We have to get out," said Blackbird. "The house is going to go." I could hear bangs and cracks as ancient beams warped in the heat, and the crash and whoosh as a ceiling came down or a wall gave way.

"It's growing," I said.

"What do you mean?" she asked me.

"It's getting bigger. It was tiny at first, but now it has a distinct size."

"Well make it stop," she said. "In fact, make it disappear altogether."

"I don't even know what it is," I said, coughing at the encroaching swirls of smoke. I extended my senses, looking into the light. It had an intensity that belied its size. "I'm going to try and extinguish it," I said.

I extended my hand and the star hovered over my palm. As a creature of the void I had a sense of the space between things. If I could collapse it, then it should vanish. I subtracted the space from it, expecting it to wink out of existence. Instead it grew brighter. I tried again, and once more it grew brighter. You could see the whirls and eddies of smoke by the light it shed.

"It's getting stronger," said Blackbird.

I let my senses extend and gathered power from the surroundings. The room cooled and warm air rushed to take its place. I could hear the flames roar nearby as the breeze I was creating fuelled it. "Niall! What are you trying to do, fry us all?"

"I have to see it," I explained. "It's operating in a space of its own. I need to be able to sense the void to see what it's made of." I continued to draw power until everything began to fade around me. Strangely the star did not fade. In comparison to everything else it grew brighter, more dominant.

With my senses extending into the void I began to see it more clearly. Whereas it looked like a point, in the shadow world between things it was a twisted knot. It writhed and turned in on itself, turning inside out and then twisting to invert again.

"Niall! We have to get out."

I reached into the knot with my sense of the void, pulling at one of the threads that made it. It wriggled under my gaze and inverted, gaining size and strength.

"Niall!"

"What? Give me a minute. I have to try and work this out."

"Niall, look at your face. Look!"

I retreated from the void and found myself looking at a twisting ball of light. In the radiance it shed, I could see my hands. They were red and starting to blister. I felt my face – it stung just to touch the skin.

"It's not hot," I said. "It isn't heat that's driving it."

"No," said Blackbird, stepping aside from the doorway. "It's radiation."

"What?"

"Whatever that thing is," she said. "It's like you have sudden sunburn. You're being exposed to some kind of radiation – maybe light, maybe more than that."

"It's a twist of space," I said. "I keep trying to untangle it, but it reforms itself."

"What did he say?" she asked.

"Raffmir? He said it was a parting gift, something for old times."

"Is that a clue?"

"I have no idea," I said. "What do I do with it? It's getting bigger."

"Bury it," said Blackbird.

"Where?" I asked.

"It doesn't matter – in the wall, under the floor. Get rid of it."

I guided it over to the fireplace where there was a solid

surface, and then coaxed it down to floor level and positioned it. I found I could both pull and push it, and that it could be guided. Using my hand I pushed it downwards into the hearthstone. It flared angrily, pulsing out white flashes of light. Each time, my sight was blurred from the intensity.

"Stop! It's not helping," called Blackbird.

"There's a hole in the stone," I called to her. "I think it's eaten into it." It was also noticeably larger.

"Anything that can be made with magic, can be undone with magic," said Blackbird.

"If it were made of magic," I said, "wouldn't it have died with Raffmir?"

Now it was pulsing, absorbing energy from the house, the fire – I just didn't know. I could feel the skin on my hands burning in the scintillating light. With my void-sight I could see that the tangle had accelerated; it was twisting, turning, inverting and re-ravelling faster now.

"I have to get it away," I said.

"Where to?" said Blackbird. "If it eats through anything it's in contact with, what will you put it in? Where will you take it?"

"Is there some sort of nuclear shelter? Maybe glass will hold it?"

"It needs to be somewhere away from anything else." I could hear the panic in her voice. "Niall, the walls are smoking, and it's not the fire."

I already knew. My sight was failing me. I could no longer see with my eyes. They had been burned away with the intensity of the light. Only with the void-sight could I sense the malignant tangle. Whatever Raffmir had done, it was his way of denying us the future we had fought for. My mind raced, trying to think of somewhere it could go, something that would contain it. Soon the house would collapse and bury it, which would only make it bigger and harder to contain. Even if I managed to get it out of the house, it would continue to grow unless I could find some way of undoing it. But then, if I released it, where would all the energy it contained go?

Then I knew what had to be done. I knew of one place where it could go where the harm it could create would be limited. I understood at last what Kareesh and Angela had meant. Finally, it all made sense.

"Blackbird?"

"Yes, Niall?"

"I'm sorry," I said.

"About what? What are you sorry about?"

"Look after the children. I love you."

"What? What are you doing?"

I embraced the tangle. There was a white flash greater than anything I've ever seen. It filled me with a burning intensity that surpassed anything I'd ever know.

So much brightness.

TWENTY-FOUR

The sky lightened out in the east. Blackbird stood on the grass, watching the smouldering, smoking remains of the house as it crumbled in on itself. Only the chimneys had survived, the blackened rickety columns rising out of the ashes. Her face was smeared with soot, her clothes charred black, and she stank of smoke. Beside her a man stood in the growing dawn light. In uniform, Secretary Carler looked distinctly uncomfortable, as if taking the place of someone else. The insignia on his arm gave it away, though. A shield with six horseshoes.

"We seek your assurance that the danger has been contained, Lady. I'll need to report to the proper authorities," said Secretary Carler.

"Don't call me that," she said. "My name is Blackbird. It's as good a name as any I've had and will serve me well enough. I didn't ask for this."

"The survivors are looking to you," said Carler. "They need reassurance."

"I'm not in a position to reassure anyone," said Blackbird. "You call us survivors, and that's all we are. Simply those who remain."

"Nevertheless," said Carler. "I would like to be able to reassure the minister that the danger has passed."

"It's gone. So has Niall. That's all I know," she said. "If I knew any more, I would tell you."

A soldier in similar uniform trotted up, saluting smartly at Secretary Carler, hesitated and saluted Blackbird as well. She sighed. "Sir, the fire is contained and as far as we can ascertain the hostiles have been eliminated. Some may have escaped - it's impossible to say. Lord Mellion is evacuating the survivors through the portal in the woods."

"They're called Ways," sad Blackbird.

"Yes, Ma'am," said the soldier.

"Assemble the men," said Secretary Carler. "Get them back on board the chopper. You can allow the fire service in now, I think. They'll want to make it safe. I expect they'll pull down the chimneys."

"What about any remains within the building, Sir?" asked the soldier.

"There was at least one human body in the house," said Blackbird. "We would like the remains recovered if possible. There should be a funeral, or at least a memorial."

"In a fire like that, Lady, the chances of recovery are small. The entire building collapsed," said Carler. "The heat…"

"His name was Big Dave," said Blackbird, "and there are those who will grieve his loss." She glanced towards Lesley who stood apart, a blanket wrapped around her shoulders, holding William.

"I will see what can be done," said Secretary Carler. "Perhaps a symbolic gesture – some ashes from the fire."

"Perhaps," she agreed. "There should be something."

The soldier saluted and trotted away again.

"You understand that it was not within our remit to intervene in matters internal to the Feyre," said Secretary Carler.

"If the night had not gone as it did," said Blackbird, "this morning's prospect would be somewhat different for all of us."

"I think you can hear the truth in my words, Lady, when I say that we had contingencies for that, but none of them were prospects I was looking forward to."

"Let's not mince words, Secretary," said Blackbird with some bitterness. "You let us take the brunt, and only became involved when it looked like we would prevail."

"The treaty—"

"The treaty is with the High Court of the Feyre, a body which I think you will find no longer exists. You chose your battle and your losses are light as a consequence. Ours are not."

"The treaty has held for almost a thousand years, Lady. We regard it as a treaty with the Feyre, rather than with the High Court."

"I can't speak for the Feyre." said Blackbird. "I only speak for myself."

"What about the gifted?" said Carler. "What about the people who have yet to emerge, those whose gifts are still dormant?"

"You could have helped us," said Blackbird. "Instead you chose to stand on the sidelines."

"I have my orders, Lady," he reminded her.

"And yet the choices we make are what defines us," she said. "We are no longer the Eighth Court for that would imply there were seven others, and after tonight I'm not even sure we can muster one, never mind eight."

"Lord Mellion—"

"Has his own concerns, though without his help we would have been truly lost. I will speak with him, Secretary, but not now. We need time."

"Of course," said the secretary.

"He's out there somewhere," said Blackbird.

"Who?" asked Carler.

"Niall. I can feel it in my bones. He did something. He's not stupid – blindly loyal, impetuous, brave to the point of recklessness, but not stupid. He found a way…"

"Let's hope so, Lady. He did say when we last met that

he would arrange for the return of certain journals to the National Archive," he said.

"Did he? What journals?"

"I think you know the journals I am referring to. They were taken after the incident with Ms Radisson in the National Archive. Is that something you'll be able to help me with?"

"The fire has destroyed much," said Blackbird. "It will be some time before we know the extent of the damage."

"I see," said Carler. "We are hoping that a new clerk may be appointed, along with the new Remembrancer."

"You're intending to continue with the ceremony?" asked Blackbird. "To what purpose? The wraithkin are here, what's left of them," she pointed out.

"The ceremony has always continued, Lady. No matter what. The journal will be useful for the new clerk. He or she will need to familiarise themselves with certain protocols and practices."

"I'll see what I can do," said Blackbird, "but I make no promises."

"We would consider it an act of good faith," said Carler.

"Is that so?" said Blackbird.

"With your permission, Lady?" Secretary Carler indicated the waiting helicopter.

Blackbird nodded as the engines of the helicopter whined into life and the noise from the rotors drowned out any further opportunity for comment. Secretary Carler saluted, and withdrew, climbing into the helicopter after his men. Blackbird moved back to where Lesley held William, who reached for Blackbird so that she took him from Lesley. He stared with wide eyes as the aircraft lifted into the air, buffeting them with the downdraft, turned, and climbed away into the sky.

"Mellion said he'd wait for you at the Ways," said Lesley, after the thudding of the rotors had faded to a distant beat.

"Tate will ask Mullbrook to send a car," said Blackbird. "I'll travel back with you."

"You don't have to," said Lesley. "I can manage." She looked pale and sick.

"It'll give me time to think," said Blackbird. "We can return to the High Court, or what's left of it. There's no one to gainsay us now."

"What about Niall?" asked Lesley.

"He's not here," said Blackbird. "Wherever he is, he's not here."

They walked slowly together back towards the drive, away from the smouldering ruins.

"Blackbird, look! You have to see this." Alex burst into the room, holding a laptop computer.

"Do we not knock any more?" asked Blackbird. She was changing, again. Somehow the smell of smoke lingered no matter how much she showered and changed clothes. It was in her skin, in her hair.

"It happened yesterday. They say it's a rare event – something special," she said. Alex went to the bed and rested the computer on the covers.

Blackbird pulled a soft cotton top over her head and went to see what Alex had found. On the laptop was a news website with images of a blurry star. "I don't understand the significance," said Blackbird. "Why are we looking at this?"

"It's a nova," said Alex. "An exploding star. It was first seen yesterday about the same time that Dad did... whatever it was. This could be it," said Alex.

"It's not your father's doing," said Blackbird quietly.

"You don't know," said Alex. "It could be..."

"A nova is an exploding star, but the light takes centuries to travel the distance to earth so that we can see it. Look, the rest of the article explains. This happened thousands of years ago."

"It might still be the same," said Alex. "We don't know what Dad might have done..." said Alex.

"It's not him, Alex. I'm sorry."

"Fine," said Alex. "Fine! If you don't want to believe in him then you don't have to. But I know! I just know, OK!" she slammed the laptop's lid shut, picked it up and threw it at the wall. It bounced and tumbled sideways, landing on the carpet. She stormed out, slamming the door behind her. Blackbird could hear doors banging as she retreated.

Blackbird went to the laptop and retrieved it from the floor. She took it to the desk and opened it, finding the screen cracked, but the blurry image of the star still imprinted there.

"I want to believe," Blackbird said quietly. "I really do."

Against the light inside me, the dark was a cool balm. I pressed the back of my bare feet into the black sand, feeling the sharp grains under my heels. My fingers brushed the surface of the beach, the gritty feel of wet sand under my hand was a welcome sensation. The rhythmic *crump* and *sigh* of the waves were a relief. There had been noise and chaos, but I couldn't remember what had caused it. My memories had been scoured clean. The utter blackness above was soothing to my eyes. All was calm. I felt my chest rise and fall with each breath, and heard my slow heartbeat echoing the thump of the waves.

I closed my eyes again and tried again to look inwards, only to find the glaring brightness coiling inside me. Every time I tried to remember who I was, where I was, why I was here, all I could see was searing light. It twisted and turned, trapped writhing within me. If I could let it out – eject it from inside of me, then I could be free, but every time I turned inwards I was forced away by the brightness there.

There was something – a memory or a dream. There had been a fire. I could smell the smoke on my clothes and feel the rawness where the heat had caught my skin. That didn't explain the light inside me, though. How did the fire get inside me?

"Cousin. I wondered if I would find you here."

I opened my eyes. Standing above me was a man I felt I ought to recognise. He wore a long coat and his features reminded me of someone I knew. I could see him illuminated against the sky until I looked away. I looked back and the light found him again. I was seeing him in the glare from my eyes. Somehow the light was escaping from inside me.

"Who?" I asked.

He sighed and then looked out towards the horizon. "Ah," he said. "So that's what you did with it."

"Do I know you?" I asked. His voice was familiar.

"I'm not sure that you ever did," he said, "and now you probably never will."

"Where are we?"

"These are the shores of night. This is the last place you will ever be." He looked around, as if enjoying the view.

"Why am I here?"

"A fine question, though the answer is probably not to your liking."

"What are you doing here?" I asked him.

"I'm here because I let my judgement get the better of me. I let sentiment come before purpose, and I got lost in the play and got careless. You learn fast, do you know that?"

"I'm having difficulty even remembering my name," I said. "Do you know my name?"

"Yes, Niall. I know your name," he said.

His use of my name brought other things back. "You're... Raffmir," I said. "And we are not friends."

"Not friends, no." He agreed. "But we have a deal in common. Come," he said offering his hand.

I took it and got to my feet. Somewhere I had lost my shoes, but the sharp wet sand under my feet was not unpleasant. "What now?" I asked him.

"Now? In due course we will discover that together,

perhaps, but for now let us walk along the shores of night, and you can tell me how much you remember."

"Should I walk with my enemy? You tried to kill me, I remember that now."

"There are no friends or enemies here, Niall. Only companions. Did you know you've been here before?" He set off along the shore and I walked beside him.

"No," I said.

"At least twice," he said, "though the memory of it will be lost to you."

"Then, how do you know?" I asked him.

"Ah, well," he said. "Therein lies a tale." We walked along the shore, the waves lapping almost to our feet. "And for once, we have time on our side…"

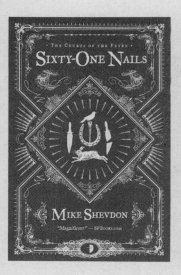

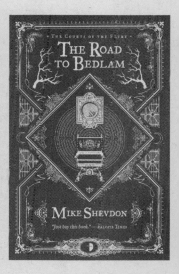

THE COURTS
OF THE
FEYRE

"A Neverwhere *for the next generation. The pacing is spot-on, the characters engaging, and the world fits together beautifully to create a London that ought to be."*

C E MURPHY